Trish Peele
12146 Mirkwood Ave.
Baton Rouge, LA 70810

Also by Ellen Gilchrist

Victory Over Japan
In the Land of Dreamy Dreams

The Annunciation

The Annunciation

✦ ✦ ✦

ELLEN GILCHRIST

Little, Brown and Company — Boston — Toronto

Sixth Printing

Any similarities to actual persons and
events are purely coincidental.

Acknowledgments of permission to quote previously published material appear on page 355.

LIBRARY OF CONGRESS CATALOGING IN PUBLICATION DATA

Gilchrist, Ellen, 1935–
    The annunciation.

    I. Title.
PS3557.I34258A82   1983   813'.54   83-800
ISBN 0-316-31302-5
ISBN 0-316-31308-4 (pbk.)

MV

Designed by Susan Windheim

Published simultaneously in Canada
by Little, Brown & Company (Canada) Limited

PRINTED IN THE UNITED STATES OF AMERICA

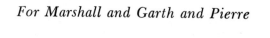

For Marshall and Garth and Pierre

"And when she saw him, she was troubled at his saying, and cast in her mind what manner of salutation this should be."

Luke 1:29

❧ ❧ ❧ ❧ ❧ *Cargo* ❧ ❧ ❧ ❧ ❧

"Amanda McCamey? Sure, I remember her. Lived up on Esperanza when she was a girl. Got famous writing a dirty book about the Church. Fell in with freethinkers. Too bad. She was a pretty girl. Prettiest girl in Issaquena County. And from good stock. Her cousin was Guy McCamey, the All-American. You remember him, don't you? Well, you would have if you'd ever seen him play."

Amanda. What she remembered was the delta, thirteen feet of black topsoil, starched dresses, Baby Doll and Nailor, the bayou, the bridge, the river, the levees, the smell of coffee and powder, her mother's whiskey, her grandmother's kisses. What she remembered was Guy smiling at her down the wide hall. He was eight years old. She was four.

All day she had been in the Packard beside her mother, driving from Tennessee. As soon as they had come to the flat delta farmlands her mother had begun to cry.

Now they were there. Amanda was standing in the front hall underneath her grandfather's twelve-point deer. She was leaning on one hip, wearing a white fur coat and hat and muff. She reached up and pulled off the hat and dropped it on the floor, her hair shining like copper in the last light of the long day.

Guy was coming down the hall holding out his hands to her.

A day in November. Amanda had been on Esperanza for a month. She had been in every cupboard, every closet, every drawer. Now she was standing on the screened-in porch leaning against the screen, getting her sweater dirty. It was a new sweater, a yellow sweater with grosgrain ribbon down the front and pearl buttons from the Chinaman's store. Amanda was waiting for Guy, singing songs to herself, pretending she was a singer on the radio. Every now and then she would press her face into the screen and stick out her tongue to taste the strange rusty taste. She had been on the porch for almost an hour. It seemed to Amanda she had been waiting for days.

As soon as she heard the trucks she came running down the stairs to meet him. He had been out hunting with the men, with his father and Harper Davis and Joe and Peter Holloman. They returned in a flurry of dogs and talk and guns and laughter, in their khaki coats and red hats, smelling of gunpowder and cold weather, the thick Delta mud called buckshot stuck to their boots like clay.

Guy handed her the box of rabbits and the dogs jumped all around trying to take the box from her hands. They were her grandfather's dogs, brown and black and white beagles and setters and terriers. She kicked one of the beagles to the ground with her sturdy legs, making the men roar with laughter.

"Look at Amanda, Guy. She's about to kill those dogs. Take her inside with those rabbits before the dogs have a fit. And come on out to the back hall. We got to clean those birds."

"You look pretty in your sweater," Guy said. He was

making a place for the box behind the heater in their grandmother's room.

"They're hungry," Amanda said. She was squatting beside the box, watching them squirm. Their little sucking noises bothered her, as though they might get on her and stick to her skin. Part of her wanted to throw them away.

"We'll feed them later when I get through with the birds," he said. He reached down and put his hand on her hair.

It was growing dark outside, the swift dark that falls in November. Amanda watched the rabbits for a while. They looked like the fingers on her hand, lying so close together, moving up and down with their soft breathing. After a while she picked up the box and wandered down the back hall to look for Guy, past the shelves of musty books she pretended to read. The books were full of silverfish. When she opened them the tiny creatures would slide across the page and disappear into the bindings.

The voices of the men were growing louder. Their voices were exciting, different from the voices of the women in the house.

Amanda followed the voices, and there was Guy, sitting on a low stool in the wide back hall that led to the kitchen. He was cleaning the birds and he was crying. The yellow light bulbs in the old wall fixtures cast black shadows all around him and the hall smelled of gunpowder and boots and the sour smell of the icebox and the smell of butterchurns and the smell of whiskey.

It seemed to Amanda that near the smell of whiskey someone was always crying.

The men were leaning over Guy, sipping their drinks.

One of the birds was so warm Guy thought it was still alive. His thumb hit a tendon and it moved in his hands. He leaned over and vomited onto the pile of feathers. Amanda stood beside a rocker watching him.

"You want to help your buddy, Miss Rabbit Trainer?" Guy's father asked. "You want to give him a hand with those birds?"

Amanda ignored him. She stared at Guy's hands. Every now and then he would look up and see the terrible stern look on her face. Her eyes were as dark as an Indian's.

Later that night she climbed out the window onto the sleeping porch and got into his bed, warming him with her small body while the owls called back and forth across the bayou.

"Don't worry," she said. "Tomorrow we'll get to the store and play the slot machine. This time we'll get the oranges. Maybe we'll hit the jackpot like Baby Doll did."

No one minded when they found her in his bed on cold mornings. Amanda thinks Guy hung the moon, they said. She thinks Guy can do no wrong. She likes Guy the best of everyone in the whole delta.

These were the people of Esperanza Plantation. These were the ones who taught Amanda everything she would always know. There were three generations of women, not counting Amanda, who made it four.

There was Amanda's great-grandmother, also Amanda, who had outlived three husbands. She wore long dresses and smelled of dried flowers and gave Amanda peppermint candy. She had come to Issaquena County as a pioneer, bringing her silver and the long gray-and-black-striped dresses she wore until she died. There were paintings of two of the husbands on the walls of her room. The third had been a simple carpenter and had built the beautiful wardrobes of Esperanza and the high bed where Amanda sometimes slept, safe in the arms and the soft snoring of the woman whose name she would carry into the future.

There was Amanda's grandmother, who never stopped moving, who ran the house with her energy. On Fridays she would get into the Buick and drive the gutted road to Rolling Fork to the Chinaman's store. Sometimes she took Amanda along and the little girl would watch through the window of the meat counter as the Chinaman cut into the meat with his fierce knives.

When they paid for their purchases he would turn to her with a smile and hand her a little paper gift, a flower or a bell or a tiny umbrella with beautiful pictures painted on it.

Guy's mother worked at the gin and left in the mornings before anyone else was up. She was always kind to Amanda but she stayed away from the other women in the house because they looked down on her and were angry with Guy's father for marrying her.

Amanda's mother didn't count anymore. She moved through the rooms like a ghost, never laying down her grief for a moment.

Guy's father, Frank, hated Amanda. Everything he had hated in his older brother was in the child. When she had only been on the place an hour she turned those black eyes upon him and it was exactly like looking into Leland's eyes. Leland, who had gone off to Ole Miss in style, then to Nashville to play ball and have his name in the papers, while Frank went to Mississippi State. Didn't even get to finish that before their father died and he had to come home to run the place.

Leland, who had come to his own father's funeral wearing a white suit. Then driven off in a Pierce-Arrow. Not to be heard of again until he died in the war, and the crazy flapper he'd married in Nashville came driving up with a chauffeur bringing the little princess and handed her over to her grandmother.

Every dish she ate had to be put on a separate plate or she wouldn't touch it. "She eats cake and sugar sandwiches all day," he said. "If you want her to eat at meals, tell Nailor to stop feeding her in the kitchen."

"Can't stop her, Mr. Frank," Nailor said. He was standing in the kitchen door listening to every word. Amanda was refusing to eat mashed potatoes because they had pepper on them. "Can't stop her. She too fast for me."

"I'm going to the back acreage until supper," Frank said, slamming out of the house. They were seated in the dining room at the noon meal. As soon as he was gone the offending potatoes were removed and some without pepper prepared.

These were the black people, Baby Doll and Nailor and Gert and Overflow and Sarah and June and Sam, who clapped and laughed when Amanda danced or threw fits. All except Kale, who never smiled at anyone, and Ditty, who was a hundred years old and could tell fortunes and make conjures and tell warts to disappear and was as white as Guy's mother.

There was Man, who did no work now but sat on the steps of the store and had his house and his living forever, left to him in writing in Amanda's grandfather's will. Man was the tallest Negro on Esperanza. He had stood beside Amanda's grandfather when the crazy man, Mr. DuBose, came gunning for him. They had stood on the bridge all morning and had shot Mr. DuBose together as soon as he set foot on the land.

They shot him together but only Amanda's grandfather stood trial that afternoon at the Grace Post Office. Leland Cincinnatus Eudoxus McCamey was acquitted in five minutes and afterwards everyone went back to Esperanza for quail. Man ate his on the front steps with a mason jar full of whiskey for a chaser.

These were the stories Amanda was told on the porch at night.

Then there was Guy, who could do anything, who had picked up a cottonmouth moccasin and slammed its head against a tree when he was eight years old, who was afraid of nothing in the world but his own cruelty. The summer Amanda was five he taught her to swim. He had work to do on weekday mornings but on Saturday Amanda would sit on the floor by his bed drinking the thick coffee Nailor made for her, waiting for him to wake up. The coffee was called Camouflage. It was a cup full of hot milk with a thimbleful of coffee and three spoons of sugar. Amanda would sit on the floor by the bed sticking her fingers down into the bottom of the cup, bringing up the little grains of coffee-flavored sugar, licking them off with her tongue, little rivers of coffee and sugar falling all over the front of her gown.

She would be quiet as long as she could. But as soon as the morning sun was visible behind the round roof of the chicken house, as soon as the first ray of sun touched the pecan tree above the sandpile, she would get up and stand over Guy, looking down into his face. She would take a sticky finger and push open one of his eyelids.

"You're playing possum."

"No I'm not, Sissy. Please go away."

"When can we go? You promised me."

"As soon as it's warm. Come on, Sissy. Please let me sleep." He would roll over and pull his head down under the sheet. She would walk around the bed and try another tack. She would pull down the sheet and whisper in his ear. "I'm going to make it to the pier. From the swing to the pier."

"If you leave me alone until eight," he said, "when Nailor says it's eight."

Then Amanda would wander back to the kitchen and get a piece of pinch cake and take it out on the back porch to eat it by the washing machine. The washing machine fascinated Amanda. It was new and only Baby Doll was allowed to run it. Only Baby Doll stood before the high white tub feeding clothes into the dangerous wringer. At any moment one of Baby Doll's hands might disappear into the rubber rollers and be flattened forever.

Amanda ran her hands around and around the smooth porcelain finish, then wandered down the steps and out into the yard to inspect the jars of frogs and lightning bugs she had collected the night before. They disgusted her now and she threw them under the house. She wandered on out to the edge of the bayou bank to look in the Mexican jars for treasure. They were tall pottery jars Frank had brought back from Mexico. They reminded Amanda of the jars in *Ali Baba and the Forty Thieves*. Every few days she checked the jars to see if they were filled with treasure. There was nothing in them today and she went back into the house and into her grandmother's room, then out through a window to the sleeping porch to see if Guy was still asleep.

"It's eight," she said.

"It isn't eight," he said. Then he gave up. She looked so forlorn. "In an hour," he said. "Go get on your suit."

Then Amanda tore into her mother's room and got her yellow bathing suit and found Baby Doll and stood very still while Baby Doll put it on and adjusted the little straps, and buckled on her sandals and found her a towel.

When Guy was ready they left the house and walked the four hundred yards to the swimming place as if they were going on a long journey. Every cypress root, every mussel shell, every dark mud-covered plant was a message, a landmark, a mystery. The bayou was a place of endless fascination for Amanda. She would stand on the bank or lie on the pier looking down at her reflection in the water, thinking about the story of Narcissus, who was turned into a flower for liking to look at himself too much. She would stare down into the water hating and fearing the gods who had such powers, wondering how far she dared go to challenge them.

There was nothing to fear when Guy was there. He would wade out into the bayou and hold out his hands to her. She followed him, feeling the thick cold mud between her toes, the roots of the trees and the sand that washed away as fast as her grandmother had it poured. Then she lifted her feet and let herself go, sliding out into the water, the heaviness of bearing herself on the earth gone. Now she was borne by the water and Guy's hands. Then she let go of even his hands and paddled up and down between the rope and the pier. "Don't guard me!" she called out, her mouth half full of water. "Don't guard me! I don't want anyone to guard me!"

She flailed up and down until she was exhausted, then

clamped her hands around his neck and he would swim out into the deep water with her hanging on to his back, letting her use him as a raft.

Amanda and Guy. Amanda and Guy. The only white children for ten miles down either road. The only white children with two pairs of shoes and shampoo. Amanda and Guy and the love that passed between them like a field of light. Everyone on Esperanza watched it but only the black people knew what they were watching. Only the black people knew what it meant.

At first they only touched each other. Guy would wake in the night and find her beside him, pretending to sleep, breathing like a sleeping person. He would rub his fingers up and down between her legs. She trembled beside him, safe in the smell of his skin, the flat hard width of his chest, the warmth of his hands on her thigh.

Later he took her hand and showed her what he wanted her to do.

When he was twelve years old Guy would have no more of it. He would not even talk to her about it and became angry if she looked at him in certain ways or came into his room at night, for the great-grandmother had died and he had his own room now.

"If you talk about it I'll tell grandmother," he said. "I'll let them beat me to death. I want God to let me be good at baseball, Sissy. I want to be on the football team next year. If I do this he isn't going to let me."

"I hate God anyway," Amanda said. "I hate his nasty old church. I hate Father Agnew. He looks like his face is blue. He was a blue baby. Grandmother said so. He can't do anything to me."

"Don't talk like that, Sissy," he said. "You don't mean that. You don't mean the things you say."

When she was fourteen and he was eighteen grown men came to Rolling Fork from Jackson and Oxford and Starkville and as far away as Nashville to watch him play football and talk to him about where he would go to college.

He had a job that year caretaking Doctor Usry's summer place on the lake. The use of Doctor Usry's sailboat was part of his pay and Amanda would go along with him on Saturdays to crew for him. Anytime it was warm enough they would take the little boat and sail out across the lake to an island of cypress and pine where Guy was trying to tame a Cooper's hawk.

One day they took the old tarp out of the sailboat and made a place to eat their lunch under the tree where the hawk nested. It was a windy March day and they had had a great sail to the island. Amanda was gobbling down chicken sandwiches, pleased with herself for the way she had handled the lines.

Then Guy showed her the letter saying he had won the scholarship to the university.

"It's the most money they can give anybody," he said. "It will pay for everything. Coach Voight said they'd even have a car I could use if I needed it."

"I knew you were going to get it. I wasn't worried."

"It will be a big help to Daddy. It means Coach Voight's going to let me play my freshman year. Anyway, it means he thinks I'm good enough. The rest depends on me."

"You'll get to. No one's as fast as you. Just because some boys are from Jackson or something doesn't mean they're going to be fast."

"Aren't you excited, Sissy? Aren't you glad for me?"

"I don't know," she said. "I think it means you won't come back here. You won't want to come back here." She turned away from him, moving over to the edge of the tarp, looking up into the trees, trying to imagine him gone.

"I'll be back all the time to visit. And you'll be coming up to see the games."

"I don't care. I still don't like it. I can't help it if I don't like it."

"You've got your friends. You've got lots of friends. Come here, Sissy. Don't act like that. Be glad for me."

Then she turned around and pulled him into her arms and began to put her hands on him.

"I can't imagine it here without you. I can't imagine what it would be like not to see you."

"The hawk's coming back," Guy said. "Look, he's circling his nest."

"You won't come back. You'll forget us." She moved her hands down his legs. Guy is ours, she told herself. Guy belongs to us. Guy belongs to me. "I want to do things with you," she said. "I want you to do things to me." She undid her short wool sailing pants and took them off. "Don't look like that," she said. "It isn't bad. Nothing's wrong with doing it to someone you know." Of course Amanda didn't know exactly what to do but she had watched the horses being bred and she had dreamed of it and once, when Gert was drunk, she questioned her about it. "He puts it in," Gert said. "And then you do it."

Afterwards, Amanda always believed it was that afternoon when they made the baby. Afterwards, it was always that afternoon she chose to remember, that wind in those trees, that great hawk circling like a black planet.

All of that Amanda remembers. All of that she can leave behind her.

Amanda. What she has forgotten. What she refuses to remember. What she must carry with her always. Her cargo. The stone house on the corner of Saint Charles Avenue and Jena and what took place there that summer and that fall.

"I sees them there in the summertime. They sits on the porch. Some of them are rich and some of them are poor. All of them are pregnant. I think doctors and nurses are there and people work there."

Later, Amanda never was sure whether it seemed like a long time or a short time, those unreal days of the strange New Orleans summer and fall. Humid days that all ran together into one long day in which she rose, dressed, attended mass, went to classes, dreamed, listened to the radio, walked in the afternoons with the other girls to the Katz and Bestoff drugstore to buy magazines and stationery and makeup. One long afternoon spent reading the names of the lipsticks, Persian Melon, Love That Pink, Cyclamen Evening, Crimson Lilac. One long summer and fall that smelled of Tigress and Aphrodisia and Coty's Emeraude and something new called Something Blue.

One long day of steady afternoon rains and nights with no stars. Mostly she read, the novels of Frances Parkinson Keyes, the romantic histories of Thomas Costain, the books of Pearl S. Buck with their terrible accounts of young girls enduring the torture of having their feet bound, of girls sold into teahouses, of arranged marriages and cruel mothers-in-law. Frightening descriptions of women giving birth, aristocratic women with bound feet giving birth in dreadful three-day ordeals surrounded by their in-laws and servants.

On Fridays Amanda would ride the Saint Charles streetcar to the Latter library and check out four books at a time, riding back past the home to the bakery at Jackson Avenue to shop for coconut cookies and petits fours, or brownies or ginger cookies. She saved the sweets to eat while she read herself to sleep at night, her mind far away in fifteenth-century England, taking sides in the War of the Roses, or in pre-revolutionary China, pitying the pagan women.

She would sprawl on the bed in the small room lit by the light of a single reading lamp. It was an old-fashioned pink china lamp with a worn silk shade cocked at a rakish angle toward the figure on the bed. A stranger passing along the wide hall outside the room, and drawn by the light to the doorway, might have stopped for a long time, entranced by the vision of the girl's bright hair in the soft light, by the concentration on the lovely profile, by the way the darkness of the high-ceilinged Victorian room seemed to close around the bed, as if waiting for the end of a story.

The smell of sweet olive trees outside the window mingled with the muffled sound of tires going along the avenue. A streetcar stopped at a corner, sounded its bell, started up again with a clang. In the background the endless hum of crickets. Amanda turned the page.

If anyone had told him there were small hands like these he would not have believed it, hands so small and bones so fine and fingers so pointed with long nails stained the color of lotus buds, deep and rosy. And if one had told him that there could be feet like these, little feet thrust into pink satin shoes no longer than a man's middle finger, and swinging childishly over the bed's edge — if anyone had told him he would not have believed it.

"Now why have you wept?" Wang Li said.

Then she hung her head and toyed with a button on her coat and said, shy and half-murmuring.

"Because my mother binds a cloth about my feet more tightly every day and I cannot sleep at night."

"I have not heard you weeping," he said, wondering.

"No," she said simply, "my mother said I was not to weep aloud because you are kind and weak and do not like the sound of pain and you might say to leave me as I am and then you would never love me."

"Jesus," Amanda said out loud, and sat up, hearing a knock on the frame of the open door.

"Aren't you burning up in all those pillows?" Sister Celestine said, standing in the doorframe, her hands in the folds of her skirt.

"You ought to read this book," Amanda began excitedly. "You wouldn't believe what they do to these girls in China. They make cripples out of them. They can't even walk. You wouldn't believe it, Sister. It makes my feet hurt just to read about it."

"I wouldn't read things that disturb me," the Sister said. "It doesn't do you any good to read those kinds of books. Aren't you ready to turn out the light now?"

"This writer's father was a missionary. She's a Chinese Christian! This book's on the *list!*"

"Still, if it disturbs you."

"It doesn't disturb me. I was just saying that."

"You really have to turn the light off now."

"A few more pages. Let me finish the chapter."

"Until I get to the end of the hall then."

"All right. Good night, Sister."

"Remember your prayers. God bless."

Amanda made a face at the empty doorway and turned back to her book.

In September the baby came.

The intern holding Amanda's hand listened to her drugged heroics with tenderness. She was a beautiful child, high as a kite on the pre-op, flirting with the young white-coated men who surrounded the hospital bed where she waited outside the operating room. He looked at the chart. She was fifteen. Reason for the cesarean, premature breech birth, a footling. Doctor Williams covering all his bases.

The hallway smelled good to Amanda, clean and antiseptic. No one was in a hurry. She was making the good-looking young men laugh. The one holding her hand rolled her into the operating room. He turned her gently on her side, her legs up against her belly. "This may feel cold for a moment, and you'll feel a little prick. It won't hurt." The needle went into her spinal column. In a second it was over.

"Good girl," a nurse said, and the young man began to tie her hands to the sides of the bed.

"You don't need to do that," she said. "I won't touch anything."

"Just in case you get drowsy and forget," he said.

"Am I paralyzed now?"

"In a minute."

"Stick a pin in my foot before they cut on me to be sure."

"All right. How's that?"

"What?"

"I just stuck your foot three times. Did you feel it?"

"No. Oh, that's good."

"You're going to be fine. This is the way movie stars have babies. Try to breathe normally. We're taking care of you."

She could hear the hemostats, like a hundred crickets. She turned her head. On the floor was a pile of large gauze pads soaked with blood. Every now and then a nurse dropped another one on the pile. She had never seen so much blood, except once, when Guy took her to a hog killing.

"Whose blood? Mine?"

The anesthesiologist held her head in his hands. "It's all right. You have plenty of blood."

"It's so much."

"Everything's fine. You're doing just fine. It won't be long now."

Then the sensation of a cow pulling its foot out of the mud. The mysterious feeling of the child leaving the body, like music, like part of herself floating free and away into space, the pull on the spinal column, as though part of her spine were leaving her. It seemed to take a long time for the baby to leave, to rise above her. As if part of her body had moved away, leaving her lighter and at peace.

Then the sight of the baby, covered with blood, still attached to the long sinewy cord. A small bloody thing wriggling in the doctor's hands, struggling for breath beneath the huge circular light. She was afraid the doctor would drop it. It looked so slick, so slippery.

"It's a fine baby, a girl," someone said. The pediatrician and an intern were working on the baby with syringes, sucking mucus out of its nostrils and throat. Then two nuns were there, wearing great white hats like birds in flight. They took the baby to a table in another part of the room. Four or five nuns clustered around the table. They looked like a great flowering shrub, in their gray dresses, their white hats.

"What are they doing with the baby?" Amanda asked.

The anesthesiologist put his hands back on her head. "They're cleaning her up and baptizing her. They always do that to preemies. Don't worry. It's good luck. Rest now."

Amanda dozed off in the strange hands that held her face.

"Now you can be a girl again," Sister Celestine said. They were sitting in the coffee shop, waiting for the train to take Amanda to Virginia. Her mother and grandmother had wandered off to see about the luggage, and left her alone with the Sister. "You'll love Virginia Sem. It's beautiful in that part of the country. I know you're going to have a wonderful time and learn so many new things."

"Is my baby all right, Sister?"

"She's fine, Amanda. She's in a wonderful home. The people who took her are very special, very devout. She'll have everything the world has to offer. Put it out of your mind, dear. You've made a barren woman happy. Now you belong to yourself again. God knows what he's doing. If you get worried, write to us."

"You sound like a nun in the movies."

"There's no need to talk to me like that," Sister Celestine said, twisting her gold ring. Her finger was swollen around it from the humidity and her predilection for potato chips.

Amanda's mother and grandmother returned to the table and handed her the tickets.

Somewhere on the train was a trunk full of new clothes

and matched set of dark green luggage. There was even a short fashionable beaver coat. Her grandmother had sold the Deadning, a sixty-acre stand of wooded land, and put the money in an account for the next six years of Amanda's life. "She will have her chance," she told the rest of the family. "She is all that we have left of Leland."

Amanda arranged her things beside her on the seat and looked around the daycoach. It was deserted except for a family of four sitting in front of her.

Jesus, I'm glad to be alone, she thought. She looked out the window. They were still there, her mother and grandmother and Sister Celestine, staring up at the train as if they were watching a public hanging.

Amanda tapped on the window, smiling down at them. They waved and smiled back. She opened the window and stuck her head out.

"Go on," she said. "I'm fine. Go on."

"Phone us the minute you get there," her mother called back.

"I will. I'm fine. Go on." She closed the window and watched them leave. Jesus, she thought.

The train smelled musty and close and exciting, like an old sofa. Amanda took a deep breath and sat up straight, running her hand across her midriff. She was filled with elation. She was free. Last night she had orgasms in her sleep, for the first time since the child was born. She touched herself through her clothes. Later, she told herself. As soon as it's dark. I don't need Guy. I can do it to myself.

She smoothed the skirt of her new plaid wool suit. Everything she had on was new, her green sweater, her gloves, her hose. Even her shoes were new, brown leather pumps with two-inch heels.

She looked down at her hand, at the diamond solitaire her grandmother had given her that morning. It had been her grandmother's engagement ring. She turned it around and around on her finger, thinking about her trunk some-where on the train full of the clothes her grandmother had bought for her, linens and underwear and gowns from The Lylian Shop, skirts and sweaters and party dresses from Holmes and Maison Blanche and Gus Mayers. There were jodhpurs and riding boots although she had never been on an English saddle in her life or dressed up to go riding. There was a fitted makeup kit with a silver-backed comb and brush. There was even a little manicure set with four different shades of nailpolish and an ivory buffer. Amanda settled back into the seat, making a catalog in her mind of her treasures, imagining herself in her new white formal, surrounded by young men in uniform.

By the time the train got to West Virginia in the morning Amanda was losing her feeling of adventure. She was even bored with looking at her diamond ring. She had slept fit-fully in the little bunk of the deserted Pullman, dreaming all night of the baby, seeing the bloody thing in the doc-tor's hands and the nuns carrying it away. In the dream the baby came and stood over her where she lay strapped to the operating table.

Go away, she screamed to the baby. Can't you see I'm not your mother? Then the baby turned into the doctor. She reached up and threw her arms around the doctor. I love you, she said. I love you. I love you.

She woke up thinking about Guy. What had they told him? Why hadn't he called her? She made up her mind to call him as soon as she got to Virginia. I can't believe I haven't called him, she thought. I don't know why I've been letting everyone boss me around. No one can keep me from calling him. No one can make me do anything I don't want to do.

She dressed carefully, taking a long time with her hair, and wandered down to the dining car. It was barely seven-thirty in the morning. Outside the windows the picked tobacco fields of West Virginia were going by, rich and neat looking in the morning sun.

There was no one in the dining car except a well-dressed man reading the paper and eating breakfast alone. Amanda played with the menu, hoping the good-looking man would notice the ring and think she was engaged. She put her hands under the table and switched it to her left hand. She took a package of Pall Malls out of her purse. She walked over to the man's table and asked him for a light. When he held out his lighter she cupped her hands around it as though she were an actress in a play.

"Looks like we're the only people on this train," she said. "I thought it would be full of people."

"It is rather deserted."

"I haven't talked to anyone since yesterday," she said. "I might forget how."

"Would you like to talk to me for a while?" he said. "I wouldn't want anyone to lose the power of speech."

"Sure," she said, taking a seat. "I'm used to being in a house full of people all the time."

"And where is that? That happy place?"

"In Mississippi. Esperanza Plantation in Issaquena County, Mississippi. I know you never heard of it."

"It has been my experience that most of the best places

in the world are secrets," he said. "I'm awfully glad you came over. I was staring at you when you came in. You look like someone I used to know. For a moment I thought it was her."

"Who was it?" Amanda said. "This person I look like?"

"Someone very beautiful." He was laughing, as if the memory was a good joke on himself. "Now, then, where are you going on this lonely train in the middle of the week?"

"I'm going to Virginia to college," she said. "I had to be late starting school because I've been sick."

"You don't look like you've ever been sick a day in your life," he said, laughing again. He had a handsome face, like a movie star, and he talked with an accent. Amanda thought he must be an Englishman. She had never seen clothes made of such fine material.

"I'm all right now," she said. "I'm fine now."

"Do you always get up this early?" the man said. "I thought girls your age slept until noon."

"Not on a train," she said. "Besides, I'm excited. I've never even seen the school I'm going to. Are you from England?"

"I'm from Charlottesville," he said. "Is my accent strange?"

"Well," Amanda said, "I guess it is. I've never known anyone from Virginia before. But all my ancestors came from Virginia."

"Did they? Then we should celebrate your returning to the land of your ancestors."

"Okay," she said. "Let's get some champagne and celebrate."

"In the morning?"

"I like to drink champagne anytime I think it up. 'Three

be the things I shall never attain. Envy, content, and sufficient champagne.' That's from a poem I like a lot."

Now he was laughing harder than ever. Amanda decided to press her luck. "Do you have a compartment?" she said. "I would like to sit in a compartment and drink champagne. I was reading this book about these people going through Spain and they were sitting in compartments drinking champagne. The minute I read something like that I want to do it."

"I suppose that could be arranged," he said, wondering what the headlines would say when he was arrested for child molesting on the Southern Railway. Perhaps it will kill mother, he thought. That would certainly be worth the price of the champagne.

They walked back to his compartment through the swaying railroad cars. It was exciting to move from one car to the next across the noisy platforms. It was wonderful to be out in the world talking to this handsome man while the train rattled toward Virginia, the sound of the wheels like a strange music.

"What do you do?" she asked, when they were settled in the compartment. She was trying to remember to look him in the eye while she talked, trying not to stare at his beautiful foreign-looking clothes.

"I don't do much of anything lately," he said. "I used to be a writer but I ran out of things to write. Actually I got tired of doing it."

"Why did you do that?"

"Because it was very hard work and it didn't seem to make much difference in my life."

"Are you famous?" she said, looking surprised, as if she had just thought of that.

"I suppose you could say I'm famous. In some circles." He told her his name but it meant nothing to her.

"I don't guess I've read your books yet," she said. "But I'd like to. I read all the time. I read everything I can get my hands on. I've never known a writer before, except Mr. Carter. He's the newspaper editor in Greenville. Do you know him?"

"I think not," the writer said.

Amanda took off her jacket and leaned back on the seat. The scenery outside the window was changing now, the small mountains of the Appalachians beginning to appear in the distance. "He's a good friend of my family," she said. "He speaks French to me. I speak French, you know. And Italian. That's three languages, counting English."

"My goodness," he said. "Three languages. At your age."

"I had a tutor. Well, I had one with some other girls. He came over to Aberdeen Plantation on Saturdays to teach us. Anyway, his name was Armand. He's Italian. He said I was so good at it I could learn any languages I liked. If that isn't bragging. I hope it isn't bragging."

"Oh, no," he said. "It isn't bragging. It's fascinating, actually."

"I could do Spanish if I wanted to but it's so easy it isn't worth fooling with. That's what Armand said."

"It has its uses. There's been some rather nice poetry written in it."

"Well, I guess so, but it just sounds like Mexicans to me."

"So you're going off and study languages. Then what will you do, get married and have children?"

"Oh, no," she said. "I won't do that. I won't ever do that. I'm going to live in New York and have a job." She pulled her eyes away from him and busied herself with her jacket, arranging it across her shoulders. "Are you afraid of dying?" she asked.

"I used to be," he said. "When I was your age I thought about it all the time. I'm more accustomed to the idea now."

The waiter brought the champagne and opened it. The writer poured a glass for her and raised his own. "To Amanda McCamey, returning to the land of her ancestors." She accepted the glass, held it up to the light and tasted it. Then she drank it and held out the glass for more. "I almost died last month," she said. "That's why I'm so late getting to school."

"My goodness," he said.

"I had my appendix out and it ruptured. I was awake the whole time they were trying to save my life. There was this sheet on the floor and they kept throwing these big pieces of gauze soaked with blood on it. You wouldn't believe that much blood was in anybody. You wouldn't believe anybody could bleed that much and not die. But I have a strong constitution. All the McCameys are real strong people."

"Look out there," he said. "The mountains are beginning." What a marvelous careless girl, he was thinking. I don't believe I've ever seen a girl that careless with her body. Amanda was sprawling on the seat now, holding up her glass as she had seen him do. She drank several more glasses one right after the other. He was trying to think of a polite way to put a stop to that but nothing occurred to him.

"This is just like that poem I was telling you a while ago," Amanda said. "This writer in New York named Dorothy Parker wrote it. Have you ever heard of her? The rest of it goes, 'Four be the things I'd be better without, love, curiosity, freckles and doubt. Three be the things I shall never attain. Envy, content and sufficient champagne.' I've forgotten how it starts. I've got the book with me if you want to borrow it."

"I know Dorothy Parker," the writer said. "She's a friend of mine. The next time I see her I'll take great pleasure in telling her a young woman who had just escaped the jaws of death was quoting her on a train."

"Are you in love with anyone?"

"Not at the moment," he said. "At the moment I'm free."

"Would you like to kiss me then?" Amanda had meant never to kiss anyone again but this chance to kiss a writer was certainly not something she was going to pass up.

"I'm sure every man you ever meet will want to kiss you," he said. "But I'm not going to. It's against the laws of the Commonwealth of Virginia for a man my age to kiss girls your age. Very short-sighted of them, I must say."

"I just thought it up for something to do," she said. She was embarrassed. The whole morning was ruined. Now he thinks I'm cheap, she thought. Now he thinks I'm terrible. Now he'll have a bad taste in his mouth whenever he thinks of me. "I better be getting out of here," she said. "I have to write some letters and things. I have a lot to do."

"Good luck at your school then. Don't let them make you forget who you are. And keep up with those languages."

"I have to go," she said. "I really have to go." She went back to her seat and ate several sandwiches she bought from a vendor and slumped down on a pillow all the way to Madden lost in gloom, thinking about what a fool she had made of herself.

⚜

Many years later on a cold Sunday morning the writer would open the book section of *The Washington Post* and read a review of a book by a woman named Amanda McCamey.

Dear Ms. McCamey, he wrote to her that cold afternoon —

When I read Jean Morrow's review of your book in *The Washington Post* I thought perhaps Jean must be turning giddy in his old age. Still, you never know, so I went straight down Wisconsin Avenue to a bookstore where a stack of your books was on display in the bestseller section.

Jean was right. You are the real thing. My concern is whether you are the real Amanda McCamey, whom I met once on a train returning to the land of her ancestors.

If you are that golden headed girl who was going off to college at about age fourteen then memory is the wonder I always dreamed it would be. If not, at least you have snatched a dreary Sunday from the jaws of despair for one jaded member of your species.

Put me down as a fan —
Monroe Preis

✢ ✢ ✢ ✢ ✢ ✢ ✢ ✢ *3* ✢ ✢ ✢ ✢ ✢ ✢ ✢ ✢

In the spring of that first year Guy came to Virginia to see her. He borrowed a car and drove all one day and night to come visit her for a few hours.

Virginia Seminary was built on a hill. At the foot of the hill was a stone wall with iron gates. Amanda had been sitting on the wall all afternoon looking down the road, waiting for him, trying not to mess up the blue and white sundress she had borrowed. The dress was a size too small. Amanda had squeezed into it by wearing it over a miserably uncomfortable garment called a Merry Widow which took all the baby fat from around her waist and deposited it under her armpits. Over the sundress she was wearing a white stole. She kept rearranging the stole to cover the fat places around the top of the Merry Widow. It was hard sitting on the wall wearing the Merry Widow but Amanda was managing it. All around her the redbuds were blooming and the mountains in the distance were turning wonderful intense shades of blue but Amanda wasn't thinking about redbuds or mountains. She was too busy hating her body. She thought of her body as some undependable animal she was doomed to carry around like a penance. Already it had betrayed her. Now, on top of everything else, it was getting fat. Amanda hated her body so much she had stopped giving it pleasure. She didn't even like to give her body anything good to eat.

Anytime she ate cookies or ice cream or candy she paid herself back by sleeping in a Playtex girdle. She had started a rage at Virginia Sem for sleeping in tight belts and Playtex girdles.

Now she sat on the wall with the stays of the Merry Widow sticking into the armpits of her treasonous body, waiting for Guy, hardly daring to believe he was really on his way to see her, driving all that way to be with her for a few hours. It seemed more like something she would do than something he would do.

As soon as she saw the car in the distance, as soon as she saw his big hands on the steering wheel of the borrowed Chevrolet, she felt a dark iron sail of love filling her chest and she scrambled down off the wall forgetting the stole and tore open the door of the car. She threw herself into the safety of his arms. "I don't believe I'm crying," she said. "I swore it would never make me cry."

"It makes me cry," he said. "I want to kill myself for what I did to you."

"How did all this happen to us?" Amanda said. "I don't know how it happened."

"It happened because we did things we weren't supposed to do," he said. "I ask God all the time to forgive us."

"There isn't any God," Amanda said, pulling away from him. "Only idiots believe in God. If there was a God I'd hate his guts."

"You look wonderful, Sissy," Guy said, changing the subject. "You look beautiful."

"No, I don't. I'm fat as a pig. All I do is eat cookies all the time. That's all there is to do around this place. I'm always campused. I never get to go anywhere."

"Tell me about the baby," he said. "I want to know about the baby."

She moved away from him. "It was a girl. It was all covered with blood. I barely saw it."

"Was it terrible?"

"It wasn't terrible. But thinking about it is terrible. I don't want to talk about it. It's over. I want to know about Ole Miss, about your games."

"I'm the best player they have, Sissy. I really am." He straightened his shoulders, smoothing one hand with the other. "Do you ever read about me in the papers? I keep wondering if you do."

"Of course you're the best. You're a McCamey. You're supposed to be the best."

"I wish you could see me play. I'd give anything if you could see a game."

"I will sometime," she said. They were quiet then, thinking about all the things they couldn't do a thing to change.

"How long can you stay?" she said.

"I have to start back late tonight. It's Coach Voight's car. I have to be there Monday for a special practice. I have to be very careful about things like that, Sissy. Because they're jealous of me. I have to go to a lot of trouble not to act like I'm special." He looked up at her and smiled a funny bemused smile.

"Why are they jealous? They're on your team, aren't they?"

"That doesn't matter at college, Amanda. It isn't like Rolling Fork High. Everybody's fighting to be on the team. I can do things they can't do. I can run faster and I can throw farther and men hate other men for that. It's been a hard year. All that terrible stuff last summer, then the hate and the jealousy. I don't know what I would have done without Coach Voight. I wouldn't have made it without him."

"I wish I'd been there with you," she said, wanting to go to Oxford and kill his enemies. "Well, come on, let's walk up the hill and I'll show you this dump. All my friends are dying to meet you. I told them they could meet you."

Because he was her cousin Mrs. Lowry gave Amanda permission to go off with him to eat dinner in town. "She has to be back by nine, you know," the fat old headmistress said, going all coy and girlish in the face of Guy's marvelous shoulders and the elegant manners that well-raised Mississippi boys wield like rapiers. "And drive very, very carefully."

"Yes, ma'am," he said. "I'm always careful with Sissy. She's the only cousin I have. She's all we've got."

As soon as they left the schoolgrounds Amanda snuggled up against him in the seat. And forgot everything else in the world, the sun going down in the trees along the road, the burning blue skies, the fear, the sadness, the warnings. All she remembered was desire, that sweet flame, that honey, that sugar to end all sugar.

"We can't do that," he said. "We can't ever do that again."

"We can if we want to. Go get some rubbers. If we get some rubbers we can do it. I know you do it. Tell me who you do it with."

"I do it with everyone. I do it with so many girls I can't tell one of them from the other. They ask me to. I don't even have to ask them."

"Then do it to me. Take me somewhere and do it to me.

Goddammit, Guy, I mean it. I want to do it. If you don't do it to me I'll start doing it with every boy I see. I'll go over to VMI and do it with the whole football team."

He stopped the car by the side of the road and put his hands on her arms and held her away from him. "If you do that and I find out about it, I'll come up here and kill you. I'll kill every man who touches you and then I'll kill you. So you can just stop that damn screaming and all that bad stuff, Sissy. I'm tired. I drove all night to get here. I love you but I won't do things to hurt you and I won't have intercourse with you ever again."

"Why not?" she screamed at him. "I want you to. I want you to do it to me. Why won't you do it to me?"

"I'll touch you. I'll touch you as long as you want me to but I won't be inside you. I won't do that. I swore to God I'd never do that again. After I went off to Oxford I stayed on my knees for two days begging God to forgive us and I promised him I'd never touch you again."

"There isn't any God," she began, then thought better of it, fearing he would go back on his promise to touch her if she started that. "I'm sorry. It's just because I've been so lonely. It's just because it's such a terrible place. I hate it here so much. You can't believe how terrible it is. Take me somewhere where you can touch me. Please do it. Please let me have you close to me."

They drove along in the darkening day down several roads until Guy found a place to park beside a pasture. He pulled the borrowed car up under a tree that was growing into a barbed-wire fence and turned to her and helped her take off the sundress and the silly undergarment and made her come over and over again with his hands and with his mouth, something he had learned to do at college.

"If you do this to a man and do it right, you can make him your slave," he told her. "It's worse than fucking, Sissy. It's worse than anything."

"What do you call it? What is it called doing this?"

"I won't tell you. I can't stand to think of you saying it." The dark was gathering all around them. A white and black spotted horse came up and stood beside the tree watching them with his big blurry eyes. Then the stars came out and then the moon and it was ten-thirty by Guy's watch. Amanda put her clothes back on and they drove back to Madden and told lies to Mrs. Lowry until they were blue in the face.

Mrs. Lowry didn't believe a word of it. She was so angry she wouldn't let Amanda walk Guy out to the car. "I trusted you," she said, when he was gone and she was alone with Amanda in the hall. "I put my trust in you."

"I'm not responsible for automobile motors," Amanda said. "I can't help it if the steering wheel got stuck." She walked upstairs with her head held high, not giving away a single thing.

She got three Milky Ways out of the candy machine and got into the bed with a book by Daphne du Maurier. She could feel the dried come between her breasts. She pulled the wrapper off the candy and opened the book. By the time she got to the layer of caramel on the second candy bar she was lost in an old English mansion called Manderley, with the sea beating down on the cliffs at the end of the lawn and the fog moving in to cover everything.

In the night Amanda had one of the attacks of cramps that had plagued her since the baby was born. Most of the time she stayed so busy and had such forward motion that she was almost able to forget the whole thing. Most of the time it seemed like something that had happened in a dream or to someone else. Except for the scar. The scar was there, stretching all the way from her navel to her pubic bone, and when she bathed she would run her finger along the length of it, feeling the hard ugly ridge. Then she would wonder at the strength of her body, for she thought that she was lucky to be alive. I will never do that again as long as I live, she would swear to herself. I will never have a baby again as long as I live. I will never marry anyone and I will never have a baby and no one will ever make me do that again. No one will ever make me do anything I don't want to do as long as I live.

The scar was there, and debilitating cramps when she menstruated. There had been several letters from her grandmother reminding her to see a doctor but she had never bothered to make an appointment. The thought of telling her story to a strange doctor was too embarrassing. The attack that began after Guy's visit lasted two days and hurt so much it brought tears to her eyes. When she was better she gathered up her courage and asked the school nurse to arrange an appointment. I'll think of something to tell him, she thought. I'll tell him I got raped. I'll tell him it happened while I was asleep.

She dressed up in her best skirt and blouse and rolled her socks down around her ankles the way the girls from New York wore theirs and started down the hill trying out stories. I'll tell him the boy I did it with had cancer, she decided. I'll say I did it because he was going to die. She walked on down the hill to the town imagining Guy in a bed, dying of cancer, calling her name. She walked faster, pleased with her daydream. In the distance great banks of clouds were moving to the west. It really is beautiful up here, she thought. I ought to start appreciating that and quit feeling sorry for myself. For all we know the world is a speck of dust on someone's cello, she quoted loftily to herself. Someone could step on us *at any moment.* They might be fixing to step on us right now. Then it would all be over. Just like that. Would I feel it? Would I know I was dying? I would have to leave this all behind. I would never see it again. I would never see her again. But I don't even want to. She's in a wonderful home. She's with very special people. I won't think about that. I'll never think about that as long as I live. That isn't important. That's all over. That doesn't even matter.

She pulled the piece of paper with the doctor's address out of her pocketbook and turned a corner onto a street lined with elm trees. The office was in a frame house. As she climbed the stairs she began to worry again. He doesn't care, she told herself. He doesn't even know you. He's a doctor. He can't tell anybody. They aren't allowed to tell anything you tell them. *It doesn't matter,* she told herself. You have to do it. You have to make sure everything's all right. Go on in. Go on in the door.

The doctor was a young man. He came out into the waiting room and helped her with her things.

"Tell me what's going on up on the hill," he said. "I haven't had a talk with a Sem girl in a long time."

"It's a crazy place," Amanda said. "I stay in trouble all the time. I get caught smoking." She pulled her Pall Malls out of her pocketbook and lit up, wondering if he would tell her to put it out. "Mrs. Lowry hates me."

"Mrs. Lowry. Tell me, is she as fat as ever?"

"Did you go up there? When you were young?"

"I went to dances," he said. "I specialized in getting Cokes for people. I was extremely good at getting Cokes passed around." He helped her into a chair. "Now then, what can I do for you?"

Amanda sat her pocketbook down on the floor and told him what she had come for.

Jesus Christ, he thought, wondering how many years he would have to practice medicine before he learned never to be surprised at anything.

Amanda went on with her story, embroidering the embarrassing parts. The young doctor laced his fingers together, trying to look unconcerned. Every stupid and pointless thing in the outworn gothic mores of the Deep South was in the garbled story she was telling him. I should have been a dentist, he thought. I should have been a ballet dancer. The north light was slanting in the windows to the left of where she sat, lighting up her wide strong hands as she made designs in the air to illustrate her story, circles and triangles and parallelograms.

"So they don't know about it at school. My grandmother promised me that. They think I had my appendix out. But what if I need to have my appendix out? That's what my grandmother is worried about. Anyway, here I am. It was pretty hard for me to come. I don't like to talk about this stuff. Bury the past, that's what my grandmother says. Well, I've been having cramps. I never used to have them. So I decided to come see you."

"Why don't you let the nurse take you into a room and I'll take a look and then we'll talk some more."

In the examining room he asked her a series of questions, going over and over several of her answers. He was trembling by the time he finished the examination. She might never conceive again, he thought. I can't believe this fucking outrage. Not even to mention taking her child away. Not even to mention that.

"Is something wrong?" she said, squeezing the nurse's hand as he removed the speculum.

"Nothing's wrong. You're in perfect health. In a minute you can get dressed and we'll talk."

"I'm glad you came to see me," he said, when they were back in his office. "I want you to think of me as a friend, as someone you can call on if you need anything. Tell me, did you ever see a psychiatrist or a psychologist or a person like that at the home?"

"Oh, God no," she said. "I'm not crazy or anything like that. My mind's just fine. No one in our family's ever been crazy, although I guess you could say my mother's a hypochondriac."

"They didn't do any counseling with you?"

"The Sisters did. The Sisters talked to us all the time. Of course, I'm not a Catholic. I was raised an Episcopalian."

"No, I mean a doctor, like a psychiatrist."

"I guess they thought I didn't need one. I'm fine. I really am."

"I can see you are. You seem like a very mature young lady."

"I read all the time," Amanda said. "I read everything I can get my hands on. That's why I'm so mature. I can read French. And Italian."

"How did you learn that? I didn't know they taught Italian at the seminary."

"Oh, no, I learned it at home. In the delta. Aurora Alford and Charlotte Myers and I had a tutor that came to the

Myers plantation on Saturday. He was Italian. Well, he was teaching us French but he just taught us Italian while he was at it. I was the only one that was any good. Well, I guess I shouldn't say that. I guess that's bragging."

"*Il me donne grande plaisir de parler avec vous,*" he said.

"*C'est mon plaisir, monsieur. Commandez le vin.*"

"Oh, my," he said. "What a tutor he must have been."

"Yeah, everyone loved him a lot. Well, Mr. Myers didn't love him. He said he was a pansy. That's why we quit our lessons. He told me all about translation. You know, most of the people in the world just think everything is written in English." She straightened up her shoulders, liking the sound of all that knowledge. "You have very nice bookshelves. I've been looking at them ever since I got here."

"Come borrow a book if you like. If you exhaust the Sem library. Here, try this. It might keep you busy." He reached behind him and took down a little book called *The Golden Apples.* "Keep it for a while. I'd like to see you again in a few months. And have that prescription filled. There's no point in a strong girl like you putting up with cramps. Aside from that, you're fine, Amanda. You're just fine. Call me if you need me." He walked her to the door and stood watching as she went on down the street, the shadows of the elms falling all over her head and shoulders like a web.

But she won't be fine, he thought, stuffing his hands down into his pockets, leaning into the doorframe, watching until she was out of sight. She won't be fine, goddammit all to hell. That gorgeous child, with a mind like that. Goddamn their crazy outworn used-up terror and ignorance and hypocrisy and fear. Imagine letting that child carry a baby to term. She'll probably never conceive again. That goddamn uterus is tilted so far back I can't find the cervix. Not to even mention the really unforgivable part.

How long until she starts seeing that baby in every one-year-old on the streets, in every two-year-old, in every three-year-old? He walked back into the surgery and picked up a hypodermic needle and held it in his hand. When I am the sheriff of the world I will bomb Rome off the face of the earth. I will watch the Vatican go sailing up to God in a million pieces. He stuck the needle into his arm and felt the rapture spread across his body until it filled the room.

Then he poured himself a drink and called a woman in Boston he liked to talk to when he was high.

✦ ✦ ✦ ✦ ✦ *Exile* ✦ ✦ ✦ ✦ ✦

✤ ✤ ✤ ✤ ✤ ✤ ✤   *4*   ✤ ✤ ✤ ✤ ✤ ✤ ✤

Amanda had not seen her cousin Guy in years. The family had kept them apart when they were young. Then, when he was twenty-one years old, Guy had left Mississippi and gone to play football for the Chicago Bears.

The first year he was there he was Rookie of the Year. The second year he injured both his knees so badly he could hardly walk. In the last quarter of a game on a freezing day he allowed a medic to shoot his knees full of novocaine and his arm full of methamphetamine and stumbled off the field a hero.

Many months later he walked out of Northwestern Memorial Hospital and looked around at a hot summer city full of men who seemed to know what they were going to do next.

Guy knew what he wasn't going to do. He wasn't going home and farm what was left of Esperanza and wait for his father to die. He wasn't going back to Mississippi and sell insurance or tractors or do any of the other things all the old football players he knew ended up doing.

He had made $35,000 the year he was a rookie and $55,000 the year after that and if he wasn't going to keep on being a hero at least he was going to keep on being rich.

He knocked around Chicago for a while looking for options. The most promising one turned out to be a sweet

Italian girl named Maria who took him home to Lakeshore Drive and introduced him to her father.

Maria's father was in the habit of buying athletes for his daughters. He bought Guy for $200,000 and a house on Lake Michigan the size of a library. It was understood there would be more, much more.

"But what will I do for a living?" Guy said.

"Don't worry about that," the old man said. "We'll find you something to do."

What they found for Guy to do didn't take up much of his time so he learned to play golf and began following the wealthy golf world around from Calcutta to Calcutta, screwing society women at night, playing golf in the daytime, coming home every now and then to Maria. It was enough for her. She had a rheumatic heart and got her love from doctors.

So the years went by. There were no children of this arrangement. For a long time Guy had liked it that way. Now he was having strange thoughts about being childless. He had begun to have many thoughts he could not control or understand. His knees bothered him when the weather was bad and he had taken to sitting alone at night watching old movies of himself on the field, watching his knees move up and down on the screen, as if somewhere in that movement was the secret of what was wrong, as if he believed what plagued him was a disease of the knees and not of the spirit.

When Amanda called him one morning to tell him their grandmother had died the sound of her voice was like a voice in a dream. It was the first time he had talked with

Amanda in many years. "Guy, she's gone. Grandmomma's gone. Please come. When can you come?"

He kept hearing the soft remembered voice all the way to Memphis on the plane and he told himself that all along it was losing Amanda that had made his life so empty and alone and without meaning.

He rented a car at the Memphis airport and started driving to the delta, hurrying to get there in time for the funeral. He drove as fast as he dared down the long straight roads, beginning to lay his plans. At Shelby the rain began.

Now he stood beside Amanda with her husband, Malcolm, holding an umbrella over their heads. The funeral was over. They had stayed to watch the gravediggers shovel the last of the dirt on the grave. We should be doing that, Amanda thought. We should be the ones to do it. She looked at Malcolm. He had his head bowed, trying to be polite and respect Christian burial excesses, trying to hold on to the umbrella and pretend he didn't care that he was standing in mud up to his shoetops.

If there was one thing in the world Malcolm Ashe was good at it was being polite. Besides, he told himself, this was why he had married Amanda, to be part of this world he liked to read about in books. He had been a Faulkner scholar at Yale and it had a big effect on his life.

Guy was looking him over, sizing him up, trying to figure out who he was, this rich New Orleans Jew Amanda had married some years ago. A million times Guy had tried to imagine Malcolm. Nothing he had imagined was anything like this handsome, well-mannered man, standing so quietly, looking so out of place in his hand-tailored Oxford suit.

Much as he wanted to hate him, Guy couldn't find anything to hate.

Amanda was counting the shovelfuls. *Une, deux, trois, quatre, cinq, six, sept, huit, neuf, dix* . . . *uno, dos, tres, quatro, cinco, seis,* one, two, three, four, five, six, seven, eight . . . She was thinking about an afternoon two days before, the last time she had seen her grandmother alive.

It was the first cold day in November and she had driven up to the delta from New Orleans on a whim, thinking she would like to see the fields turned under and lying fallow for the winter. Thinking she would show her grandmother an article she had published in a magazine and make her proud. As it turned out she had never gotten around to getting the magazine out of the car.

Her grandmother was waiting for her on the porch when she arrived, standing at the top of the stairs with her hands on her hips, her glasses dangling on a silver chain, her shirtwaist dress with its uneven hem hanging in waves, her tireless shoulders as straight a a girl's.

They had eaten lunch in the dining room on unironed placemats, then gone to sit in a little sewing room on the back of the house. It was pleasant there, with a fire in the grate and the cold weather pressing against the windows. I don't come home enough, Amanda thought. I need to get up here more often.

"I've taken to sleeping back here now that I'm alone," the grandmother said. She stretched herself out on the daybed and propped her Red Cross shoes up on a pillow. She was tired now. She had outlived both her sons. Guy's father had died in the spring and his mother had gone back to her own people in Tupelo.

"Duke sleeps here with you, doesn't she?" Amanda said. "We're paying her to sleep here at night. I don't know why you won't come on down to New Orleans where I can watch after you."

"Well, of course you know why. I'm perfectly comfortable right here in my own house, thank you. And Duke sleeps right next door in Guy's old room and we're doing just fine. Put some coal on that fire, would you? I love a fire in the daytime." Amanda did as she was told and the two women settled down, her grandmother lying on the daybed reading *The Daily Word*, Amanda sitting in the wicker rocker looking through old copies of *The Progressive Farmer*.

"How is Malcolm?" her grandmother asked, looking up from her reading. "I don't know why he never drives up with you anymore."

Amanda sighed and stuck the magazine down into the side pockets of the chair. "That isn't going too well, Grandmomma. You were right. I shouldn't have married a Jew."

"Oh, Amanda, I never said that. I never said any such thing. It was just such a surprise to me. You know very well I think Malcolm's a wonderful man."

"Well, that's because you don't have to live with him. He's having a fit because I went back to school. He's jealous of everything I do. Oh, shit, it's just that goddamn city. Jesus, I hate that city."

"Please don't say those ugly words in front of me. I can't believe you let those things come out of your mouth. Do you say things like that down there in New Orleans? No wonder Sudie couldn't get you in the Junior League."

"Oh, shit, there isn't any way to talk to you. I didn't want to get in the goddamn Junior League. That was all Sudie's idea. All I want is to get my work done and learn to be the best translator in the world. That's all I'm interested in now. So I can leave Malcolm and get out of that goddamned city."

"I don't know why you always talk so bad about New Orleans. You were dying to marry him and move down there. You couldn't stay away from there. You used to go see Sudie every time she opened the door. . . ."

"Well, that's because I was crazy. Now I hate it. Ever since I quit drinking I can't stand to live there. All anybody down there does is drink and be snotty to each other. And quit bringing up that goddamn Junior League stuff. That was years ago. You and Sudie can't get that off your minds a minute. I'm sick of hearing about it. Besides, the reason I didn't get in was because I married a Jew. That's very touchy stuff down there in that old whore of a city."

She poked around in the fire, rearranging the coals, then poured herself a cup of tea. She went over and sat on the floor by her grandmother's bed and laid her head down beside her hand.

"I'm sorry. I shouldn't do this to you. I mean to just come up here and tell you how great everything is. Don't pay any attention to me. I'm really very happy. I love the work I'm doing. And Malcolm's okay. He gives me anything he knows how to give."

"It would have been different if you'd had children. That would have made a difference."

"That's the other thing about that place, Grandmomma. I think she's there. I just can't stop thinking she's there, somewhere in that city."

"Don't dwell on it, honey. It was so long ago. We did what we could. We did what we had to do." She laid her hand on Amanda's head, stroking her hair. "Look out there, honey. It's such a perfect day. Clear as glass. Listen, I'll read you today's lesson." She opened the book and adjusted her glasses on her nose. "I will lift up mine eyes unto the hills," she read. "From whence cometh my help. My help cometh from the Lord, who made heaven and earth . . ."

"I think I'll go for a walk," Amanda said. "I want to walk up to Miss Hattie's and speak to her while I'm here."

"You aren't ever going to find any peace until you accept the Lord as your savior, Amanda. He doesn't make —"

"I know," she said. "I know, I know, I know."

In the night Duke came into Amanda's room and stood at the end of the bed. "You better come on," she said. "I think she's gone. I think she's gone away. I been shaking her and nothing happen."

Amanda flew down the hall into the little room. She stood beside the bed looking down at the cold face. "Why is the window open?" she said. "It's too cold in here."

"I open it to let the spirit out. Can't keep the spirit in after it leave the body."

"All right, all right," Amanda said. "What happened, Duke? What did she say? What did you hear?"

"She just making a noise like trying to push a baby out. Big old sucking noise. Then I woke up and come running in here and she's daid. All the breath gone out of her, just like that. That's a lucky death, go off like that in yo sleep."

Amanda sat on the edge of the bed holding her grandmother's hand until she was trembling with the cold. Then she took her grandmother's old blue wool robe off a chair and put it on and went out into the hall and started making the phone calls.

At dawn she called Malcolm and told him to come down

and help her. Then she looked up the number in her grandmother's address book and called Guy. Then she walked down to the bayou bank still wearing the robe and stood for a long time staring down into the cold brown water, thinking about a story her grandmother used to tell her about an old dog and his bone, how the dog lost his bone by trying to bite the reflection of it in the water. Old greedy yellow dog, Amanda was thinking, seeing him right there in the water, where she had left him as a child. Poor old dumb thing.

The bayou bank was overgrown with weeds now. It had been years since anyone had had a fish fry or gone swimming there. All gone now, Amanda thought. The black iron pots waiting for the catfish, the wild sons and winter fires, the McCameys of Issaquena County.

Her mind returned to Greenfields Cemetery. *Une, dix, tres, cinco, seis, seven, eight, nieve, diez, ocho, nieve, diez.* She looked down the levee road to the little house built on top of an Indian mound where her grandparents had lived while they built Esperanza. The Episcopal priest lived there now. He was the only one brave enough to live that near to Mayersville, which had a black woman for a mayor and was suspected of being a hotbed of revolution.

Dix, tres, cinco, seis, siete, ocho, nieve, diez. Guy moved closer and took hold of her arm. After that the only thing she was paying any attention to was his hand on her arm.

"Now they're all gone," she said. "Now it's only us. Mother used to bring me out here every Sunday after church until Grandmomma put a stop to it," she said, turning to Malcolm. "One Sunday Grandmother picked me up and carried me into the house. 'Leave Amanda here,' she said. 'I can't stop you from going if you have to, but don't ask a child to live with a dead man.' She was a powerful woman, wasn't she, Guy?"

"The only person in the world I was ever afraid of. Not Amanda though. Amanda wasn't afraid of anything, not even Grandmomma. Is she still like that, Malcolm? Is she still that way?"

"Let's get out of here before she catches pneumonia," Malcolm said, taking her other arm.

Later they all got drunk at Beth's house. Everyone got drunk except Guy. Guy never got drunk. In the world he lived in it was stupid to get drunk. Stupid and dangerous. Besides, he was doing something more interesting than getting drunk. He was watching Malcolm.

Malcolm was having a good time. He had forgotten all about being at a funeral. He was getting drunk and listening to Mr. Rife Chaney tell delta stories.

"His name was Hank," Mr. Rife was saying, "after my dentist from Rolling Fork and he was a mussel eater. He'd dig up a mussel and bring it up and set it out in the sun until it opened, then eat the meat. He'd do that all day long, run down to the bayou bank and dig a mussel. He was the sweetest dog in the whole world, named for the sweetest man."

"Who was the dressed-up black man at the funeral," Malcolm said, "the one with the big hat?"

"That was B. C. Ward, Gert's husband. There's a nigger farmer for you. Can't even read and write. Can't write his name but he's got a Cadillac and four tractors and a six-acre fish pond he built himself. I was fishing his pond last week."

"They say gold's going up every day now," Shine Carey

put in. "There's a man in Jackson buying anything gold he can get his hands on."

Mr. Rife ignored Shine and went right back to nigger farmers. "He bought this old frame house and built him a brick room on it. A real nice old frame house on Panther Burn Plantation that Mr. Courtright built in my grand-daddy's time. Well, he just built him a brick room on the back of it. Porches falling off, steps rotting, roof leaking. He just builds on another room."

Malcolm was all over Mr. Rife, bringing him drinks, asking questions, being the best listener in the world.

"Who built the Indian mounds around here?" Malcolm said. "I never saw so many in one place."

Mr. Rife began. "Well, there were Chickasaws and Choc-taws, and before that the mound builders, but nobody knows much about them. Guy McCamey's got Indian blood. Look at his face. His momma was half-Chickasaw. Guy's got a real Indian face. You should have seen him play ball. He looked just like an Indian playing ball."

"Indians make great athletes," Malcolm agreed.

"If you can keep them sober," Mr. Rife said. "Guy can't drink. He'll tell you so himself. He told me he got drunk in Chicago one night and nearly killed a man with his fists."

"You really think it's *Indian*," Malcolm said, "that it's genetic?"

"Sure. We used to play Indians on the colored ball teams in the old Plantation League. It never worked out. There'd always be plenty of whiskey around and you couldn't tell them they couldn't have any. Give them two drinks and they'd be laid out foaming at the mouth. *I've seen them covered with flies.*"

"What kind of colored ball teams?"

"Colored ball teams, son. Regular colored ball teams. Amanda's grandaddy had one. Well, we played some Mexicans. And like I told you, we tried Indians."

"Tell me about the Mexicans," Malcolm said.

"Well, there was a big controversy about playing Mexicans at first. Colored people don't like associating with Mexicans. Mr. Audrey over at Bear Garden Plantation *worked* Mexicans. He *liked* Mexicans. Had the inside of his house all fixed up like you were in Mexico. Rugs hanging on the walls and clay plates and everything Mexican. Well, Mr. Audrey had a Mexican team one year but they never did win a game. Smoked too much marijuana."

"Where did they get it?" Malcolm asked.

"They grew it. Nobody cared. It wasn't against the law. Mr. Audrey let his Mexicans grow it right in the middle of a cotton field. They had a patch the size of a baseball diamond and it grew taller than a man's shoulder all summer long. No one cared if Mr. Audrey played Mexicans. If he wanted to put up with Mexicans it was all right with us. Of course, colored people wouldn't have anything to do with them."

"I'd love to have seen those ball games," Malcolm said.

"We had us some great times," Mr. Rife said. "Still do."

Maybe Mr. Rife will tell him about the Jew peddlers that used to come through the delta selling needles, Amanda thought. Maybe if he gets drunk enough he'll tell Malcolm all about the International Conspiracy of the Elders of Zion.

Everyone was in the kitchen. Amanda wandered off into the living room and sat on the piano bench playing with Beth's old metronome.

In a minute Guy came out from the kitchen and stood beside the piano. "You want to talk?" he asked.

"I don't know if I can," she said. "I don't know where to begin."

"I'll know where to begin," he said, and he picked her up in his arms as though she were a child and carried her out the front door and put her into his car and drove off down the street.

"I don't believe you did that," she said.

"It doesn't matter," he said. "Nothing matters."

Amanda looked out upon the darkened streets of the little community, then across the seat at the serious face of her cousin. It was the same old impassive face she had loved all her life. He was the best football player in the state of Mississippi, she thought. And I never even saw him play a game.

Guy parked the car by the gin and held her while she cried, blowing her nose on his tacky monogrammed handkerchief and getting the front of his pin-striped suit all wet with her tears. It was a suit that would have looked good on a French decorator. Guy's shoulders were so wide that none of the suits he liked ever looked right on him. She remembered him in the boys department at Nell's and Blum's with that glum look on his face when their grandmother would take them shopping in the fall. She could just imagine him somewhere in a Yankee city standing in front of a mirror being talked into that suit and somehow that cheered her up.

"Where in the world did you get that suit?" she said, beginning to laugh.

"Maria bought it. What's wrong with it?"

"Oh, Guy. Nothing's wrong with it. I'm sorry. I'm just being mean. I've been mean all day. I was mean to Malcolm and now I'm being mean to you." She had started to cry again, making little strangling sounds. "Jesus Christ," she said, "oh, Jesus Christ."

"Sissy," he said. "Little Sissy. I think about you every day of my life. Sissy, where is the child? I want to know where she is. I want to see her."

"My God, Guy, don't start that. I don't know where she is. I live in horror that she'll come and find me. Every time I read about children being allowed to see their adoption papers I get terrified she'll come for me. And she's not a child. She's a grown woman."

"I don't believe you don't want to see her."

"Don't talk about it, Guy. I've spent my whole life doing penance for this. Don't make it any harder on me."

"She's my child too. The only one I have."

"It's not the same thing."

"I have loved you all my life, Sissy. And no one else. I would have helped you if I could." He was touching her now, rubbing her arms and her shoulders and her soft fair graying hair. "Shit, I couldn't even help myself. That was the worst summer of my life. Not that the rest of them have been so good. Sometimes I feel like I haven't known what I was doing for years. But I want to find that child. I know that."

"*Don't talk about it.* There's something terrible about it. She's blind or crippled or dead. Or she'll come for me and kill me for deserting her. Shut up about it, Guy. Don't talk about it."

She moved closer to him, moving her hands across his

shoulders, then laying the palms of her hands against his chest, ready to do anything to make him stop talking about it.

"Oh, God," he said.

"It doesn't matter. It's all right. It's raining and Grand-momma's dead and you're supposed to fuck your cousins at your grandmother's funeral. Don't they know things like that in Chicago?"

Then the old desire rose between them and they gave into it while outside the rain poured down upon the houses and the streets and the levees, upon the sidewalks and sheds and graves and clotheslines and fences. The old rain falling and falling all over the little town of Glen Allen, Mississippi.

"Well, we shouldn't have done that," she said, when it was over. "But we did it." Now that it was over she wanted to be away from him. It was too sad, sad and impossible, like trying to fit into a dress she had worn in another life. She moved away from him, back to her own side of the seat.

"How has life done this to us?" he said.

"Life doesn't do things to people, Guy. Life happens. And it's good. Most of it is good."

"Where do you think she is?" he said. "I have to find her. I have to know she's well. I have to know there's something of me left on this earth."

"I think she's in New Orleans. Imagine what it's been like for me to live there all these years knowing that. Guy, you have to take me back now. I can't do this to Malcolm. Mr. Rife will get drunk and start tracing his bloodlines or something."

"Let me come to New Orleans," he said. "Let me see you. We can at least have that after all these years."

"No," she said. "I won't do that to myself. Besides, I may not be there long. I've gone back to school, Guy. To Tulane."

"I heard you were doing some kind of writing."

"I'm a translator. I translate poems from French and Italian into English. I'm getting sort of famous in a limited way."

"What about Malcolm? What will you do with him?"

"I'm going to divorce him. Or let him divorce me, whichever comes first. He's a good man, Guy. He's been good to me. It isn't his fault I don't love him anymore. It's that goddamn city. Jesus, I hate living in that city. It never changes. It never gets to be fall or spring or winter. And you can't see the stars. There're these goddamn clouds all over the sky all the time. Well, now that I have some money I'll be free to make a life for myself."

"Let me leave with you," Guy said. "I'll leave Maria. We'll go somewhere together. We'll be happy. You know we'd be happy." He reached across the seat and pulled her back into his arms. "I need you, Sissy. There hasn't ever been another woman for me. Do you know that? All the women in the world, all the women I've fucked and it's still only you."

"I don't want that, Guy, even if it's true. I don't want to be anyone's woman, yours or Malcolm's or anyone's. I want to find out what I really want in the world."

"I can give you anything you want. I can give you anything that goddamn ingratiating Jew can give you."

"I'm not talking about money. I've had all of that I can stand. I want something else. Something I don't know the name of yet. Oh, well, I don't mean to say things that hurt you."

"What's this work you're doing?"

"Different things. I'm writing for a newspaper. And studying translating. I'm fascinated right now by what happens when you move things from one language to another. Well, all I'm really trying to do is find out what I'm good at. So I can be a useful person, so I can have some purpose."

"You could have me for a purpose."

"And we'll find our little girl and live happily ever after. Is that the scenario? Jesus, Guy, I'm the romantic and even *I* know better than that. Look, you have to take me back now. I can't do this to Malcolm."

"Please say I can come see you in New Orleans."

"No," she said. "Whatever happens from now on, at least it won't be this old sadness." She looked out the window. The rain was falling harder. "I hope the rain doesn't wash all the dirt off the grave," she said. "What if it washes the dirt off the grave?"

"I can't believe you can make love to me like that and then just disappear again. Doesn't this mean anything to you, Sissy? Don't you know the difference between this and the rest of it?"

"I know how sad it is. Don't worry. I know about that. Now take me back. I mean it, Guy, take me back there."

Malcolm was furious with her. When the party broke up and they were back in her grandmother's house, he was so angry he wouldn't let her get in the small walnut bed with him.

"My God, Amanda, I thought you'd wandered off to the river to drown yourself. You've been acting weird ever since we got here."

"Of course I'm acting weird. My grandmother's dead, Malcolm. I'm taking this very hard."

"So you run off from the party with a man without even telling me you're leaving."

"Good God, Malcolm. He was closer to me than a brother. He's my oldest friend."

"You didn't have to go off with him in the car."

"I needed to talk to him about Esperanza."

"I'm taking care of all that. I told you I'd take care of that."

"Look, can I get in the bed now? I'm bleeding again," she said. "I'll have to go see Dr. Friday as soon as we get home. I guess he ought to go on and do a hysterectomy."

"Don't say that. You know how that scares me."

"Look, just let me get in the bed."

She climbed in beside him and held him to her. Keep it on the road, she told herself. No one is happy. We are outside of nature. Nothing outside of nature is happy. Only idiots are happy. She held on to the tight angry body of her husband and fell asleep to dream of wandering in a forest, the child's face looking out at her from behind every tree. The child was glad Amanda was lost, glad she was lonely, glad she was frightened. Amanda walked on and on, pushing aside the thick undergrowth as the light began to leave the sky.

It was one thing to sit in a car in the rain and brag to Guy about leaving her husband and going out into the world to be useful and simple and wise, no longer attached to money and power.

It was another thing to actually divorce Malcolm Ashe. He didn't want a divorce. He was a well-raised Jew. He thought divorce was a terrible dusty Christian sin.

Besides, Amanda liked Malcolm. He had never done an unkind thing to her. He had never told her a lie or denied her anything he had the power to give her or threatened her or broken a promise to her. For years he had devoted himself to Amanda morning night and noon whether she wanted him to or not.

Amanda had met Malcolm at a cocktail party at Delgado Museum. It was the night before her birthday and she was in New Orleans visiting her cousins and trying to decide what to do with her life.

There was Malcolm leaning up against a marble pillar with an oil painting of a pope on the wall behind him. He was wearing a rumpled tweed jacket he had bought years before at the Yale Coop and he was smoking a cigarette so small it was about to burn his fingers. He was just what Amanda had been looking for. She had become enchanted with Jews during the civil rights movement and thought every Jew she met was a crusading liberal.

Amanda and Malcolm proceeded to get drunk together at the benefit and before the night was over she dragged him off to a dive on Royal Street where tourists gather to sing corny songs around a piano bar. Amanda pulled up a stool next to the piano player and announced to everyone at the bar that she and Malcolm had been married an hour before.

"Had to do it," she told everyone. "Got to give this baby a name. Can't have babies running around without daddies to fight off tigers."

Everyone in the bar was delighted to be in on such a brave and fruitful romance and bought them drinks and serenaded them until four in the morning.

Malcolm had lived a sheltered life. He had never been with a woman who had that much energy or that much imagination. He had never been with a woman who seemed to be in that much danger. He wanted to follow her around and protect her. He wanted to see what she would do next.

When the bar closed he took her to the Royal Orleans Hotel and rented a suite of rooms and held her in his arms while she slept off her martinis. He held her in his arms dreaming of tall redheaded sons who weren't afraid of anything. By the time the sun rose Malcolm was in love. He decided to marry Amanda as soon as he could talk her into it. He was very wealthy. He could buy anything he wanted, even a wild Christian girl from Mississippi.

"What do you do for a living?" Amanda asked. They were sitting cross-legged in the middle of the bed taking big drinks of the milk punch the Royal Orleans bartender had made for them and little bites of the lavish breakfast the

Royal Orleans chef had cooked for them. It was one o'clock in the afternoon and already they were getting drunk again.

"I represent minority groups," he said, smiling his charming boyish smile. It was a joke he was fond of telling people. What he was was a management lawyer. What he meant by minority groups were the owners of the restaurants and factories and newspapers he represented.

"Oh, God," Amanda said. "That's wonderful. I wish I had done more to help the civil rights movement. I never did feel like I did all the things I should have done."

"As soon as we get moving let's go out to the lake and sail my sailboat," Malcolm said. "I've had it a month and barely had time to sail it. Can you do that? Can you call the people you're staying with?"

"I don't have anything to wear," Amanda said. "I only brought dress-up clothes."

"We'll buy you some," he said. "Gus Mayers is just down the street."

In the next few months Amanda started going down to New Orleans to visit her cousins every chance she got.

"I've run through all the available men in Mississippi," she confided to her cousin Sudie. They were out at the New Orleans Country Club eating sandwiches by the pool, watching Sudie's children show off on the diving board. "Everybody worth a damn is either married or gay. I'm not getting any younger, Sudie. I'm starting to get fat on the back of my legs. I am. I saw it in the mirror the other day. I think I ought to get married."

"Stand up," Sudie said. "Let me see."

Amanda stood up. "They're not fat," Sudie said. "But I see what you mean. There's something starting up there."

"I really am thinking about getting married."

"Well, for God's sake, find somebody with money," Sudie said. "Being married is bad enough without having to be poor at the same time. Whenever I get tired of Johnny's allergies I just go look at his Merrill Lynch portfolio. It turns me on. I swear it does."

"Malcolm Ashe has plenty of money," Amanda said. "I'll say that for him."

The next afternoon she went with her cousin to Langenstein's to buy cheese for a party they were having that night. A tall mannish-looking woman in a tennis dress came up to them as they were leaving and started talking to Sudie about a book fair they were planning.

"Remember," the woman said, patting Sudie's arm. "This is your big chance to show your stuff." She smiled conspiratorially and moved on off into the imported coffees.

"What was that all about?" Amanda said.

"That's Coleman Riley. She's grooming me to be president of the league next year. But don't tell anyone. It's very hush-hush. Usually it has to be a native, but, well, I've got the skills they're looking for."

"You mean because you're so good at bossing people around?"

"No, that's not what I mean. Chep's got his eye on me. And, well, a lot of men in this city are in love with me. It oils the wheels when you want something done."

At the party that night Sudie's little children were all over the place in their school uniforms, passing napkins, looking like children in an English book. The man who owned Defraites Parish was there and the man who owned the governor and the man who owned the football team.

The man who owned the parish was telling African safari stories but he was too drunk to remember the end of them. He kept starting new ones, then forgetting the end.

"*Town and Country* is coming to do an article on the hundred most prominent New Orleanians," the tennis dress woman was saying. "They're going to film it at Marti's. Can you imagine. Everyone's scared to death they won't get in. I heard Jean deMontluzin offered them her house to make sure she'd get Herbert in but they turned her down."

"Who would film anything in that old thing? They never even cut the yard."

"But, darling, they're never here. They stay on the Coast all the time."

"Did we tell you Mark got into Princeton? Oh, yes, we're terribly pleased. He was in the top percentile."

I could live here like this, Amanda thought. I could have beautiful little children and send them to wonderful schools with blue and white uniforms and wear my tennis dress to the grocery store and have my picture in magazines like Sudie. All I'd have to do is marry Malcolm. She looked over at him, leaning on the stair railing being charming to everyone. They wouldn't mind that he was Jewish. It would be a famous mixed marriage. She's so brave, they would say. So advanced. She married a Jew. Oh, yes, she's very liberal. She's a brilliant girl. We must groom her for something special.

One afternoon she went with Sudie's husband to Galatoire's to talk about it. "If he asks me should I marry him?" she said. "Would you do it if you were me?"

"Why not?" he said. "He's got a good reputation. We'd adore to have you down here with us. Sudie's so fond of you. And when you got bored with him, well, I'll always be here if you get lonely." He reached his pudgy fingers across the table and gave her hand a little squeeze.

"Are you worried about the election?" she said. He was running for district judge.

"Not too much. We might have to buy the black vote and that's a bore. But then, it's always for sale. Last time I ran I had two black leaders in the kitchen the night before the election practically going crazy trying to sell me votes. Come on, let's have another martini before you catch your plane."

"Why not," she said. "Whyyyyyy not."

A few weeks later Amanda and Malcolm flew off to Bermuda and got married. They had a bottle of wine before the ceremony and two more before they even bothered to make love to each other.

Amanda really liked Malcolm Ashe. She liked his boyish smile and his Yale degrees and his beautiful house on Henry Clay Avenue. She had visions of extravagant cocktail parties with Christians and Jews and black people all running around getting to know each other better. Malcolm would be running for office, senator maybe. She would be president of the Junior League or the Council of Jewish Women or both at the same time. "Have a drink," someone was always saying. "Come on, have another."

She could never remember when her vision cleared, when she began to see past the designer gowns to the women who couldn't even comb their own hair. "Darling, she's never combed her own hair. I swear it. Well, she has those Mexicans, you know. She has three or four. They're just like slaves."

"She told her brother she was pregnant and he said, good, he'd go on safari and bring her back a little Negro."

"The Puerto Ricans are pretty good, if you can find one that's devout. Oh, fix that room in the basement. They'll live anywhere. Of course, Hondurans are also nice."

Perhaps it was the faces of the children. She watched them run in and out of the houses on Henry Clay and Webster Street and State Street and Exposition Boulevard. Why do they look so worried? she asked herself. Why do children this rich look so scared?

Then she began to hear the voices. Then she began to really listen.

"Did he get into Newman? Did he get into Country Day? Do you think I should have her tested for Trinity? What if she has to go to Saint George's? I'll die if he doesn't get in this year. Well, we've got him working with a tutor. Well, she'd better make it this year or I don't know what we'll do."

These people hate their children, she decided. They use their children as counters in the games they play.

"Did she get into Sacred Heart? Oh, that's a shame. Well, she'll probably like Saint Stephens. It's a nice little school. There's always Ecole Classique. There's always Montessori. There's always boarding school or that new place out in Metairie."

"Perhaps another weekend. We're packing him off for Europe. Oh, yes, he's off on a tour. I know, isn't it absurd. He's only thirteen and already he's been around the world."

"She's going sailing in the BVI. Oh, yes, it's darling. They have these little regattas just like grown people."

"My dear, did you hear who's queen of Oberon? I heard

they had to lock her in a house in Covington for two weeks to keep her from eating so she'd fit in her dress."

"She's suing the hospital and both the doctors. She's furious because they didn't finish her nose. I mean, her heart stopped while she was on the table. What could they do? Well, she's suing. I swear she is."

"She stole all the drugs out of the medicine cabinet. Oh, it was dreadful. Then she stole the car. Oh, no, they were in Vail. The housekeeper didn't know what to do."

"Shot himself in front of his girlfriend's house while the party was going on. Oh, yes, barely sixteen. They don't know where he got the gun."

"Hung himself in the closet at Covington."

"Jumped off a bridge. Just like his daddy before him."

"Oh, he's disappeared into the Quarter. Won't even take calls. Of course, everyone's known for years. I heard it was a high school boy, an Italian."

"Darling, no one sees him anymore. He's in hiding on Philip Street. Well, the maid goes in."

"No, he hasn't written anything in ages. Just comes over to stay at his cousin's in that old fortress on Camp Street. Just lies out on the lawn drinking and looking at the stars."

What am I doing here? Amanda thought. What am I doing in a place where people hate each other? No, that's wrong. They hate themselves. That's who they really hate. Oh, well, I'll have a drink. I'll call up some people and have a party.

Malcolm's dreams didn't fare much better. Amanda's body wouldn't cooperate. No matter how many times he made love to her, no matter how many mornings she took her temperature or let Dr. Friday blow out her Fallopian tubes, Amanda never got pregnant.

Amanda wanted to get pregnant. She wanted to give Malcolm a baby. She had a UNICEF calendar with a painting of a small black-haired girl on the cover and she would look at it and imagine herself the mother of a child radically different from herself, a small dark-haired girl who was quiet and composed. Amanda's imagination created all sorts of small dark-haired children that could come from her womb. In her dreams she bathed and dressed and loved them, her perfect dreamchildren with their perfectly wonderful genes.

"I wouldn't allow one of my children to marry another Jew," a pediatrician told her at a party. "I'm sick of all the little children at Newman running around with their thick glasses. It's from intermarrying all these years. I *might* let one of my children marry a *Russian* Jew. If they could prove to me their people hadn't had anything to do with French Jews for a thousand years."

"What does all that mean?" Amanda said.

"That the recessive genes disappear when people from different racial groups marry. You and Malcolm would have a wonderful child, for example. Your mania would disappear into his nailbiting."

"Oh, Drusy," Amanda said. "You're insane."

Amanda and Malcolm waited and waited for the baby that never came. Many times Amanda's menstrual period would be a week late, even two weeks late. Then Malcolm's face would light up every time she entered a room and if he touched her she would tremble. Once she was three and a half weeks late. Malcolm came home one afternoon carrying a package and hurried into his bedroom and hid it on a closet shelf. After she started menstruating Amanda took it down from the shelf and looked at it. It was a poster with a picture of a pregnant woman on it. *Pregnant is beautiful* the poster said. Taped to it was a diamond bracelet.

That night she had a talk with Malcolm. "I'm going to get an IUD to regulate my periods," she said. "I won't spend my life waiting for something that isn't going to happen. I'm plenty good enough to love, just like this, me, Amanda McCamey Ashe, singular. I'm tired of the obstetrician's stirrups. I'm tired of Dr. Friday's Fallopian tube torture machine."

"You're going to do what?"

"I'm going to put an IUD into my poor confused uterus and get on with being alive. I'm not an incubator. I'm bored with this baby project."

"I don't believe you'd do that to me."

"Well, you might as well believe it. Because tomorrow I'm going to do it."

After that, whenever Malcolm made love to Amanda he was always thinking about Onan, a man God punished for spilling his seed on the ground. Every time he was inside Amanda he could see God standing over him frowning and looking sad. After a while he quit making love to Amanda altogether.

And what of Amanda's real child? Every time Amanda drove down Saint Charles Avenue she passed the home, a stone building surrounded by oleander bushes. Sometimes she hardly noticed it. Other times, especially on days in early fall, it would loom before her or the sight of the girls standing beside the gate waiting to go to the drugstore would haunt her for hours.

One afternoon she was driving home from a drunken lunch at Brennan's. She stopped the car and got out and walked up the stairs into the front hall. Five or six girls were gathered around a library table. A young man from the Tulane sociology department was helping them fill out forms about their dental habits. Amanda walked up to the table. She put her hands on a girl's shoulders. She had come into the place with the drunken idea of telling the girls not to give their babies away. The sight of them so earnestly filling out the pointless forms took all her resolve away. She had not known they would look so helpless.

"Are you coming here?" the girl she touched asked her. "Are you going to come here?"

"No," she answered. "I came to see about my little sister coming here. Is it a good place? Would it be all right to send her here?"

"I guess so," the girl said. "They've been okay to me."

A sister appeared in the entrance to the room and Amanda made a hurried exit. The girl she had touched followed her to the door. "Come back to see us," she said. Amanda stopped at the door and looked up the wide stairs leading to the dormitory rooms. Her room had been at the top of those stairs.

She walked across the street to the K&B and bought a bottle of wine and went out to Jefferson Parish and drove drunkenly around until she passed out in the parking lot of a Piggly-Wiggly.

Amanda touched her daughter one night without knowing it. It was in a hall behind the back rooms at Antoine's. Wealthy New Orleanians all have special waiters at Antoine's. They call ahead and the waiter meets them at a side door and takes them to one of the rooms on the back of the restaurant. No one who is anyone in New Orleans would be caught dead eating in the front rooms of Antoine's with the tourists.

The night Amanda touched her daughter was a Saturday in February. Amanda and Malcolm were at a party in the Mystery Room arguing politics with two of his partners and their wives. Amanda was arguing. Malcolm was getting drunk and trying not to listen. The room was dark, lit only by candles and a fireplace.

Everyone at the party was good and drunk. Even the waiter was drunk. He was a Frenchman named Bernard who was famous for being drunk. You could depend on him to be drunk any time after five in the afternoon. But anything Bernard lacked in efficiency he made up for in servility and he was in great demand, especially among the wealthy Jews. The wealthy Christians were partial to a black man named Twilight, who was good at rolling his eyes back into his head.

"I don't give a goddamn," Amanda was saying. "Your vested interests are the welfare of mankind, Arthur. Your vested interest is the survival of this planet. You can't just cut half the people in the world off at the trough. Goddammit, you can't let people go hungry."

"You're such a little bleeding heart, Amanda. And you've never worked a day in your life. You don't know what in the shit you're talking about."

"I know you can't go bomb villages off the face of the earth and not have to pay for it in karma. I know that, you bastard."

"Jesus, Amanda, you're getting to be such a pain in the ass. Can't you control this woman, Malcolm? Can't you control your wife? What's getting into you lately, Amanda? Who've you been running with?"

"I read, Arthur. I read books. I read something besides the *Times-Picayune* and the *Wall Street Journal*."

"Amanda," Malcolm said. "That's about enough of that." Arthur's father was a power in the *Times-Picayune*. "You really go to far."

"I'm going home," Amanda said. "That's what I'm going to do. I won't stay here and eat with a bunch of warmongers. I'd catch bad karma from you like a disease. Like a fucking virus. Like flu." She picked up her pocketbook and started out the door, nearly knocking over the waiter who was carrying a tray of d'filet en brochette Medici. He almost dropped it on Malcolm's head.

"Get them some more booze," she screamed in his face. "And get the hell out of my way."

In the hall leading to the phone booths she passed a girl in a navy blue silk dress. The girl was crying. Or about to cry. Walking toward the ladies room holding her pocketbook in front of her like a steering wheel.

"Can I help you?" Amanda said, reaching out her hand, touching the girl's sleeve. "Can I do anything to help you?"

"No, thank you," the girl said, pulling her arm away. "It's nothing. It's just a mistake. Thank you anyway." It was dark in the hall, the girl lowered her eyes. She had been taught never to get into conversations with strangers, not even at Antoine's. She pushed open the door to the ladies room and went on in.

What a place to live, Amanda was thinking. The faces of these dismal French Catholics. Goya could have painted that young woman's face. She shook her head, pulled open the door of the old-fashioned wooden phone booth, and called a cab. Then she called a couple of people she knew, trying to find somebody who wanted to drink with her the rest of the night. Finally she got a journalist from Greenville on the phone. "Well, wake up anyway," she said. "I can't stand it, Joe Lee, I've got to talk to somebody. Well of course I'm drunk. Would I be calling you up if I wasn't drunk? . . . Well, I'm coming over anyway so just go on and open the door."

Inside the ladies room, the young woman, whose name was Barrett Clare, and who was Amanda's daughter, fixed her makeup, took thirty milligrams of Valium, and pulled herself together. When she opened the door to the hall her husband, Charlie, was waiting for her, towering over her in his blond good looks. He was furious with her.

Inside the phone booth Amanda hurled one last demand at her buddy Joe Lee, hung up the phone, and started to open the door. Then she stopped, not knowing what to do, trapped in the corner of the hall by the scene she was overhearing.

"Are you going back to that party and act like a lady?" he said. "Or do you want me to have you sent home?"

"It's not fair," Barrett said. "It isn't fair. You know it isn't fair."

"Life isn't fair," he said.

"You didn't really invite that woman, did you?" She squeezed her pocketbook until her fingernails went through the leather. "You didn't really do that to me?"

"I had to invite her. She wants to come. She works for me, Barrett. She doesn't sit around on her ass all day in a psychiatrist's office feeling sorry for herself. She's going to

Comus and you're going to call her up tomorrow and tell her you'll pick her up and take her with you to the ball. You can use mother's chauffeur."

"I won't do it, Charlie. I just won't do it."

"Then you can pack up and get your ass back over to that mausoleum on Prytania where I found you. How about that?"

"All right. Katherine'll be glad to have me."

"And you go alone, Barrett. You aren't taking Charles with you."

She lowered her chin into her chest until it touched her breastbone. "I will take him anywhere I go. He belongs to me. No one could take him from me."

"You just try me, baby. You just try me and see."

Amanda could stand it no longer. She slammed open the door of the phone booth, making as much noise as she could. Tell him to get fucked, she wanted to say. Tell him you read the Napoleonic Code. But she didn't say it. She had already been rebuffed.

She brushed past the couple as quickly as she could and wandered out the side door and down the narrow passageway and out onto Saint Louis Street. She stood leaning against an iron column, picking off pieces of the peeling green paint.

The air was moist and full of the smells of the river and the sacks of oyster shells piled up by the banquette. The sweet smell of fish and spilled wine was all around her like a cowl. Three drunk college boys came by drinking Hurricanes and falling all over the sidewalk. The taxi was taking too long to come. A band started up across the street, four bored musicians playing dixieland. All I need now is a couple of little black boys to tap dance for quarters and I'd be all set, she said to herself. Way down yonder in New Orleans, in the land of the dreamy dreams.

Inside the restaurant Barrett and Charlie Clare returned to the party. The party they were enjoying that night was in the Rex Room. A senior partner of Putney, Carroll was having a surprise fiftieth birthday party for his wife. She was surprised, all right, but she wasn't having any fun. She had given orders to everyone she knew not to give her a birthday party. She had taken an Antabuse that morning and planned to spend a quiet evening getting used to the idea of getting older. Instead, she was sitting at the end of a U-shaped banquet table watching forty people get drunk and pretending not to be mad about the presents they had given her. They had given her a bottle of Geritol and a bottle of hair dye and a pair of support hose and a lot of stupid cards and some inexcusable book called *How to Be Hip over Forty.*

She was sitting at the end of the table in a brown tweed suit, being pissed off and refusing to talk to anyone. The only interesting thing that had happened all evening was when Clayton Paige let it slip that Charlie Clare had invited the receptionist to Comus. Of course it was accepted practice for men in the crewes to send invitations to their little sweeties so they wouldn't feel left out at Mardi Gras. Still, one arranged for someone else to do the inviting. It really wasn't done to invite your own mistress yourself.

"Did you hear Stella Marcus was going to the balls this year?" someone was saying. "I saw her at Oberon and she was dancing with everyone at Proteus."

"What did she do with Sidney?"

"Oh, he sits upstairs and watches her dance like a good little well-raised Jew. Can you believe it?"

"Of course he can't be on the floor committee because of his religion. So he just goes along and *watches*. Isn't that the limit?"

"Oh, balls are such a bore, anyway," someone said. "I don't know why we keep on doing it."

"We have to do it. It's our responsibility. I mean, after all, sweeties. It's what we do."

Down the hall in the Escargot Room the floor committee of Momus was eating Pompano en Papillete and arguing about whether to start serving drinks to ladies at the ball. "Let them drink in the ladies room like they've been doing for years," Claiborne Redding was saying. "For God's sake, Paine, they love to sneak in there with their little bottles. You'll take all the fun out of the ball if you start serving them drinks."

"He's right," another man said. "Susie's the cutest thing, finding all the little train bottles in the house and sticking them in the pockets of her mink. She had a quart of whiskey hidden on her last year. I said, 'Susie, you'll be the most popular girl in New Orleans tonight.'"

✤ ✤ ✤ ✤ ✤ ✤ ✤ ✤ ✤ *6* ✤ ✤ ✤ ✤ ✤ ✤ ✤ ✤ ✤

Amanda had an ally during the years she was married to
Malcolm, a black woman named Lavertis, a beautiful Creole
who had come with her husband to New Orleans to escape
the sugar mills of South Louisiana. By the time Amanda
knew her, Lavertis was alone with small children to support
and could only do work that allowed her to be home early
in the afternoon. In New Orleans that meant housework,
wearing a white uniform, washing a white lady's underwear,
standing all morning ironing linen sheets and Brooks
Brothers shirts and white tablecloths.

The day Amanda moved into the house on Henry Clay
Avenue Malcolm's mother sent Lavertis around to help
with the unpacking. "I'll give her to you if you like," she
said. "She's too clever to be a laundress. She has nice manners and she's honest, but uppity. Too uppity for me, but
she might work out for you. Well, see what you think. If
you like her you can keep her."

Amanda kept her. Or the other way around. Amanda and
Lavertis loved each other from the start. They liked the
way each other looked. Lavertis *was* beautiful. She had
lovely erect posture and a wonderful face. Everything she
did in the world was done with courtesy and with love. If
she opened a box she opened it with ceremony, one flap at
a time, as if it might contain a surprise. If she ironed a lace-

trimmed sheet, it was not as a servant irons, with resentment or impatience, but as a person in the business of augmenting and admiring the lace-maker's art. "Look a here," she was always saying to Amanda. "Look at this pretty thing. Imagine making something like that. I bet that come from Paris, France."

Lavertis thought Amanda looked like a movie star, flying all around the house unpacking everything at once, drinking orange juice out of a wineglass, her hair falling all over her face, unpacking and redecorating. Unpacking and talking and complaining about her hangover, pushing furniture around and asking Lavertis a million questions about herself.

All day that first day they pushed and shoved furniture around and opened windows and unpacked boxes and sorted sheets and towels and pillowcases.

Around four in the afternoon they sat down in the sun room to survey their work. "Well," Amanda said. "What do you think?"

"It looks a lot better," Lavertis said. "It doesn't look so much like a museum."

"Wait till I paint it. Wait till I get rid of those gray walls."

"They likes that color," she said. "His momma and his auntie got everything painted that color."

"Do they keep the drapes closed all the time?"

"Most of the time, unless we're dusting. I guess they don't want the sun coming in and fading things. Of course, they're old people. They got old ways."

"Well, we're new people," Amanda said. "We're going to have all the sunlight we can get."

Later, when Lavertis was ready to go home, Amanda

insisted on driving her. "So I can see where you live," she said. "In case I need to get you for something."

They walked out to the car and Lavertis opened the back door. Amanda sighed and put her hands on her hips. She looked down at the ground, trying to decide what to do. "Look," she said at last. Lavertis wasn't looking. "Look here, Lavertis, we've got to get some things straight between us. I can't have you sitting in the back seat. I used to be a civil rights worker. Well, not much of one, but at least I helped. Anyway . . ."

"I knew all about that," Lavertis said. They were standing by the car beneath the live oak trees with the evening traffic going by down Henry Clay. The rich men were coming home to dinner. "I was right down there in Abbeville praying to the Lord every night that you all wouldn't get me killed."

"Oh, my," Amanda said. "I never thought of that. How old were you?"

"I was in high school when it was all in the papers. I was scared to go to school. I thought somebody was going to come and shoot me."

"Oh, my," Amanda said. "I'm sorry. I never thought of it that way."

"Well, it was for a good cause," Lavertis said. "Now I'm glad it happened."

"Well, come on," Amanda said. "Get in the car. Look, let me put it this way. Where do you want to sit?"

"I'll sit up there," she said. She very formally got into the front seat and put her pocketbook in her lap, and the two women drove off down Saint Charles Avenue looking straight ahead, getting used to being new people in the old museum of New Orleans, Louisiana.

✤

Lavertis ran the house on Henry Clay Avenue to perfection, hiring other servants when she needed them, telling the gardener what to plant and when to trim the hedges, taking care of small repairs, making grocery lists.

It left Amanda plenty of time to drink.

Lavertis took care of her when she had hangovers, pretending they were colds or sinus headaches or flu. She would come into Amanda's bedroom bringing glasses of chocolate milk or iced tea, and sit on the bed listening to Amanda's morning-after remorse. By noon they would be together in the library watching *As the World Turns*. Lavertis would be ironing, Amanda lying on the couch beginning to feel better, comforted by the sound of the steam rising from Lavertis's tireless iron.

The hangovers might have gone on forever. Amanda might be lying on that Henredon sofa watching *As the World Turns* right this minute except for a series of accidents that even Amanda's ability to rationalize couldn't overlook.

Of course, even before the accidents Amanda hated being drunk. She hated never knowing where she left her car or her pocketbook or her evening wrap. She hated calling people up and apologizing for things. Dozens of times she swore off alcohol. A week or so would go by. She would start lecturing her friends on the evils of alcohol. Then there would be a party. Then she would decide to have a glass of wine. Then she would be drunk again.

When the accidents began they happened one right after the other. First she fell down a flight of stairs. She quit for two months after that. Then she turned the car around three times on a rain-soaked road and plowed into a power line pole. Then she got drunk at a bar called The Saints and went upstairs and started interviewing the hookers. She had been writing articles for a local paper and had the idea that a press card would take her anywhere. The first hooker liked being interviewed. The second hooker hit her in the face and knocked her down.

But the worst thing of all, the thing that caused Amanda to quit drinking forever, was the night Coretta Scott King came to New Orleans and the Ashes were invited to meet her.

The party was held in a famous French Quarter restaurant. The owner of the restaurant had given Mrs. King $200,000 to start a scholarship fund in her husband's name. She was in town to accept the gift at a ceremony at Dillard College.

Amanda started getting drunk before she even left the house. They had been invited to the party because Malcolm was the restaurant owner's labor lawyer. He would never have told her about the invitation if he had dreamed she was going to accept it.

"Why are you going downtown to see that woman strut her black ass all around Knoll's Restaurant acting like the great martyr's wife when everybody knows her husband screwed half the women in the South. She probably wanted to shoot him herself. Hell, she might have done it. Why are you going down there, Amanda? Will you just tell me that?"

"You don't have to go if you don't want to," she said. "I happen to admire her very much. I don't want you to go with me anyway. I wouldn't be able to talk to her with you around."

"How much have you had to drink?"

"None of your goddamn business." She was putting on her shoes, getting up and starting to leave. "I wouldn't let you go with me if you wanted to. I wouldn't want Mrs. King to know I was with someone who does what you do for a living."

"As opposed to what you do for a living?" he said.

Amanda slammed out of the house, got into the car, and drove on down to the Quarter. She stopped on the way and bought a bottle of wine and drank most of it out of the bottle. By the time she got to Knoll's she was good and drunk. She sat down at the bar and started talking to the black bartenders in a conspiratorial tone. "Do you guys really think Mr. Knoll likes black people? Do you think he gave Mrs. King that money because he's such a good guy? He should have used that money to raise your salaries. Let me tell you something. I'm married to the man Mr. Knoll loves, the man who fixes it so you guys never get a union. I'm married to the man who oversees the hiring and firing of every single man and woman who works in this place. And if you think Jodie Knoll gives a damn about Dillard University or any goddamn thing in the world but his own profits you're just as crazy as he hopes you are. And the minute Mrs. King gets here I'm telling her so. I know Jodie Knoll. I know all about him. I know his humanitarian ideals and his fascist heart and his racist jokes."

Amanda was surrounded by black bartenders. They didn't know what to think. They knew this crazy white woman was fixing to get them fired. Beyond the circle of bartenders a group of well-dressed people were giving each other horrified looks and trying to decide what to do. Mr. Knoll knew what to do. He came charging across the room through a sea of black and white faces and took hold of Amanda's arm.

"Let go of me, you son-of-a-bitch," she said. She thought he was a bouncer. "I'm Mrs. Malcolm Ashe. I'm married to Mr. Knoll's labor lawyer and I'm here to organize your goddamn kitchen help."

"Get this woman out of here," Mr. Knoll said. "Somebody get this woman out of here. Willy, get over here and help me out with this."

"Where's Mrs. King?" Amanda was yelling. "I want to talk to Mrs. King."

Mrs. King was being escorted into the restaurant by an entourage of Dillard professors. She turned her head and looked Amanda's way.

"Coretta," Amanda called out. "Come here. Come over here. I've got to talk to you. I've got to tell you where you are. I have to tell you who these people are who have you. *Coretta!* I've got to talk to you!"

But the real bouncers were there now and three Secret Service men. "Take your hands off me, you sons-of-bitches," she was yelling. "Don't you dare touch me, you goddamn fascist pigs. Coretta, come help! Coretta, come let me tell you where you are!"

The men took Amanda out a side door and put her into a car. They drove off through the crowded streets of the French Quarter. Halfway home she passed out in the lap of a Secret Service man. When the car got to Henry Clay the driver helped Malcolm carry her into the house.

"That's it," she said when she woke. "That was the last straw. That was really the last goddamn straw." As soon as she could get out of the bed she pulled on a robe and went wandering around the house looking for Lavertis. She found her in the sun room watering plants.

"I've got to quit drinking," she said. "Lavertis, you wouldn't believe what I did last night. I can't even stand to tell you what I did."

Lavertis put the watering can down and took Amanda into her arms. "Oh, Mrs. Ashe," she said. "I been waiting so long to hear you say that. I've been praying and praying for that. Every Sunday I go down to the prayer circle and pray you'll stop doing yourself that way."

"What will I do?" Amanda said. "How will I do it? I don't know how to do it."

"First you got to find something else you like to do," Lavertis said. "You got to get you a baby or a job or something so you hadn't got so much time on your hands."

"It has to stop," Amanda said. "I'm going to end up like my mother if I don't stop. I'll end up spending my life in a back room where the sun can't even get in."

"You'll do it," Lavertis said. "I know you'll do it. You can do anything you want to do. A lady as smart and all as you are."

It was not easy to stop drinking. *I am a pocket of habits in a burning universe* Amanda read somewhere and stuck up on her mirror. The hardest part was going to parties. The hardest part was not actually being there. The hardest part was thinking about it beforehand.

"You're mindfucking, Amanda," the behaviorist she went to said. "You're spending more time dreading the party than you are being there. The party's only going to last two hours. Just suffer those two hours instead of thinking about it for days beforehand. Or don't go. You're a rich lady. You don't have to go anywhere you don't want to go. Are you listening, Amanda? Listen to me. Please listen to me."

"Do you want to fuck me?" she said.

"No, I want to make you well. Do you want a tranquilizer to take before you go to parties? To use for a month or two?"

"I don't think so. I don't like to take drugs."

"Alcohol is a drug."

"No it isn't, Walter. Alcohol is a way of life."

"All right. It's a way of life."

"It's a religion. It's Dionysius."

"I'm going to tell you something, Amanda. You can serve that god sober. You can do anything sober you can do drunk, including ecstasy. You were capable of ecstasy when you were a child, weren't you?"

"Oh, God, yes. When I was little I lived in the water. I am deliriously happy in water. I go crazy in water."

"Do you want some Antabuse for the parties?"

"No, I wouldn't be caught dead taking that stuff. Let me see how much longer I can do it this way."

Needless to say Amanda's friends were horrified that she quit drinking. What did it mean, they whispered among themselves. Did it mean she would be wandering around their parties listening to every word they said?

"Oh, come on, Amanda," Dr. Lovett said. He was the Ashes' family doctor. "You can have a glass of wine."

"Leave me alone," she said. "I don't want a goddamn glass of wine. I quit drinking. I told you I quit drinking. Don't talk about it."

"What's that you've got in the glass? Is that water? In a wineglass?"

"I'm made out of water, Drusy," she said. "I'm ninety-eight percent water and the rest is a finely balanced highly sensitive delicately tuned chemical mix and I'm tired of pouring alcohol into it so I'll be as dumb as all the rest of you."

"Jesus Christ, Amanda, you ought to hear yourself. You sound like some kind of evangelist. Well, there's nothing worse than a reformed whore, they always say."

"I'm trying to save my life, Drusy. I'm sick of having hangovers all the time."

"People have been getting drunk since the dawn of time, Amanda. The first thing men did with the first grain they stored was find a way to make alcohol out of it."

"So it's time to find something better to do," she said. "Time to climb down out of the trees."

"Are you still drinking water?" Monroe Frazier said, coming up to them, trailing his mannerisms. "Dear heart, that's getting to be rather a bore."

"Excuse me," she said. "I have to be somewhere else. I have to collect Malcolm and get out of here."

"Now don't go off mad, Pussy Faye," Monroe said. "Don't go off in a huff."

"Fuck you, Monroe," Amanda said. "You'd give anything in the world if you could quit being a drunk. You're just mad because I'm doing something you can't do."

She pushed him out of the way. She put her hand on his pin-striped Christian Dior suit and shoved him out of her way and made for the door, leaving her coat and purse and Malcolm behind. She headed down the stone stairs to the sidewalk. I'm leaving this behind me if it's the last thing I ever do in my life, she told herself, moving on down Philip Street like a tank, head down, hands in the pockets of her three-hundred-dollar skirt, scuffing up her leather boots on the bricks. I'm leaving it. I hate them. I hate every goddamn one of them. I hate those goddamn little drunk Frenchmen and drunk Jews and drunk white Anglo-Saxon Protestant princes and princesses. I know there's something better to do in the world than hang around doing numbers on each other in this fucking dead old anachronistic world. Goddamn it, I know there's something to do in the world besides get drunk. . . .

"Did you really shove Monroe into a mirror?" Malcolm said. "Did you really insult him in his own house? I don't know about you, Amanda. I don't know . . ."

"Don't you dare talk to me about that," she said. They were fighting it out in their bedroom. "You goddamn self-righteous bastard. Don't you dare say a word to me about anything. I hate this goddamn place. I hate this life. I hate it, Malcolm, do you hear me? And I'm getting out. I'm getting out of here if it's the last thing I ever do in my life."

"I hate their guts," she screamed at her behaviorist. "You don't know what it's like. You can't imagine what it's like at those parties."

"Then don't go," he said. "Don't go to the parties."

"How could I not go? You have to go. I hate Drusy. He's the worst one. Every time he sees me at a party he starts in on me about it."

"Are you getting plenty of exercise, Amanda?"

"God, yes. I'm doing ballet and yoga and swimming an hour a day. All I do is exercise. Goddammit, Walter, what am I going to do about those parties?"

"You're going to quit going. Now get in the chair. I'm

going to hypnotize you and put some good ideas in your head. Then I'm going to take you to lunch."

"Are you sure you don't want to fuck me?"

"I never said I didn't want to, Amanda. I said I wasn't going to. And that's another thing. I want you to find somebody to fuck. It's unhealthy not to fuck anyone."

"I can't fuck anybody. I'm married. Malcolm would kill me."

"Then stop being married to him. Come on, get in that chair."

"Shrinks don't talk like that, Walter. They're going to kick you out of the club for saying things like that."

"They already did," he said. "Come on. Get in the chair. And I'm serious about you finding someone to fuck. If you keep putting it off, when it finally happens it's going to hit you like a ton of bricks."

"What a nice idea," she said, settling down into his chair, imagining a love affair falling down on top of her like a disintegrating skyscraper. "I've been waiting all my life for that to happen."

"Everything happens," he said. "Anything we can think of happens."

"I've stopped going to parties," she told Malcolm. "I mean it. Not a single one."

"Are you going to the firm dinner with me on Saturday night?"

"Nope. Those people bore the shit out of me. When they're all in a room together it's like some vast superego sucking the juice out of my brain. Or when we're all sitting down at the tables like good little lawyers and wifelets. I always think maybe Jesus will come and nail us all to the chairs to punish us. . . ."

"Well, you're going with me to that dinner, Amanda. I don't care whether it bores you or not. It's something we have to do."

"I don't have to do a goddamn thing but get myself well. Besides, the Ballet of the Americas is in town. It's the first time it's toured in years. I'm going to see Maurice Béjart dance. He's going to dance *The Firebird*."

"I don't know who you are anymore, Amanda," Malcolm said. "I look at you and I can't find the girl I married. I don't know what you're talking about half the time."

But she had left the room.

"All I ever wanted from the stuff to begin with was the sugar," Amanda told Lavertis one morning. "I think now I was in it all along for the sugar. So anytime I want a drink I'm going to eat all the candy and ice cream and cake I want. I guess I can work my way up to protein later."

That afternoon Lavertis walked down to the store and bought all the ingredients and made a yellow cake and left it sitting on the counter in the kitchen. It had real caramel icing an inch thick that was made from scratch in an iron skillet. There was a note in Lavertis's careful handwriting propped up on the cake cover.

I am so proud of you. Lisa's husband came back. I think he's planning on taking her child away. Grandpa got out the flower boxes for spring. Bob is back on the staff but he's still mad at David. He and Lisa are going to get together for lunch. More next week.

It was something Lavertis had started doing to keep Amanda up with the events of *As the World Turns*. Amanda never had time to watch *As the World Turns* anymore. She had taken Lavertis' advice and found something to do to fill up all the time she used to spend having hangovers. She had walked across the street to Tulane and signed up for five classes in the foreign languages and English departments. She was getting up at dawn to begin her work, sitting at the dining room table covering pages of paper with her huge illegible scrawl, relearning two languages and the craft of translation all at once, learning fast.

"I think I have enough left," she said to herself, meaning her brain cells. "I think I have plenty."

Soon she was the golden girl around the Tulane foreign languages department. Small magazines were accepting her translations almost by return mail.

Lavertis was as excited about Amanda's new career as Amanda was herself. It was Lavertis who thought up turning a spare bedroom into an office.

"You can't move those papers on and off the dining room table every time you want to have a meal," she said. "Make Mr. Malcolm send you out a desk from the office. They got a hundred desks down there."

"I think that old table in the basement will be fine," Amanda said. "Go call Clarence and tell him to get over here and help us move it."

Lavertis began to change her role in Amanda's life. She brought endless cups of coffee into the room on trays as she had seen secretaries do on television. She answered the door and the phone and told everyone Mrs. Ashe was working and couldn't be disturbed. She noticed if Amanda's spirits got low.

"I haven't heard that typewriter going lately," she would say over her shoulder as she dusted the piano. "I read about some big translator coming to talk at UNO," she would mention as she got out the vacuum. "Guess you'll be going out there to hear him. Guess you'll be traveling around giving speeches before we know it."

Amanda began signing her maiden name to her translations. *Amanda McCamey*, it said. *Translation by Amanda McCamey*. The first time she saw her name in print it excited her so much she took the magazine home and hid it.

After a few days, she got it out and showed it to Malcolm.

"Oh, my God," he said. Malcolm knew what he was seeing was more than a twelve-line poem in *The New England Review*. "Now you're going to start that. Why don't you go on and stop wearing my rings, while you're at it. Go all the way. Stop spending my money." This was an uncharacteristic thing for Malcolm to say. He never mentioned money to Amanda. He and Amanda just pretended money didn't exist.

"I would if I knew some other way to get some." She started out of the room. Then she came back and took his face in her hands. He was sitting in a high-backed Queen Anne chair looking so tired, looking so forlorn.

"Start thinking about a life without me," she said, relieved to be saying it at last. "I was the Wasp princess and it didn't work out. You don't have to stay here forever with an idea that didn't work. Get out of here and find a woman with black hair and have yourself some babies."

"Don't say that," he said. "It's like telling me my mother just died."

"I'm not your mother," Amanda said. "Your mother's

right over there on State Street waiting to welcome you home."

"I'm sorry I said that about the money," he said. "I didn't mean that. You can have all the money you want as long as you want it. You know that."

"It doesn't have anything to do with money," Amanda said. "It has to do with us not having anything in common, not a single dream or idea. It has to do with the future. I want there to be one for me. As long as we stay in this dead marriage the future can't happen for either of us. Pretty soon I'm going to have to leave here, Malcolm. I feel it coming like a storm across the delta."

"Where are you planning on going, Miss Weather Barometer?"

"I don't know. I just know life isn't supposed to be a holding action."

The next month Amanda's grandmother died and left her half of Esperanza, seven hundred acres of delta land under cultivation.

Now, she said, driving home from the funeral. Now there is not a single thing to keep me from being free.

When he got back from Chicago after the funeral Guy couldn't stop thinking about Amanda. He thought about his body deep inside of hers, long ago and last month and in every sort of dream and predicament. He began to dream of her, something he hadn't done in years. Every woman he fucked became her. Finally he stopped seeing all the women he fucked in Chicago. Finally he only thought about Amanda, and about the child, the girl, the woman. He thought about the girl with different faces, at different ages. He imagined he saw her on the streets, in movies, in restaurants.

He began to cry in odd times at odd places and became so cold and distant to Maria that her whole family stopped speaking to him. He began to imagine that her father would have him killed, that he would turn a corner at any moment and the hit man would be laying for him.

One night he could stand it no longer. He had been off on a business trip during which he was barely civil to the men Maria's father had sent him to see. When he got home Maria made him a late supper in the kitchen. He ate it in slow disinterested bites, listening to her ramble on about her sisters and their families. How did I get here with this ugly Italian woman, this big-nosed woman sitting across a table from me? Is this what I bought with my talent and my skills? This foreigner, this idiot, this invalid. Thank God there are no children. Thank God life didn't do that to me. Imagine children with skin like that, with hair that thick and coarse, with eyes that stupid and permitting. This is what I sold out for? And for what? None of the power has passed to me. None of the money has come to me. It is all in her name still.

Across the table Maria rambled on, knowing he wasn't listening to a word she said, content to have him there.

After Maria went to bed Guy walked around the house touching the dark shapes of the furniture. Light from a streetlamp poured in the windows of the living room.

"Goddamn that streetlight," he said for the thousandth time. "It fucks up the stars."

He sat down at his grandfather's desk. It was the only thing in the house Guy felt was really his. Maria and her decorators tolerated it like some sort of an indictment, this old handmade plantation desk taking up a perfectly good wall in the contemporary splendor of the Mies van der Rohe living room.

Guy sat at the desk all night pushing the little drawers in and out, thinking of Esperanza, of the old days, of Amanda, and of the girl who was his daughter, asleep somewhere in a stranger's bed.

At dawn he made some phone calls, drove out to the airport, got into a small plane that belonged to the family, and flew out over the lake, then banked and turned, headed for New Orleans.

Vaiden Canizaro was waiting for him on the porch of his lakefront mansion. He looked like the old emperor he was, watchful, intense, impossible to intimidate or overpower or fool.

He took Guy into his study and held out a manila envelope. "It is here," he said. "I hope it will set your mind at ease."

Guy could not move his hand. He stared at the folder. He could not reach out his hand to take it. "Tell me," he said. "Tell me what it says."

"That she is a grown married woman. That she is well. She was raised by the Allains here. That's sugar plantation money. She's married to a lawyer, a young partner in Putney, Carroll, the society law firm."

"Where does she live?" Guy said. "I have to look at her. I have to see what she looks like."

"I arranged for that. She plays tennis. My correspondent says she plays nearly every Sunday at a club. I arranged for someone to take you there. A man named Todd Denery, who moves in those circles, an asshole but you can tolerate him, I suppose. He thinks you're looking the town over to see if you want to live here. He was impressed by your name. Of course, there's no assurance she'll be there tomorrow."

"What is her name? What do they call her?"

"Barrett. Barrett Clare."

"How will I know which one is her?"

"You'll find a way."

"I won't forget this, Vaiden."

"These things happen to all of us. We help each other. We fix them up. We go back home. It all works out."

Sunday was a clear bright day. Guy had refused Vaiden's offer of a bed and taken a suite at the Pontchartrain Hotel on Saint Charles Avenue. He was waiting in the lobby when Todd Denery came to pick him up.

"I used to watch you play," Todd said, helping him into the car with elaborate courtesy. They drove off down Saint

Charles Avenue. Guy hadn't been in New Orleans in years. He was surprised at how little anything had changed. "The city never changes," he said. "I had forgotten how quiet it is."

"I was quite a fan of yours," Todd continued. "I'll never forget that Sugar Bowl when you played Nebraska. What a football game. It was freezing cold that day."

"It's kind of you to take me to your club. If we move here my wife will need someplace to play."

"It's the oldest lawn tennis club in the United States, you know. We're proud of that. There's a waiting list. But it wouldn't apply to you, of course. We'd figure out something for you."

"Who are the good women players around here?"

"Oh, Diana Davis is about the best. And Anne and Sally Waters, they're sisters. They take turns winning things."

"There's a woman my wife met somewhere named Barrett plays down here. Clare, that's her name. Barrett Clare. Do you know her?"

"Barrett Clare?"

"I guess that's her name."

"Oh, yeah, Barrett Allain. That married Charlie Clare. She's pretty good. She's a queer duck. She's some kind of a poet. She doesn't mix much with people at the club. Well, the Allains are funny folks, intellectuals, liberals, you know the kind."

They turned off Saint Charles at Jefferson and crossed Magazine and pulled into the parking lot of the new Lawn Tennis Club. It looked like a motel.

"I wish you could have seen the old club before they built this one," Todd said. "The old club was one of the most beautiful things in this city. It's a nigger tennis club now. The city bought it. They let this old black player run it as a city playground. He's a nice old guy but he's got all these blacks and Chicanos playing there, trashing the place. You ought to see what they did to the swimming pool, which had tiles made for it in Mexico. One of the Palafox boys gave them to us. Sent them from Mexico City. Well, times change."

Guy sighed, wondering if the man ever stopped talking. Jesus, he thought, Jesus Christ. The South. I had forgotten.

"I grew up playing," Todd was saying. "It's a way of life for me. Of course, all the tournaments are ruined for me now. You have to let anybody in. They'll wear anything. They don't care how distracting it is. Last week I had to play a man who wore a shirt advertising his business."

I am on my way to see my child for the first time in my life and I have to listen to this idiot, Guy thought. He smoothed the knuckles of one hand against the other, breathing as softly as a cat.

They went into the building and on into the snack bar to get a drink. As soon as they entered the door Guy began searching the faces of every woman who was walking by. The snack bar was the center of the Sunday morning club activity. Women were walking by in lovely fresh tennis dresses with matching ribbons and headbands and hats, all going in and out of the doors zipping and unzipping their racket covers, sipping Cokes, talking to each other. Any one of them could be her. Guy was sure he saw his dark eyes on one woman. He saw Amanda's smile on another. Once he saw his grandmother's shoulders. Todd kept chattering away, introducing him to people, talking about the club.

"A hundred years ago this place was started. Well, you

have to be at the old club to get the full effect of that. Think of playing tennis on top of a hundred years of tennis history . . ."

"Look," Guy said. "If you don't mind I'll just wander around by myself and get the feel of the place. You don't need to introduce me to anyone. They're all getting ready to play."

Todd went off to the locker room and Guy walked carefully over to the board where members signed up for courts. He looked down the list of names. It was there, halfway down the page. *Barrett Clare*, it said in careful legible handwriting. *Barrett Clare/Shelly Brunstetter — Court 4*.

Guy moved out of the glass doors and up the stairs to the balcony and looked down on the neat green rectangle.

Two women were on the court. One of them was tall and blond, with long braids down to her waist. As Guy watched she returned a serve with a beautiful clean down-the-line backhand and moved quickly to the net, laughing with delight at her good shot.

Across the court from her a young woman swung easily and without haste, without even any apparent interest and put the ball away in a corner far from the blond girl's reach.

"Nice shot," the blond girl called out. Then the girl who was his daughter turned her face his way. It was an impassive, humorless face. It was Amanda's face with all the gaiety and passion gone. The girl wore Amanda's face as if it were a shadow. This is real, Guy thought. This is true. And he watched his child as the game went on.

All of her moves were exactly right. She played like someone who has had thousands of dollars' worth of tennis lessons. She made almost no mistakes. Because of that she was beating the blond girl badly.

The blond girl played as Amanda would have played, fiercely, with much gesturing and cursing and hitting her racket on the ground. And across the court the child he had dreamed of a million times picked up the tennis balls one by one with the edge of her racket, gave each one a careful precise bounce and served or returned them as if she were a tennis-playing machine.

For almost an hour Guy watched his child, watched the muscles in her legs, watched the arc of her arm as she hit the flawless serves. There had never been anything in his life like the hour he stood on the balcony of the New Orleans Lawn Tennis Club watching the breath enter and leave the body of the strange young woman who was his only child.

Her legs were lovely and well formed, her breasts were full, her hands were graceful and sure. There was no motion wasted. There was nothing excessive anywhere. Even her hair stayed in place, tied back with a brown and white checked ribbon that matched the trim on her ladylike tennis dress. She is like me, he thought. She is careful, like me.

A strange thing was happening to Guy. In some absurd way he was starting to root for the crazy blond girl with the braids. She was losing so badly and trying so hard not to.

Finally the match was over. Barrett came up to the net. She reached out and the two women shook hands. They poured water from a steel pitcher and drank. As they were gathering up their things to leave the court, a child came to the gate behind them. A wild fat little redheaded boy. He came bursting out into the court yelling about something, and as Guy watched, his daughter gathered his grand-child into her arms, put her face down into his wild curly hair. Now she was smiling. Now her face had come alive. I have to hear her speak, Guy thought. I have to hear her voice.

He leaned over the railing and dropped his glasses into the path of the women and the child. "Could you help me, please," he said, leaning over the railing. "I dropped my glasses. Would you throw them to me please."

"Of course," the blond girl said. She picked them up. "You're lucky," she said, "they aren't broken." She threw them up into his waiting hands. Barrett turned her face to his. He caught the glasses. "Nice throw," he said to the blond girl.

"Nice catch," the blond girl said.

It was hot for February. Hot and humid, one of those languid midwinter New Orleans days. By the time Guy got back to the hotel his golf shirt was soaked with sweat. He pulled it off, then lay down on the bed with his hands on his chest, letting the knowledge sink in, letting it run, letting it go.

It was two A.M. when he got back to Chicago. He parked in the driveway, went inside, took a Browning thirty-ought six out of a closet in the hall, walked back out the side door and around to the front of Maria's eight-hundred-thousand-dollar house, took careful aim, and splattered the street-light all over the top of a silver maple tree. Then he sat down on the lawn to look at the stars.

Amanda was in a strange elated mood when she got back to New Orleans from the funeral, full of a sense of power that owning part of Esperanza gave her. I could sell it and live on the money for ten years doing anything I damn well pleased, she thought. For ten years I could do anything I wanted to without asking anyone's permission. I could live in Europe. I could live in Paris.

What she wanted to do was work. She threw herself deeper than ever into her studies. "She's got the blue flow," her teachers said. "She's got the touch. She's got the thing we can't teach."

She began writing feature articles and stories for magazines around town and working on translations with a serious young man named Brummette. He was part of a group of writers and artists who had all studied at one time or the other at the University of Arkansas at Fayetteville. People at Tulane called them the Fayetteville Mafia because they always walked off with all the grants and prizes.

Amanda was comfortable with these people. They reminded her of people in the delta. She began bringing them home with her to the house on Henry Clay Avenue, among them a tall, eccentric potter named Katie Dunbar who was at Tulane for a year working on a grant project.

Brummette was in bed with a cold the day Katie arrived in New Orleans. He called and asked Amanda if she would meet the plane. "I can't," she said. "I'm going to a wedding. My housekeeper's getting married. Oh, damn, I really want to meet Katie. Is she the one that did that white vase in your living room? The one with the cross on top?"

"The very one, the one and only Katie Vee-for-Victory-over-Japan Dunbar. Well, damn, I was really hoping you'd meet her."

"What time's she coming?"

"At twelve-thirty. To Moissant."

"All right. The wedding isn't until two. I can make it. What does she look like, this great potter, Katie Dunbar."

"Like a state champion drum majorette, which she was. Like the Alma Homecoming Queen. She dresses like no one you've ever seen in your life. You'll know her. It won't be hard."

Katie was not a disappointment. She came striding down the aisle in a group of passengers, passing everyone in sight, wearing a purple jacket over a white silk halter and what might have been a skirt or might have been a sari. She was tall and broad shouldered with a dazzling smile and a yard of wild blond hair.

Amanda was enchanted. "I don't usually dress like this," she said as soon as she introduced herself. "I know I look like some fucking uptown matron but I've got to go to a wedding as soon as I let you off."

"How do you usually dress?" Katie said. Depend on Brummette, she was thinking. He can find them. He can ferret them out.

"I don't know," Amanda said. "But I wish it was in whatever you're wearing. Is that a skirt?"

"It's something I made to wear down here. Brummette said it was hot as the gates of hell. Where is he?"

"He says he's got a cold. I guess he's either got a cold or a new graduate student. He runs through a lot of graduate students." She giggled. "Anyway, I'm delighted. I love your work. I've been dying to meet you."

They were at the baggage carousel. Katie picked up a fat duffel bag and a heavy old-fashioned suitcase and Amanda helped her lug them out to the car. "What time's your wedding?" she said. "I don't want to make you late."

"Well, to tell the truth I'm going to be late if I try to take you to Brummette's first. I was thinking maybe you'd go with me. It might be a great introduction to New Orleans. Part of the city you'd never get to see."

"Sure," Katie said. "I'm up for anything." From the looks of the car she imagined Amanda was going to take her to a society wedding where she could meet all the eligible bachelors in town.

"Well, put on your seat belt then," Amanda said. "And don't worry about my driving. I've never had a wreck in my life except once when I was drinking. Actually I have this really good hand-eye coordination that makes up for it if I stop paying attention." She pulled out onto Veterans Highway and started driving as fast as she could go, weaving in and out of the lanes of traffic.

"Well, damn, I hate for anyone to see New Orleans from this ugly highway. I know you hear all your life about how pretty this place is, but driving in from the airport you'd never know it. Well, most of it isn't pretty anyway. Most of it is a tenement and a swamp." She turned off Claiborne Avenue, then down Washington through the old Creole neighborhoods. At Saint Charles she decided to waste a few minutes and go through the Garden District. "I can't give you much of a tour right now," she said. "But at least you can get a look at what people mean when they speak of the beauty of this city. It's this overpriced bunch of monuments to slavery they're talking about. They worship these old houses. There're people down here that spend every cent they've got to keep up these old mausoleums. And, of course, there isn't a single plaque anywhere with the names of the people who actually *built* them."

"Is this where we're going?" Katie asked, looking out at the beautiful antebellum homes with their gorgeous gardens blooming like crazy. She was starting to worry about the way she was dressed.

"Oh, no," Amanda said. "We're going to the Saint Thomas Street project. It's near here though. As a matter of fact it's right next door. My best friend's getting married. She's my housekeeper, I'm ashamed to say."

"You don't have to justify having a servant to me," Katie said. Amanda had slowed the car down. That's all she was really interested in.

"I have to justify it to myself. Well, I do a lot of things I can't justify but I'm getting better. Anyway, don't think of me as some rich New Orleans cunt. I love your work. That vase of Brummette's blows my mind."

"I wish I was a rich New Orleans cunt," Katie said. "It would make my life a lot easier. I could really throw some pots if I didn't have to make a living at it. Well, throwing pots is easy. What you and Brummette do is what blows my mind. I had a big crush on a translator once. I used to go over to the translation department and take the worksheets down off the shelf and read them all the time. I was so crazy about this guy I worshipped his poetry. Anyway, I'd go read the worksheets and there would be this poem in Spanish or something and then four or five different translations of it. It was fascinating. I could really get into doing that if I was good with languages."

Amanda had come down Coliseum and turned onto Jackson Avenue, a main street that runs beside the Garden District. "I've been able to speak different languages since I was a child," she said. She stopped at a street light by the Sara Mayo Clinic. Black women with children were lined up by a side door.

Across the street black men loitered outside a bar. By turning a corner the whole atmosphere of the city had changed, thickened and darkened. Finally the light changed and they proceeded on down the street, moving in the direction of the river.

Katie had never seen that many black people in one place in her life. All the old scary movies about the South were playing in her head. "I guess I should have worked harder at it when I was young," Amanda was saying. "But I was too busy drinking and running around being wild. I was the wildest girl in Mississippi. All I wanted to do was relive the life of Zelda Fitzgerald. No one ever told me she wasn't happy. Can you believe it? I used to read those books and all I got out of them was that it was exciting. I thought *The Beautiful and the Damned* was about some people having a wonderful time. Well, so much for the power of the printed word. At least when you throw a pot you don't have to worry about influencing someone's life. . . ." Amanda stopped, seeing the expression on Katie's face. "Oh, shit, I forgot about that pot with the cross on top. Goddamn, that's the most irreligious statement I've ever seen." But the expression on Katie's face had nothing to do with the relative social values of clay sculpture or literature. Amanda had turned off Jackson Avenue onto Rousseau, a narrow street between tall yellow buildings. They were near the river now. Everything was the color of the river. The streets were covered with dried mud, the courtyards so bare she could not tell the difference between the concrete and the earth. Even the shrubs were covered with dust. In three blocks they had come from the lush tropical beauty of the Garden District to a floodplain. No one could live here, Katie thought. No one could live in such a place.

Amanda turned down Barrow Street to Nuns, then to Celeste. They were deep into the heart of the Saint Thomas Street Project. "Well, now I have a new start," she said, bringing the car to a stop before a courtyard where a group of men were drinking beer around a statue of Martin Luther King. A child walked by carrying an empty bottle. He ran his hand across the hood, then stopped and stared into the car. The men by the statue turned and looked their way.

"I was almost forty years old before I started to use my talents or gifts or whatever you call them," Amanda went on. "I hope it isn't too late." Katie was trying to open the car door. She had her hand on the door handle but her fingers wouldn't work. She kept wanting to roll down the window and yell, "It's not my car. I marched at Little Rock. It's not my car."

"Don't be afraid," Amanda said. "We're under Lavertis' protection. No one will hurt you here." As she was talking a tall black man came down off the balcony where the wedding party was going on and escorted them into the building. Lavertis had been watching out a window and sent her brother to bring them inside.

The rest of the afternoon was wonderful. Lavertis and her daughters were dressed in beautiful shades of pink organza and the ceremony was full of surprises. The preacher tied the bride's and groom's hands together with a white ribbon saying this wedding would be one they couldn't get out of without a fight. Then the musicians arrived and the dancing started. Lavertis' children took the white women and started teaching them dance steps. Katie learned fast and soon was dancing with everyone at the party. Amanda couldn't get the hang of it. "It's this goddamn skirt," she said darkly. "Who could dance in a thing like this?"

Then the bride, who was cutting her wedding cake, put down the knife, came across the room and held out her hands. Amanda rolled her skirt up around her waist, took off her shoes, and the two women began to dance. They danced and danced, holding each other's arms, laughing up into each other's eyes, while everyone clapped and cheered them on.

"She's really something," Katie told Brummette the next afternoon. "She isn't afraid of anything. I don't think I ever met anyone that fearless."

"Or oblivious," Brummette said. "Unless they're the same thing."

"Well, I like her. And I'd know she was a writer without anyone telling me. She just makes up the world as she goes along."

"I knew you'd like each other," Brummette said. "That's why I sent her out there to get you."

So the two women became friends, real friends, with things to teach each other. They spent a lot of time together the year Katie lived in New Orleans. They were both working very hard that year, and they would meet in the afternoons and go for long walks around Audubon Park, then back to Amanda's house to lie on the floor and listen to jazz, telling each other the stories of their lives. Amanda even told Katie about the baby she had given away. It had been on her mind a lot since Guy brought it up at the funeral.

"Why don't you find out where she is?" Katie said. "It's easy to do that now. I don't know how you can stand not knowing."

"Oh, I would never do that," Amanda said. "I would never in a million years do that."

"Don't ever say you wouldn't do something," Katie said. "Don't set traps for yourself."

"Let's go over to Tyler's and get some oysters," Amanda said. "Johnny Vidocovitch is going to be playing later. I heard he has a great new bass player."

A strange thing happened to Katie one afternoon that fall. She was out jogging in the park and fell in behind two women as she passed the flower clock. One was a chubby blonde, the other a tall foreign-looking girl. Katie was a few feet behind them, looking for a polite way to pass, when she began to overhear an intense conversation. She slowed up so she could listen.

"You ought to go over there sometime if you can get invited. You wouldn't believe that house. She's got art hanging all over the walls. I mean, every wall is covered with paintings. It's like a gallery. She's got these artist friends who make things for her. Oh, yeah, they're all painted especially for her."

"I heard she said terrible things to some people I know."

"Oh, she talks all the time. She's always telling someone something they don't want to hear. She told me it was a waste of time to have children. That all they did was break your heart."

"You don't mean it! She didn't say that."

"Yes, she did. She told it to me at a Yellin, Ashe picnic in Mandeville. She said I could forget being a painter if I had children. Well, listen, what she really said was worse than that. She said it in front of CeCe Mullin. If you don't believe me, just ask her."

"What did she say?"

"She said when the child is born the parents start dying. Something like that. I can't remember the exact words."

"What a terrible thing to say. It's like that article she wrote for that French Quarter paper. About the mixed marriages. I know that embarrassed the Ashes to death. All about Negroes that live with whites."

"Oh, I heard about that. But I haven't read it yet."

"Did you like her at all? I mean, he's such a doll. Jim just loves working for him. Why is he married to her if she's like that?"

"Oh, I liked her. You can't help liking her. There's something about her. Like she's, well, like she's glad to be here."

⚜

Later that evening Katie reported the conversation to Amanda. They were lying on the sun room floor listening to Ravel. "Do you think they meant me?" Amanda said, sitting up on one elbow, looking surprised.

"Of course they meant you," Katie said. "Who else in New Orleans could they be talking about but you?"

"It must have been some of the associates' wives," Amanda said. "I feel so sorry for them. They're expected to live up to such unbelievable standards of mediocrity."

"They said they liked you. The one that knew you said she liked you."

"Well, that's something," Amanda said. "I guess that's something."

Malcolm stayed in the back of the house when Katie was there. Of all of Amanda's new friends Katie bothered him the most, towering over him with her long crazy hair, wearing her clay-spattered sweatshirts any time of the day, laughing at everything that happened. He was haunted by the sight of her unpainted toenails in her hippie sandals, by her wild language. "You're starting to talk just like that woman," he said to Amanda. "You two sound like a pair of sailors. You ought to hear yourself."

"Then don't listen," Amanda said. "Besides, I was talking that way long before I met Katie Dunbar. I don't need her to teach me language."

"Well, it's worse when you're with her. You ought to hear a tape of yourself talking to her someday."

Malcolm began to wonder if Amanda and Katie were queer for each other. In a way he liked the idea. It was better than the fears he had about her being over at Tulane.

Malcolm was a proud man. The thought of being married to a woman who ran all over town not wearing a wedding ring drove him crazy. The thought of never knowing whether his wife would be there when he came home from work in the afternoon drove him crazy.

The sight of his mother holding his brother's children in her arms broke his heart. Maybe she's right, he began to think. Then he put that idea aside. Malcolm had been brought up to believe that divorce was an unforgivable evil, a sign of weakness, a thing Christians did because they didn't have enough sense to make a marriage work. He decided to try one more time to make Amanda love him.

Amanda came home one night from a seminar very excited about a piece of writing the other students had praised. She couldn't wait to get to her workroom and start making the revisions they had suggested. I'm going to make a pot of coffee and write all night, she said to herself as she turned off Saint Charles onto Henry Clay. I'm going to be the best translator of Middle French that ever walked the face of the earth. She started to turn into her driveway, then stopped. Malcolm's Audi was parked on the sidewalk blocking the steps going up to the front door. Someone had driven Malcolm's car right up onto the yard. What in the shit is this all about? she thought. Goddammit, what's going on? There must have been an accident or something. What has Malcolm done now? Well, I just hope he isn't dead. Then I'd never get to finish my poem.

She gathered up her papers and walked across the yard to the car. Now she could see the signs. The Audi was locked and the windows rolled up. There were handprinted signs in all the windows. *I love you Amanda Ashe,* they said. *I love you and I don't care who knows it.*

She shook her head. It was a part of Malcolm she hadn't seen in years. It was a part of him she had forgotten existed. She climbed around the car and went up the steps and opened the door. There was a chair blocking the front hall with a manila envelope from the office lying on the brocade seat. She opened it up. It was two airplane tickets to Paris for Saturday. And a letter.

Dear Mrs. Ashe,
Mr. Aschaffenburg has made you reservations at the Ritz. He says it's the only place in Paris silly enough for you. He says they still talk about you running out of there at dawn in your jogging suit and he says if you and I don't get out of this town and enjoy life he is going to do it for us.

Amanda, please go with me. I am pretending to sleep in our bed. Please come get me warm.

"Oh, shit," Amanda said, and sat down on the chair. She sat there for a long time holding the letter. He can do it, she thought. He can really do it when he wants to do it. After a while she went back to the bedroom and sat down on the bed and put her hand on the back of his head.

"I have to work all night," she said. "I have something important to do. And I can't go to Paris. I'm in the middle of a semester. I have important work to do."

"I'm not important," he said, keeping his face turned to the wall, not looking at her.

"I guess not," she said.

"What's going on, Amanda?" he said. "What's going on in this house?"

"The end of a marriage," she said. "Go find a woman to love, Malcolm. Go find a woman to bear you a child and cook you dinner and care whether you live or die. It isn't me. I don't think it ever was."

"Where are you, Amanda?" he said. "Where are you going?"

"I don't know," she said. "I'm on my way somewhere, though. I'm going to find the other places. That's a line from something I read the other day. It goes . . ."

But Malcolm had pulled the pillow over his head. There was a tone Amanda got in her voice when she was going to start quoting something that made him want to tie her jugular vein to her carotid artery.

She went into the kitchen and made a pot of coffee and carried it into her workroom and went to work. I don't know how to love, she thought. I'm hopeless. I can't even love a man who would drive a car up on his own tulip beds for me. Later that night she wrote him a letter.

Dear Malcolm, I don't know what it is I'm looking for. I know it is wrong for me to take your love and life and use them as props — I know it's wrong of you to let me.

This is a cold letter. This is a dead serious letter.

All I'm interested in is my work. I don't know what is wrong with me or right with me. I didn't make my nature. I didn't create my needs and ambitions. Neither will I deny or regret them. I am what I am. So be it. Find us an out.

Amanda

P. S. The quotation goes: "A traveler who has lost his way should not ask, Where Am I. What he really wants to know is, Where Are The Other Places. He has got his own self but he has lost them." — A. N. Whitehead

✠ ✠ ✠ ✠ ✠ ✠ ✠ ✠ *9* ✠ ✠ ✠ ✠ ✠ ✠ ✠ ✠

When Katie went back to Fayetteville at the end of the year Amanda was lonely for her. Within a month she had gotten in the habit of going up there to visit.

The first time she drove to Arkansas she left before dawn, planning on making the long drive in one day. She drove up through Mississippi, coming within a few miles of Esperanza without giving in to the desire to go and look at it. She crossed the Mississippi River at Greenville so close to home she could smell it, then drove on up through the Arkansas delta all the way to Little Rock without stopping.

In Little Rock she stopped at a Waffle House for an omelet, pouring maple syrup all over the eggs like a bad child, eating the last bites with her fingers, full of some outlandish feeling of freedom. She licked the syrup from her fingers and began the last leg of the journey.

As soon as she saw the hills of northwest Arkansas she fell in love. It was an October day and the red maple trees were a brilliant carpet all the way from Little Rock to Alma. *This is where a person could live a real life,* she told herself.

At Alma the real hills began, the Boston Mountains, the oldest mountains in the United States. As Amanda drove up into the mountains they reached out to her and took her heart away as nothing had ever done, not the Tetons, not the Rockies, not the French Alps. Something about the lay of the land seemed exactly right to her, as if she had been here before, as if she had been on her way there always.

It looks like Scotland, she said to herself. *It looks like where I am supposed to be.*

From Alma to Fayetteville the mountains got higher, the bluffs black in the afternoon sun, the beautiful views appearing around any curve making her laugh with pleasure and surprise.

"I don't know why you're so infatuated with Fayetteville," Katie said, laughing at her. "There's nothing to do here but work and wait for the mail."

"It's the way it looks," Amanda said. "Like someplace I've been before. I lived in Indiana, before my father died. Maybe it looks like that. Or maybe it's an older memory, Katie. My family are Scots, the McCameys and Torreys and Purcells. Maybe this place is like Scotland. Maybe my DNA feels at home."

"It's a good place to make a stand," Katie said. "If you can put up with the winters. And if you have some money. There isn't any money. You have to bring it with you or do without it. Well come on, I want to take you to meet some people." Then Katie put Amanda into an old van she used to haul her pots and drove her around town showing her the sights. She took Amanda down Maple Street to sit on the Alberts' swing and talk literature, then over to the Whiteheads' to argue politics and philosophy, then down to the Morrisons' to see the paintings and over to Calabash to watch Angele throwing plates and out to the river to go wading. They ended up at the Restaurant On The Corner eating omelets and helping plan the victory celebration for a local girl who had just run a triathlon in Hawaii.

"We're going to have thirteen guitars," Margaret Downing was saying, "and two dobo players. Do you think that will be enough?"

"They had thirteen for Anderson winning the Medal of Honor," Jodie Whitehead said. "I think a triathlon ought to get more than a Medal of Honor."

"That's just like you, Jodie," someone said. "Always trying to turn every goddamn thing in town into a contest. Anderson's medal of honor hasn't got a damn thing to do with Sylvia's triathlon and if you don't think thirteen guitars are enough well you just go out and get some more yourself."

At night Amanda slept in Katie's waterbed looking up at the skies through Katie's homemade skylights. Katie's house was an old stone ruin with a high roof like a wing. In one room there was a brick kiln with copper tubing going in and out at strange angles.

"It's designed to hold the vases I was painting that year," Katie said. "At that time I intended to paint Chinese love scenes on vases forever."

"The first thing I saw of yours was one of those vases," Amanda said. "I saw one in a house in New Orleans. It was the wildest thing I ever saw on a piece of pottery."

"That was the year I went back to men," Katie said. "After the movement cooled down and we let men back in. Jesus, what a relief that was."

"That's wrong," Amanda said. "The first thing I saw was the vase Brummette has. The one with the cross on top. I really love that vase, Katie. That vase gives me cold chills. It gives me chills just to think about it."

"You're always talking about that vase. Well, come on.

Put on your shoes. I'll show you where the idea came from. Come on, we're going for a walk."

They walked down a dirt road and up a hill until they came to a wide place in the road with a beautiful view of the valley. Right in the middle of the view was a huge tin cross, fat and squat and riddled with uneven punctures designed to let the lights show through at night.

"Welcome to Arkansas," Katie said. "Methodist heaven. For fifteen years I have had my view of the valley ruined by that goddamn cross. It's like a bad marriage. I'm so used to it I've forgotten to want to blow it up. I used to spend a lot of time figuring out ways to blow it up. Finally I just made the vase instead. I'm glad you like it."

They sat down on a bench to look at the cross. A storm was brewing to the east and south, great horizontal streaks of lightning beginning to appear in the distance so far away they could not even hear the thunder.

A car full of graduate students drove up, coming to watch the lightning. By the time the storm arrived there were several dozen people. They had driven up from all over town to watch the storm approaching.

It was that kind of trip.

That fall a coincidence occurred. Amanda was only a few months away from finishing her graduate work. Brummette had put her in touch with some young French poets and she was studying their work, but none of it seemed really serious or beautiful to her.

"It's just words," she told Brummette. "There isn't any heart in any of it. It's all either surreal or nihilistic. I can't find any reason to bring that to English. I want something that means something. I want something with a moral heart to it, or some passion, or something worth passing on."

"I thought art wasn't supposed to mean anything," he said. "I thought art was supposed 'to be.' "

"That's not enough," she said. "I won't serve abstractions. Whoever started that idea did the world a big disservice. A rock has being. But I don't learn much from it."

"Come over to the seminar at Loyola this weekend," Brummette said. "I want you to meet my old teacher, Marshall Jordan. He's going to be here lecturing. He thinks like you do. You'll have fun talking to him. Maybe he can put you on to something."

"I've heard of him," Amanda said. "All his old students tell wild stories about him."

"They're all true," Brummette said. "He's something else, oh, God, it'll be fun introducing you to Jordan."

"Why do you say that?"

"Oh, he'll just adore you, that's all. If he asks you for a piece of ass don't feel insulted. He lived in Italy too long. Promise you'll come. You'll love meeting him."

"Oh, fuck," Amanda said. "You drive me crazy, Brummette. I never know when to take you seriously."

"Never," he said. "Never take anything seriously if you can help it." He turned to a girl who was standing in the door holding a notebook. She was an expensive-looking girl, so well dressed she looked like an advertisement for a college shop. Everything she had on was perfect: Bass Weejuns, madras skirt, oxford cloth shirt, careful makeup. She was obviously embarrassed at the conversation she had just overheard.

"Come on in," Brummette said. "This is my new tutorial student, Amanda. Barrett Clare, Amanda McCamey. I was telling you about Barrett the other day, Amanda. Remember, I told you I liked her poems."

"Oh, sure," Amanda said. "Well, I'll be around on Saturday then." She leaned across the desk to give Brummette a kiss. "I'll see about this guru. Can we get together afterwards?"

"Of course," he said.

"I like your work," the girl said, refusing to be ignored. "I read the portfolio *The New Orleans Review* published last month. I was hoping I'd get to meet you around here."

"That's nice," Amanda said. "It's nice of you to say so. I've got to be going, Brummette. You be a good boy. I'll see you on Saturday then. Nice to meet you, Shelley. I'm glad you liked my poems."

"Barrett," the girl corrected. But Amanda was gone before she got it out of her mouth.

"She's beautiful," Barrett said.

"She really is, isn't she? Did you see her piece in Sunday's paper? I thought it was so good. Quite a coup to get to write about that stuff in the T-P. I don't know how she got that interview past the editor."

"Do you think she'd look at my poems?"

"I don't know about that," Brummette said. "She's pretty busy. Why don't you just let me go on looking at them? What's that you've got in your hand? Come on, out with it."

"They're new ones."

"My God, Barrett, you must write all night every night."

"No I don't. It's just that lately I seem to have a lot of things to write about."

He put the folder down on his desk and opened it, trying to act enthusiastic. Jesus, what a profession he thought. A fucking dream merchant. Why don't I go on and tell her how dull this stuff is? Why am I leading her on like this? Jesus, I hate this job. He pushed his sleeves back up above his elbows and pretended to concentrate.

"Nice title," he said. "Very nice title."

NOTES FROM THE CRYING LESSONS

First Lesson, Alphabet Blocks

Answer me
Blame me
Curse me
Damn me
Eat me
Fuck me
Goad me
Help me

I am in jeopardy   Kiss Me   Lay with me
Make me whole   No Oh Please Quiet Rest Satan Time

Universe   I am Valid   Say I am Valid

Swear you will come to my deathbed. Swear you will
be there.

Answer me   Answer me
Answer me   Answer me

"This must have been hard to write," he said, raising his eyes from the page. He thought he was going to cry. There she sat in those careful clothes with all that terror. How armored she is, he thought. Armor by Perlis, Your Uptown Store, Where The Elite Meet To Shop. I would not tell that girl to stop writing for anything in the world. For all

I know this goddamn poetry is the only thing that's keeping her alive.

"Is it good? Do you think it's good? Is it poetry?"

"Of course it's poetry. It's the best thing you've shown me."

"It's just a rough draft. It needs working on. You think it's a poem then? You're sure it's a poem?"

"It's a poem, Barrett."

"There're a lot more of them. They're for him, for Gustave. He's my doctor. I want to surprise him with them. Get them published. Then surprise him."

"Come back Wednesday and bring them all and I'll have a look at them."

"You're so nice to do this for me. It's so good of you to do this. So kind of you."

"It's what I do," he said. "It's my job."

On Saturday afternoon Amanda dressed in some old slacks and walked over to Loyola to the translation seminar. Jordan was not a disappointment. He came sweeping into the lecture room wearing a broad-brimmed black hat and a cape. Amanda had never seen a grown man seriously wearing a cape. He must have been seventy-five years old but he was as straight and supple as a dancer and full of wonderful energy. He took off the cape, dropped his hat on top of it, pulled some papers out of his pants pocket and went to work to mesmerize the audience, talking about a manuscript he had smuggled out of Italy the previous summer. *The Lost Wedding Songs of Helene Renoir* he called it. *Les chansons mystiales perdues d'Helene Renoir.* He had bribed a Jesuit to steal the poems from the cata-combs of the Vatican. Jordan was obviously having the time of his life being involved in the intrigue and would throw out his hands and lapse into Italian talking about the secret meetings in every café in Rome. "The Italians take themselves so seriously," Jordan said. "Here I was sitting in a café talking to a man who actually believed he was selling his soul for two thousand American dollars."

Amanda was fascinated by Jordan and by his story. That night she dressed in her most seductive clothes and went around to Loyola to the cocktail party being held in his honor. As soon as she got a chance she lured him off to the solarium and started asking him questions about the manuscript.

Jordan leaned happily against a marble pillar, gazing down the front of her pink silk blouse, telling her anything she wanted to know.

"My favorite is called 'Moon on My Breasts in Winter.' *'La lune d'hiver sur mes seines.'* Isn't that lovely? Almost oriental. Imagine, she wrote that in Aurillac in seventeen thirty-three. She couldn't have known Chinese poetry. And yet, there you are. Like Sappho. Dazzling clarity. The good ones are always alike, you know. Well, I've got to appoint a translator. I mean, I found the damn things."

"Let me try it," Amanda said. "I'm good. Ask anyone. I'm really good."

"Well, if I were here I would take that under serious consideration," he said. "Alas, I am far away in Fayetteville and I really don't like to work with anyone through the mails. It takes all the fun out of collaborating on anything."

"I'll come up there," Amanda said. "I know all about Fayetteville. I have a friend up there, the potter, Katie Dunbar. I'll come up there and live and work with you."

"My goodness," he said. "I don't know what to say to that."

"I could translate those poems better than anyone in the world," Amanda said. She turned her great black eyes upon him. "They're mine. I know they are. Please let me try."

He smiled down the blouse and sighed, wondering how old a man would have to be to be safe from those breasts.

"Send me your credentials. I'll see what I can do. It wouldn't be official, you understand. There wouldn't be a guarantee that you could publish."

"Let me get you another drink," Amanda said. "You're all out of wine."

That was in October. As soon as Amanda heard from Marshall Jordan that she could do the translations she walked into the bedroom and asked Malcolm very formally for a divorce.

He had been polishing a Celestron telescope he almost never got around to using. He laid down the polishing cloth and walked over to his closet and got out his tripod.

"What do you want?" he said, opening the door to the back porch. "What can I do to help you?"

"Give Lavertis some money. Fix it so she doesn't have to go to work for some asshole."

"What else?"

"Forgive me. Be my friend and forgive me."

"So far I've given you everything you ever asked me for, Amanda. I don't know why I should stop now. How much money do you need?"

"The house will do. Give me the house and I'll sell it. You wouldn't want to keep on living here."

"What else?"

"The Walter Andersons. And 'Country Doctor.' "

"Not 'Country Doctor.' "

" 'Walk to Paradise Valley'?"

"No."

" 'Moon Over Half Dome'?"

"Okay."

"Did we love each other?"

"Probably. Look, will you plug that cord in and bring it on out here. I want to see the moons of Saturn. I've been waiting all week to see the moons of Saturn."

Malcolm looked through the telescope for a while, then he took a small bag and went over to his mother's house and walked into his old room. Everything was just where he left it when he married Amanda. His lunar globe, his bronze statue of Diana, his old desk, his old chair, his old bed. He turned back the beautiful linen sheets and climbed in and slept like a baby. He was glad to be home.

Barrett was lying on her analyst's couch with her eyes closed and her hands lying lightly on her waist. She almost never lay on the couch. Mostly she sat in a cross-legged position with her back against the wall and looked at him, babbling on and on and on about the petty details of her boring uptown New Orleans life. She was the most intractable patient the doctor had ever treated. She couldn't seem to learn a thing. No matter how many hours she sat on the couch or lay on the couch or squirmed around in the chairs she always seemed to come out as helpless as she had been the first day he treated her. He leaned back in his chair and tried hard to listen, to care and not to care.

"Let's face it," she was saying. "I'm an unsuccessful poet.

No one wants to publish my stuff. The editor of the *Oak Mountain Review* told me I should stop writing. Brummette said he ought to be put in jail for saying that to me. Brummmette really likes my work. He couldn't fool me about that. *I know.* I know he needs the money I gave him for the magazine. I know that, Gustave. You don't have to remind me of that. But he wouldn't lie about poetry. He really thinks I'm good.

"He says I'm good. He tells everyone I am. Why would he tell me I was good if I wasn't? Why would he let me go on spending all my time on something like this? Writing and writing and writing if it wasn't going to get me somewhere. He said I just have to keep trying. I'm going to be an associate editor of the magazine he's starting. Did I tell you that? Well, it isn't certain yet. Of course Charlie doesn't care. He doesn't give a damn. Nothing I do matters to him. Did I tell you what he did? I can't believe what he did. At the one hundredth anniversary of the club. He passed out these cards saying 'Would you like to fuck me?' With his office number on them. He gave one to Donald Coleman's wife and she called and told me about it. He put it in her pocket and she got it out when she got home and her husband almost saw it. Printed cards, Gustave, printed cards. He's gone too far this time. I won't put up with much more of it. I don't love him. You know that. Why do I live there? Daddy practically supports us. I told you that. It's my house. Why do I live with him? I beat Shelly Brunstetter Sunday. I beat the shit out of her. Well, I'm sick of it. When are you going to get me out of it? Oh, I know, I know. I have to get myself out of it. I'm going to. I'm going to get out of it. You know so much. But you don't know what it's like to be me. You can't imagine what it's like to be locked up in this marriage. I don't know what's going to happen to Charles if I divorce Charlie. I think I'll go on and try to find out who my parents are but you can't know who they'll turn out to be. It might be somebody really awful. Really bad. They might be anyone. I beat Gail Harris Tuesday. I think she wants to be my doubles partner but first I'll have to get rid of Norma. I can't keep on playing with Norma. She never practices and one of the kids is always sick. Well, I'm sick of Norma. I want Janet. But no one can get Janet for more than a month. She's always moving around.

"What I want is a book of poems published by a respectable press. Is that too much to ask? Well, I don't care how long it takes. Brummette says I have to pay my dues. I'll get there. You just wait and see if I don't.

"Why won't you ever help me? I wouldn't even think you loved me except you cried that day I told you I dreamed about my mother. You cried. I saw the tears. You know you cried. What difference does any of it make? I ought to go on and have another baby. Except that I hate Charlie. You'd hate him too. I'm tired of the looks everyone gives us. He's not going to be beautiful forever. He's getting fat and there're these little places coming on his skin from being in the sun all the time. He's so blond. Maybe he'll get skin cancer. I know where his apartment is. It's in the building with Al Hirt's apartment. The whole law firm's got herpes now. Isn't that a riot? I ought to write a poem about that. Putney, Carroll, Davies and Weems and all their goddamn secretaries and half their wives and their wives' boyfriends and I heard the obstetric group at Ochsner's was going crazy trying to do something about it. Well, he isn't giving it to me. I don't even sleep in the same room with him since he got it. I'm scared to death he's going to give it to Charles.

"I know, I know, I know. It's just a virus. It's just like a cold. It doesn't matter. It doesn't matter. Well, I watched Sally Lucas when she got it and it isn't funny, Gustave. She couldn't urinate for three days. She didn't even know it was a venereal disease. That's why she told everyone about it. Now there've been nine cases at the firm that we know about.

"I wouldn't make love to him if he was the last person in the world. I'm going down and see Daddy this afternoon about the divorce. I really am. I won't live with a diseased man. I don't care how good-looking he is.

"What time is it? Do I have time to tell you about the match with Darby? It was a riot. I wish you could have seen me. I was so cool. I slaughtered them. I wish you could see me play. I wish you could see me do something besides sit in this room."

The monologue rolled on and on. The gentle middle-aged Freudian laced his fingers together, listening to every single word as if it were the most important thing in the world.

"What difference does it make to you," she rambled on. "Your kids go to Newman. Your kids get good grades. They aren't going to let Charles in Country Day. And Charlie went there. But John Jenkins is trying to help me get him into Trinity. Maybe I ought to try Newman again.

"I have to get him in somewhere. I don't know what I'll do if he has to go to some trashy second-rate place. I can't stand it if he does. Oh, well, who cares. I guess it doesn't matter. I know he's bright. You can't miss it. I mean he's twice as strong as anyone his age. He just can't sit still. There's nothing wrong with that.

"You can only be the kind of mother you had. That's

what I read somewhere. Well, mine was nonexistent. And of course Katherine doesn't love me. You ought to see how she hugs me. I think they're sorry they adopted me. I've told you that. They love Terry and Danielle so much. If it wasn't for me they wouldn't have had them. They could love me for that, couldn't they? They could at least pretend to love me, couldn't they? I know, I know, they give me money. They do that. They sure do that."

She rolled over and put her head down in her arms. "I know you get tired of hearing this same old bullshit over and over and over."

"I never get tired of anything you tell me," he said, unlacing his fingers. "Go on. Tell me how Katherine hugs you. I know it's hard, Barrett. I know it isn't easy." He sighed.

He was tired. He had flown home that morning from committing a fifteen-year-old adopted boy to a home for juvenile incorrigibles in Houston, Texas. It was the second patient he had lost. In seventeen years it was the second patient he had ever committed to an institution. It was driving him crazy to think about it.

"Three-fourths of the juveniles in homes for permanently disturbed children are adopted," the head of the home had told him. "You know that, Gustave. Stop acting like a bourgeois. We do what we can. He'll kill someone, you know that. We do what we can."

What do I care, he thought, looking up at Barrett's crazy confused face. She was sitting up on the couch putting on her shoes. Now she was bragging about some tennis match she had saved at the last minute. When she left the Folger boy would be here. Then it would be over. Sixty-three more minutes and it would be over for the day.

The Annunciation

It was the last Christmas Amanda would ever spend in New Orleans. She woke up all alone in the almost empty house on Henry Clay Avenue. She woke up feeling wonderful. She was drunker than she had ever been on whiskey. She was drunk on an idea.

She pulled on an old red bathrobe with ruffles down the front, turned on the radio and went to work. She had spent the last two months selling everything she owned. She had sold the house on Henry Clay and a cottage on the coast and all the silver and all the china and her mother's engagement ring. She had sold everything she owned but Esperanza. What she couldn't sell she was throwing away. The long front hall was piled high with the stuff she was throwing away. *Adeste fideles* . . . the radio was playing . . . *Joyful and triumphant . . . Oh, come ye . . . Oh commmmmmmmmmeeee ye to Beh . . . eth . . . leee . . . hem.*

I'm going to join the poets, Amanda hummed to herself as she moved across the bare floors throwing cookbooks and heated rollers and cocktail dresses and curtain rods on the piles of stuff in the hallway. . . . *Glory to Gaaaaddddddd . . . in the highest glory. . . .* I'll be the Margaret Mead of Fayetteville, Arkansas. Oh, God, I'll be so simple and humble and wise. I'll wear shirtwaist blouses and old jeans and learn to be a good listener and if I get famous I'll pretend I don't want to be. I bet I'll win the Pulitzer Prize for that book. . . . Oh, God, Malcolm will just die. . . . *Glory to Gaaadddddddd . . . innnn the highest glory . . .*

She added a muskrat stole to the pile of things for the Metairie Park Country Day Drama Department and stepped back to survey her work. It's got to be at least eight-thirty, she thought. Surely Katie is awake by now.

"You're going to do what?" Katie said. She was still half asleep. She rolled out of Clinton's long black arms and sat up on the edge of the waterbed holding the phone to her ear with a shoulder, rubbing the sleep from her eyes.

"I'm coming up there to live," Amanda said. "I'm going to help Marshall Jordan translate these incredible poems he sneaked out of Italy."

"It's Christmas," Katie said. "I'm not even awake yet."

"Aren't you glad? Aren't you excited?"

"What's going on? When did all this happen?"

"It started this fall. I wouldn't let myself tell you until everything was settled. I'm so excited, Katie. This is the best Christmas morning of my life."

"How do you know you'll like it here?" Katie said, waking up, starting to worry. "It's cold up here."

"I'm not going to be any trouble, Katie. You won't have to take care of me. I'm going to be busy morning, night and noon with the poems."

"Amanda, let me plug in the coffee, will you? Now," she said when she returned. "What's going on? What's all this about?"

"I'm coming up there to live. It's all set. A realtor found me a house on the mountain around the road from you.

I'm going to get to translate these incredible poems some Jesuit sneaked out of the Vatican. Marshall Jordan's letting me. Say something, Katie. Say you're glad I'm coming."

"Of course I'm glad," Katie said. "I'm stunned. I just don't know what you're going to find to do all winter in Fayetteville, that's all. There's not an available man in town except this one in bed with me, and he's on loan from the high school athletic department."

"I'm coming up there to work," Amanda said. "I'm coming there to get my work done. Who's in bed with you, Ms. Dunbar?"

"The high school basketball coach," Katie said. "I'm tutoring him in art. Next year I'm going to teach him how to read."

"I'm going to teach your scrawny little white legs how to be a knot," Clinton said, starting to do things to her rib cage.

"Oh, Katie," Amanda said. "I can't wait to be there. I can't wait to see you."

"Well, hurry up, then," Katie said. "There's always room for one more eccentric in the Ozarks."

"Oh, God," Katie said, hanging up the phone, settling her long legs into the warm place between Clinton's. "Now we're in for it. Amanda's coming."

"Who's Amanda?" Clinton said.

"Wait and see," Katie said. "Just wait and see."

Fayetteville, Arkansas. Fateville, as the poets call it. Home of the Razorbacks. During certain seasons of the year the whole town seems to be festooned with demonic red hogs charging across bumper stickers, billboards, T-shirts, tie-clasps, bank envelopes, quilts, spiral notebooks, sweaters. Hogs. Hog country. Not a likely place for poets to gather, but more of them kept coming every year. Most of them never bother to leave. Even the ones that leave come back all the time to visit.

Fateville. Home of the Hogs. Also, poets, potters, painters, musicians, woodcarvers, college professors, unwashed doctors, makers of musical instruments.

Fayetteville, Arkansas. Beautiful little wooded mountain town. Lots of poets. No money. Clear air, clean rivers, wonderful skies. Nothing to do but go to school and make things and wait for the mail.

Fayetteville, sitting on its hills and valleys in the extreme northwest corner of the state of Arkansas. The Ozarks, high ground. Where weather from four directions meets. An escarpment, Marshall Jordan calls it, although the dictionary would not agree with his use of the word. Hard to scrape a living from those hills. Hard to leave once you learn to love its skies and seasons. Seasons appearing right on time like seasons in a children's book. Fall, a riot of red and yellow maples, winter, with enough snow for sleds, spring, coming over the hills like a field of dancers, bringing jonquils, dandelions, violets, pussywillow, celadine and sedge and trout lily, turning the creeks into rivers.

Stars, clouds, storms, rain, snow, eagles. Wild weather and people who work for a living and women who wash their own underwear.

Amanda had fallen in love with the world where the postman makes stained glass windows, the Orkin man makes dueling swords, the bartender writes murder mysteries, the waitress at the Smokehouse reads Nietzsche on her lunch break.

"Where in the name of God are you going?" everyone in New Orleans kept asking Amanda.

"To Fayetteville, Arkansas," she replied. "My Paris and my Rome."

Christmas morning in Fayetteville. The town was going about its business as if it never heard of Amanda McCamey. The two hundred rich families were giving each other rich presents and worrying about whether they would stay rich another year.

The 34,678 regular and poor families were giving each other what they had to give and worrying about paying the bills. The university slept in the sun. Most of the professors wished they did something else for a living. A few of them still dreamed that knowledge would change the world. Marshall Jordan, who ought to have known better, was one of those.

Once, at a party for graduate students, he dragged a young professor out into the yard and made him look in the kitchen window at the small house crammed full of crazy young writers. "Look in there," he demanded in a somber serious secret voice. "That is a time bomb I'm fixing to unleash on the world."

"Who's this woman you've got coming up here to mess with the Renoir sonnets?" the dean demanded. He was in a terrible mood. He had spent four days trying to get Marshall to answer his phone.

"Wait and see," Jordan said. "It's a hunch."

"*Wait and see*," the dean demanded. "I've got every translator in the country begging to have a go at them and you let some nobody in on it."

"She's not a nobody," Marshall said. "They told me at Tulane she's the most intuitive student they've had in years. She won the Rawlings last year."

"You could have had Maxine," the dean said. "Denise would have done it."

"We have Amanda," Jordan said. "Wait until you meet her. She speaks romance. She smells like a garden. She has shoulders like Athena . . ."

"You know Duncan's planning on the press bringing out that book this fall?"

"I know," Jordan said. "I know what Duncan wants."

The minute Amanda drove into town she went straight to Marshall's office, driving right up into the yard of the stone building that housed the translation department, running up the steps two at a time to present herself.

"I'm here," she said, allowing him to cradle her against his chest.

"What *is* that perfume?" he said. "What is that marvelous stuff?"

"I'm not telling," she said. "You'd give it to all your girlfriends. Then where would I be?"

"Come in, come in," he said. "Have a cup of tea. Tell me about your trip. When you're moving in your house and all of that."

"The movers are coming tomorrow," she said. "There isn't much. A bed. A piano. A lot of paintings. I threw everything away. You wouldn't believe what I threw away. Christmas tree decorations. Everything. I had to — I had a vision of myself trekking up here like that man in Thoreau with all his possessions on his back, clanking along the highway trailing vacuum sweepers and heated rollers and coat hangers. *Marshall,* I want to see the manuscript."

"It's right here," he said. "I had copies made for you. But, Amanda, I have to warn you about something. You aren't the only one working on these. I couldn't do that for you."

"Who else has it?"

"The only one that's any good is a woman in Albuquerque. A nice woman. You would like her."

"Is it a contest?"

"Not exactly. I just want you to understand there's no guarantee what you're doing will be published. So make it good, Amanda. Make it really good."

"I will," she said. "Don't worry about that."

"I hope you'll find time to write some things of your own now that you're here," he said. "I liked the things you sent me, especially the Egyptian poems, in the Egyptian persona. They're very nice."

"I'm not interested in much of anything right now but this manuscript." She was eyeing the folder on his desk, wanting to reach out and grab it.

"I wish we knew more about Helene," Marshall said. "They're supposed to be sending me a copy of the maid's diaries. I don't know what the holdup is. It would be nice if you had the diary before you start work on these, but what can we do. Art is long and slow. Thank God something is." He picked up the folder and held it out to her. "Here you are, my dear. The French is bizarre, to say the least. It's all hers. Well, now it's also yours." He laid the folder down on the desk between them. Amanda was sticking the pins in and out of a small bronze cribbage set. She was dying to pick up the folder but she didn't want to seem that eager so she just kept rearranging the pins. It was a game Marshall had going with his secretary but he didn't say anything about it. "There's something else," he said. "A list, an inventory of the things she took with her to Lyons when she was imprisoned. I can't figure it out. Perhaps you'll do better. Perhaps a woman will know why she took a cloak lined with peacock feathers to a nunnery. Well, go on. Take a look."

Amanda picked up the folder and opened it. *Les Chansons mystiales perdues d'Helene Renoir,* the title said. By Helene of Aurillac, Helene Renoir. 1713–1734. Amanda held it in her hands. "It's so exciting," she said. "I can't believe how exciting it is."

"Of course," he said. "That's why we do it. This strange craft or art, this old service."

"I can't wait to get started."

"Where are you staying? Would you like to stay with me?"

"I'm going to Katie's. Will you come tomorrow night to my housewarming?"

"Of course I will. And I'll see you Monday. We'll get started on the work."

"I love you for doing this for me," she said.

"That perfume," he said. "That perfume is really something."

Amanda moved into her new house in the snow. She woke at dawn and pulled Katie out of bed. "Come on," she said. "I'm so excited I can't stand it. Come on, get up."

"I thought you weren't going to be any trouble to anyone," Katie said and dove back under the covers. In a few minutes she relented and the two of them put on all the warm clothes they could find and drove around the mountain to build a fire in the fireplace and wait for the movers.

Amanda's new house was built into the side of a small mountain. A stone cottage with an addition on top like a wooden wing. The main floor was one long room with windows that opened out onto a balcony overlooking the town.

Amanda and Katie sat on the hearth drinking coffee from a thermos and eating doughnuts, shivering with the cold.

"The thing I love about the world," Katie said, "is never knowing what's going to happen next. Look out there, Amanda. Look at that goddamn snow. That stuff never ceases to amaze me."

"The thing I like about the world is doughnuts," Amanda said, licking the sugar from her fingers. "Maybe I'll get fat, Katie. Maybe that's what I came to Fayetteville for. Maybe my destiny is to start a fad for getting fat."

"Have another one," Katie said, handing her the sack. The snow was really starting to come down now. They watched it blowing in through the mountains, filling the branches of the huge old liveoak tree outside the windows.

"It's like living in a treehouse," Amanda said. "I can't believe I found this house without even looking for it. Well, lately everything I do seems charged with meaning, Katie. As if the world had decided to give me wonderful gifts and all I have to do is allow it to happen."

"There's your moving van trying to make it up that hill," Katie said. "You better get out there and start turning on the charm if you think they're going to move you with this stuff falling."

⚜

The truck somehow or other made it up the hill. In a few moments the driver was standing in the door, snow melting all over his leather cap. A very tall young man with blond hair stood behind him smiling at Amanda as if he were coming to tell her some news she'd been waiting to hear.

"Will Lyons," Katie said, recognizing him. "What are you doing here?"

"Picking up some money to make it through the winter," he said. "Even guitar players have to get an honest job every now and then."

"We've got to move that baby grand on in here, lady," the driver said. "This stuff's really starting to come on down."

The men carried in a stack of boxes and cartons and then, as Katie and Amanda watched, they loaded the big harp-shaped body of the piano onto a dolly and pulled and shoved it across the wooden bridge leading to the front door.

"Only you, Amanda," Katie said, watching them shoving and tugging, with the snow falling all over the canvas tarp, "only you would move a baby grand piano all the way to Arkansas when you don't even know how to play it."

"I'm going to learn how to play it," she answered. "I'm going to have a piano teacher. It's what I'm going to do at night while you roll around on the waterbed with Clinton."

The men moved the piano to the far side of the living room and began assembling it. Amanda was unpacking the boxes, searching for a pair of Katie's vases she wanted to put on the mantel.

"I know they're here," she said. "They have to be in this

box because I packed them myself. I wrapped them up in an old negligee." She tore open the tops of all the boxes, muttering about not bothering to write the contents on the outside. The vases were in the last box. She pulled one out and began polishing it with the black silk gown she had wrapped it in.

Across the room the young man sat down at the piano and began to play ragtime. The music filled the room, then stopped as abruptly as it started.

"Don't stop," Amanda said.

He played a few more bars, looking right at her as he played. Then he got up and walked across the room. He had a wonderful walk, as if he thought wherever he was going would turn out to be a good idea.

He took off his jacket and handed it to Amanda. "Keep this for me, will you?" he said, "I'm burning up in all these clothes." Amanda took the jacket, letting her eyes meet his, then moving them down to his careless waist and hips and legs.

Maybe I won't get fat after all, she thought, and took the jacket and hung it in a closet. Later, when she went to look for him to return it he had been paid by the driver and gone off down the hill.

"In the snow?" she said. "Without his jacket?"

"He said he had to get to a class," the driver said. "He said he was in a hurry." Amanda hung the jacket back in the closet. She meant to ask Katie the young man's name but she got involved in unpacking and it slipped her mind.

Amanda had done a good job of throwing everything away. The things she had brought with her fit easily into the new house and by five o'clock that afternoon the books were stuffed haphazardly on the bookshelves, the liquor cabinet was full, and people were beginning to arrive for the housewarming party. They were people Amanda had met in New Orleans or when she visited Katie.

A woman named Caryn came in bringing cheesestraws, talking a paragraph a second, asking a thousand questions. "I don't believe you really moved up here. And what's this about Marshall stealing a manuscript from the Pope? Well, he'll do anything. When he was in Vienna, after the war, he opened a university without asking anyone's permission. He just declared it open. He was only a major.

"What I want to know is how you got hooked up with him. No one here can even get him to come to dinner. He's living with this eighteen-year-old student. Someone he found in a piano factory and took home to educate. I swear to God. He took her home the night he saw her and started sending her to school. He said she had intelligent eyes."

"He's pretty incredible for seventy-five," Amanda said. "Or however old he is."

"Well, everyone says he sleeps with her," Caryn said. "You'll see. If he comes over he'll bring her with him. He takes her everywhere."

"Amanda," Clinton said, interrupting them. "Come and tell me about that painting over the piano. I want to know who did that."

"Oh, look," Amanda said, "Marshall's here."

Marshall was standing in the doorway with snow falling all over his cape. He was a man who liked *occasions* and knew when to show up with flowers or wine. Now he handed her a box of candy, smiling widely. "Almond Roca," he said, as if he were offering her the distilled evil of the world. "To welcome you to your new home."

"Oh, my," Amanda said.

"May I present Elderwind," Marshall said. "Named for the I Ching."

A young girl stepped up and took Amanda's hand. "What is your name?" Amanda said.

"Elderwind. Do you like it?"

"I think it's extraordinary," Amanda said. "I wish it was my name."

"Well, come along then," Marshall said. "Let's see this famous house on the mountain."

There were several graduate students in Marshall's retinue and behind them a sculptor named Teddy O'Connor bringing new music. "Ry Cooder," he said. "That's all anyone is listening to this winter."

A woman named Sandy was holding the floor in the living room. "I had the strangest thing happen to me in New Orleans once," she was saying. "I was visiting a friend who lived in one of those old fortresses on Palmer Avenue. I had my little boy with me, he was seven at the time. Quinn. You'll meet him, Amanda. Everyone in town knows Quinn. Anyway, we went down to the Quarter and left Quinn with my friend's parents. He was sleeping right next to them in the guest room. I mean, he was asleep when I left. At exactly a quarter to twelve we sat down at a table at the Top Of The Mart. The waitress had just put our drinks on the table when I had this terrible sense of foreboding, oh, no, it was more than that. It was a message, as clear a message as I've ever received in my life. Something was wrong with Quinn. I knew it like I know my name. I ran out of there without even waiting for my friend. I didn't wait for anything. I ran out of the Trade Mart and got a taxi. I don't even remember riding across town. I was so sure something was wrong. It was like being on fire. Anyway, when I drove up in front of the house there was Quinn sitting in the front seat of my car crying his heart out."

"What had happened?" Amanda said.

"He woke up in the night and remembered these big jars of candy that were sitting around the living room. So he wandered down there to get some. Then, because he's used to living in the country where no one ever locks anything, he walked out on the porch and this huge door slammed behind him. It was dark and there he was, out on Palmer Avenue all alone, so he found my car and got in it and started crying. He was crying his little heart out. He was just terrified. Well, anyway, that night changed my view of reality. I can't tell you how clear the message I got was. Well, no one ever believes this. Don't you see! We're all sending and receiving messages all the time. Real messages, the ones the subconscious deals in. It means we're all hooked up to everyone else, all sending and receiving all the time. Then up on top we're bullshitting each other with words, well, not everyone is."

"That's what Merwin says poems are," a graduate student put in. "They're shorthand, points where the subconscious breaks through the bullshit."

"But of course," Marshall said. "You're talking about the mystery. Everything outside and all around the tiny point we experience as conscious life. All around us unimaginable energy, the real stuff. It's all energy. And I certainly can't think of anything more energetic or able to send and receive than a child in distress."

"He hears me," Elderwind said. "He reads my mind all the time."

Is she sending me messages? Amanda thought. All these years has my child called out to me in pain or terror? *Did I hear her? Did I know?* "Once a friend of my husband's sat in my living room and told me his company had invented a computer that could translate poems," she said. "God, that made me mad. I was so goddamn mad at that man I almost stabbed him with the cheese knife."

"I remember that," Katie said. "I had to listen to her bitch about that for days."

Someone put the new Ry Cooder album on the phonograph and the party kept on growing until the house was full of friends and strangers. Then everyone asked Amanda to swear she would have lunch with them, and she promised everyone she would have lunch with them, and then, one by one the guests left, even Katie and Clinton, and Amanda was alone.

She picked up all the glasses and cups, turned off the lights and sat down on the stairs by the long row of windows leading to the bedrooms.

This is it, she thought. This is what I dreamed of. The old sugar maples outside the window moved in the wind, sending shadows onto the wall behind her. That doesn't scare me, she thought. Nothing scares me. That's only the wind I'm watching. That wind has traveled around the world a million times to be with me. That wind was alive when Helene Renoir walked the earth.

Amanda went downstairs carrying the box of Almond Roca and got into bed and opened the folder Marshall had given her. She took a big bite of the candy and started to translate the first poem.

In the white garden
time is the circle of your arms
We sing together one song
Nothing outside the garden
has dominion
Outside the garden only dreams
falling like snow
on the towers of Lyons

There was a note in Marshall's handwriting. She studied it for a while, thinking it might give up its secrets if she looked at it long enough.

Helene of Aurillac, called Helene Renoir. Locked away with the sisters of Lyons for an illicit love affair. After her suicide a maid took the poems to a priest for safekeeping. The poems disappeared. Forty years later the maid described them in her memoirs, which were published during the French revolution.

Good luck. Have fun. Take your time.

Marshall

Amanda put the folder on her dressing table, turned off the light and snuggled down into the sheets. She took one last bite of Almond Roca. She was all the way under the covers eating the candy when she had a vision.

In the vision she was an earthworm working its way through a sea of creme-colored percale, eating everything that got in its way, moving through the earth chewing and swallowing.

Maybe that's all we really are, she thought, cold determined organisms moving through our days, chewing and swallowing, feeding, shivering, subterranean, secret, alone.

☙

Now Amanda was happy for the first time in many years. Nothing about the life of the small college town seemed boring or provincial to her. She threw herself into the work of translating the poems, going straight into her workroom as soon as she woke every morning, working until one or two.

In the afternoons she visited Katie at the kiln or walked down the hill to the university to talk to Marshall or sat around the student union gossiping with the other graduate students.

She spent long afternoons on her balcony watching the skies, fascinated by the great banks of clouds traveling across the hills breaking the sunsets into a thousand colors.

In the evenings there were readings or lectures at the university or films at the union. Amanda gained five pounds and cut her hair and even started wearing her glasses in public.

Then January wore on into February and she was content with her life.

"I adore it here," she told Marshall, stretching her hands out to his little office fire. "It's what I dreamed of. While I was waiting to come up here to live, running around New Orleans selling everything, I used to dream of being here, of walking around the buildings with many books in my arms."

"You were dreaming of the Academy," he said. "A dream of order. A good dream. Look out there," he said, pointing out the window to where the engineering school and the library rose up on the hill. "Sure, it's a hokey little place with a football team they call the Razorbacks and a Greek theater that's only used for pep rallies, but those buildings and their contents represent the cultural history of our civilization. Oh, . . . my," he said. He took off his glasses and rubbed them on his wool tie. "I am sorely given to rhetoric in my old age, Amanda. I had meant to escape that fate by fearing it, but, there you are, I preach on and on."

"Look at this, old pedantical thing," she said. "Look what I did today."

> *Snow snow snow devours the air*
> *and one red bird*
> *my flag in a white tree*
> *God's ring, heaven's song,*
> *flight's memory*
>
> *The ones without wings*
> *do not touch me*
> *with their dark songs*
> *I know whose shoes they worship*
> *whose purposes they serve*

Amanda was reading over his shoulder. "I'm going to be her nun," Amanda said. "I'm going to devote myself to these poems." The nice thing about Marshall Jordan was you could say things like that around him without being embarrassed. Besides, Amanda meant every word of it. She meant to devote the rest of her life to a dead poet's imagination.

The twentieth of February was Amanda's birthday. It fell on a Friday and she gave a little dinner party for herself at a Chinese restaurant out in the country. It was a bright little house on a creek beside a waterfall, with red flags flying from the roof. The party was on a patio overlooking a series of stone ledges. It had rained in the afternoon and water was pouring down over the ledges adding to the gaiety of the party. Amanda looked around the table. Marshall and Elderwind were there and Katie Vee and Clinton. So this is Bohemia, she thought. I finally made it to the free people. My wild bohemian friends, those four gentle people unwrapping their chopsticks.

The waiter brought soup and wonton and egg rolls, then Peking duck and lobster Cantonese and Chinese vegetables and beautiful blue porcelain bowls of steaming rice.

"I picked out this place for the name," Amanda said. "Only in the Ozarks would someone name a restaurant Susie Wong's."

"There might even be a Chinaman in the kitchen," Marshall said. "This duck has an authentic ring."

"Get Katie to tell you what she's going to call her new show," Clinton said.

"The One Hundred Names for Red," Katie said. "Isn't it great? The glazes are going to be every shade of red I can cook up."

After dinner the waiter brought fortune cookies. "Read them out loud," Elderwind said. "Marshall first. He's the oldest."

" '*You will step on the soil of many free countries,*' " he read. "My goodness, what a remarkable fortune." He sat up straight in his chair, as pleased as a child, and put the piece of paper away in his pocket.

"Oh, damn," Katie said. "Marshall always is the luckiest

man in the world. I'll bet mine won't be worth a damn. '*You should be able to undertake and complete anything,*'" she read. "See there. What kind of a fortune is that?"

"I'm afraid to open mine the way the team's been playing lately," Clinton said. "Well, here goes. '*Get your mind set. Confidence will lead you on.*' Hey, that's not bad. I'll take that."

"'*A partner in business will not put an obstacle in your way,*'" Elderwind read. "I'll have to think about that one," she said. "Read yours, Amanda."

Amanda was holding it in her hand, imagining the Chinaman at the Rolling Fork store folding the little strip of paper into the dough, making a little package of her destiny.

"'*Your most secret desire is about to come true,*'" she read. "Oh, my God," she said. "You guys planted this. I know you did."

"It's all right, Amanda," Marshall said. "You can have a good fortune. It doesn't have to be a trick."

"I guess it means the poems," she said. "I guess it means Duncan will publish the book when I get through." On the way home in the car she kept reaching her fingers into her blazer pocket to feel the little paper fortune. When she got home she read it over again several times, sliding her finger across the words. Then she put it carefully away in a porcelain powder box on her dresser.

The first of March was a bright Sunday. Will Lyons woke up on his sofa and lay for a long time watching the pattern of light coming through the venetian blinds, making the ceiling tiles look like something out of the Museum of Modern Art.

Not that Will had ever been to the Museum of Modern Art. He had hardly ever been out of the state of Arkansas except to visit his cousins in Texas.

Might as well get the show on the road, he thought, whistling a little tune to cheer himself up. Make some coffee, smoke a joint, see what's happening. Maybe I can throw some shoes with Jodie if it warms up.

He made some breakfast, straightened up the sofa, and wandered into the little bedroom he used for an office meaning to spend what was left of the day on calculus but he picked up his old plumb bob instead and let it out on its line, watching it dangle in front of him, heavy and hard and cold, moving with the earth. Will liked to think about gravity. He could think about gravity all day. He just wasn't much on learning to measure or control it.

He opened the calculus book and sat down at his desk and worked out a couple of problems. Then he put the book carefully away and lit a cigarette. How in the name of God did I get hooked with this engineering school to start with? he thought. He leaned back in the chair seeing his father's face the day his father talked him into quitting his surveying job and going back to college. Surveying was good enough for him, Will thought. I don't know why he won't believe it's good enough for me.

He put the plumb bob carefully back in its leather case, straightened up the pencils on his desk, pulled on his old plaid shirt and decided to wander downtown to see if his guitar was still where he left it in the health food restaurant where he played gigs for tips during the dinner hour. That's all I'd need now, he thought. Lose my guitar on top of my driver's license. Lose my guitar in a health food restaurant. A goddamn health food restaurant, hell of a comedown for a headliner at Jose's. Well, what can you do. It's the price you pay.

Will swung himself out the doorframe and headed on down Tin Cup to Dickson Street, making up a country and western song about himself.

> *Well, they took off my license*
> *and stole my guitar*
> *Stopped me from singing*
> *and driving my car*
> *Stopped me from calling*
> *when they ripped out my phone*
> *Now no one can stop me*
> *from being alone*
>
> *It's a terrible ending*
> *a terrrrrrrrrible ending*
> *for the best loved and brightest*

for the saddest and meanest
for the loneliest son
of the homecoming queen

He sang the song over to himself a few times, adding
verses, then picked up a rock and sailed it up into the power
lines above the post office, making a direct hit on the flag-
pole. All in all he was feeling a lot better than he had any
right to feel as broke as he was today.

But, then, Will Lyons had a knack for not worrying about
things. Something always turned up. While he waited he
used whatever was available in the world he lived in. He
used booze or marijuana or shooting pool or friendship.
Will had a gift for believing one thing was just about as
good as another.

He walked on down Dickson Street admiring the afternoon. It was the first really warm day in months and the
sun shone down out of a cloudless sky, lighting up the little
valley that holds the town, lighting up the square and the
football stadium and the chicken-plucking plant and the
bank and the park, lighting up Will as he came walking
down the street singing about himself, past the Baptist
Church and the Methodist Church and the Episcopal
Church, past the post office and the drugstore and the pool
hall, then up the next hill past the Library Dance Club and
the House of Books and on down to the Rainbow Restaurant where the sun was pouring in the windows onto a table
where Amanda was deep in conversation with Katie Vee.
Amanda had been restless all weekend, tired and irritable.
The work was going poorly on the sonnets. Something was
wrong and she couldn't put her finger on it. She kept want-

ing to get on a plane and fly to New Orleans to hear some music and eat dinner at Le Ruth's or Moran's. This morning she had given up and called Katie to come and save her. They had gone for a long walk in the hills, then downtown to eat carrot cake and drink coffee and talk. They were deep into one of their favorite subjects.

"I only fucked him on Wednesday nights after the Joyce seminar," Katie was saying. "It wasn't an affair. It was just something to do."

"Then why do you think he's acting like this?" Amanda said, leaning over the table to get in closer.

"I don't know," Katie said. "I can't imagine what he's up to."

"Men are crazy," Amanda said. "You never can tell what they'll take seriously. I tell you one thing, Katie. Living alone is the most wonderful thing that ever happened to me. I wouldn't marry God if he asked me."

"Can you believe he's threatening to tell Clinton?" Katie said. "I mean he wants to break up my relationship with Clinton."

"What's happening?" Will said, walking up to the table, giving Katie a kiss on the head. "I've been missing you, Katie. You haven't been around school all winter."

"Hello, Wild Child," Katie said. "What are you doing in a health food restaurant?"

"I came to pick up my guitar," he said. "Besides, the pool hall's closed on Sunday." He turned his eyes and looked at Amanda.

Later, she was to spend many hours trying to remember that moment, the dark humor of his face in the dark café, the careless slant of his shoulders, trying to understand what had been in his face that had made the blood pour down her arms and legs and into her face and fingers.

And sometimes she believed it had been his soft voice and sometimes she believed it had only been her own loneliness.

"I know you," he said. "I moved a piano into your house last winter."

"You're the one that left the jacket," Amanda said. "I kept meaning to find out who you were so I could return it."

"I was wondering where I left that jacket," he said. "I knew it'd turn up sooner or later."

"Go get some coffee and join us," Katie said.

"Who is he?" Amanda said, when he left for the coffee.

"He used to play basketball for Clinton. He plays music around town. He played with the Mike Summler band before they made the big time. He's good. He's a good musician."

"I love the way he looks," Amanda said. "Tell him I'm a famous writer, Katie. Tell him I'm a talent scout."

"I'll tell him you haven't had a piece of ass since you left New Orleans," Katie said. "How about that?"

"Amanda's a writer from New Orleans," Katie said when he returned. "She went crazy and came to live in the Ozarks."

"I know your work. I've seen your work in magazines."

"Oh, my," Amanda said. "You must read some funny magazines to run into my little translations."

"I read them at the library," he said. "I like to read everything. What are you working on now?" He was watching her quick nervous fingers which were moving as she talked, touching everything on the table and then her clothes and then her hair.

"Oh, something that was terribly exciting last week," she said. "This week I'm no good at it. This morning I was going to run away to Paris till my money ran out but instead I called up Katie."

"I don't understand translation," he said. "I was twenty years old before I knew there was such a thing. I just figured everything was written in English."

"Oh, God," Amanda said, as if that was the funniest and most wonderful thing she had ever heard in her life. "I did too. I mean, there everything was, all in English waiting for me to read it. I didn't know how much trouble it was to get there. Well, translation's mysterious. It's like being a spy into another person's mind. It's really nice for me because in real life I'm not a very good listener." I'm talking too much, she thought. *Stop talking so much.* "Does that guitar really work?" she said. "Can you really *play* that?"

"I was able to last night," he said. "Do you want to hear it?"

"Of course I do," she said.

Then slowly and carefully, as that was how he did things in the world, he took the beautiful old Gibson out of its case and cradled it in his arms. He fiddled with the frets, then began to play chords, humming along with himself. After a few minutes he raised his eyes to Amanda's and began to sing. "Dance with me," he sang. "I want to be your partner. Dance with me."

I wouldn't have missed this for the world, Katie thought, getting horny just watching it, starting to wonder when Clinton would be getting back from Little Rock.

"The music is just starting," Will was singing. "Night is calling and I am faaaaalllllllling. Dance with me. Dance with me. Dance with me." When the song was over he sat very still with his hands still on the strings. Will was a good performer. He knew how to size up an audience.

"I know what let's do," Amanda said. "Let's go up the mountain to my house and you can play your guitar while the sun goes down. There're wonderful sunsets from my balcony and wine to drink. I'll fix supper if you'll play for me. I haven't heard any live music in so long."

Then the three of them trouped out of the café, squeezed into Amanda's MG with the top down and the guitar case standing on end and drove on up the mountain.

I'm sixteen years old if I'm a day, Amanda thought. I'm crazy as a loon.

This redheaded lady is fixing to take me home and fuck my eyeballs out, Will was thinking. Well, what the hell. I haven't got anything else to do till Monday.

I'll fill the kiln tomorrow, Katie was thinking. Who knows, maybe I won't have to hear any more lectures about solitude for a while.

When they got to the house Amanda settled her guests on the balcony with a bottle of wine. Then she went into the kitchen and made a plate of small brown rolls filled with ham and lettuce and sliced olives. She brought it out on the balcony and put it down between Will and Katie. The sun was beginning to set, filling the clouds with purple and orange and wild magentas.

"I've got to find a yoga teacher," Amanda said, stretching her legs out, propping them on the railing so Will could see how nice they were. "The only thing I miss about New Orleans is my yoga teacher. I was learning so many wonderful things from her."

"Like what?" Katie asked, playing along.

"Like how to do a headstand. Can you believe that? Well,

anyway, I adore it here, Will. Fayetteville, Arkansas is my Paris and my Rome."

"I've lived here all my life," he said. "I wouldn't know how to love anyplace else."

"Amanda thinks Fayetteville is an artists' colony," Katie put in. "Because of the way the women dress."

"Well, I do love the way they dress. They dress like they don't give a damn who's looking at them. Like they aren't for sale. It's one of the first things I noticed when I first started coming here."

"How do women dress in old New Or-leans?" Will asked.

"The black women are the best. I used to go down to Canal Street just to watch them on their lunch hours. They're very tall and wear the most extraordinary colors."

"That's where you're from? You're from New Orleans?"

"Oh, no," Amanda said. "I'm from the delta, from the smallest county in the state of Mississippi."

"My mother was from Mississippi," he said. "From a place called Rosedale. I always wanted to go down there and see where she came from."

Amanda didn't know what to say to that. She was afraid he was going to offer to introduce her to his mother. "Well, I'll take you with me sometime when I go," she said. "Don't get me talking about the delta or you'll be sorry. It makes me homesick to think about it. This time of day in the spring, when the fields have just been turned, you wouldn't believe how it smells, you wouldn't believe how it shimmers in the sun after a rain." Her face had grown serious as she spoke of it, soft and sensuous, and Will began to desire her.

She got up and filled the wineglasses.

"None for me," Katie said. "I've done enough damage to my gorgeous body for one day. I'm going home."

"Don't go," Amanda said.

"Don't leave," Will added. But neither of them wanted her to stay and all three of them knew it.

"Is she still living with Clinton Dottley?" Will asked when Katie left. "He was my favorite coach. He was my idol."

"She's living with him. Right out in the open. Right here in Fayetteville."

"Do you live with anyone?"

"No."

"Do you get lonely?" He was waiting for her answer as if he had every right in the world to question her.

"I'll tell you something," she said. "But don't tell anyone. It would ruin my reputation. Lately I do get lonely. This time of day, when the sun is leaving the earth, I get lonely. And I wonder what I'm doing here, so far away from everything I used to love."

"Katie said you came up here to work with Marshall Jordan."

"I think I really came to see the stars. I lived in New Orleans for such a long time, Will. You can't see the stars there. There's always a cloud cover over the city. Because it's on the coast, you know."

"I've been lonely all my life." He poured the rest of the wine into his glass and held it out in front of him like an offering. "I wouldn't know how to stop being lonely."

In the light Amanda could see him better. He was a beautiful young man with hazel eyes and ears that stuck out through his unkempt hair. But the thing she was falling in love with was his mouth, which was wide and full and seemed right on the verge of laughter. He lowered the hazel eyes to a pile of rocks sitting in a blue pottery dish beside the railing.

"What are those rocks for? It looks like you're building a pyramid."

"Well, you probably won't believe this. But I'm using those rocks to prove a theory. Don't get me started on my theories. I get very wordy about theories. *Anyway*, what I *do* with them is throw them at the knot holes on that tree."

"What's the theory?" he said. He picked one up and threw it right into the center of the hardest target.

"Oh, God. Hand-eye coordination. I'm a sucker for hand-eye coordination. I think it's a metaphor for the whole psyche."

"What's the theory?" he said.

"My theory." She picked up a rock, took careful aim, and threw it a few inches away from the target. "Oh, good, that proves it. *My theory* is that however close I can come to that target is a barometer of what sort of mood I'm in."

Will picked up a handful of the rocks and threw them, one at a time straight into the target. He threw the last one far out and over beyond the tree, then turned and smiled at her.

"I live right down there," he said, pointing to the south. "I can almost see my street from here."

"Where?" Amanda said, as though that were the most extraordinary coincidence in the world.

"Right down there on the edge of Tin Cup. That's where I was this morning."

"And now you're here."

"Now I'm here." The sun was almost gone now. A wind came up, making them shiver.

"Let's go inside," Amanda said.

Will sat down on her piano bench still holding his guitar. He was wishing he had bathed. Aside from that he didn't care what happened. This crazy woman from a world of tennis clubs and ski resorts and yoga schools was a lot of excitement for a Sunday afternoon in Fayetteville. It never occurred to him that he might fall in love. He had never even read a book about a man loving someone old enough to be his mother.

"Do you play this piano?" he said.

"I'm learning. Maybe I should have started with a guitar."

"Come sit by me. I'll show you some chords."

She put down the glass she was holding and sat beside him. He reached his arm around her and held down the chords while she touched the strings.

"This is an old trick guitar players use to put their arms around women they fall in love with," he said. "Has anyone ever done this to you before?"

"I've never known a musician before," she said. "I always end up with lawyers."

"How does it feel, knowing a musician?"

"It feels very nice so far," she said. Then Will put the guitar away and took her into his arms with the gentle manners he had learned from his mother and Amanda gave up thinking and allowed herself this strange excitement as if she had every right in the world to tenderness and to joy.

"We might as well go on and do this," she said finally. "Since it looks like we are definitely going to do it."

"Do we have to hurry?"

"We don't have to hurry. On the other hand we don't have time to do anything as foolish as get to know each other."

In the night Amanda started menstruating for the first time since she'd taken out the IUD. Now she stood on the bathroom floor staring down at the towel in her hands. She stared down at the white towel with its red stains mixed with semen.

Oh, God, she thought. I'm still alive. I'm not old yet. She took a deep breath, feeling her rib cage rise up out of her waist, looking up at the ceiling as if to thank someone, anyone, God or Jesus or the Gautama Buddha or Albert Einstein or her grandmother's weird tough little genes.

"Sometimes that happens," Dr. Kincaid told her later. "Sooner or later the estrogen level rises and one of the leftover eggs drops. It isn't unnatural. Especially with an early menopause."

But Amanda wasn't in a mood to believe in estrogen levels. It's because he touched me, she told herself. He touched the part of me that wants to live.

When she woke again in the morning, Amanda was sleeping in the beautiful hazel-eyed young man's arms. His body was strong and still beside her, his skin was warm against her skin. The curves and volumes of his body fit against her own as if they were made of the same material. Wordlessly and perfectly they made love again.

"It seems so easy," she said.

"It's you," he said.

"Oh, no," she said. "It's you."

"It's us," he said and Amanda smiled to herself. She would never in a million years have said such a romantic thing. But Will was a small-town boy who listened to songs on the radio. He wasn't afraid to say anything.

❧

"Oh, God," Amanda said, rolling over on her stomach, pulling the pillows over her head. "I feel like that poor woman in *The Last Picture Show*. Maybe I better get up and start redecorating the bedroom."

"Which one?" he asked. "Cloris Leachman or Ellen Burstyn?"

"Ellen Burstyn," she said. "Ellen Burstyn's looks and Cloris Leachman's role."

"Where are you going to be when I get out of school this afternoon?" he said.

"Right here painting this room baby blue," she said. "Going crazy waiting for you to call me."

As soon as he left for school she called Katie. "Look what you've done to me," she said. "I'm in love with him. I swear I am. Katie, I am not teasing you."

"Oh, God," Katie said.

"Tell me about him. Tell me who he is."

"You already know more than I know," Katie said. "He's a good musician. I know that. And he's a local boy. Oh, I'll tell you something else. Clinton used to coach him. I told Clinton last night I'd just left you on a balcony with Will Lyons and he said that's one of the few men in this town he'd trust you with."

"Listen, Katie," Amanda said. "Would you believe this? Would you believe I didn't even know that I was lonely."

On Monday night he had dinner with her and spent the night. On Tuesday night he had dinner with her and spent the night. On Wednesday he had dinner with her and spent the night.

"Why do you always cry when I make love to you?" he said, smoothing her hair with his fingers. The moonlight was pouring through the window, covering the bed with silver.

"Because it makes me remember death," she said. "Because when you love someone you can't bear to think of ever leaving them."

"Don't talk like that," he said. "I hate to think about things like that."

"That's why loving someone younger than you are is so sad and dramatic and *poignant*, if there still is such a word." She was trying to keep it light but she was warming to her subject. "Because you know from the start it's a limited engagement. We can't fool ourselves about how long this will last."

"Don't talk about it," he said. "It makes me sad."

"You started it. You asked me why it made me cry. Because I've already made up my mind what it's going to be. I'm going to love you as hard as I can for as long as I can and then I'll give you to someone your own age and you can have babies and lead a normal life."

"I don't need a normal life," he said. "A normal life would bore me to death."

"I'll tell you what," she said. "I'll love you until I'm fifty years old. How about that? When I'm fifty years old I'll give you up and go back to work."

"If I kiss you will you stop talking?" he said.

"I hate my lips," she said. "They aren't big enough. I have skinny English lips. I want lips like yours. I want thick rich lips to kiss you with."

"Hush," he said. "I'll make them grow."

❦

On Thursday he broke the spell. He came walking into the kitchen where Amanda was cooking Creole sauce in a copper skillet. She had just added green peppers to the tomatoes and was watching the good-smelling steam rising in the cool air of the small kitchen. A bowl of biscuit dough was sitting in a sunny window. Amanda was thinking that it was the nicest day she had ever known. *All the pieces have fallen into place,* she was thinking. *My most secret desire, my most secret desire is about to come true.*

"I have to go home for a few days and think this over," he said. "I have to get some studying done. I can't keep this up."

Amanda turned the fire off under the skillet and looked away. All the armor fell into place and clamped shut. She put on her city voice.

"Of course," she said. "Whatever you want to do. I'll see you Sunday then. Or Sunday night."

"I'll call you," he said. "I'll let you know."

"Great," she said. "That's wonderful. I was going to be out of town for a few days anyway. I need to go to Eureka Springs to see an old friend from New Orleans. I've been meaning to go ever since I moved up here. It's this old friend of mine, this great guy I love like my own brother."

"I just need to be alone for a few days," he said.

"Of course," she said. "That's wonderful. That's great. I'll call you when I come back then. Or you call me."

When he left Amanda threw the Creole sauce and the biscuit dough into the sink and wandered downstairs to the room that was her office and stood looking at the piles of papers on her desk. She hadn't been in the room since Sunday. What am I doing? she thought. What in the name of God have I been up to?

She picked up the page she'd been working on Sunday morning, a fragment she was making a trot from.

> *Where are the hands that brought me*
> *water from every stream*
> *Where are the psalms and bells*
> *The well at the root of the tree*
> *How long until even thirst*
> *will seem a stranger*

She played with the verbs for a while, then dropped the paper back down on the desk. He might never come back, she thought. I might never see him again.

She sat down in the middle of the workroom floor and pulled her legs into a yoga posture and closed her eyes. After a while she was deep into a long stretch and she could see Garth Hotchkiss's sweet face smiling at her over the cash register at the Tulane Book Store, telling her about his plans to move to the Ozarks. I really will go see Garth, she thought. I really will go see him. She got up off the floor, found his phone number in Eureka Springs, and called and told him she was coming. She stuffed some warm clothes into a bag, locked the house, jumped in the car, and started driving as fast as she could go down the mountain.

I'm going to Garth, she told herself. Garth will save me with Zen. Surely Garth will save me.

Garth Hotchkiss was an old college friend. One spring they had owned a houseboat together on the Tennessee River where they held "literary afternoons," chugging up and down the river with a borrowed ten-horsepower motor, drinking sherry and discussing Albert Schweitzer. Garth had later gone to India as a Peace Corps worker, then knocked around New Orleans running a bookstore while he saved up money to make a dream come true.

Every time Amanda ran into him in New Orleans he talked to her about a dream he had to buy the old schoolhouse in Eureka Springs, Arkansas, and turn it into a Tai Chi academy.

The only thing wrong with his dream was that it wasn't making any money. He had taken to running the early morning paper route in Eureka to pay the light bill. He had just come in from delivering his papers when Amanda called.

When they finished talking he put the phone neatly back on its pedestal, shook his head from side to side several times, sat down on the floor and began massaging the neck of the German shepherd he had rescued from a commune at Loyola and brought to Arkansas to enjoy nature. The only thing wrong with that was that the dog didn't like to go outside.

"Krishna, Krishna," he said to the dog. "Amanda Mc-Camey's in the Ozarks. What a world we have lived to see. What a long way we have all come from our beginnings." A bell was tinkling in a tree outside the window. It was a tiny brass bell on a string Garth had found one day outside the Five Happiness Restaurant on Carrolton Avenue in New Orleans. He kept it around to remind him of why he was in the Ozarks. Sometimes it reminded him of the dirty crowded streets of the city. Other times it reminded him of all the good restaurants he had left behind.

Garth moved his hands across the dog's body. Garth was very interested in the fields of energy that surround living bodies. He waved his hands around over Krishna's back for a few minutes, then stretched them out to the pile of bills lying on the table.

"Open Sesame," he said out loud. "Make bad bills shrink up like hearts of stingy people." He moved his hands closer to the stack, trying to lift the top one from the pile without touching it. He tried for a few minutes, then put his hands back on his coffee cup. He was very relieved that the envelope had stayed in its place.

Amanda came driving down off the mountain onto Mission Road and followed it until it turned onto Highway 45 leading into the hill country to the north. The hills were steeper here, the farms more desolate, the farmhouses farther and farther back from the road.

"Those tapes are playing in my head," she sang as she drove, "all those silly goddamn love songs. Shopgirl sorrows, jukebox tears, low-rent rendezvous. Where or when, September songs, the clothes you're wearing are the clothes he wore, the smile you are smiling he was smiling then, but I can't remember where or when. Oh, to love again and again and again . . . It's always the same thing. Always the same goddamn silly thing.

"Oh, Garth, oh, good buddy, save me from the fierce grip of Karrrrrrrmmaaaaaaa, from the dark heart, from the fatal heart of Metro-Goldwyn-Mayer and Twentieth Century–Fox and George Gershwin and Cole Porter.

"Calm down, Amanda," she said to herself. "Calm down before you drive the car off the road."

Eureka Springs was a strange little Victorian town where two centuries of white men and before that the Indians believed the waters to have healing powers. All sorts of strange groups call it home, hard-core Baptists and witches' covens, a lesbian community up in the hills, a group of wealthy dilettantes who move back and forth between Eureka Springs and New Orleans, believing there are bands of energy that connect the two places and tell them when it is time to move from one to the other. Even the skeptics admit the mountain on which the little town sits like a cuckoo clock might be a magnetic field. Even the skeptics know something is going on.

Now Amanda drove into the city limits and followed the winding road through the town. She turned onto a narrow cobblestone street, then up an unbelievably steep hill to a brick building perched on top among its overgrown gardens.

She turned into a makeshift parking lot and came to a stop beside a marble statue of Diana, overgrown now with blue cornflowers.

Garth was waiting in the yard with his hands deep in the

pockets of his old gray corduroys. He took her into his living quarters, made her a cup of peppermint tea, and listened while she poured out her love story.

"*So* I went to all the trouble to fix it so I could come up here and translate the Renoir sonnets. Now I've fallen in love with this boy and you've got to save me from it. He's much too young. It's terribly inappropriate."

"If you say so," Garth said.

"Stop that," she said. "Don't pull that enigmatic stuff on me. I have to figure this out before I go off the deep end again. Remember that law student I fell in love with? Remember that? It took me five years to get over that."

"Why don't you let me show you something I learned last week," Garth said, putting out his cigarette. "See, I still smoke. I'll never get to heaven either, Amanda. Much less Nirvana. Let me show you something I learned to do."

He took her into a large room with windows on two sides. The only furnishings were a small bed, a Persian rug with figures of animals worked into the design and a row of simple bookshelves against a wall. Light was pouring in the windows, picking up the golds and reds of the carpet.

"An enlightened man was here this week," Garth said, "a master who came to teach a class for me. He stayed in this room. I think he's the only person I've ever met who was really enlightened. It was the strangest thing. There's an exercise he showed me that I can't stop doing. Let me show it to you." Garth moved his lanky body around in a shuffle. "Watch," he said. Then his whole posture changed. He became as graceful as a girl. He reached his hands up into the air, brought them down in an attitude of prayer, then extended his arms out in front of him in a semicircle. "You hold your arms out like this and then you bend your knees.

Then you stay in that position for as long as you can. You have to keep practicing it every day until you can do it for an hour. I'm very taken with this, Amanda. I can't explain to you how powerful it is."

"You don't have to convince me," Amanda said. "I know what's in those Eastern arts. I get spooky every time I start fooling around with Zen or Tai Chi. Every time I start getting good at it I always quit. It scares me. I need the concept of self to do my work. I want to do my work, Garth, whether it makes any difference to the world or not. When I get around this stuff from the East I lose sight of the reason to do anything at all. The idea of recording anything or saving anything for the future seems so ludicrous."

"Like falling in love," Garth said.

"What is the sound of one hand beating the shit out of you?" Amanda said.

"Friends can't talk true anymore?" he said.

"Okay," Amanda said. "Okay. God, it's good to be with you. Now show me your exercise again. Come on. I want to try it."

Garth moved to the center of the room and resumed the posture, holding his arms out in front of him and bending his knees. "This is all you do," he said. "Only you have to keep it up for a long time. And you have to imagine the bands of energy flowing around the inside of the arms and the great band of *ch'i* energy, the sexual energy of the universe, which flows in a circle from the shoulders to the crotch." He took his big hands and described the circles.

"It feels great," Amanda said, doing as he did.

"This exercise is five thousand years old," Garth said. "It's stored up a lot of power."

"I want to see how long I can do it," she said.

"I have to go now to teach a class," Garth said. "Go on and practice. I'll find you after a while."

When he left Amanda moved to the exact center of the room and resumed the posture. Her arms became heavy, then lighter, then very light. What a peaceful place, she thought, feeling the room all around her. She smiled at her hands, concentrating on imagining the circles of energy. Amanda was a very good person to teach something mystical to. As old as she was she could still talk herself into believing anything she wanted to believe. She stayed in the posture until she thought her arms were going to break off at the shoulders.

Then she put on her running suit and walked down the stairs and into a large high-ceilinged room that was used in the afternoons for ballet classes. A piano concerto was on the record player. Amanda turned it on and made lavish bows to the four corners of the room. Then she began to dance. She danced a dream of dancing. Every movement she made seemed perfect to her, perfect and free. She rose up on her toes, turning and swooping as if this were something she did every day of her life, as if she had been rehearsing her dance forever. She remembered seeing Margot Fonteyn dance the year Nureyev defected to be her partner. She danced that time and that place. She danced Margot Fonteyn and Rudolf Nureyev and herself and all their dances made into one dance. She danced on and on, raising her hands high over her head, feeling as graceful as a tree in the wind, turning and turning and turning.

A little group of five-year-old girls began appearing in the doorway for their class. Amanda bowed deeply to each one and invited them to join her. One by one the little girls dropped their coats and hats on the floor and began to dance with her, turning and swooping and gliding, moving their fat little arms and legs as they saw her doing.

Amanda turned the record over and they went on dancing, Amanda in her blue velvet running suit, the little girls all around her in bright leotards and sweaters.

The mothers stood against the wall, leaning on the practice bar, smiling at the scene. A little girl in tights the color of emeralds walked primly off the dance floor to her mother, took her year-old brother in her arms, lugged him across the floor and set him down in front of Amanda for a gift.

The teacher appeared and the dance was over. "How beautiful," she said to Amanda. "That was a lovely thing to do."

"I made it up," Amanda said. "I don't know how to dance."

"You won't believe what I did this afternoon," she told Garth later. They were having dinner in his kitchen, bright steamed vegetables, kale and carrots and okra and thick brown bread, everything arranged on white plates like a painting.

"I heard," he said. "Sally was talking about it. She said you were wonderful. She wanted to know who you were."

"I *was* wonderful," Amanda said. "I don't know what happened. It was the strangest thing. I was doing your exercise and I thought about the dancing rooms you had shown me. I wanted to dance and all of a sudden I knew how, as if I had always known and had just remembered."

"Maybe my enlightened man left you something in the room. He slept there."

"Maybe it's my new boyfriend," she said. "Could getting

laid by a twenty-five-year-old guitar player turn you into a mystic?"

"What do you think that smile on the Buddha's face is all about?"

"Well, a lot of very strange things have been happening to me lately. Besides, he'll probably never even call me again. If I had any sense I'd be praying to the Buddha to keep him from ever calling me again."

That night Amanda slept in the room the enlightened man had used. Sometime in the night she woke up with the moon shining in the window and got out of bed and walked over to the exact center of the room and fell on her knees in an attitude of prayer. She stayed that way for a long time with her head bowed to the moon, then got back into the bed and slept again.

In the morning as soon as she woke she walked back over to the same place and stood there in her bare feet. In a moment she started doing the crazy exercise again. I'm going nuts, she thought. This is what it means to be crazy.

Then she thought of Will and it dawned on her that he was as caught up in this mystery as she was herself. He's afraid of this too, she thought. For all I know he might even love me. It takes two people to do the kind of stuff that we've been doing. Goddammit, he's in this thing as much as I am.

Garth fixed lunch and they carried it on trays out to the garden and ate on an old stone table. "I hope you can stay until tomorrow afternoon," he said. "Father Provosty is coming over from Huntsville to teach fencing. He's an interesting man, a Jesuit. I'd like you to meet him."

"A Jesuit. You're running around with a Jesuit?"

"You're so intolerant, Amanda. I'd forgotten about that in you. You never have had any tolerance for anyone else's beliefs."

"I haven't got any tolerance for stupidity. For goddamn religions."

"Not everyone in the world is as fortunate as you are. There are weak people in the world. They need religion. They need something to believe in."

"The hell they do. They need someone to teach them to be strong. They need someone to tell them the truth."

"What do you propose to do with all those people out there, then? The dumb, the sick, the powerless?"

"Well, to begin with I'm not going to condescend to them and tell them lies. I'm not going to patronize them and take advantage of their weakness like the goddamn R.C.s do. That's the main reason I'm translating those poems. So people will know one more nasty thing the R.C.s have been up to. I hate them. I really hate them."

"You're going to take on the Holy Roman Church with a book of translations?"

"It isn't a joke, Garth. They have manuscripts from six centuries from all over the world locked up in Rome. They won't even let anyone in to catalog them. Not to mention paintings and God knows what all else. They stole those things, confiscated them down through the centuries. Well, I hate the Church so much anyway. I can't believe you're running around with a Jesuit."

"Come on," he said. "Eat your strawberries. I fixed them just for you." She's really impossible, he thought. She'll never grow up.

⚜

Sunday they picked up the argument again. "Why pick on the R.C.s?" Garth said. "They aren't any worse than anyone else. I mean, the Catholic Church does a lot of good in the world."

"What good? Scaring the shit out of little children before they can even read? Making them hate their bodies? Listen, Garth, I've had lots of friends who were Catholics. Remember James Tilling? He was afraid to hold his dick in his hand until he was twenty-two years old. He had a Jewish roommate at Princeton who finally taught him to hold his dick in his hand so he could pee standing up. He used to have to sit on the john to pee. I swear it. He told me that himself."

"That's just one case, Amanda. That's not enough reason to condemn the whole Church."

"The hell it isn't. You know what they do in their schools in New Orleans? They make the little boys keep crucifixes in their pockets. In case they should accidentally touch their dicks when they put their hands in their pockets they have to feel that fucking cross with a dead man nailed to it."

"Still you can't condemn the whole Church. Look at that wonderful nun in India taking care of all those babies."

"Oh, God, I can't believe you, Garth. I don't want to even talk about it anymore to you."

"All right, let's don't talk about it. Let's talk about love. Tell me about this paragon you've fallen in love with in Fayetteville."

"He's just someone I've got the hots for. Let's face it. He's a beautiful young man with a guitar. A cliché. And I'm scared to death he'll never call me up again. I mean, there's a good chance he'll never call me up again."

"You could call him up," Garth said.

"That's true," she said. "But I'm going to."

It was almost fifteen minutes before she went in the other room and called him.

It had been a long weekend for Will, restless, sleepless. He had ended up in a fight at the pool hall. Now he couldn't even remember who it had been with or what it was over. He got up and made up the bed, hearing the bells of the First Methodist Church start up in the distance, then the bells of the small black church on the corner, thinking of his father fastening his tie back in the days when he dragged him off to Sunday School.

A third set of bells began, coming from the direction of the university. Will finished making up the bed, picked up some clothes off the floor, carried them around in his hand for a moment, then dropped them in the closet on top of a box of squirrel shells. He picked up his mechanical drawing book and stood in the middle of the room looking at the cover, but the bells were louder now and he couldn't concentrate.

He shook his head and lay back down on the bed with his hands spread out beside him, thinking about Amanda.

I wasn't ready for this, he thought.

He lay on his stomach thinking about her, listening to the church bells fill the morning air. He had almost fallen back to sleep when the phone rang.

"I'm bringing a cat home," she said when he answered. "A gray cat with eyes like the sea. Don't you want to come over the minute I get home and see my cat and eat supper and make love to me?"

"Where are you?" he said.

"I'm in Eureka Springs," she said, "taking tolerance lessons and I'm never coming back to Fayetteville, Arkansas unless you missed me."

"I missed you," he said. "Don't worry about that. How long will it take you to get here?"

"As soon as I catch this cat," she said. "Garth gave me a cat."

"I'm waiting," he said. "I'm right here waiting."

Amanda drove home from Eureka Springs in a state of pure ecstasy or plain old-fashioned spring fever or just plain old-fashioned love. She was so high she was barely subject to the laws of gravity. She had lost eight pounds. She had hardly slept for days.

He wants to see me, she sang to herself as she drove madly home down the curving road from Eureka Springs to Fayetteville. He missed me. He's waiting for me.

I will take anything that I can get, goddammit. I will take as many days or hours or years as I can have.

Once more before I die I will have this thing which is better than anything else on the green earth and everyone knows it and anyone with any sense would travel anywhere to have it if they knew where it was hiding.

Goddamn, the world is beautiful today. Rain and leaves, sky and wind and rain. Rainbows. I haven't seen a rainbow in years.

I will take Will to the island of Granada to see the rainbows. I will take all my money out of the bank and we will get on a plane and fly to the Spice Islands and sit in the sun watching the rainbows on the green hills, drinking cocoa, watching the rain come and go on the ocean, feasting on lobster and lime pie, sleeping all night to the sound of crickets in the cocoa trees.

When she got to her house Will was waiting, leaning against the wooden fence, wearing a sweater as blue as the summer sky, smiling at her as if she were the most wonderful thing in the world.

"What's happening?" he said, taking her bag.

"The cat wouldn't come," she said. "The goddamn cat wouldn't get in the car."

Then he touched her and he kept on touching her while they walked across the bridge and while she unlocked the door and while they moved into the living room.

"First I'm going to build you a fire," he said. "First I'm going to get you warm." He built a fire in the stone fireplace and Amanda spread a quilt on the floor and they knelt before the fire and began to undress each other.

Then for a long time he would only hold her in his arms, touching her with great tenderness, for Will Lyons was a real musician and he made love the way he played music, without caring where it led or if it led anywhere.

"I love thee," she said at last. "Thee and thy hand-eye coordination, thee and thy music."

"Tell me one thing," he said, lying back with his hands behind his head. "Was there really a cat?"

"Of course there was a cat," she said. "Would I lie about anything as important as a cat?"

It was late the next afternoon before Amanda even remembered to get the mail out of the mailbox. She was dressed in a soft dress with a yellow sweater tied around her shoulders, waiting for Will to come and pick her up. They were going to an Italian restaurant on the edge of town for dinner.

She got the mail out of the mailbox and settled down on the steps at the edge of the bridge, arranging the sweater just so, thinking about how nice she would look when Will came walking up the hill. The mailbox was stuffed with mail and she sorted out the magazines and advertisements. There was a letter from the editor of *The Paris Review* saying they had accepted a group of her translations. There were letters from friends in New Orleans, saying what they always said. "Where are you? What in the name of hell are you doing in Arkansas of all places? When are you coming home? Can I come and visit? How in hell do you get there from here? Why don't you ever answer your phone?"

There was a letter from Malcolm, his small precise handwriting on law firm stationery. Amanda saved it for last. When she had finished all the other mail she opened it.

Dear Ms. McCamey,

How is the trout fishing in the Ozarks? Hope you are catching whatever is biting.

Here at the old Whitney Bank Building we are answering the phone for you. Mother wants to know what you want for your birthday. She has tried to call several times with no success.

Amanda, please send back my grandmother's jewelry as per our agreement. Amanda, don't sell Mamaae's jewelry. If you need money just let me know, I'll be glad to send it to you.

Are you serious about not giving out your address to *anyone?* Your cousin the quarterback has been calling. He was in town several weeks ago and called twice trying to get it out of me. I suggest you get in touch with him.

Go on and get the divorce up there and I'll pay for it. We can get married again later when you get tired of pickup trucks or whatever it is you are currently patronizing.

Your obedient servant,
Malcolm

Amanda's good mood went away. She shivered and stuck her arms into the sleeves of her sweater, her face going all tight and old and wrinkled.

What is Guy doing in New Orleans? What is he doing down there? Goddamn him, he went to look for her. Goddamn Malcolm, how dare he write to me. Goddamn them all, why can't they leave me alone? Why can't I ever have anything? I'll throw the goddamn telephone in the lake. I'll get a mailbox downtown and never pick up my mail. I'll hire a graduate student to go through it for me and send back all his letters.

No, I know what I'll do. I won't pay any attention to it. I'll just forget it. I'll pretend it doesn't exist. It can't get in if I don't let it in.

I'll stay on top of it. They cannot have me anymore. None of them can have me anymore *for any use* for any price.

She hurried into the house and threw the mail down on a desk and wadded up Malcolm's letter and dropped it in a wastebasket. She found the key to her lockbox at the Whitney Bank and stuck it in an envelope with a note.

Dear Malcolm,

Please get your grandmother's jewelry out of my lockbox so you won't worry about me selling it on the street. Don't

give anyone my phone number or my address. My friends
know where I am. Guy only wants to talk about Esperanza.
He wants to talk me out of selling my half. And I'm too
busy to think about that now.

Love,
Amanda

She stamped the envelope and walked down the long hill
to the mailbox on the corner of Water Street.

Will was coming up the hill. She ran down the rest of the
way to meet him.

"What have you been up to?" he said, taking her hand,
walking along beside her.

"I've been waiting for you to come home and kiss me,"
she said. "How can my lips get bigger if I don't practice?"

"I want to take you somewhere before we go out to dinner," he said. "If I can find it. It's something I've been
thinking about showing you ever since the first night I was
sitting on your balcony. You can see it from there."

"What is it?" Amanda said.

"Just come along. I don't have much to offer you,
Amanda. Except to show you things around here you'd
never find for yourself. Come on. Stop talking."

They walked down Spring Street and turned onto a
gravel road that led along the side of the mountain past the
big green tanks that held the city's water supply, past a row
of small houses with gardens just being turned for the
spring planting.

"What's wrong?" Will said. "Something's wrong."

"No, it isn't," she said. "I was thinking about how crazy
it is to love you. It's just like something I would do. Now
what's this surprise?"

"Just wait," he said. "If it's still here."

They walked past the houses and back into the deserted part of the mountain, land that had never been cleared, a stand of red maples still bare except for a few leaves on the low branches.

They walked along the path to where it opened onto an apron of land with the ruins of a chimney at the far end.

"We used to come up here and ride bikes when we were little," Will said. "Once we came up here and cooked on that old fireplace. I'll never forget that night. We thought we were such outlaws, cooking on Methodist property."

"Oh, God," Amanda said, for she had just spotted what he had brought her to see. Beside the ruined fireplace a long bank of small yellow flowers were waving in the March breeze, a field of yellow flax.

Amanda ran down the hill and knelt among the flowers.

"It's what they make linen from," Will said. "I knew it was the right time of year."

Amanda ran her fingers across the delicate waxy blooms of the flax. A whippoorwill called in the woods, then called again. "People lived here," she said. "Slept and ate, talked and dreamed, raised this chimney, right here where we're sitting."

"They worked their ass off raising this chimney," he said, examining the caulking. "These are big stones."

"What are the bright yellow bushes by the chimney? I've never seen any of these flowers, Will. All these flowers are new to me."

"It's called Scotch broom. When the Plantagenet kings came to Scotland they wore it in their hair. Or so Mrs. Jansma taught me in the fifth grade." He smiled up at her and she had a vision of him on a fat horse riding across the meadows of Scotland, a great sprig of yellow flowers in his hair.

"Redbirds, mockingbirds, robins," she told him later. "One event leading to the next event. And time, what we call time, a sea we swim in. We swim along the surface, all of us together going God knows where. We swim along the surface. Below us the past in thermocline after thermocline, moving, pulling, tugging us down. We keep on swimming. We keep on moving forward or we drown. Forgive the metaphor."

"You think such sad things."

"That's what you get for running around with old women. We have a lot of sadness, a lot of old baggage."

"Don't say that," he said. "Don't call yourself an old woman."

"Why not?" she said. "That's what I am. I want to start liking the sound of it."

She cuddled down into his arms, thinking about time. A triangle, a pyramid of time and space. Me, *whoever I am*, in the middle like a buried pharaoh, no more important than the sand on the bricks on the steps leading to the quarry where the stones were cut . . . the smile you're wearing is the smile he wore. We looked at each other in the same way then but I can't remember where or when.

"We played everywhere back then," he was saying. "Applegate's, Jose's, you name it. If we wanted it we had it. We were the richest kids in Fayetteville for a while. The year I was eighteen I had a brand-new Volkswagen van . . . well, those were the good old days."

"You're only twenty-five years old," she said. "There aren't any good old days."

"Mike and Jim and Leonie and me," he went on. "Jesus, we were wild. Well, at least I had my turn. They're all in California now."

"Why'd you quit?"

"My old man talked me into it."

"He made you quit? Your father made you quit?"

"No one can make a rock-and-roller do anything, Amanda. That's what it's all about."

"I don't understand it. It doesn't sound like music to me. Well, it really doesn't."

"It isn't about music. It's about being free. Jerry Lee used to set his piano on fire. One time he shot his bass player. The music didn't matter. What mattered was the wildness. Well, in the end the world won out. I hurt a blood vessel in my thumb and couldn't play for a long time. Then I got bronchitis from staying up all night in bars. It was just one thing after the other. I started running lines for this poet that killed himself. I ran lines for him all one winter. I loved him. Jesus, I loved that man. Well, he shot himself and it scared the shit out of me so I went to work for my father. Next thing I knew I'd sold all my amps and signed up for school. It makes me hot every time I think about it." His voice was soft now, as plaintive as a ballad. Amanda was a wonderful audience for this sort of thing.

"I'm sorry," she said, pulling him into her arms, pouring herself like melted butter into the story of his golden lion-hearted youth.

"You don't have to be sorry," he said, cheering up at the sadness in her voice. "I had some great times. I'll have some again."

"We'll have them together," she said. "We'll bring back fun. We'll start a fad."

Now two weeks had gone by since Amanda was in Eureka Springs. Will had moved half his clothes into her house and they were stacked in a cardboard box on the floor of her closet. Every time she passed the box she felt giddy and silly, as if the boundaries of what passes for reality had broken down entirely and the proof of their dismissal was that cardboard box holding Will's unironed clothes sitting on her closet floor.

One event leading to another event. First his clothes on the floor of my closet, then his guitar beside my piano, then a toothbrush and a razor. God knows what everybody's thinking. At least my friends have read about such things. What do his friends think?

"Will and I are going to bring back fun," she told Katie. "We're going to start a fad."

"That's great," Katie said. "That's what we need, some more fun."

"It is what we need. I'm tired of misery. People are crazy, Katie. They don't have enough sense to be happy. We all starve to death all our lives. Starve to death in the middle of a feast. Here it is, more beauty than the eye can bear to see, miracle after miracle after miracle. *And I could not even see it.*"

"That's it," Katie said. "A clinical definition of love."

"What's *that* supposed to mean?"

"That you're in love. And that's a good thing to be. As long as you keep on working. Don't stop working, Amanda. The work will be there long after the boy is gone."

"I can work and be in love at the same time. I got a lot done this morning. I translated the whole inventory of things she took to Lyons. You ought to see it. It's really something."

"That's great," Katie said. "Actually it's revolutionary. If you can work and be in love at the same time, you're the first woman I ever knew that could. Maybe you're the missing link, Amanda."

"Maybe you ought to get a job for the *Ladies' Home Journal*. They like simplistic shit like that."

"All I know how to do is tell the truth," Katie said. "It's the only challenge there was down in Alma."

"Well, I'm not interested in truth this month," Amanda said. "This month I like lucky charms and fortune cookies."

"Hot tips and long shots?"

"Yeah, stuff like that. Incense and votive candles."

"Call if you need me."

"Phone calls," Amanda said. "True Romances. Dreams of order."

One day during these weeks a friend sent her a Chinese prayer-poem in the mail from San Francisco, a little gold and red piece of rice paper with Chinese characters on it. *Write a secret wish on the back and burn it,* the directions said. That night Amanda took the poem outside and burned it in the moonlight on the balcony. The fire crackled into tiny points of light on the railing. Above, the stars were bright in a blue-black sky. She could not make a wish. Life is the wish, she thought. Life is enough.

She really did try to work. But she couldn't concentrate. Amanda was in love, deep into a mystery darker than the mass. She could make fun of the mystery to Katie but the mystery did not lose its power. Will's skin against her skin in the night, his laughter rising with hers to the heavens, hope like a sail in the wind. She had no defenses against power like that.

Marshall sent her a copy of a translation the woman in Albuquerque had done. It wasn't bad. Much as Amanda wanted to hate it, she had to admit it really wasn't bad.

Well, it's not a contest, she told herself. Art and literature are not a competition. But of course Amanda didn't really believe that for a moment.

She got out her own trot of the poem and went to work on it.

> *Those days that fell from my hands*
> *like Spanish music*
> *Oh, burning, burning*
> *you have consumed my bright days*
> *By what right do you consign me*
> *to this winter place*
> *By what power will you keep me here*

Consumed, she thought. *Brûler,* burned up, eaten away, *consommer,* completed. You have wasted my bright days, completed my bright days. Oh, that's good, that's really good. *O, brûlant, tu consummais mes jours ensoleillés.*

Ensoleillés, sunfilled days. I wish I could hear her voice. Well, Helene will speak to me. I know she will. If I do the work. If I listen.

Amanda was staring out the window, sending messages across several centuries. Don't go to Albuquerque, she was saying. You don't want some housewife in Albuquerque messing with your poems while she does the dishes. Give me time. Wait for me. She pushed her glasses back up on her nose and went back to work. *Brûler,* yes, that's the one. That's the one I need. Just as she was getting the feel of it Will came into the room. Came breezing in and put his hands on her hair.

"Let's go over to Spider Creek and go swimming on the bluffs while there's still light."

"It's too cold to go swimming," she said. "We'll freeze."

"Who cares," he said. "It's almost April. It's time to test the lake."

The bluffs were gray and wonderful in the afternoon sun. The water was clear, like green silk, cold and delicious.

Amanda took off her dress. Underneath it she had on an old brown bathing suit. "This," she announced, "is a one-piece bathing suit. This is what grown women wear when they go swimming. You may have seen photographs of such wearing apparel. You may have read of such suits in old books. Well, how do I look?" She stood grandly on a rock ledge, allowed him to look at her old brown bathing suit for several seconds, then dove into the cold water. When she scrambled back up the ledge he reached out both his hands to help her. "That," he said, "is showing off."

She pulled off the bathing suit and dropped it on the ground. "Well, come on in," she said. "You're the one that thought this up."

Then they were in the water together. Amanda dove deep down into the water, down along the stone ledges. The visibility was marvelous. It was as clear as a reef in the islands. She came up beside him and pulled him against her in the water, warm and smooth against his chest and arms and legs.

Above them the bluffs rose five hundred feet. Below, a series of wide stone ledges led down into the water. They held on to the ledges, moving close together, then moving away, then back together. Amanda was pretending she was a porpoise. She looked out across the still surface of the lake to the woods on the far side. The sun was going down in the water, making a path all the way to their ledge.

She moved away from him and swam out toward the sun, doing her very best Australian crawl, going as far out as she dared, feeling like she did when she was a child and would swim away from Guy in the bayou.

She kept on swimming, getting farther and farther away, until he called her back to him. "Amanda," he called out. "Come on back here. Come on. That's enough. That's enough of that. I'm freezing. Come on. Let's go get dinner."

She dove, going far down and staying as long as she could, then swam languidly back to the shore.

They left the lake and drove to a little German restaurant and feasted on veal and dumplings with a marvelous Mandeltorte for dessert. Amanda licked the last of the whipped cream from her spoon and sighed. "This is where heaven starts," she said. "In a spoonful of almonds and whipped cream."

"I've never seen anyone like sugar as much as you do," he said. "It fascinates me to watch you eat it." He sipped his brandy, wishing he could tell her about the letter he had folded in his shirt pocket. It was a letter from the dean saying he was flunking out of school. I'll tell her tomorrow, he thought. I can't stand to make her unhappy. She's so wonderful to be with when she's happy.

"It never occurs to me that anyone is watching me do anything," she said. "The next time I do yoga I'm going to meditate on you watching me."

Will ordered another brandy and they talked to the proprietor for a while, then drove home in the moonlight through the hills. Will had forgotten about the letter and was singing all the way home in the car. He was singing a song he thought of as his theme.

"I used to think of myself as a stranger," he sang. "Holding my own against impossible odds. Badly outnumbered and caught in a crossfire, of devils and gods."

"Those are nice lyrics," she said. "That's a nice song."

"It's Dan Fogelberg," Will said. "He's my hero."

My hero is Albert Einstein, Amanda thought, looking out the window at the stars. My hero is Margaret Mead. My hero is Johann Sebastian Bach. Well, I guess I'm going to learn some new music.

When he came home from school the next afternoon she was out on the balcony getting a tan. "My last tan," she said. "One more year and I'll quit and be a white girl forever. I *meant* to quit this year. I *meant* to get old this year."

"You're the youngest person I've ever known," he said. He meant it. He'd never known a human being as free as Amanda.

"How'd it go at school?" she said. "How was the calculus test?"

"Great," he said. "I'm making A's. Nothing to it. A piece of cake. Come on. Get dressed. I want to show you Goshen where I used to survey. Come on. I want to show you the Goshen Post Office while it's still open."

He got a beer out of the refrigerator and drank it while she dressed. He had already had two. He took a six-pack with him and set it down between them in the car.

"I like to drink beer out of bottles when I'm with a woman," he said, to take her mind off the six-pack. "When she's close to your mouth it's sexier that way."

"You're kidding," she said. "You must be kidding."

They drove out to the Goshen P.O., a small frame building with a huge American flag above the door. The postmaster was sitting on a chair beneath the flag reading a book. Inside the walls were hung with a collection of posters from museums all over the world, Vermeer and Titian and Whistler and Fra Filippo Lippi and Turner and Redon and Leonor Fini.

"Let's buy a house in this town," she said. "I want to get my mail here always. Only good mail could come to a place like this."

"Come here," he said one morning. "I want you to hear something." Then he sat her down on the sofa with a cup of peppermint tea and went to work to teach her his music. He started with Led Zeppelin.

"This is the greatest record ever made," he said. "This record changed music forever."

"What kind of music?" she said.

He got a wild look on his face, then moved over close to her and tried again. "Don't worry about that," he said. "Look, you've got to imagine what this sounded like twelve years ago when nothing like it had ever been made. There hadn't ever been any music like this, *anywhere in the world.* I was thirteen years old and I remember holding this in my hands and saying *this will last forever.* As long as they make these plastic things in these cardboard covers this record will be there."

"I can tell your mother was from the delta," Amanda said.

"Just listen to it," he said. He put the record on and Amanda closed her eyes and opened her mind and it did sound good. It sounded wonderful. Especially with Will sitting on the floor beside her with his long legs curled up underneath him waiting for her approval, looking like a wild thirteen-year-old boy and the grown man she went to bed with and a whole world she had never even visited and the morning sun was all over the room and nothing can go wrong with a day that starts like that.

"Here's what it's all about," she told Katie later. "Loving someone that much younger is like taking a trip to a foreign country. All the manners and customs are different. Even the language is different."

"Here's what it's all about," Katie said. "His fingers in between your fingers. His palm on your palm. His hand in your hand. You sigh. He smooths your wrinkles with his fingers. He touches your hair. He is always touching you. He can't keep his hands off you. I don't know how you're getting any work done."

"Where are you going?" he said. "Don't work tonight. I want you with me."

"I promised Marshall I'd type up some fragments for his seminar. I really ought to do it."

"Not tonight. Come sit by me. Come let me hold you."

"Oh, Will, you make me want you just talking to me. You make me want you just saying anything you say."

"Do you still have the cramps?"

"No they're better now."

"I'll be more careful."

"Don't be careful. I don't want you to be careful."

"Are you my baby?"

"I'm your anything. I belong to you."

"Do you want to go downstairs with me?"

"Or on the floor, or anywhere."

He knelt beside her and took the blue robe off her shoulders.

"Hold me," she whispered.

"Come to me," he said. "Come to me. Come to me."

Amanda opened the bedroom windows and looked down the hill at the trees swelling with spring, at the town spread out below her in the morning sun.

She turned and looked at herself in the mirror. She was as thin as a girl.

She picked up Will's clothes off the floor and put them in the laundry room, then sat down on her workroom floor and started playing with the line breaks on a poem.

> *Shall we sing a song of Joseph*
> *sweet cuckold of history, on his way*
> *to such fame as the meek inherit*
> *I would as soon worship the donkey*
> *as a God so powerless he allowed*
> *his own subjects to torture him to death*

Now, damn, there's no connection between the ideas. Half the time I feel that she left out a line. Well, I could fix that. All I'd have to do is make it say "I would as soon worship Joseph's donkey." Well, then I'd just have to add one word to the French. She was covering a page with pencil marks when Will came in. She didn't hear him until he was there beside her. He turned her around to face him, put his finger to his lips, then opened a sack and took out a blue and white baseball shirt. He pulled it down over her head. He adjusted the sleeves around her wrists, straightened the seams, then moved back to survey his work.

"It's spring," he said. "It's baseball season."

"Make love to me," she said. "Now, here, this instant, this minute."

"I wish I could," he said. "I came back to get some papers. I have to go see my professors. I'm so far behind I might as well forget this whole semester."

"Oh, God. I'm sorry. It's my fault, isn't it?"

"No. It isn't you. It started before I knew you."

"Tonight you have to study. I'll fix supper early and you can study all night. I'll work too. I'm in as much trouble as you are. I'm afraid to even talk to Marshall on the phone."

"Does he know I'm living with you?"

"I guess so," Amanda said. "I guess everyone in town knows it by now."

"Do you mind?" He was holding her wrists in his hands, wondering if he could tell her how broke he was, wondering what she would think if she knew.

"I don't care what anyone thinks about what I do," she said. "I make my own rules."

"I've got to be going," he said. "I'll call you later."

"When is later?"

"I don't know. I'll call you. I'll let you know." He paused at the door. "Do you have any money? I need to borrow some money."

"Of course," she said. "How much do you need?"

"Enough to buy gas and get a haircut. I have to go find a job."

"You can't find a job," she said. "You're taking sixteen hours of classes. How can you find a job?"

"It doesn't matter how," he said. "The point is I'm broke and I have to do it."

"Not this week," she said. "For God's sake don't do it this week." She pulled a checkbook out of a drawer and began scribbling on it. "Here," she said. "Take this. Promise you won't look for a job until we talk about it."

She handed him the check, knowing she should not do it. Doing it anyway, doing it against her own reason.

She handed him the check. He took it out of her hand without looking at it and stood holding it between his fingers, moving his fingers across it as though it were a small dangerous message he was carrying into enemy territory. He kept holding it, trying to decide where to put it. Then they both turned away, pretending to be busy with other things.

When he was gone she tried to get back to work on the poem but the mood was gone. I have to tell him not to bother me when I'm working, she thought. I can't have him doing that to me. Even Malcolm knew better than to come in a room when I was working.

She sighed, standing in the middle of her workroom in the baseball shirt with her hands on her hips. She took off the shirt, folded it neatly and put it in a drawer. She put her own shirt back on and walked around the mountain to find Katie. She walked up the road seeing the wildflowers that had begun to appear here and there in the woods. White first, she thought. Then yellow, then purple, then red, then orange, then blue and gold and then it's summer. It smelled wonderful here on the edge of the woods. She walked on up the gravel road to where it joined the asphalt on top of the mountain. From there she could see the slanted roof of Katie's pottery. Smoke was rising from the thin black chimney of the kiln.

Amanda walked faster. Katie Vee is an anchor, she thought. The world around her gets crazier and crazier and Katie Dunbar just gets up every morning and goes out to her shed and goes to work.

Amanda turned down the path and opened the door. There was Katie, her overalls spattered with clay, hot coffee on the stove, wild South American jazz on the stereo. She was kneeling beside the kiln, humming along with Gato Barbieri's saxophone, pushing the cones in and out with a piece of folded burlap.

"Can I bother you?" Amanda said.

"I've been expecting you for days," Katie said. "Come on in. What's going on? You still shacked up with that kid?"

"He's twenty-five," Amanda said. "He's not a kid. Oh, Katie, I don't know what to do. It's getting crazy. It's getting out of hand."

"Well, you look like you've lost ten pounds," Katie said. "Whatever you're doing at least it makes you thin."

"How could I eat?" Amanda said. "Can you believe this is happening to me? As old as I am."

"Being old doesn't have anything to do with getting laid," Katie said, wiping her hands on her pants. "You were lonely, baby. There's nothing wrong with that. Just don't let it carry you away."

"It's carrying me away."

"*The body is not on your side,* Amanda. Remember that."

"What's *that* supposed to mean?"

"I mean it isn't him, you know. It's the activity. *It's fuck-*

ing. Aphrodite, passion, love, sex, whatever you want to call it. *It's still fucking.*"

"No, it isn't. You don't understand. You don't know how intelligent he is. I don't have to explain anything to him. He has a mind like mine."

"So he speaks metaphor. So do I. But it's still fucking, Amanda. And it's because you've been living like a nun all winter, playing Georgia O'Keeffe or whoever it is you're playing."

"Georgia O'Keeffe has a husband young enough to be her grandchild. Well, never mind."

"As long as you keep this thing in perspective."

"I don't want it in perspective."

"Look," Katie said. "Have you got a minute? I want to show you something I just finished for my show in Dallas. Come on. Have a look."

She took Amanda into a room where a large rectangular piece of black Plexiglas dominated a wall beside a window. Six rows of life-sized baby bottles with silver nipples marched along the Plexiglas in neat lines. The cheerful shiny little bottles marched along as though they were headed straight for the viewer. "It's called *Concept,*" Katie said.

"I don't know what to say. It's wonderful. It's as stark as a Goya."

"Yeah, I like it. I think they'll go for it in Dallas. How're the poems coming?"

"I've got an idea to write a novel about Helene's life when I finish them. The strangest thing happens to me sometimes when I work in the French. I start thinking I can hear her voice. And I see her. I see her world, the clothes, the woods, the weather. I think that's how a historical novel takes shape in the mind, like a haunting. So I'm making notes on that as I go along. I'm really pretty amazed at how much I'm getting done, all things considered."

"That's good. I don't want you to forget who you are, Amanda. I don't want you to forget what you set out to do. Work is the thing that stays. Work is the thing that sees us through."

"I'm going to have my work and Will too. I don't have to choose between them. I've waited all my life for this, silly as it may sound. That goddamn kid knows how to love, Katie. It's the strangest thing. It's a gift, like a singing voice. He loves my wrinkles, soft spots, sugar addiction. It's life, Katie, real life. And I've been cold a long time."

"Are you giving him money? Are you supporting him?"

"No. I know better than to do that."

"Don't do it. Don't get tempted to do it."

"Oh, shit," Amanda said. "I'm older than he is and I have more money and I have a career. It's hard for me not to give him things. I keep wanting to do things like buy him a new guitar."

"I know," Katie said. "But don't do it. He's a proud man, Amanda. He's an Arkansas mountain boy. They don't come any prouder, except in the hills of Tennessee."

"Okay," Amanda said. "I'm listening. I swear I am. And I'm staying rational, whether I seem to be or not."

She hugged her clay-covered friend and walked back around the mountain thinking about the expression on Will's face when she handed him the check, thinking about the bottles, the cheerful, shiny little army of bottles.

I'll make Hungarian goulash for dinner, she decided, thinking that would solve everything.

⚜

Will Lyons walked into the bank building and up the stairs beside the escalator. He stood for a long time looking around at the high vaulted ceilings, trying to decide which teller to use. He felt like he did the first time he went into a drugstore to buy rubbers. Finally, he walked up to a woman with gray hair and handed her the check. He took the bills she gave him, stuffed them in his pocket and walked back down the stairs and out onto the square. He walked all the way down to Dickson Street without changing the expression on his face, went into two places and paid his tabs, then walked over to the Bar and Grill. He pulled up a stool and ordered his first drink.

Fuck it, he thought, watching his face in the mirror above the row of bottles. "Fuck every goddamn motherfucking bitch of a woman in the whole fucking world and fuck their mothers."

"You're in a nice mood," Talley said, handing him the drink.

"I'm fixing to get in a better one," Will said. "Starting right this goddamn minute."

"She's manic," Katie Vee told Marshall when he came looking for news. "She's high as a kite. Well, what can we do about it? We'll stand by and let it run its course."

"What do you think she'll do?" Marshall said. "She hasn't been by school in weeks."

"Who ever knows what Amanda'll do. But she'll sort it out. She's designed for speed. That's how she operates. She always pulls it out at the last minute. Well, she's in deep. You ought to see her. She's got these little burns all over her fingers from trying to cook without her glasses.

"I thought she had given up cooking," Marshall said. "She told me she was going to eat out from now on, even for breakfast." He clasped his hands together, shaking his head and smiling down at his fingers. Human nature was a source of endless pleasure to Marshall. He meant to live forever, just to keep on watching it repeat its patterns.

At seven o'clock Amanda put nine thin brass candlesticks with ivory candles on the little table she had set up beside the piano and went back into the kitchen to finish the salad. The goulash was simmering in a copper pan. She added a cupful of Burgundy and took a breath of the dark sweet smell as the wine settled into the hunks of beef and carrots.

She looked at the clock, then went into the living room to read while she waited for Will to call. She picked up a book that was heavy with her underlinings.

All good things were formerly bad things; every original sin has turned into an original virtue. Marriage, for example, seemed for a long time a transgression against the rights of the community; one had to make reparation for being so immodest as to claim a woman for oneself. The gentle, benevolent conciliatory and compassionate feelings — eventually so highly valued that they almost constitute 'the eternal values' — were opposed for the longest time by self-contempt; one was ashamed of mildness as one is today ashamed of hardness. . . . Every smallest step on earth has been paid for by spiritual and physical torture. . . .

Will wasn't there by eight-thirty. He'll call, she thought. He might be studying. I'm not his keeper. He'll call in a minute. She forced herself to keep on reading the book.

⚜

Nothing has been bought more dearly . . . than the modicum of human reason and feeling of freedom that are now our pride. It is this pride, however, that makes it almost impossible for us today to empathize with that vast era of the 'morality of mores' which preceded 'world history' as the truly decisive history that determined the character of mankind: when suffering was everywhere counted as a virtue, cruelty as a virtue, dissembling as a virtue, revenge as a virtue, slander of reason as a virtue, and when, on the other hand, well-being was counted as a danger, thirst for knowledge as a danger, peace as a danger, pity as a danger, being pitied as a disgrace, work as a disgrace, madness as divine, change as the very essence of immorality and pregnant with disaster.

She laid the book down, thinking about something Clinton had said to her about Will: "Whatever else there is about him or what it looks like on the surface that young man has never bowed his will to any man in this town. That's a hard thing to do in a place like this. He won't work for 'the man' and he's got enemies because of it. You don't get popular in Fayetteville by acting that way."

At ten she put the food away in the refrigerator, took the Japanese mats off the table, went downstairs and got into the bed.

She was almost asleep when the phone rang. She tore up the stairs to answer it, almost pulled the cord out of the wall groping for it in the dark.

"Will," she said. "Will, is that you? Are you all right?"

"Sissy," the voice said. "It's me, baby. It's Guy." Amanda sank back against the wall. She didn't even let him finish the sentence before she started yelling at him. "Why are you calling me up? Why are you doing this to me?"

"Please listen to me, Amanda. Please let me talk."

"I won't talk to any of you," she said. "I won't have anything to do with any of you. I'm happy for the first time in my life, Guy, really happy. And no one is going to ruin it for me and no one is going to take it away from me, not even you." She was shaking now, talking louder and louder. "I'm going to sell my part of Esperanza whether you like it or not. I'm going to sell it to the Arabs or the blacks or anyone who wants it. I'm going to have my own money and live my own way and never have to ask anyone for anything. What do you mean calling Malcolm behind my back? What are you two plotting together? Because I'll tell you one thing. I have . . . I am not here . . . I am here to stay . . . I'm through with the past and the terrible decadent south and everything it represents. I'm going to have a new life for myself and I'm not going to have it ruined by you or Malcolm or anyone. . . . Don't call me ever . . ."

"Sissy, calm down a minute. Just listen a minute. I need to see you. Please let me fly up there and see you. I have to talk to you. I'm not going to hurt you . . . all I want is to talk . . ."

"What were you doing in New Orleans?" she screamed. "What were you doing down there!!!!"

"I was down there for a golf tournament. I won the NFL alumni tournament for my region and I went down to play in the finals."

"I don't believe you. I think you went looking for the child. You told me you wouldn't do it, Guy." Amanda was crying now. Guy's voice still had the power to do that to her. All night she had kept from crying over Will. Now Guy was doing this to her. "Oh, shit," she yelled at him.

"Now I'm crying. Goddamn you, you always make me cry."

"I don't want to make you cry, Sissy. I only want to love you."

"Then leave me alone. For God's sake leave me alone. I'm going to hang up, Guy. I'm up here working my ass off trying to figure out how to live the rest of my life and I want you to leave me alone. I want you to leave me alone forever . . ."

She hung up the phone, took one of Will's cigarettes out of the package and went out onto the balcony. She lit the cigarette and took a drag on it, feeling the hot assault to the lungs. Jesus Christ, she thought. Now I'm smoking.

She heard the door open behind her. Will was there, drunk, barely able to stand up, twenty-five years old, confused, drunk, wounded, crazy and wild and drunk and *hers*, hers to love and try to understand and try to care for, hers to sleep with all night long.

They got into bed and he sobered up enough to hold her in his arms while she sobbed out the story.

"Then they took the baby away. What could I do? I was fourteen years old, for Christ's sake. I didn't know I had a choice. I thought they were doing me a favor. God knows, maybe they did me a favor. All I know is that I don't want to think about it. And if Guy goes and finds that girl he will ruin my life with it. He's already ruined his own life. Now he wants to ruin mine. I saw him at my grandmother's funeral and he promised me he wouldn't go and look for her. And, goddammit, I know he's done it."

"It's all right," Will whispered. "It's going to be all right. I'm here, Amanda. I won't let anyone hurt you."

"Hold me," she said. "Hold me close to you, Will. Make me sleep. Let me sleep. For God's sake, let me sleep."

They slept until late afternoon. When they woke they took coffee out onto the balcony and sat with their feet propped up on the railing, acting as if the night had never happened. The weather was getting warmer every day. The maple trees were filling with leaves. The crocus and daffodils and wild sedge were making.

Amanda's balcony was surrounded by a wood railing. Along one end the oak board had split and a line of tiny orange mushrooms were coming up in the cracks, surrounded by bright green moss.

"Thank you for not being mad at me," he said. "You're different from anyone I've ever known."

"This place is worse than New Orleans," she said. "Look at those mushrooms. Talk about sultry. That's downright indecent. This place is more verdant than the tropics."

"A couple of more rains," he said, "and it will be time to float the rivers."

"Tell me about the rivers."

"I've floated most of them," he said. "They're all different. The Mulberry's the wildest, the White, that's for trout fishing. And, of course, the Buffalo, that's my favorite. The Buffalo's really something. If these rains keep up it'll be ready soon. I'll be the first one down it if I can."

"Will you take me with you?" she said.

"If you'll open me a beer," he said. "Don't you know by now I'll do anything you want me to? Don't you know that yet?"

"I'll make you a shirt the color of these mushrooms if

you'll take me down a river," she said. "I'll sew a hundred buttons on it. I'll sew a thousand buttons on it."

"Then I'd look like Conway Twitty," he said. "I could wear it in my act. Make that a scotch and water, Amanda. I think I'll have a drink instead."

"How old is he?" Marshall asked. He and Katie were having lunch together at Bruff Commons.

"Oh, I'd say their combined age is about thirty. Fourteen for her, sixteen for him."

"He plays a guitar?"

"Oh, yes, and he's good at it. He's a home-town boy, Marshall. A real Fayetteville iconoclast. Baseball shirt and Roger's Pool Hall and everything. He has these long legs like a dancer's. Well, it all stands to reason if you think about it. She was already in love with the town. And Clinton likes him. Clinton thinks he's great."

"A basketball guitar player," Marshall said. "Well, it wasn't what I expected but it suits her somehow. I think I like it, Katie. It should liven up everybody's spring."

It divides and divides and divides, then it folds. It becomes the spinal column and the brain. The vascular system is laid down, the center forms, the veins and arteries, the rivers of life flowing in and out of the great soft red pump of a heart.

In April Amanda started menstruating again and she thought she should go see Dr. Kincaid but that seemed like a silly thing to do. Besides, there never seemed to be time for anything anymore.

Will was playing music several nights a week in the little café. Amanda would go along with him, carrying a portable tape player to record his performances, sitting at a table near the bandstand, changing the tapes while he played every song to her.

"I can't do this," she said. "I'm too old to be a groupie. This is ridiculous."

"No it isn't," he said. "It's whatever we want it to be. Besides, I like to have you where I can look at you. You can pretend you're my music coach if you like. Or my manager. How about that?"

"Your aunt," Amanda said. "That's the one I like this week."

"You could be my aunt," he said, smiling at her. "You look like my mother's sisters."

"How about her?" Amanda said. "Do I look like her? Like your mother?"

"Of course you do," he said. "She has hair like yours. Didn't I ever tell you that?"

The little café was a favorite haunt of Will's old friends from high school. They would come and sit at the table with Amanda and she would talk to them as she would to any other young people, hanging on to as much dignity as she could under the circumstances, trying not to be caught looking at Will, trying not to return his looks as he sat across the room on the bandstand playing every song to her.

"Dance with me," he would sing at the end of each performance. "I want to be your partner. Dance with me. Dance with me. Dance with me."

"Do you two live together now?" a blond girl asked her one evening.

"I guess so," Amanda said. "I guess you could call it that."

"I think it's neat," the girl said. "I think it's way out. My grandmother out in Texas lives with a young guy she isn't married to. She doesn't even make him leave when we go to visit."

"That's great," Amanda said. "That's really wonderful."

One night two little six-year-old girls came to the restaurant with their parents and started dancing in the cleared space before the bandstand. They were lovely messy little girls wearing long skirts and cowboy boots and they danced the whole time they were waiting for their dinners, moving their limber little bodies enthusiastically to Will's music, completely fascinated by his guitar.

After a while they brought their little brothers out onto

the dance floor to use for partners, dragging them along, holding them around the middle like fat sacks.

"Those are the cutest little girls I've ever seen," Will said. "They're really nice to their little brothers, aren't they?"

"Sure they are," Amanda said. "As long as they get to be in charge. As long as it's *their dance* and *they get to lead.*"

"What you got there?" Will said, turning to one of the little girls. She was standing beside the bandstand still holding her little brother.

"It's Charles," she said. "He's three."

"Go tell your daddy to come put some money in my jar. Then I'll sing some more. Tell him the nice man needs some money."

"Okay," she said. "I'll be right back." She got a better grip around Charles's middle and carried him over to her mother. In a minute she returned holding her father's hand and stood primly by while he put a dollar in the tip jar and thanked Will for the music.

"Nothing to it," Will said. "They're nice kids. You're a lucky man."

Later, the waitresses started wiping off the tables and stacking the chairs in the aisle. Will put the guitar in its case, snapped the fasteners and came down off the bandstand. He picked up the big-mouthed mayonnaise jar and poured the change out into his hand.

"Cheapskates," he said. "Well, what can you expect? It's hard times, baby. Money's tight. Everyone's hurting."

They walked across the street to George's and sat in the outdoor beer parlor under the trees listening to jazz. Will was withdrawn, leaning up against the board wall drinking beer. The musicians were old friends of his from the days when he was making a living as a musician. Now they seemed far away, as if they had gone to a new country leaving him behind.

"What's wrong?" Amanda said.

"Nothing you can do anything about," he said. "Nothing I want to talk about tonight."

"How do you know I can't do anything about it?" she said. "Please tell me what's bothering you."

"What are we doing together?" he said. "Will you just tell me that? You're older than I am and you're wealthy and you're good at what you do. I'm twenty-five years old and I'm flunking out of school and I don't even have a job. I made three dollars an hour for four hours tonight. That wouldn't pay your water bill."

"Don't talk like that. Don't say those things."

"Why not? They're true. You asked me what was wrong. I'm telling you some of the things that make me look this way." She was trying to think of an answer to that when some of his friends came and joined them.

In the morning it started again. Will woke up with Amanda's body in his arms. He cupped her breasts in his hands. He put his face to her soft hair. He breathed deep of the clean April morning. It was almost a full minute before he remembered the letter from the bank.

He sat up on the edge of the bed and lit a cigarette. Will Lyons was young and proud and broke. What did it matter to him that the wonder of spring was happening all the way down the mountain and across the whole state of Arkansas.

"Is something wrong?" Amanda said, touching his back.

"It's money, Amanda. I have to find some money to start paying back the student loans I owe. I've got to find a job. I don't have fifty dollars in the bank."

"I'll lend you some money," she said. "Please let me. I'll lend you whatever you need."

"I don't know," he said. "I don't know if we should do that again. I'd better just go on and take the first job I can find, doing anything I can find to do."

"Why not?" she said. "Just because you got wild the last time I lent you money. I mean, for Christ's sake, can't we learn from our mistakes?"

"I don't know," he said. "Let me think about it. I'll let you know."

"Bullshit," she said and walked upstairs to her desk and wrote out a check and walked back downstairs and handed it to him.

"Now don't dare thank me for this," she said. "Or get mad at me. Just take it and go get your affairs straightened out. And stop looking so sad. I can't stand it when you look sad." He wasn't smiling so she went on. "It isn't my money, anyway. It came from the Mississippi delta. It came from land that was cleared and worked by black people whose children and grandchildren are dying in the slums of Detroit and Akron. I don't have any right to it anyway. It's money someone *gave* me. Now I'm giving part of it to you. Please just take it and don't think about it anymore."

Will took it. He took the check and stuck it in his pocket. It was worse than the last time. It was terrible. All the rationalizations in the world couldn't make it any better.

Here I stand, he was thinking. In her living room, on her carpet, *taking money from a woman*. My daddy would have me killed.

By two o'clock that afternoon Will was drunk. By dark he was in Hot Springs at the races.

When he finished losing all the money Will hitchhiked back to Fayetteville. He was tired and hung over and broke and dirty. He felt better than he had felt in weeks.

"I can't believe you did this to me," she said when he called her. "I can't believe you would treat me like this."

"I'm going to pay you back the money," he said. "You can depend on that."

"I don't give a fuck about the money. It isn't that."

"Well, it is that. It's what's wrong between us."

"I'm sorry I gave it to you then. It was a stupid thing to do."

"Can I see you?"

"No. I don't want to see you. I want to go back to my own life. I want this to all stop."

"All right," he said. "I'll call you then. I'll call you up. We'll go see a movie."

"Fine," she said. "Or I'll call you."

She hung up the phone and went storming around her house cleaning everything, planning her monastic life as a great translator. She cleaned up the living room and the dining room and the bedroom and the workroom. She straightened up all her papers. She sat down at the dining room table and made a list of all the things Will Lyons liked that she had outgrown and grown contemptuous of. The title of the list was *Junk Food*. Pizza, television, *Playboy* magazine, music with words, beer, whiskey, marijuana, American movies, pinball machines. The list went on and on. A week before those things had been a trip to a foreign country. This week they were junk food.

✤ ✤ ✤ ✤ ✤ ✤ ✤ *16* ✤ ✤ ✤ ✤ ✤ ✤ ✤

All morning Amanda had been agonizing over two lines of a poem. It was a poem she had been arguing about with Marshall for several weeks. *Faces of stone, faces of stone and underneath their skirts the same machines as mine must surely grind and itch all day, the same sweet sea.* I know that's what she meant. Walls of stone, faces of stone, what's the difference. Except you can't say stone walls now because it means Watergate. Well, Marshall will just have to listen to reason. What difference does it make if we fix a few of them to make them better? It's stupid to leave them like this. Well, I'm not going to do what he wants. Goddamn, he's not going to boss me around. No man is going to boss me around ever as long as I live.

Amanda sat at her desk with her face in her hands getting madder and madder. She hadn't seen Will in a week. She hadn't made love or even had a hot meal for a whole week. For a whole week all she'd been doing was sitting at her desk covering pages of paper with French words and English words. She'd been sitting at her desk fooling with the translations for so many days she'd begun to think the pieces of paper lying all around her on the floor were more important than real life.

Now she sat at the desk with her face in her hands thinking of people to blame for the fact that the translations weren't as wonderful as she wanted them to be. She was blaming Malcolm Ashe and Marshall Jordan and Duncan Walker and the American Academy of Arts and Sciences and the poor taste of the American public and whoever it was in Paris that was holding up sending the diaries to her. Not to mention the woman in Albuquerque, that bitch.

Faces like stone, names like stone, "names like water poured from stone jugs," no, that's *Philip Levine's, blank faces, stones like walls, water like stones.* "Oh, shit," she said out loud.

Amanda got up from the desk, put on her shoes, drove down to Marshall's office and laid the offending lines before him on the desk.

"I won't leave this like this," she said. "I can't."

"I'm glad you came over. Now, listen, Amanda. I have to have a manuscript soon. Have you fixed the things we talked about last week?"

"I can't fix them," she said. "It's bullshit to leave them like that. They sound terrible. She wasn't much of a poet, Marshall."

"Well, we can't change that, my dear."

"Why not? We can change the French too. I mean, it's our book."

"We can't change the poems."

"I don't mean really change them. Just make them better. Just make the crazy ones make some sense."

"Well, we just can't do that, my dear. It isn't how it's done. Even if I'd put up with it we'd never get Duncan to go along."

"I hate translating. I ought to be writing my own stuff."

"I couldn't agree with you more. You aren't suited for this temperamentally. Still, let's finish this thing we've started. Let's see this through."

"If I were sure it was going to be published. If you'd give me some guarantee."

"I told you I couldn't do that at the beginning, Amanda. I told you it was a gamble."

She sighed and looked glumly down at her hands. It was true. He had told her that from the beginning.

"How's your love life?" he said, thinking it would cheer her up.

"What have you heard?"

"That you're in love. Is there more? Is there blood on the lintel? Is the vice squad at the door?"

"He's twenty-five, Marshall. He's only twenty-five years old."

"Good for him. That's quite an accomplishment. Tell me about it. Tell me what's going on."

"There isn't anything to tell." She was looking at the sign over Marshall's desk. *Everything Will Happen*, it said. "Last night I got so mad at myself I got out the *Symposium* to see if I could learn something to cure myself."

"What did you learn?"

"That Socrates was as crazy as I am."

"I saw him at the Heaney reading, your young man. He looks nice enough."

"He's beautiful and he's brilliant and he's talented and he's twenty-five years old and he's driving me crazy. Marshall, if there was one thing in the whole world I swore I'd never do, it was fall in love with a young man. I don't know how I've been justifying what I've been doing."

She looked up and caught his eye and the two of them started laughing.

"Why do I think it's funny?" she said. "Why in the name of God am I laughing?"

"I don't know," Marshall said. "But it's all we have, the fairest of the gods."

"Well, it's just been an unbelievable spring. I don't know what I've been doing. I'm about as disciplined as Niagara Falls. I don't sleep. I cry when he makes love to me. I listen to the Led Zeppelin. The other day I actually thought about buying a television set so I could watch the ballgames with him. I swear to God. I was in the grocery and they had those little television sets on sale and I almost bought one. Well, it's probably over. We had a big fight."

Marshall pulled his chair closer and took her hand. "Now, Amanda, go on and love your young man if you have to. Just try not to *need* him. Then you won't be disappointed if he isn't your perception of him. It's your perception of him you love, you know."

"You mean he's a fiction of my mind? Like a hologram? Jesus, Marshall, if that were true I could decide to love a refrigerator or your desk or something."

"It would be hard to love a refrigerator," Marshall said, leaning back in the chair. "But not impossible. I remember once in London I fell in love with a Burberry raincoat in a shop window. I was a young man on a small allowance and I had visions all one winter of walking around London with that raincoat on my arm, of draping it over chairs, of pushing my arms down into its lining, of going back to Arkansas wearing it, knocking everyone's eyes out getting off the train wearing my Burberry. I used to go out of my way to school just to walk by the store window where it hung, so perfect, so British, alone on a headless manikin.

"Aphrodite gathering her yellow ray flowers," he went dreamily on. "Your competition, meanwhile, has sent Duncan a completed manuscript of the first ten poems. He got them in the mail yesterday."

"Have you seen them? Are they any good?"

"I don't know. I haven't been over there."

"You said it wasn't a contest."

"It isn't a contest. I only told you because I thought you'd like to know." He was hiding behind his beard, not giving a single thing away.

"If it isn't a contest, what do you call it then?"

"It isn't a contest because you can do it better than she can. If you do it. When you do it."

"I have eight finished pieces, and one I was working on today. That will be finished if I go on and trust myself."

"Then do it."

"They're my poems, Marshall. You know they are."

"I know they are. Let's make sure Duncan knows they are. Now, stop worrying so much about the poems and just go on and do the best you can. It's better than you think it is, actually. Wait till it's all finished and then we can criticize it. For now, just go on and do it. Please stop trying to rewrite the poems and just go on and translate what's there."

"All right," she said. "I'll try. I'll go on home and try it again. But if I hate it I'm going to put somebody else's name on it." She leaned over the desk and gave him a kiss on the beard.

⚜

To hell with love, Amanda walked home thinking. I've got work to do. Then Amanda walked home faster and faster, climbing the long hill to her house planning the great book she was translating and the great books she would write, spurred on by a seventy-five-year-old poet and a phantom enemy in Albuquerque, New Mexico and an old dream of glory. *Guess you'll be going around giving speeches before long,* she could hear Lavertis's voice saying. *Guess it won't be long till we'll be seeing your name in the papers.*

Hi-Octane. Kundalini rising. The feet of Athena, Diana's girdle, Wonder Woman and Dorothy Parker and Margaret Mead and Brenda Starr and all the fated gifted blessed crazy driven ones, the darlings of the gods, their playthings.

When she got home she went straight to her workroom and sat down to work. It was four o'clock in the morning and the floor was piled with papers and dictionaries by the time she got to a stopping place. She had added one adjective and raised the first line to be the title.

Faces Like White Stones

Underneath their skirts the same machines as mine
must surely grind and itch all day
the same sweet sea
Sister Clara would fill my cunt
with stones from the dark mountain she calls God
She prays to where no water is

Soon the flower I planted in her eye
will bloom, red as fire, red as the tongue of vengeance

Cunt, Amanda was thinking as she fell asleep, what a wonderful old word, cuntess, cuntessa, cunted, couunt, count, Count, cune, cuneus, cuniculus, kunte, wedge, woman, wife, woe, fill me with woe, you cunt, you no count cunt, and she fell asleep singing a song to Baby Doll about cunts and wedges and Baby Doll clapped her hands and laughed and was not ashamed of Amanda or anything at all for Baby Doll was not afraid of music.

Supply and demand. Supply and demand. The economics of love, no different from the rate of exchange between the lire and the yen.

Ambiguity, excitement. Booms and recessions. Two trillion, six billion cells in Will's body. For whose benefit was this data put together?

In the end she went to look for him. One afternoon the light took a certain tilt through the clouds and the spring woods were fragrant outside her bedroom window and Amanda woke up from a nap so full of longing that nothing could keep her from going to find him.

She called around the few places she thought he might be but no one had seen him. She dressed and went down to the pool hall to see if he was there.

She walked into the stale smell of beer and cigarettes and looked around. Three or four regulars were leaning on the bar lost in a harmless sort of stupor.

"Can we help you, little lady?" one of them said, turning his gray pleading face her way.

"No, thank you," she said. "I was just looking for a friend."

"You looking for Will?" the bartender said, recognizing her.

"Oh, no," she said. "I'm waiting for someone else. Why, has Will been here?"

"Not in a while," the bartender said. "We been wondering where he is."

"I don't know where he is either," she said. "I don't have any idea."

"Maybe he's gone to his granddaddy's place out by Goshen. Sometimes he goes out there and stays."

"Where is it? Tell me where it is."

"It's out by the Goshen P.O.," the man said. "Down the road from the P.O. Used to have a mailbox said Lyons on it. I guess it's still there."

The bartender was a good guesser. Will was holed up out at his grandfather's deserted farm. He had cleaned up a bedroom, stocked the kitchen with groceries, plugged in his radio, and gone to work to think things over. He had even been doing some studying, thinking maybe he could salvage something out of the semester if he could pass the finals.

It was a nice house, as farmhouses go in Arkansas. A frame house built on a stone foundation with a dirt yard and a bright pink cherry tree in full bloom beside the steps. When Amanda drove up he was sitting on the porch with his feet propped up on the railing watching a field of yellow daisies and Queen Anne's lace move in the wind. A horse and its foal were coming across the field toward the house. Above their heads a crow moved like a broken glider. Will was trying to think of a way to work all that into a song lyric when he saw her car come over the hill and dip down and come to a stop by the gate.

How in the name of shit did she find me way out here,

he was thinking. He pushed his hat back off his head, beginning to desire her before she even got out of the car.

"Ms. McCamey," he said. "As I live and breathe. If I'd known you were coming I'd have worn my white suit."

He's on his own territory here, she thought. This land belongs to his daddy.

"Come on in," he said, not getting up. "You want some coffee?"

"What are you doing, Will?" she said. "What are you doing here?"

"I'm not doing a goddamn thing," he said. "That's what us hillbillies do. We sit on the porch and wait to see if anything's going to happen. That's all, by God, any man needs to do. And it's all I'm ever going to do."

"Are you drunk?" she said. "Are you stoned?"

"No, Ms. McCamey. I am not drunk and I'm not stoned. I'm thinking. I'm thinking things over."

"What did you decide?" she said.

"I don't know. I haven't finished thinking yet. I'm still making up my mind. Look over there. That's Straw, daughter of Bess, the first horse I ever rode. I named that horse. I think I named her. Either I named her or Felton named her. Maybe we both named her. My granddaddy Lyons built this place. He was a Welshman. Someday it'll be my place. When I'm about eighty it'll be mine as the Crouchs and Lyonses live forever. Part of it'll be mine, anyway."

"I like this house," she said. "I really like it."

"No you don't," he said. "You don't *like* it and if you lived here you wouldn't *like* it but it's where I live and *I* like it. You can sit on the porch but don't go getting any ideas about *liking* it."

"I just wanted to see if you're all right," she said. "I didn't come out here to start a fight."

"You're starting one. You're starting one by driving up in my yard."

"Do you want me to leave?"

"Maybe so," he said. "Maybe that would be the best thing for everybody."

"Why can't people love each other?" Amanda said. "Why does it always end like this?"

"Are you writing a country and western song?" he said. "If so I think you're on to something with that line. *Why does it always end like this*? Hey, I like that. That'll catch on, baby. We can go with that."

"Don't do that," she said. "Don't pretend to be cynical. I can't stand it when people do that." The shadow of a branch of cherry blossoms was falling across his chest like a birthmark. Amanda kept looking at it as she talked. "I'm not very good at loving people, Will. I know that. I knew better than to give you that money. I knew that was a stupid thing to do and I went on and did it anyway. So I didn't have any business getting mad at you. I know that. I know it was my fault. God knows. Maybe my subconscious is trying to protect me from really loving you."

"Have you been rehearsing this speech all the way from Fayetteville?"

"Yes, so let me finish it. I want to love you, Will, really love you. But my subconscious is plotting all the time to keep you from being important to me . . . to keep you from having any real power over me." She was watching his expression, which never changed. "Oh, well, I give up. Maybe there aren't any ways for a man and a woman to make it work. Maybe we're all too fucked up. Our systems don't work. Nothing works. Why is it nothing ever works?"

"Nothing works for us because you've got more money than I have."

"It isn't that."

"It is that. Jesus, Amanda, I'm a romantic and even *I* know that. It gives you all the power. Talk about someone having power over someone else. Shit. And I'll pay you back that money by the end of summer, you can book that."

"Are you going to see me anymore?"

"I don't know. I don't know what I'm going to do."

"All right then," she said. "Do whatever you want to do. I don't give a damn what you do. I have work to do and I'm going home and get to work doing it."

"How's the work coming?"

"It's okay. It's half done. I turned half the poems over to Marshall yesterday. I guess I knew I'd go find you as soon as I got to a stopping place."

"Well, it's nice to be an amusement parlor, for when you're in between projects. And I'd like to read the poems sometime. If you have copies."

"I think I'll be finished with the whole book by July."

"Then what are you going to do?"

"I'm going to write a novel, about Helene. I told you that."

"I thought you were joking."

"Why not? Just because I don't know how. I believe people can do anything they want to do. You could do anything you want to do."

"No, I can't. You can't do what you want when you're

broke. You have to work for the man. You have to let the man use you. Well, I'll come over one day and read what you're doing."

"Do that," she said. She pushed one of the straps of her yellow sundress back up on her shoulder. "I'm going on home then," she said.

"Thank you for coming out." He wasn't making a single move. He wasn't giving up a thing. Amanda admired that even as she suffered.

"I love you," she said. "Whether you believe it or not."

"Well, if you say so I guess that makes it true."

"All right," she said. "I give up." She walked across the yard thinking he would follow her but he didn't even take his feet down off the railings. She turned around at the gate. He pushed his hat farther back off his forehead and folded his arms across his chest.

As soon as her car was out of sight over the hill he went into the house, took a beer out of a six-pack, got out his guitar, and sat down to write a song about the horse and the colt and the crow. He found some chords, hummed a little melody and began. "Now you've got crows and my old horse Bess and the place my granddaddy left for me. Now my own granddaddy's pasture isn't safe from the sight of you." It was ten o'clock that night before he finished the six-pack and the song. He folded the paper neatly into squares, put it inside his guitar case, cranked up his car and went on over.

"I wrote you a song," he said, when she came to the door. "Well, do you want to hear it or not?"

"What are we doing to each other?" she said when he was beside her in the warm bed. "What is going on between us?" He was touching her hair with his hands. Outside the uncurtained windows a full moon was lighting up the yard, shining in the room, covering them with silver.

"I'll tell you how it is with me," he said. "When we're together I feel like a rubber band that's being stretched thinner and thinner. The longer we stay together the worse the tension gets. Then something happens to put a stop to it and the sound stops and I fold back into myself. Then nothing. Then it all starts up again. Like this . . ." He moved his hands down her face, beginning to put small sweet kisses all over her face and neck.

"It's your drinking," she said. "That's the part I can't accept. I can't stand to watch it. I spent twenty-five years fucking up everything I tried to do with alcohol. It's like living it over again to watch you."

"Well, I can't quit drinking," he said. "There isn't anything else to do in Fayetteville. If I quit drinking there wouldn't be anyplace I could go. No one trusts a man who won't drink with them."

"In order to be liked you have to agree to weaken yourself, is that what you're saying? Have to lose your driver's license, get in fights, wreck your car? Jesus Christ!"

"It isn't all that bad," he said.

"It is that bad. It's the whole world conspiring to keep everyone at bay. It's as if there isn't any use in the modern world for real power and real energy and one of the ways the powerless people . . . oh, shit, what good does it do to talk about it. Well, they won't do it *to me* anymore. I'm going to use myself. I'm going to do my work and I'm going to have all my power and all my energy and a strong healthy body to do it with. *And all my brain.* The whole thing. What's left of it, anyway. God knows what part I left in all those martini glasses."

"I sure am glad I came over," he said. "I was lonely for your mouth. I haven't had any advice in days."

"I'm not finished," she said.

"What's the alternative?" he said. "What are the options?"

"Loving yourself, not letting your self-esteem be in the hands of other people. Being in touch with the phenomena of yourself, being aware of your place in the phenomenological universe. Your place in a universe of air and water and light, this holy place and time in which you are *conscious*, perhaps the only conscious thing in all the universe."

"I thought we were talking about drinking," he said, moving his hands down her ribs and across her hips and thighs and into the warm phenomenon between her legs.

"I don't know what we're talking about. Except you're here and I'm here and I want you to keep on doing that and I love the way you smell and sometimes I even believe you love me. And I adore my song. My song's the best present I ever had."

"Believe I love you, Amanda. Please go on and believe it."

"I don't know what happened to me, Will. I don't know why I can't love anyone. I don't know why other people can do that and I can't do it."

"You can do things other people can't do, Amanda. Maybe that's the reason."

"Don't say that. I can't bear to believe that. It's like saying I'm doomed to never love anyone."

"Maybe you ought to go on and find that girl, Amanda. Maybe you ought to put that behind you. Maybe your cousin's right and you ought to go on and do that. I don't know much about psychology but even I can see . . ."

"Don't talk about that, Will. I can't talk about that."

"Go to sleep then," he said. "I'm here. You're here. It's all right. It's going to be fine. You'll see."

"It's going to rain tonight," Will said. "I love to make love to you when it rains. Every time it rains it makes me lonely. Every goddamn time it rains I start thinking about you."

"Now you're going to start giving me credit for the rain?"

"Every single drop," he said.

She looked down at his intense face, wondering how in the name of heaven he had fallen that much in love with her. Wondering why it terrified her so.

The storm came from the south. And from the west and east. Outside the curtainless windows the lightning was breaking in three directions, a bowl of storm clouds surrounding northwest Arkansas.

Around two-thirty Will pulled her into his arms. "I know you're awake," he said. "Let's go watch the storm. Let's go upstairs and watch the lightning."

They took pillows and quilts and made a pallet on the floor before the long glass doors that opened out onto the balcony. They sat up half the night watching the storm, snuggled together in quilts on the floor.

"Let's have a wonderful breakfast," Amanda said when they woke. "Katie Vee brought fresh blueberries yesterday. Let's have blueberries and English muffins and café au lait out of china cups. And then," she said, "let's fly to New York City and spend all my money. I want to take you to New York, to the Village, to Donovan's and Gregory's and Sweet Basil and the Eighth Street Playhouse. And the ballet. And croissants, croissants on Seventh Avenue before a show. Oh, Will, it would be such fun to be there with you."

"Let's go," he said. "I'm ready."

"I can't believe you've never been. I want to show you the Metropolitan Museum of Art and the Museum of Natural History and the Vermeers at the Frick and Steuben Glass.

I want to show you The Sword in the Stone. Oh, Will, I want to give you The Sword in the Stone."

"Let's go," he said. "I can do anything you want to do. Until Wednesday. On Wednesday I'm going out and get a job. Well, you want to go to New York until then?"

"We can't," she said. "It costs too much. We'd have to spend my money. You told me not to do that to you."

Then they were quiet, wishing they hadn't talked of it. They were eating breakfast at a small table by a window, blueberries and muffins and orange marmalade and real cream.

He is so beautiful she thought, watching the light from the windows fall across his cheekbones, the light on the brass bowl of blueberries, the light on his hair, the light on the parquet floor.

She reached out her hand to touch him, then picked up a blueberry instead and held it between her fingers, wondering how anything could be so fragile and so blue.

"Going to New York isn't the only thing to do," he said. "We could go down a river. Look out there, every river in the state is running like crazy after that rain. You're always talking about wanting to float a river."

"Could we go down the Buffalo?" she said.

"We can do anything you want to do," he said. "We can do the top reaches of the Buffalo after this storm."

"Then let's go," she said, standing up. "Let's go right now. What do we have to do to get ready?"

"It will take two days," he said. "We'll have to sleep out one night."

"That's wonderful," she said. "I'd rather do that than anything in the world."

"Okay," he said. "Get dressed. Let's get going."

⚜

They drove out of Fayetteville into the soft green beauty of the hills, the country becoming wilder and more sparsely populated, the old Boston Mountains getting higher and higher as they moved upwards into the escarpment, to the place where the rivers begin, to Ponca where the Upper Buffalo is only full enough for floating for a brief time in late spring.

"Where will we get a canoe?" Amanda said.

"There's a little store called White Deer. I used to know the guy that runs it. A crazy guy that had a commune up here in the seventies, a guy named Jeter. I don't know if that's his real name or not."

"What kind of commune?"

"A bunch of kids that came up here when they got fed up with the Peace Corps. They all left except Jeter. I guess he's still here. Be watching out for a sign."

By noon they came to Ponca, a little town spread out along a narrow creek valley, four or five frame houses with chickens and goats and sleepy dogs and porch swings. There was a hand-painted sign stuck on a fencepost with a picture of a fat white deer. CANOES, it said, Jeter Mayhew, Whitewater Guide.

"That's it," Will said. "That's the guy. He'll rent us something that won't leak."

They turned a curve, went down a hill and came to a stop in front of a log cabin with red and yellow canoes piled haphazardly around the yard. A huge dog the color of rust was lying on the path to the door.

"What is that?" Amanda said. "It looks like a Shetland pony."

"It's one of Jeter's dogs," Will said. "Don't be afraid of them. They won't hurt you."

"That's the biggest dog I've ever seen in my life," she said, getting carefully out of the car, keeping her eye on him. He was standing now, at least three feet tall, standing right in the middle of the path, looking up at her out of his great soft sad face.

"It's okay," Will said. "Take it easy."

Amanda squared her shoulders, walked politely around the dog and hurried into the safety of the little country store. She looked around at the shelves of camping gear and racks of colored life jackets. Then she saw the other dogs, four more of the great silent rust-colored creatures. They seemed to be everywhere. Two were lying beside a white freezer, one was asleep on an old sofa and the biggest one of all was standing by the cash register being fondled by a tall man wearing glasses.

"The dogs won't hurt you," he said. "Don't be afraid."

"They're the biggest dogs I've ever seen in my life," she said.

"That's Trevino outside," he said. "And that's Allie and Luke by the freezer. And Rose, there on the sofa. She's hurt. Somebody shot her, took her for a deer. It's been a bad year for the dogs. Someone stole Carl Orff but we got him back."

"They're beautiful," Amanda said. "I'm starting to like them."

"Be careful what you say around them," he said. "They're very sensitive. They're worse than children."

"Hey, Jeter," Will said. "What's happening? How's the river?"

"It's the best week we've had all season," he said.

"Where've you been? You haven't been in these parts for a while."

"I went back to school," Will said. "Wasted a lot of time and money." He reached out and pulled Amanda to him. "This is Amanda McCamey, Jeter. Get her to tell you about how she tamed the Colorado. She says she's ready to take on the Buffalo."

"I did not," Amanda said. "You're the one that thought this up." She moved his arm and walked over to a rack of T-shirts, pretending to be looking through them.

"Come back here," he said. "I want Jeter to show you his worm farm."

"What on earth is a worm farm?" she said.

"It's how I make a living," Jeter said, leading them back through the store to a room with a concrete floor. A great pile of loam and peat moss was spread out on a canvas with fat earthworms crawling through the openings. At the far end of the room a waterfall came out of a wall and poured down into a long concrete pond.

"Look at Jeter's waterfall," Will said. Amanda walked to the back of the room and stared uncomprehendingly at the arrangement.

"What's it for?" she said.

"To listen to," Jeter said. "I like to hear it while I'm sleeping."

"Where does it come from?"

"It's from springs," he said. "The pipes take it back to its course. Sometimes I keep fish in the tank. There might be some in there now." He leaned over and stirred the tank with a broom handle. One lazy-looking catfish swam to the top and then sank again. Every time Jeter moved Carl moved with him, keeping close to his leg. Now Rose, the wounded dog, hobbled out of the other room and joined them. Jeter reached down, caressing them while he talked.

"We better get going," Will said. "We want to make camp before sundown."

"You're going to have a hell of a day," Jeter said. "You couldn't have picked a better one."

They drove down a little winding road and there it was, spread out before them, the Buffalo, a bright, curving line of fast-moving white water, rushing down out of the mountains, breaking out of its canyon, so fast and full now it almost covered the little concrete bridge leading to the put-in place.

"Well, what do you think?" he said, smiling as if he had just handed her a piece of the moon.

"It's wonderful," she said. "It's moving so fast. Jesus, Will, when I told you I knew how to canoe I meant *at camp* or on a little bayou. I didn't mean in anything like *that!*" She was looking at the place where the rushing water went in two directions around a tree. It didn't look as though there was room for a canoe on either side.

"We'll do fine," he said. "Just remember what I told you about diving out on the high side if we capsize. Everything else will be all right."

"Are you sure you know how to do this?" Amanda said.

"I don't guess I forgot how since September."

"Did you ever turn one over?"

"Not on purpose," he said.

"What does that mean?" she said.

"You're safe with me," he said. "I wouldn't let anything happen to you." He was tying their gear into the center supports of the big soft-bottomed yellow canoe.

She watched his hands, thinking of them lying so still

beside her while she slept, on the strings of his guitar or skipping stones on the flat surface of the lake or throwing rocks one right after the other into the knotholes on her tree.

"The opposable thumb," she said. "Imagine a creature who could develop that being too stupid to be happy."

"I'm happy right now," he said. "Now then, are you getting in this canoe or not?"

"All right," she said, striking her chest with her closed fist like the old Indian in *Little Big Man*. "It's a good day to die. Show me what to do. I've never seen anything like this river in my life, Will. Isn't there an easier place to start?"

"Put-in," he said. "It's called put-in. And you have to do it here. Don't worry. All you have to do is paddle as hard as you can and remember, for God's sake, which side to fall out of in case we turn over."

"All right," she said. "I'm counting to three and then I'm getting in." She took a breath, stepped into the front of the canoe, picked up a paddle and looked straight at the tree. "Let's go," she said. "Vaya con dios, Holy Mary Mother of God, whatever one says."

Will stepped into the back of the canoe, and they shoved off into the sudden violence of the river. "Paddle," he yelled. "Paddle like a son-of-a-bitch."

Amanda paddled. She sat up straight, pulling her torso up out of her rib cage, leaning over the side, paddling as hard as she could. Will tossed away his cigarette and guided them around the tree and down a little three-tiered waterfall and they were off down the winding spinning first half-mile of the high Buffalo.

"Paddle," he yelled, "you're doing great." Amanda paddled harder. After a while the water smoothed out and they coasted past a rock-covered beach and on down to where the river became a pool with huge black and gray bluffs rising up like eagles' wings.

"Look at the bluffs," Will said. "Is that as good as Steuben Glass?"

"Steuben Glass couldn't hold a candle to this river."

"It smells so good," he said. "I'd forgotten the smell. And she's running. She's running like a dream."

The canyon narrowed. The water became swifter again. "Listen," Will said. In the distance Amanda could hear the rapids. She leaned into the paddle. In a moment they were upon a rush of water falling over stone ledges. She felt the adrenaline pour down into her arms and fingertips. They were through a couple of long exciting chutes, then the river ran down to a shelf of level land. Around them and behind them were dense unbroken woods. A jungle of trees met over their heads like a green tunnel. It was quieter here, darker, and Amanda sat back, letting Will do the work for a while.

I feel safe with him, she thought. I think he can take care of me. She felt a sharp pain low on her left side, thinking for a moment she had pulled a muscle, then recognizing the old quirky pain of ovulation. Don't be silly, she told herself. You're too old to ovulate.

"Is something wrong?" he said.

"No," she said. "I was just thinking about form. Like the way you handle this canoe. Making it look easy."

"Well, you don't have to worry about what you look like out here."

"Can I take my shirt off?" she said. "You have yours off."

"Take it off for all I care," he said. "If we get arrested

I can always say you're from New Orleans and don't know any better."

"Is there anyone out here?" she said. "I mean, to arrest me?"

"Of course not," he said. "It's Monday. There isn't anyone for miles. Take your pants off too for all I care."

"Well, that might be going too far." She reached up and pulled off her old gray and white striped boat shirt and Will guided the canoe on down the river thinking about her lovely smooth back, thinking about the night.

Thirteen days, she was thinking. No, twelve, I guess. Let's see, Monday, Tuesday, Wednesday, Thursday, Friday, Saturday. Well, it's absurd.

"Amanda," Will said. "Quick. Look up there. To the left." She turned her head and saw a waterfall pouring down over rock shelves to the river. Beside it a fat, white-faced steer gazed out through the trees.

"You see everything," she said. "You're always showing me something."

"That's because I look. Most people never look more than thirty feet in front of themselves. That's one thing I got from all those days I spent surveying. I'm always picking out landmarks, walls, ditches, fences. I'll be glad to get back to doing it."

"You're definitely giving up on school?"

"I don't like to go to school, Amanda. All I want to do is get a job and be a happy man. I don't care about that other stuff. I never have. All I want is some work to do and a band to play with on the weekends."

"I don't believe that's all you want, Will. I don't believe that for a minute."

"Hear that," he said. "That's white water up ahead. You better be watching out for where we're going."

By late afternoon they had passed Three Points, an unmarked place where the river splits around a small island. They came upon it unexpectedly, sailing down the incline and around the curves yelling like Indians. They went around a final bend and Will guided them into a small lagoon beneath some willow trees. "How's this, Ms. McCamey?" he said. "Will these accommodations do you for the night?"

"I'm with you, Captain," she said. "Whatever does for you does for me." They pulled the canoe up on the rocks and Amanda went to work hanging their wet things on the persimmon trees along the bank.

"I'm going to walk up into the woods and see where we are," Will said.

When he left she took a box of animal crackers out of the supplies and sat down on the edge of the bank biting the heads off tigers and lions, looking up at the ancient twisted junipers growing in the cracks at the top of the bluffs, pretending she was an eagle perched on the junipers, looking down on herself sitting on the riverbank in her old gray shirt, munching the little cookies, content as any housewife.

Will walked up the path into a stand of birch and water oaks, breaking off dry branches as he moved along, making a little bundle of twigs. I'll make her an Indian fire, he thought, remembering his grandfather squatting beside him in the woods teaching him to build the small hot fires of the Cherokee. He shivered, feeling the cool beginning of evening. We should have brought blankets, he thought, but, shit, I was afraid if I let her go back in the house one more time she'd change her mind. Jesus, she's changeable and hard to figure. All I really know about her is the way her skin feels. She's got the softest skin of any woman I've ever touched. Sometimes I wish she'd take those big eyes and all those goddamn words and ideas and go on back to New Orleans and just leave me her skin to hold. Goddamn, I can't even drink around her. What kind of a deal is that? He walked on into the woods, thinking about her strangeness.

It was growing darker now. He had moved almost half a mile into the underbrush. He turned and walked back the way he had come, caught up in the cool green of the woods at dusk, getting used to the feeling of being alone in the world. The darkness was gathering faster turning the leaves black all around him. He looked up and saw her sitting on a fallen tree trunk with her head tilted up to catch the last light.

"Are you going to make me a fire or not?" she said.

"Wait till you see this fire," he said. "This fire will knock your eyes out." He walked down to the beach and found stones and arranged them in a circle, tore a paper sack into fat strips, laid pieces on the stones like a Maltese Cross, then added the bundle of twigs, then a log. She sat on a sleeping bag, watching him without speaking. In a moment the fire caught and began to blaze hot and quick, sending a thin stream of smoke straight up into the windless night. He held out his hands. The smoke sailed up through a hole in the overhanging willows, becoming a small cloud as it hit the air currents above the trees.

"I wish I had some eagle feathers," he said. "The Cherokee bring up the fire with eagle feathers. When the smoke reaches the sky it becomes an eagle. And the spirit of the firebuilder can fly with the eagle wherever the night winds carry him. In the morning the spirit returns through the fire and goes back into the man."

"What if the fire goes out?" Amanda said.

"I won't let it go out," Will said. "Not tonight anyway."

They ate a cold supper sitting beside the fire, then lay down together to watch the constellations appear in the sky.

Amanda woke in the night. There was mist all over the water and the little rock peninsula. She stirred in Will's arms, moving her body against his until she woke him. Then, half asleep on the hard bed of the earth they made love as softly as ever they could in the world. Love me, Amanda's body sang. Dance with me, his body answered. Dance with me, dance with me, dance with me.

Now the darkness demanded. And Amanda surrendered herself to the darkness and the river and the stars.

It divides and divides and divides, then it folds, and becomes the spinal column and the brain, *then the center forms*, the vascular system is laid down, the veins and arteries, the rivers of life flowing in and out of the great soft red pump of a heart.

A light rain woke them again at dawn. Amanda stumbled over to the supplies, found the plastic sheeting and shook it out over them like a flat tent.

They lay in the makeshift tent giggling, naked and freezing. Amanda sneaked an arm out, reached over by the ice chest and found the chewing gum and stuck a piece of it in her mouth and began to chew it.

Then Will reached down to where his clothes were

wadded up in the bottom of the sleeping bag and found a cigarette and lit it and they lay like that with the soft rain falling on the plastic sheeting, chewing gum and smoking.

"Very fucking romantic," Amanda said.

"Do you want to stay here until it storms," he said, "or go on while it's only raining?"

They ate the rest of the Fig Newtons and peanut butter, packed the canoe and headed down the river to Pruitt.

"Once I was out here with my grandfather," Will said. "And when we woke up in the morning the canoe was covered with yellow butterflies. That canoe was *painted* with yellow butterflies."

"Steer the canoe," Amanda said. "Watch out where you're going."

They paddled in rain for an hour, then pulled the canoe up into a cave under a bluff and rode out the storm wrapped in the sleeping bag, watching the lightning flash and break all around them so close it turned the trees white.

"Are you scared?" Will said, pulling her close to him.

"Hell no," she said. "I'm not scared of anything. I'm too old to be afraid of things. What a way to die this would be." And she burrowed her head down into his chest thinking wonderful brave thoughts, smelling the river and the cold mossy smell of the limestone cave and the clear smell that lightning gives to the world.

Around eleven the skies cleared and they got back in the river. Amanda took her shirt off and tied it around her breasts like a halter, throwing her life jacket down on the bottom of the canoe.

"I can smell civilization," Will said. "We're not too far from Pruitt."

She turned around to face him, meaning to get a scarf out of the duffel bag. Amanda was bored with the river now. She was thinking of ways to look glamorous. I'll tie a scarf around my head the way Patsy Wainwright wears hers in ballet class, she was thinking. I'll braid it into my hair.

"Amanda," Will called. "Sit up. Paddle, Amanda, goddammit, start paddling."

She reached in the bottom of the canoe for the paddle but it was stuck under the sleeping bags. She struggled to pull it out but it was too late and they were on top of Trumpet Falls, a series of stone ledges falling fourteen feet in twenty yards. The river was having its own way now.

"Goddammit, Amanda," he was calling. "Get low. Don't do anything. For God's sake, get low." But she couldn't hear him or she wasn't listening and she had the paddle in her hands and stuck it down into the water and it caught on a ledge and threw the stern around in a circle and they were turning and turning and then they were in the water.

Will was in a pool near the bank. Amanda was in the current, her life jacket floating in the water a few feet away from her. She grabbed at it and caught one of the strings and pulled it to her as her head went under. Then the current took her and pushed her on down the river and she felt a boulder hit her shoulder. She was being sucked and pulled and pushed by the river. She had never known such helplessness. All the thousands of hours of swimming she had done in her life, all the beautiful strokes, all the water lore in the world was of no use to her now. She was choking. The water was so cold she could not get her breath. She was being tossed and pulled in three directions and down. I will go down, she thought. She came to the top and caught a glimpse of the big yellow canoe. Then it was gone. She was as alone as if she had been abandoned on Jupiter.

Everything in the world was cold green water, so cold, so very cold. The whole world was singing in a higher key. She could not breathe, the pressure of the water against her chest was so deep, so hard and dark and cold and full. I am here forever, she thought. This is what it is to die, this pressure, this powerlessness. Then Amanda let go of fear, surrendered, gave in to the water, gave in to her death.

The current turned her around like a dervish and slammed her against a tree that grew down into the water. Her head was above the water now and she was furious with the river and began to grab and claw her way up the roots of the tree. When she had her torso up on the roots she looked back across the river and saw Will struggling with the canoe. "Will," she called out. "Help me. For God's sake, help me."

"I'll be there," he called. "Stay still. Hold on. I'm coming."

Breathe, she thought. For now she was freezing. Breathe, goddammit. Live. Let me live. Get me warm. Let me live. Let me be.

He had the canoe now and was dragging it back to the pond. "Don't yell," he called. "Save your energy. Don't let go. For God's sake, don't let go."

Then he had the canoe and a paddle, the extra paddle his father had taught him to tie into the bedroll no matter how his grandfather laughed at them for doing it.

He beached the canoe downriver from the tree where Amanda was clinging to the roots. Then he worked his way back to the tree and down the roots and held out his hands.

Then she was on the bank and he was massaging her arms and legs.

He sat beside her massaging her, working furiously to get her warm. There was a pile of brush beside the tree, debris that the river had washed up. He pulled it onto the rocks and managed to set it afire with his cigarette lighter. He made her sit by it while he dried out their clothes, stopping every now and then to work on her legs.

"I thought you weren't coming. I thought you couldn't save me."

"I didn't save you. I don't know what saved you. Goddammit, you scared me to death. My father told me never to go floating with a woman."

"Oh, God," she said. "I'm sorry. It was all my fault. I forgot what to do."

"Never mind," he said. "It's all right. You did the best you could. You did what you knew how to do."

Later, when she was warm and some of the clothes were dry, he wrapped her up and took her on down the river to Pruitt. At a shallow they found Will's baseball cap. At another, her scarf wrapped around a rock.

The car was waiting for them in Pruitt just where Jeter said it would be and they drove home on a winding road along the perimeter of the national forest, not talking very much.

It was dark by the time they got to Fayetteville. "Do something for me," Will said when they got to her house. "I want you to get in bed and stay there. I know you're bruised. Tomorrow you're really going to feel it."

She did as she was told and he tucked her in like a child and kissed her on the forehead. Then he went upstairs and poured himself a water glass full of scotch and went out to sit on the steps. He was worn out and he was tired of being sober. He was tired of not knowing what he was supposed to do.

Well, I guess I love her. I guess there isn't any getting away from her. But I'm not living in her house any longer, no matter how much I like to fuck her. Have to sneak around to drink. He sighed and took a drink out of the glass.

By two o'clock the bottle was empty, he was out of cigarettes, the sky was full of stars, and Will had decided what to do. He wrote her a note and left it at the top of the stairs and walked on down the hill to his own house. *I am going home to get my life straightened out,* the note said. *I need a few weeks to think things over. I'll call you soon. I'm a small town boy, Amanda. I have to know what the deal is between us. I have to know what's going to happen next. I'll call you as soon as I get some work to do.*

Katie Dunbar is luckier than most people. When she wakes up in the morning she is almost never thinking about herself.

This morning she woke up thinking about a kiln she promised to design for the Alma Orphans' Home. Goddamn Momma for volunteering me for everything in the state of Arkansas, she was thinking, wondering if she could get them to build a really big one, thinking how mad she was about orphans in general and the poor irresponsible helpless mothers of orphans and how much she wanted to kill everyone who helps make orphans.

She started making up the bed, thinking about everyone she blamed for orphans, blaming Baptists, strangling a fat Baptist minister with her bare hands as she tucked the pink sheets into the edges of the waterbed.

I might be able to make them a little wheel, she was thinking. They could learn how to throw their own little doll dishes. Clinton and I ought to go down there and run the place. We could get married at the cleaner's. Then Momma'd have to retire.

She was thinking about her momma leaning over one of the ironing machines with a cigarette in her mouth, a look of intense concentration on her face. Katie smiled, remembering herself eating a stick of peppermint candy, watching with admiration as her mother overpowered the big machine. She could hear the steam hissing, could smell the hot starch, could hear her momma yelling orders at the tall black woman who assisted her.

A happy childhood, Katie thought. I had a happy childhood. Jesus, I've got a lot to do today. She stretched her arms over her head, pulling herself up to her full five feet ten inches.

She moved the soft flannel curtains back from the windows and looked out on the day. "Oh, God," she said. There was Amanda, sitting on the stone wall with her arms clamped around herself.

Katie tapped on the window with her hand, tied one of the sheets around herself for a robe and walked out the door to her friend.

"What's going on?" she said. "What time is it anyway?"

"I don't know," Amanda said. "I thought you'd never wake up. I saw Clinton leave. I hid from him. Oh, Katie," she said and fell into her friend's arms. The sheet gave way and Katie held her friend against her breasts.

"Come on in," she said. "Let's get some coffee going. Goddamn, you look terrible. Where's Will?"

"He's gone. We had an accident on the river. I almost got killed. I really did. Then I went to sleep and he left. He's gone. Just like I always knew he would be. And it's because of money. Goddammit, it. It's money. Money did this to me."

"Well, come on in. Start at the beginning." Katie settled her friend on the waterbed. "Start over. Tell me what happened."

"I nearly got killed on the Buffalo. You ought to see my shoulder. Then Will got drunk, I guess. Anyway someone drank a bottle of scotch while I was sleeping. Then he left me a note saying he was leaving. It's money, Katie, just like you said it would be. Money's ruining it. And I don't know what to do about it. I can't give him my money. And I can't live with him when I have money and he doesn't have any. There isn't any answer to it."

"There really isn't," Katie said. "Jesus, I feel sorry for young men. When I was young I thought they had it so easy. I thought young women were the ones to feel sorry for. Now I think young men have it worse than girls do."

"Well, he flunked out of school. I think he did it on purpose. He doesn't want to be an engineer. He likes to survey land. He likes to walk around in the country with a couple of ex-convicts running lines for him and survey land. Well, that's what he says he likes to do. He swears that's all he wants to do with his life. What can I do about it?"

"Nothing," Katie said. "You have to let men do what they want to do. Because they are going to do it anyway. One way or the other they'll do what they want to. Like everybody else. Or if you make them do something they don't want to do they'll sabotage it."

"He isn't going to see me until he gets a job. It might be weeks before I hear from him again. Well, at least I've got my work to do. Thank God for that. At least I've got that. It was so beautiful on the river. Before the bad part started. I hate money, Katie. I hate and fear it."

"Don't go off the deep end, Amanda. All money is is power. A way to store power. The Rosetta Stone is a record of money transactions, did you know that? So many bushels of corn for so many sheaves of wheat."

"It's power over other people's lives. Someone planted

that corn. Someone harvested that wheat. I'm sick of it. Look what it's doing to Will and me."

"So where's he gone?"

"Back to his little place in Tin Cup. He's going to call me when he gets a job. Katie, how can I let him go work at some terrible dirty job when I have enough money for both of us? Would you tell me how I'm supposed to think that's a good idea?"

"It isn't a good idea, Amanda. But supporting a man is a worse idea. Believe me, it's a worse idea."

"Oh, God," Amanda said. "Nothing works, nothing ever works for me. Oh, goddamn, now I'm whining. I'm whining like Alice Little."

"Who is Alice Little?"

"A girl who lived on Panther Burn Plantation that whined her life away. When I was small my grandmother always said, 'Don't be like Alice Little who whined her life away.'"

"Well, you're welcome to stay around here and whine if you want to but I've got to get to work."

"I'm sorry. I don't mean to come over here this early and do this to you. I'm just so confused, Katie. I'm trying so hard to figure it out. To do the right thing for once in my life. I thought it would be enough to have work to do. Then Will came along. And he's too young. He's just too young. I don't know what to do about any of it. I don't know why I can't be happy to just live alone and do my work."

"In loneliness you assume a responsibility for yourself which you cannot fill."

"That's beautiful. Who said that?"

"Wendell Berry. It's from a poem a friend of mine typed

up and gave me once for my birthday. Maybe I'll make you one. I'll write it on clay. Meanwhile, I really have to get back to work. Let's go for a walk this evening. Or have dinner."

"I love you, Katie. I don't know what I'd do without you."

"And I love you. It's all right to be confused, Amanda. Everyone gets confused. Just don't stay that way. Call me later and read me something. You never have shown me that inventory, you know. You said you were going to show it to me."

Amanda walked home the long way. By the time she got to her corner the postman was coming down the road in his jeep and stopped and handed her a stack of letters tied with a rubberband. On top was a letter from Lavertis. Amanda pulled it out from the rubberband, meaning to sit on the walkway and read it. Then she saw the other one. It was a letter from Guy.

You have to see me. Here are three phone numbers where you can call me night or day. Please, Amanda, please call me. All our lives I came when you called me.

She stuck it in the pocket of her shorts and opened Lavertis's pale blue envelope.

Dear Mrs. Ashe,
Seems like every day I turn around and start to tell you something and you aren't there. I know you're busy with all the work you have to do but if you get time write and tell me what's going on. I can't wait to see the book. I bet it's going to be a best seller.

Every Sunday I go down to prayer circle and pray you get whatever you want out of life. Well, that's about all for now. Here's a picture of Layman and me in our Easter outfits. Look how fat I am from not keeping up with you.

Amanda kissed the photograph, looking into the eyes of her friend. I'll dedicate the book of translations to her, she decided. I don't know why I didn't think of that a long time ago.

Amanda took the photograph down to her workshop and taped it up on the lamp above her typewriter and went to work.

"Sing a song of Jesus," the new trot began.

> *Sing a song of Jesus,*
> *so powerless he allowed his own subjects*
> *to torture him to death.*
> *Sing Jacob, ready to hack his own kid*
> *and blame the blood on God*
> *Sing Joseph, sweet faceless cuckold of history*
> *All on their way with Sister Clara*
> *to the land the meek inherit,*
> *the ones whose shadows tremble in the sun*

Lavertis may not want this book dedicated to her, Amanda thought, sitting back and wiping her hand across her face. Lavertis may not like this stuff about Jesus worth a damn.

Will woke up on his sofa. He was dreaming of her again. In the dream he was running a cement mixer out in front of her house. He was making her a sidewalk but the pieces he made were too big to move. They kept piling up all around him, great square pieces of concrete. No matter how he pulled and tugged and shoved he could not move them into place.

9:30. A new day. Time to get the show on the road. He rummaged around in a box of clothes and found a blue oxford cloth shirt that had belonged to his father. It was a size too big but it was the only thing he had that was ironed. He put it on, smoothed out the wrinkles in his corduroy pants, and started out to look for work. There was hardly a surveying or carpenter's job in town that he hadn't already had at one time or the other but he was ready to try again.

He was feeling good about things. It was a beautiful day to do anything, even look for a job. At least I'm through with that goddamn school, he thought. At least I won't be shut up in a building listening to theories.

He stopped on Water Street to admire the Morgans' fence, a line of fifteen old bedsprings strung together along the back of the property. There was a blue one and a pink one and a bright green one and many white and rusted ones, all hooked together with baling wire.

Will shook his head, thinking about Amanda dragging him down to see it. Amanda thought the Morgans' fence was "art." She thought Ray Morgan had built the fence to be "nonmaterialistic." It never occurred to her that he couldn't afford any other kind of fence. Let's face it, Will thought. She can't imagine anyone not being able to afford anything.

Amanda. Will sighed and stuck his hands deep in his pockets, thinking about her. *Well, the best piece of ass I ever had,* he thought. *I guess I've got to go with it. Don't want to fuck anybody else. Can't fuck anybody else. I guess I'll have to ride it out wherever it's going.*

He went by the hardware store and borrowed a hundred dollars from Jodie and walked down to Dickson Street to pay his bills. "There aren't any jobs around here worth having," Jodie had said. "You've got to get out of this town unless you want to end up broke all your life, Will. I've told you that. You won't ever listen to anyone. All your life you won't listen. What can we do? No wonder your old man gave up on you. I'd give up too but I'm a soft touch. Now get this back to me by the first of the month. And stick with something. You never stick to anything. It's a sign of weakness. Don't be weak. I can't stand a weak man."

It had been a hundred bucks' worth of listening. Well, he loves me, Will thought. At least he loves me. What can I say. Let's see, $45 to Roger's and $37 to the Bar and Grill and $10 to Lorraine. *Then I'll be even. Nothing wrong with being even.*

Coming out of Roger's he ran into an old poet named Elton who used to run lines for him. He was a great fat dreamy man who had published poems in *The New Yorker*. Once when he was making a lot of money he had invited the town to a poetry reading at the U-Ark. Instead of reading the poems he had thrown three hundred silver dollars out to the crowd. He wasn't even a drunk, he was just a poet.

Now he lived around town the best he could, renting a room from this professor or that one, never staying in one place very long, leaving boxes and suitcases full of half-written poems and novels and plays behind him wherever he had been.

"Now about those Pindaric Odes I'm working on," Elton said. "I've got it worked out that the coaches over there ought to be in on it. I could read some of them before the games. I was talking to Clinton about it last week and he said he thought they'd jump right on it. That's where all the money is in this town, Will, right over there in that gym."

"Go with it," Will said. "They'll love it. They'll do anything around here for the Razorbacks. I think you're really on to something this time, Elton."

"The idea came to me years ago but I didn't get around to it till this winter. Well, I'm glad you like it. What you been doing? You playing any music?"

"Not much. Right now I'm looking for work so I can make it through the summer."

The big poet moved in closer, giving Will a good whiff of the baloney sandwich he was carrying in his pocket. He put both his hands on Will's shoulders. "You take care of yourself," he said. He was looking Will straight in the eye. It was hard to put anything over on Elton. He had spent too many hours at a typewriter to be fooled by anything.

"I'm okay," Will said. "I'm just in a hole I got to climb out of. It's nothing serious."

Will finished paying his bills. *That leaves seven dollars* he thought. *That's fifty cents a day for fourteen days.*

He looked up at the clouds, watching one until it passed beyond the farthest ridge of blue mountains, then walked down to Sutton Street to see if Lester would give him his old job back.

"I could put you on a framing crew," Lester said. "It doesn't pay much and I can't guarantee how long it'll last but it's something. You can have that if you want it."

"Come on, Lester," he said. "You know I'm too good for that."

"No one's too good for anything, Will," the contractor said. "I've got college kids begging for work. It's tight around here. Money's tight."

"Tell me about it," Will said. "I'm scraping to keep a roof over my head and have enough left for cigarettes."

"Stop smoking," Lester said. "Then you'll be ahead."

Will laughed like he thought that was the funniest thing he'd ever heard in his life. "Well, maybe I'll dig out my tool belt and be around in the morning," he said. "It might feel good to be climbing a scaffold."

He walked back down to Roger's and had a beer. Then he had two more, then walked around to his father's office to pay him a call.

"I've been expecting you," his father said. He leaned back in his chair letting Will admire his muscles. "I figured you'd be around," he added. "Davis told me you'd flunked out of school."

"How'd he know?" Will said.

"Everybody knows everything you do, Will," his father said. "This is a small town. A very small town."

"You got any ideas about what I ought to do next?" Will said. "I'm asking for help, Daddy."

"I'm through helping you, Will. I'm fed up."

"Just like that, huh. No possum, no sop, no taters."

"Whatever that means."

"It's something I learned at that school you talked me into going to."

"I didn't talk you into learning any damn thing like that. And I'm pissed off at you for wasting my money and not doing a good job for me at the school. There's no use talking to me. I'm not giving you another cent."

"I didn't come to get money," Will said. "I came to get a job. I want to get my hands on a transit. I want to get to work."

"I've got someone running all my crews. I can't just fire my men anytime you get in the mood to work."

"Well, I guess that's that."

"Unless you want to go out on the rigs as a deckhand. Nickles Oil is looking for some hands. I'll call New Orleans about that if you're interested."

"It's that or join the army," Will said. "I can't stay here. I've got to do something. I've got to make some money."

"Think it over," his father said. "It's good clean work. You'll see the ocean."

"Make a man of me," Will said, smiling to take the edge off of it. "I'll let you know. I'll call you up."

"Do that," his father said.

"I miss seeing you," Will said. "Let's go fishing some weekend."

"When I get time," he said. "I'm snowed under right now. I can't make plans for anything."

"You work so hard," Will said. "You make me proud."

"Make me proud," his father said. "Go make me proud."

Will walked out into the heat of the day. He started down the street to the square thinking he might look into Dillard's to see if they needed a stock clerk. He was going over in his mind all the jobs he had had in his life in Fayetteville.

He was walking along beside the McElroy Bank Building, thinking about his old jobs. No possum, no sop, no taters, he said to himself, pulling his shoulders in, letting his spine curve into the hill as he walked up. He caught sight of himself in a window. He stopped dead still on the sidewalk staring at his reflection in the angled windows of the huge bank. There Will stood, in the exact center of a dark glass painting, surrounded on all sides by sidewalks and buildings and storefronts he had known every day of his life, this small town all around him like a vise.

He stood there for long moments staring at himself. When he started moving again, he moved fast. He ran back down the hill and into his father's office without knocking and asked him to start making the phone calls.

In an hour there was an offer from Nickles Oil Company out of El Dorado to hire him as a deckhand on a boat that serviced rigs off of Morgan City and Port Sulphur, Texas. They were expecting him on Wednesday. That gave him twenty-four hours.

He called Amanda, his voice bright with excitement, and asked to see her that afternoon.

Will came walking up the hill an hour before she was expecting him. She was still in the bathtub. When the doorbell rang she wrapped herself in a towel and went running up the stairs to let him in. She stood at the top of the stairs dripping all over the place, holding on to the doorknob.

He handed her a letter.

"What's this?"

"It's a letter asking you to marry me. As soon as I can afford it. This year or next year or when I'm eighty or when you're eighty. You can do anything you want to with that letter except throw it away. Promise me you won't throw it away."

"Let me get a robe," she said. "I'm dripping wet."

When she came back up the stairs he was out on the balcony inspecting the mushrooms. "I'm going to New Orleans to go out on the rigs," he said. "My dad got me the job. I'll be working off of Morgan City, Louisiana. I'm leaving tonight."

"I'm glad," she said. "That's what you need to do."

"I don't have any choice. It's four hundred and fifty dollars a week and room and board," he said. "That's big bucks for me."

"I'm glad you're going," she said. "It's what you ought to do."

"I talked to the guy on the phone," Will said. "He said if it worked out I might end up getting to go to Africa with a crew they're sending over there. They're opening an operation in the Sudan. You can't ever tell where something like that will end up. I might even get to do some surveying as soon as I get a foothold."

"That's good," Amanda said. "It's what you ought to do."

"It isn't easy leaving you."

"You're leaving me one way or the other," she said. "It was just a matter of time."

A long time went by while he smoked a cigarette. The sun was near the horizon now. "That sunset's almost tacky," she said at last.

"It's pollution," he said. "Those clouds look great from a distance but all they are is smoke from Chicago." He looked down at the little mushrooms which were full and fat now after the rain. He wasn't saying what he wanted to say. Stop blaming me for your past, he wanted to say. Stop blaming me because you used to be an alcoholic. I'm not an alcoholic. I'm not your lost child or any of your old lovers. I'm not your husband or the child you lost or your cousin who was killed by a drunk driver. I'm William David Lyons of Fayetteville, Arkansas trying to make it through the day. Stop getting me mixed up with your ghosts.

"I have to go," he said. "I have to get packed."

"Then go on. Don't stay here making me sad. Do you want any of the clothes that are here?"

"I've got enough. I'm not taking much. When I know what's going on I'll write to you."

"I'll be right here," she said. "I'm not going anywhere."

Then he was gone. And Fayetteville was lonely without him. The streets looked dirty. The houses looked shabby and uncared for. There wasn't anything Amanda wanted to eat. There wasn't anything to do. School was winding down for the semester. It was a bad time of year to try to stop being in love.

Well goddammit, I've just got to stop being in love with him, she told herself. That's all there is to that. Fini. The way out is through the door. One rock is just like another. It's all in my head anyway. All I have to do is get busy and stop thinking about him. All I have to do is find someone else to love.

She went downstairs and got out all her beauty supplies. She plucked her eyebrows. She painted her toenails. She put on a white linen skirt and a silk blouse. She went upstairs. She ate some vanilla wafers. She made some coffee. She went downstairs and worked on a poem. She threw the poem away. She walked around the house.

She drove out to the Mall and went to a movie. She walked out in the middle of it. She stopped off at the grocery store. She picked up a carton of ice cream. She put it back in the freezer. She picked out some apples. She decided the line was too long. She put the apples back in the bin and stuck her hands down in her pockets and stalked out of the store. She went back home and picked the poem up off the floor and started working on it again.

> *Perhaps the sandman will come tonight*
> *and take me to you,*
> *sixty days of drilling each other*
> *like tin soldiers, then six thousand nights*
> *with no sand, and no trips. . . .*

What a lot of bullshit, she said, and threw the poem away again. She put her shoes back on and drove down to an automatic drive-in. She ordered a hamburger and some french fries and a vanilla milkshake. "And a package of animal crackers," she told the machine. "Make that two packages."

She drove off down the highway eating the crackers. She went home. She walked around her house. She called Katie. Katie was in Alma. She called Marshall. He was away at a writers' conference. She called Garth. An answering device gave her a rundown on the spring flowers coming up in the schoolhouse garden.

It was getting hot in Fayetteville. Two weeks went by. Three weeks went by. Then four. She thought about calling Malcolm and getting him to take her sailing. She thought about calling Guy. She thought about it a lot. Finally one afternoon she went downstairs and got the letter with the phone numbers out of her jewelry box.

"I'm sorry I yelled at you," she said. "I'm sorry I was mean to you. I'm lonely, Guy. Things aren't working out for me. I feel terrible. This isn't like me. You know this isn't like me."

"Let me come there," he said. "I'll fly up there. I'll come whenever you let me."

"This weekend," she said. "No, that's too soon. I have to get some work done. My work is all that's keeping me from going crazy."

"I'll keep you from going crazy," he said. "When can I come?"

"Sunday," she said. "Come Sunday."

"I'll leave Sunday morning as soon as the sun comes up. Be waiting for me, and take care of yourself, Sissy. Don't let anything happen to you until I get there."

✤ ✤ ✤ ✤ ✤ ✤ ✤ *23* ✤ ✤ ✤ ✤ ✤ ✤ ✤

Garth kept thinking about Amanda. He began to dream strange dreams about her. Finally one day in early June he drove over to Fayetteville to pick up some printing and stopped by to take her to lunch.

"Garth," she said, pulling him in the door. "What are you doing here?" He was standing in the doorway looking down at her out of his sweet face. Around his neck was a long red and purple scarf of some handwoven material. The ends hung down all the way to his crotch and he was pulling them up and down with his big freckled hands as he talked. "Where on earth did you get that shawl?"

"Someone brought it to me from Peru," he said. "I can't stop wearing it."

"Just look at you," she said. "You're getting more eccentric every day. Jesus, I'm glad to see you."

"Come along to lunch then," he said. "I've been worrying about you. You come tearing up to Eureka and tell me all about this great love affair you're having, then you disappear and don't even drop me a card."

"How's my aura?" Amanda said, giving him another hug, pulling him into the room. "Sit down and tell me about my aura."

"Your aura is dazzling," he said. "The clearest aura in the world." Actually he thought Amanda looked terrible.

"It's because I stopped reading newspapers."

"Well, get on your shoes and come along," he said. "I want to try out the new health food restaurant on the square."

"I heard it was dreadful," Amanda said. "I heard everything tastes like rainwater."

"It's called the Anahat Chakra," Garth was saying. They were driving down Dickson Street. Amanda was settled back in the seat thinking about her aura, imagining people looking into the jeep and seeing her there, strapped into the passenger seat surrounded by her great soft pink aura.

"I think I'll start wearing pink," she said. "It cheers people up when you wear bright colors."

"Anyway," Garth said. "It's all I'm working on now. It's here by the heart and it's the center of compassion and intelligence and universal love. It's the place that sends the best of us out into the world. It's goodwill and humor and real tenderness and real joy."

"What makes evil people?"

"They lose their sense of humor. Then they get scared. Then they want to kill everybody. I wasn't teasing about your aura, Amanda. It's dazzling today."

"I can't imagine why. I haven't been laid in weeks. I think I'm turning back into a virgin. How long do you think you have to go without being laid before you revert to a virgin?"

"Getting laid is very nice," Garth said, thinking about the librarian's hair all over his shoulders. "Between that and smoking I may not make it to the Bo tree." He sighed, thinking how hard it was to reach perfection. "I don't know about the virgin thing. A few weeks at most in today's world. Four to six weeks I'd say."

They were at the restaurant now, sitting cross-legged around a table. It was a nice room, with plants in the windows and charts of mushrooms and wildflowers on the walls.

"So I'm saving money to go to India," Garth said. "Bob was telling me all these stories about Tibet and it's stirred me up to want to go."

"Tell me one," Amanda said.

"Have you ever heard of Towel Drying?" Garth said. "It's one of the excesses the Communists are trying to put a stop to in the high lamaseries. When the novitiates are ready to enter the order the old monks take them up to the highest parts of the Himalayas, to places where the rivers are free-flowing down through snow. On moonlit nights the young men stand out in the snow beside the rivers. The old lamas dip towels into the freezing water and the young men hold them against their bodies and dry them by raising their body heat. Some men can dry, oh, twenty or thirty towels a night." He reached in his pocket for a cigarette.

"You have such wonderful stories," she said. "You have the best stories of anyone I know."

"How's your work going?" he said. "How're things in the war on Roman Catholicism?"

"My part's going all right. But dealing with Marshall is getting to be a pain in the ass. He's such a stickler for the rules of translation. He wants . . . Oh, I never can figure out what he wants. You can't change the original but you can if you can prove it's what the author meant to say. I mean how can you prove anything, much less anything about language. The thing is, you can change the original if you can get away with it. I had this great idea to change the French too. I mean, why not? But Marshall won't let me do it, of course."

"Well, which are you supposed to do then, change it or keep it the same? I don't understand what you're saying."

"You're supposed to do both. How do you like that? Well, it's very frustrating. It's a bitch. They call it the art of failure. Isn't that great? Imagine picking out something like that to do for a living. As soon as I get through with this book I'm going to write a novel about Helene. Then I can change anything I damn well please. Not to mention all the stuff I'll get to say about the Church."

"God, I can just imagine what you'll say."

"No, you can't. The part I'm going to like writing is when Helene and her maid start planning to murder all the nuns. I'm going to dream up some really gruesome ways to kill them. I think I'll kill off at least five or six. Historically, all she did was poison a couple. This salad's really terrible, Garth. What do you think they made this salad dressing out of?"

"Nun's blood," he said. "Actually, I think the strange taste is the bee pollen."

"Bee pollen?"

"It's the latest thing. Everyone's putting it on everything in Eureka. One day I had this vision that everyone in town was going to sprout little wings from eating it. It's a marvelous evil little taste. Try some more. It grows on you. How's your love life coming along? That's what I came up here to see about. How's your troubadour?"

"My troubadour is gone. I think he's on his way to Africa.

Anyway, I haven't heard from him. So I don't want to talk about it. He said he wasn't going to write me until he knew what he wanted to say."

"Is he in love with you?"

"Yep. I guess he is. Yeah, I think he is. But he isn't here. So I'm back to being me. My friends and me. My work and my friends and me."

"I loved an older woman once," Garth said. "I didn't get over it for a long time."

"Who was it?" Amanda said. She was surprised. She had never known Garth to be in love with anything but ideas.

"My piano teacher in Anniston, Alabama. I used to go over there every day as soon as I got out of basketball practice. She'd been away up north to music school and she came back to Anniston because her daddy got sick. I was seventeen years old. I guess I meant a lot to her."

"What happened?" Amanda said.

"You know those red books of piano music?" Garth went on, "The Home Library Series. Well, I know five of them by heart. She was twenty-nine the year I loved her, an old maid by Anniston standards."

"What became of her?" Amanda said.

"She married Judge Nelson McCauley in a double ring ceremony on the third of June the year I graduated from Vanderbilt. I wrote her a letter that morning and had it delivered by a messenger. She wore it in her bodice to the wedding."

"Did you go?" Amanda said.

"Oh, yes. I had to go. The next day I joined the Peace Corps." He came back to the table from India or Anniston or wherever he had been.

"You don't look well to me, Amanda. You look tired. You're

too thin." He was looking at her very curiously now, staring at her eyes.

"I have been tired," she said. "I can't seem to like anything I eat. Well, I've never been tired in my life. You know that about me. Why, do I look terrible?"

"No, but you look tired. I want you to do something for me. *I want you to promise you'll do this.* I have a friend who's a massage therapist. He's a brilliant man. He was at Johns Hopkins before he quit to practice holistic medicine. He has a little place on a ridge above town. It's worth the trip to see his herb garden. Anyway, he owes me some massages and I want you to go for me. I'll call and tell him you're going to call him. Will you do this for me? Will you promise to do this?"

"You know I'll do anything for you," she said. Garth handed her a slip of paper with a number on it. "His name is Luke Haverty," he said. "You will like him."

Amanda kept her promise. Wednesday afternoon at four she drove out into the hills above Hogeye and found the Sun Life Center, an old farmhouse with a wooden sign over the door. It was a handpainted sign with a picture of some mysterious plant in the center. She went bravely in.

"What's the sign for?" she said. She was facing a small bearded man with intense black eyes, overwhelmed by the hot sweet smell of his sweat. He had been working in the garden. An unwashed doctor, she thought. Well, Amanda, here you are at the hippie commune you always dreamed of joining.

"It's Comfrey," he said. "Heal-all, Bone-knit, as the Indians called it. I took it for my sign, instead of a snake."

"That's good," she said. "I like that. What's the music?"

"It's Pachelbel," he said. "The Canon in D. I deliver babies to that music. One of them was just here with his mother. We were playing it to see if he remembered."

"Did he?" Amanda said.

"He was awfully excited about something," Luke said. "If you like, we can leave it on while we do your massage. It's good music for that too."

"I've never done this," Amanda said. "I don't know what to do."

He led her into a sunny room with long windows and asked her to take off her clothes and lie down on the table. "Cover up with that sheet if it bothers you to be naked. I'll be right back."

She took off her clothes and lay down on the table. The music started over again, a beautiful orderly piece, the notes floating above her like bright translucent boats, filling the warm air of the sunny room.

"Did Garth tell you about me?" she said as Luke's hands began to massage her, caressing the long bones of the fingers, then moving up into the strong square hands. His fingers caressed and outlined the bones of her wrist, then moved up into the long muscles of her arm. "Trust me, Amanda," he said. "Concentrate on my hands. Learn about your body from my fingers."

All right, Amanda said to herself. I won't make a joke of this. I'll let him show me what he knows. His hands had moved across her shoulders now and deep into the space above the collarbone, then down across the ribs and into the soft places between her hipbones.

Amanda closed her eyes, following his hands with her mind, strangely at peace for the first time in many days, lying on the table with the bright afternoon sun pouring in the windows onto her skin, the music all around her, the smell of Luke's sweat, the comfort of another person's hands on her skin. He asked her to turn over onto her stomach. She did as she was told, sighed, and fell into a deep sleep. When Luke finished the massage he ran his fingertips softly up and down her back and buttocks; his fingers were as soft and soothing as a breeze.

She woke up and sat up on the table with the sheet around her breasts. It was a crazy printed sheet, dark blue with stars and moons. Luke was standing beside her with an ophthalmoscope in his hand. "You have wonderful eyes," he said. "May I look in them a moment?"

"Of course you can," she said. Then he adjusted the scope and looked a long time into her eyes. "That's quite a sight," he said. "Now would you like to look at mine?"

"Do you mean that?"

"Of course," he said. He put the instrument on her forehead and she looked into his eyes.

"That is quite a sight," she said.

"Better than the stars," he said. "More mysterious."

When she was ready to leave she tried to pay him.

"Oh, no," he said. "It was a favor I owed Garth. But I'd like to work on you again. To finish what I began. I was working pretty deep in some of the muscles. You might be sore tomorrow."

"I'd like that," she said. "How about Friday?"

"Fine," he said. "On Friday then. At four."

When she left he called Garth. "It's there," he said. "As clear as a dream of zero. How did you guess?"

"I saw it every day in India. That's what I did there. Well, did you tell her?"

"No, I thought I should talk to you first. She's coming back on Friday. Will you be around, in case she needs to call someone?"

"I'll be here," Garth said. "Waiting by the phone. But she won't call me. That isn't how she deals with things. She'll hole up with it for a while. She'll keep it to herself."

"What are you up to now?" Amanda said, picking up a bowl from the table. Katie had just emptied the kiln. The new firing was spread out on the table. The bowl Amanda picked up was bright terra-cotta with the dark red shadow of a bird's wing in one corner.

"It's the beginning of the show," Katie said. " 'The One Hundred Names for Red.' "

"Like the one hundred names for Allah?"

"Don't do that, please. Don't go dragging God into my soup bowls."

"May I buy it?" Amanda said. "This wonderful godless red bowl."

"After the show," Katie said.

"Then put a sticker on it," Amanda said. "And don't break it until I collect."

"You sure are in a good mood."

"I'm feeling better physically. I went out and got this great massage from a friend of Garth's named Luke Haverty. It taught me a lot of things about my body. I can't stop thinking about how incredibly intricate my hands are. I'm going back on Friday."

"I've heard about that guy. He worked on Clinton's knee. Are you all right, Amanda? You sound mighty high. I get worried when you start sounding high."

"I'm fine. I'm better than I've been in weeks."

It was almost dark when Amanda got back from Katie's. It had been a beautiful day, dandelions the size of daisies all over the yard, the trees all fat and full with summer. A brand-new moon appeared in the sky just as the sun went down behind a bank of clouds. Amanda was in one of those moods where everything seems to make sense in the world. She put some slow jazz on the record player and started doing yoga postures.

At first she couldn't concentrate. She kept thinking about Will. Wondering where he was. Wondering what he was doing. Imagining him on the ocean so far away. Why hasn't he written to me? I can't believe he hasn't written me.

She did some long slow twists and rolls, then pulled herself forward across her legs. She settled her head down into her knees. She was going further down than she was usually able to go. She laid her arms down on the floor beside her legs. The skies outside were turning darker blue now. The light was almost gone, the moon was clearer. *The stars*, she thought, soon the stars will be there. The real stars, not ones on a chart. I am tied up to all of that, tied up to the sky. Why couldn't it be true that our destiny is hooked up to the stars? Why couldn't astrology be true? Certain plants grow in February and other ones in May. Different plants for different seasons. Why wouldn't the body know how to make different kinds of people to be born at different times of year? It wouldn't have to start out there in the cosmos. It might be going on right here.

She pulled herself further and further down into the posture, her breathing coming long and slow. She began to see an imaginary sign in the sky, two fishes, swimming like twins in a womb. A sign, she thought, my sign, up there with the stars. Not stars in a book, not stars on a piece of paper, real stars in the real sky, the cold and beautiful real sky, the real universe. Of course I'm hooked up to everything. Of course everything in the universe touches everything else . . . how careful I must be . . . if only I'd been more careful . . . all the people who have been affected by me . . . it scares me to death . . . the child . . . Will . . . Guy . . . don't think about that . . . don't think about it . . . She pulled herself further down along her legs and the pictures went away and only the sign remained.

Then her mind was quiet, as if a needle had been lifted from a phonograph record. She stayed that way for a long time, not even aware of her own breathing.

✤ ✤ ✤ ✤ ✤ ✤ ✤ *24* ✤ ✤ ✤ ✤ ✤ ✤ ✤

"*Are* you sure?" She was watching Luke's face. One of her hands slipped into her lap. She caressed it with her other hand.

"As sure as I can be of anything in the world," he said. "Of course, you can have a chemical test if you like."

"How do you know?" she said, moving her fingers across her palm and up along the veins of her wrist.

"There's a little configuration that appears in the eye. You can see it with a simple magnifying lens. It's been known for thousands of years. Of course, the old Chinese doctors could see it with the naked eye."

"You knew Wednesday, didn't you?" she said.

"I apologize for that. I wanted to be sure before I told you."

"Can you feel it? With your hands?"

"Yes. There's a baby there. There's no doubt of that."

"I have to think this over," she said. "I have to be alone for a while."

"Is there anything I can do to help you? I'd like to work on you while you think this through."

"I'll call," she said. "I'll call you soon. I'll keep in touch."

"It's a special case, Amanda. Perhaps it will be a very special child."

She got into the car and sat up very straight and drove

home gathering her forces. *I will throw away all the bad food in the house, and turn off the air conditioning. I will dress in simple loose clothes. I will take long walks. I will be very quiet. I will go down to the heart of myself and find out what I'm thinking.*

She turned onto Highway 71, the long strip of fast food joints and motels and gas stations. Even the mountains on either side could not save it from being as ugly as the strip in any small city. Fateville, she thought. Land of dreams. Eureka. I was blind. Now I can see. Water, I have found water.

And Luke Haverty, the med school dropout, the unwashed hippie doctor of the hills with his gorgeous tan. Is he to be the angel of the Annunciation?

His hands were folded at his chest. He might have dropped to one knee. But then of course he couldn't have seen me, lying all fat and hot on his massage table, covered with oil. Maria Amanda Luisa, the gray-blue virgin of the middleweights. Vision a little fuzzy around the edges but wearing blue and white, the virgin's colors. Blue shorts, white T-shirt. I should wear these colors for the duration of my confinement. Confinement! I should be confined! *A special case. A very special child.* And Will Lyons, is he my Joseph leading the donkey? Except of course he is not here. Except I have not even heard from him and there is no donkey. Of course what we were doing might be called a visitation. Might be. Ought to be.

Okay, Amanda. That's about enough of that. It's time to think straight. This is a real problem. This is probably even true.

She parked the car and walked into her house and began to straighten up all the magazines she had left lying on the sofa. Then she went downstairs and made up the bed with clean sheets and threw all the dirty clothes in the washer.

She stopped for a moment in the hall and looked up at the ceiling and started laughing. For no reason on the earth. Just stood there laughing.

Stop that, she told herself. Stop that silly goddamn laughing.

She put on her running shoes and went up on the mountain. She ran around and around the top. She ran seven miles. She went home and began work on a sonnet.

> *I have heard them on the stairs*
> *coming for us while your body*
> *breathed in me. I have lain in your arms*
> *feeling the sword between our ribs,*
> *flames around our arms, our cries*
> *lost in unimaginable din.*
>
> *I had not imagined this narrow bed*
> *or Sister Clara farting at Matins*
> *The sweetmeats she proffers*
> *seeing I am sad.*
> *How beautiful the wind is in the trees*
> *I tell her, tomorrow walk by the tree*
> *There will be gifts, something you didn't*
> *know you needed.*

It was the last poem. The next morning Helene hung herself at dawn. The diary of her maid had arrived finally from Paris. It told a terrible story. "They locked her away at Lyons, and when she had given birth, they took away my lady's child, fruit of her only love. Death to Rome. Death to all that rule and do evil in her name. Writ in my hand for all to see forever. *Sign, Alma of Aurillac, freewoman."*

Amanda sat back in her chair and sighed, thinking of all that. What good did she do anyone by killing herself? Why didn't she run away and look for her child instead? Or poison the nuns. I'm sick of all this old depressing stuff. I'm sick of Helene Renoir and Medea and Anne Sexton and Sylvia Plath and Berryman and Will's old buddy Alter and the whole goddamn life-hating death-wish trip. To tell the truth I'm about sick of poetry.

The sword between our ribs. Jesus, well, maybe it sounded better back then. I can't concentrate on this stuff. I couldn't really be pregnant. I know it's just some hysterical thing. Well, I've never been hysterical in my life. I'm going down to the drugstore and get one of those kits. I'm not thinking about believing that hippie doctor even if Garth does think he's a genius.

She put the papers in a neat pile, straightened up all the pencils on the desk, turned out the light, drove down to the drugstore and bought a Pregnancy Home Diagnosis Kit. She pretended to read the directions on a bottle of Listerine while the young athlete behind the counter took her money. I could tell him it's for a friend, she thought. I could look at him but I'm not going to.

"Do you think Listerine is any good for a sore throat?" she said. "I don't think it helps much, do you?"

"I don't know, lady. I just take vitamins when I get a cold."

When she got home she opened the kit and set the pieces out on the washstand where she could see it first thing in the morning. She read the directions several times. She slept. She rose at dawn and wandered into the bathroom. She took a clean jar and urinated in it. She added three drops of urine to the test tube containing the chemicals. She added the contents of the vial. Vial, it said on the directions. Vial, she thought. I haven't heard that word in years. She put the stopper on the test tube and shook it three times and put it back in its container and tried to think of something to do for two hours. She went upstairs and pulled all the books off the bookshelves and started arranging them in alphabetical order. She put a symphony on the stereo and arranged the books on the shelves and played the symphony over and over without giving in to the desire to go downstairs and look at the test tube. All of the books had her name written on the flyleaf. Amanda McCamey, Amanda McCamey Ashe, Amanda and Malcolm Ashe, Amanda Ashe, A. M. Ashe, this book belongs to A. McCamey unless Grace Finch steals it.

When two hours had gone by she marched down the stairs and put on her glasses and looked into the test tube. The circle was there. It was really there. It was definitely there.

She threw the whole thing into the sink. She went upstairs and began to write lists.

Sanity, she wrote at the top of every page. Sanity, no quick decisions. No being influenced by anyone. Sanity, stars, clean air, exercise, meditation, logic, intelligence, rationality, sanity. No astrologers, unwashed doctors, no hippie bullshit. This is the real world. This is a real problem.

And Guy is coming tomorrow. On top of everything else Guy is coming.

❧ ❧ ❧ ❧ ❧ ❧ ❧ *25* ❧ ❧ ❧ ❧ ❧ ❧ ❧

Amanda *thinks Guy hung the moon, they said. Amanda thinks Guy can do no wrong. Amanda likes Guy the best of anyone in the whole delta.* The delta, shimmering in the sun, rapidly being turned into one big catfish pond as its owners have found a more profitable crop than cotton. The richest land in the world, oblivious to its lost children, oblivious to everything but the sun and the rain. Amanda had been thinking about the delta all morning as she waited for Guy's plane, thinking about the land, how it smelled this time of year, how it felt beneath her bare feet. Thinking about the river and the levees rising like the tombs of the pharaohs all the way from Memphis to New Orleans.

Guy had called from the airport as he was leaving Chicago. "The weather looks good all the way down," he said. "It shouldn't take long."

Amanda was out at the little airport an hour before he was supposed to land, waiting on the runway, pacing up and down wearing a skirt and a wide straw hat that made her face look pretty.

She was pacing up and down in a pair of high-heeled sandals she bought at a discount store on her way to the airport. I'm a whore, she thought. A forty-four-year-old pregnant whore and I don't even care. A *shameless* forty-four-year-old pregnant whore.

She was pacing up and down the runway listening to the shoes click on the pavement.

Maybe I ought to get my ears pierced while I'm at it, she thought. And catch syphilis. Then there wouldn't be anything that I forgot to do.

She fell into a daydream, pacing up and down imagining herself in a hospital in France dying of childbirth and syphilis all at the same time, all alone with only the nuns coming in and out of the room with their hands folded. She had just gotten to the good part where she refused absolution when the small speck of the plane appeared in the sky, banked and circled and banked again, and made its approach to the runway.

It landed easily, rocking on two wheels, and coasted to within two hundred yards of where she was standing, a twin-engine Beechcraft Bonanza, a shiny silver toy. It seemed like a long time before the propellers stopped, before Guy opened the hatch and stepped out onto the wing, smiling at her as if his eyes had never left her face. Then she was in his arms.

"I need you," she said. "I have never been so glad to see anyone in my whole life."

"You look wonderful, Sissy," he said. "You don't ever get old. You're the prettiest girl in the whole world. You know that, don't you?"

She followed him into the building where he made arrangements to have the plane cared for. Then they went out to her car and she handed him the keys. "Please drive," she said. "Please take care of me. I'm tired of taking care of myself."

"I used to come up here to play," he said. "We had some great games up here."

"I don't know anything about that part of Fayetteville," she said. "I hardly know where the football stadium is."

"It's always broken my heart that you never saw me play," he said. "Someday I'm going to take you to a reunion and let you see some of the films. We have a good time at those things, believe it or not."

"I never did really believe that part of your life," Amanda said. "Especially after you went to Chicago. It was always something I didn't want to think about. You up in Chicago being famous. Maybe I was jealous of you."

"It didn't last long," he said. "After I ruined my legs. But they don't forget. Other men don't forget. Once you wear that jacket you never really take it off. Will this stuff you're doing make you famous, Sissy? Do you get famous doing the kind of writing you do?"

"Not in a way you'd understand," she said. "But it might. If I ever finish it and if I do it right. Especially this manuscript, because it will be sort of scandalous. Besides, the poems are funny, some of them, and it tells a story. I'm going to write a novel about it, when I get through with the poems."

"Watch out for fame, Sissy. It ruined my life. I've spent my whole life watching men be jealous of me. It's dangerous to do something everyone else wishes they could do, to be the thing they wish they could be."

"It wasn't that way in Rolling Fork," she said. "You loved playing then. I remember you and Terry Brown and Phil Lake, and Callen, remember funny old Cally with his cowlicks?"

"That was different," he said. "We were a team. I sparked them. We hardly had enough boys to field a team half the time and we won everything in the state. It only takes one man to spark a team. To light up the others. Well, those were the best years, the best memories I have."

"We still have them," Amanda said. "Time doesn't go in just one direction. It's all there. All there forever."

They were almost to her house now. "Why were you in New Orleans?" she said. "Why did you call Malcolm to look for me?"

"Because I was lonely," he said. "Like you are now."

"I'm sorry I yelled at you when you called that day. That wasn't fair. Forgive me for that."

"It's all right," he said. "You told me not to call you. I should have done what you told me."

"You went to look for her, didn't you?" Amanda said. "Tell me straight, Guy. I know you did. I know damn well that's what you were doing there."

"Let's go to your house," he said. "I don't want to talk about this in the car."

"Then stop the car," Amanda said.

He pulled the car over to the curb and turned and took her hands. "She looks like you. She's all right. She's married."

"What else?" Amanda said. "Tell me. Tell it all to me. She's blind, isn't she? I know she's blind. I've always known she would be blind. I remember when she was born her eyes were stuck together. I remember seeing them stuck together."

"She sees as good as you or me. She does everything. She was playing tennis. She won. I went to the New Orleans Lawn Tennis Club and watched her play."

"Then what is it?" Amanda said. "Tell me what you aren't telling me. Why do you sound like this?"

Guy turned his eyes away and let his hands drop from

her arms. "She's very pretty and very ladylike and she's married to a young lawyer. You were right about one thing. If you'd kept on living there you would have met her sooner or later. You probably passed her on the street a thousand times."

"She looks like me?"

"Yes, but with dark hair. She's quieter. Well, I don't know that. I didn't get to talk to her. I just watched her play tennis. I kept thinking she looked like Grandmomma might have when she was young."

"She won?"

"Of course," he said. "Of course she won." They looked straight at each other then, the old pride rising between them, like desire.

"Let's get off this street," he said. "Let's get out of here." Then Amanda reached out and touched him, put her hand on his marvelous shoulders. He was the same old Guy, direct, impenetrable, true. How could I have been expected to love an ordinary man like Malcolm or Will after loving a man like this? she thought. Now, because she had touched him, she came within the circle of his power, forgetting as she always did when she was near him where she began or he began. McCameys, she thought.

Guy stayed for three days. They drove up to Eureka and spent the night in a crazy old Victorian hotel. They drove up into the Ozark wilderness, driving all day on the winding roads, eating cheese and crackers they bought in a country store, drinking canned iced tea, singing old hymns and love songs.

"If you have to sell Esperanza, sell it to me," he said. "I can buy it. Let me know what your best bid is and I'll buy it for that."

"Of course," she said. "But you have to give me all the money right away. I have to have an income to live on while I write."

"I'll give it to you right away," he said, trying to imagine Amanda turning into a businesswoman.

Several times she asked him about the girl. Each time he would go over the story from the beginning. He told her everything except about the boy.

"Then Vaiden promised me he would put her under his protection. That means she is safer than the President of the United States. Please go with me to meet her. Please say you'll go."

"No," Amanda said, every time he brought it up. "Absolutely not. Not under any circumstances. No." Then he would draw back. Wait, he told himself. Wait. Be patient. Let it take. Let her get used to the idea.

Amanda couldn't bring herself to tell him she was pregnant. She would get right on the verge of telling him, then talk herself out of it. It might hurt him, she thought. It might be more than he could bear. It might not even be true. For all I know it isn't even true. I'll probably start menstruating any day now.

Several times they made love, but it was different now, full of sadness and the secrets they were keeping, a darker kind of love than the bright music Amanda's body made with Will.

"It's me," Guy said. "I'm losing it."

"It's both of us," Amanda said. "We're getting older. So the fuck what. I'm damned if I'm going to care."

"It's better with you," Guy said. "Believe it or not I'm worse than this with other women."

"It's a phase," Amanda said. "You just need a new girl-friend. It'll be better when you get the hots for someone new."

"I don't want a new girlfriend," Guy said. "I want you."

"Come on," she said. "Don't talk that way. I love you as I have always loved you. Like I was loving my own self. But we can't live together. We don't have anything in common. What would I do? Follow you around to golf tournaments? I couldn't live in that world, Guy. I don't even wear those clothes anymore."

"Then just go with me to New Orleans," he said. "Get in my plane and we'll fly down there and find her and tell her who we are. Will you do that for me?"

"Guy, don't drag me into that. I have to finish what I've started here. I have work to do. You don't understand what it means to me to have real work to do for the first time in my life. You don't —"

"Amanda, it isn't just the girl. It's something else. I tried not to tell you this. Look here. Look at me." He turned her face up to his with his hands and all the pain and longing of his life was there for her to see. It seemed to Amanda that all her life Guy had been turning that lonely face up to her, asking her to get him warm with the light that was in her.

"There's a little boy, Amanda. She has a little boy that looks like you. He looks so much like you I almost went crazy when I saw him. I could almost smell him. I could smell that crazy smell you had when you were little. You always smelled like dandelions. Every time I ever saw one it made me miss you."

"Oh, God," she said. "Don't tell me that. How big a boy? How old is he?"

"I don't know. Maybe five. Or six or four. I was up on a balcony. I couldn't see him very well. I won't go through my life without knowing that boy. I'll move down there if I have to. I've already made up my mind. I'm going to get rid of my wife. I could play at the country club and see him all the time. You have to go down there with me. You have to help me with this."

"You can't do this to me," she said. "I won't let you do this to me. You break my heart. All my life I see you and you break my heart. What am I supposed to do? Cry my whole life away? I have walked through my life for thirty years dealing with this every day. Every time I saw a girl her age, every time I heard the word adoption. Every time my body bled another useless egg. And I didn't give in to it. I didn't die. I didn't end up a drunk or a suicide. I made it. And now you bring me this. How can you bring me this? You don't know what you're doing. You make me want to go out and get drunk. You make me want to cry forever. You make me want to die."

Then Amanda did cry. She went down to her bedroom and rolled up in her old eiderdown comforter and cried her heart out. Guy lay down beside her on the bed. "Let me call a doctor," he said. "Isn't there someone I can call? Amanda, please stop doing this to me."

After a long while she fell asleep. Guy lay beside her, going over in his mind every play he had ever memorized, every run he had ever made, every pass he had ever caught. It was the only way he knew to stop thinking about things he didn't want to think about.

When Amanda woke it was dark and she was starving. "I'm sorry," he said. "I'm so very sorry."

"No, you aren't. You aren't sorry or you wouldn't have

done this to me. You're just sorry I won't give in to you. You've figured out a way to be miserable and you want me to keep you company. Well, that's human. Come on, get up. I'm starving. I know a place that's got fresh oysters and shrimp. It's very expensive and they don't know how to serve them but I'll let you take me there to pay me back for making me miserable."

She tied a towel around her head and got into the shower. She was just getting warm from the water when she made up her mind to tell him. She pulled on an old velour robe and went upstairs and sat cross-legged on the floor beside the sofa where he was waiting, looking through her magazines.

"Haven't you got anything in this house with a sports section?" he said.

"Guy, I don't want to talk about sports, okay? I want to tell you something that you're going to find hard to believe. I'm pregnant, Guy. I got knocked up by this kid I had an affair with. A nice kid. But he's gone now. He's gone away.

"Anyway. *Don't talk.* Let me finish what I'm saying. I don't know what I'm going to do about all this. I might just have an abortion and forget it. Then again I might not.

"But I do know this. I'm going to live in the present, *and in the future.* I am going to live in the present tonight and tomorrow and for as many years as I have left to live. I will not pay out my life for something that happened when I was fourteen years old.

"You think that girl down there is going to be so thrilled to see us. You think we're so grand because we're Mc-Cameys. No one in New Orleans knows who the McCameys are. That girl lives in a very tough, very snotty world. We would embarrass her to death. An old athlete who married a Mafioso's daughter and a woman who has boyfriends her age. I've seen that world she lives in. They don't like people like us. We scare them to death.

"I can just see DeDe Dalton's society column. 'All work and no play makes Janie Junior Leaguer a dull girl, so Barrett Clare, née Allain, entertained Saturday night at Antoine's for her natural parents who are here for a quick weekend peek at little Buddy Clare. A good cry was had by all.'

"Don't you understand, Guy? This isn't our life we are talking about. It's her life. We might destroy her self-image. Let her go on dreaming I'm some sweet Creole girl who got in trouble and the man died or whoever she dreams we are. What would we do after we met her? Disappear again? Go visit on holidays?

"I'm glad there's a little boy who looks like me. I guess I'm even glad you told me about it. But I won't go see them. I'm going to stay right here on this mountain with this life I made for myself and finish finding out who I am."

Amanda had gotten up off the floor now and was facing him, holding the robe around her.

"What do you want me to do?" he said.

"I want you to go back to Chicago so I can get to work."

"Are you really pregnant?"

"I'm really pregnant."

"Do you want to go to Chicago with me and see my doctor?"

"No, I have a doctor. I have everything I need. I know how your mind works, Guy. I know you've got this scenario all worked out where you and I go live on Esperanza and no one ever gets old and your dick never gets soft because I'm the magic elixir and my face never gets wrinkled and the black people all come back from Detroit and bring coffee around on trays.

"And down from New Orleans for the summer comes this nice little boy to see his granddaddy. Then we go up to Ole Miss for football games and read your unbroken records on the back of the program and everyone thinks we're wonderful. I know what you're thinking.

"It's a nice scenario. Except that even if it came true I wouldn't like it. That's not the life I want for myself. Those aren't the people I want to talk to.

"I'm going to translate the goddamn crazy poems I'm working on and then I'm going to write a novel about the woman who wrote them. Then I'm going to write a book of essays, then a play, then whatever I think up next. I'm going to do the hardest and most exciting things there are to do in the world. Because I'm not afraid of life anymore. I'm not afraid of my power or intelligence or energy. The only thing left in the world that scares me is being afraid of things. I used to believe the past was the present, that we could never live it down, never leave it behind. Bullshit. The past is the past. You can dwell in it or you can move forward. I've thought a lot about all that. I've thought a lot about why I used to drink. Trying to learn something from all those years I wasted.

"And I figured out that what I loved about being drunk was that it made the tapes from the past quit playing in my head. I'm going to learn to do that sober. Well, anyway, it is true that I'm pregnant. Maybe the way I feel now is just some sort of euphoria produced by that."

"Then why are you afraid to see your daughter, if you're so brave?" He was trying one more time.

"Because if she needs me she'll come find me. Because I

leave her to her own life. I won't go pour out my needs on her."

"I'm going to New Orleans and meet her. I'm going to see that boy if it costs me everything I have. I want you with me. But I'll do it alone if I have to."

"Then it's a stalemate. I wish you hadn't come up here and done this to me right now, but it's all right. I have forty more years to live. You know, a strange thing went on between me and that kid I lived with. *We gave each other joy.* I'm going to have some more of that before I die. I'm going to make a life that leaves a place for that to happen."

"Who was he?"

"Just a kid I idealized. But he had this grace about him. He knew how to love. He knew how to be happy. Not many people can do that anymore. Not many white people anyway."

"You won't ever see me again, will you?"

"Of course I will. I'll always be seeing you. Sooner or later, one way or the other."

The next morning she drove him to the airport and watched until the plane vanished from sight behind the far mountains. Until it was the size of a bird, then the size of a ball, then gone through a hole in the clouds. Then the sadness was there, the same old sadness, the bad gift she and Guy had given each other for so many years, and Amanda was sick of the sadness and the face of the girl was before her now. No longer a blank accusing face that could be anyone at all but a face with a name, a name she could not stop saying over and over all afternoon. Barrett, Barrett Allain, Barrett Allain Clare. A woman named Barrett who could win. *She won? Of course she won.*

And now it seemed to Amanda that she had seen her somewhere in New Orleans but she could not remember where. It could have been anytime, anywhere. At Langenstein's, at The Prytania, at a party or a parade or walking down the avenue or around the park. And the little boy? He could have been in any baby carriage, in any stroller, on any playground, anywhere.

A boy, a child, *un enfant*, a boy with hair like her own. A child. Another thing to mourn. A *grandchild. Un petit fils*. She could hardly breathe to think the word and thought to take its power away by rendering it in French.

She put the word away. She drove home from the airport and lay down on her bed and watched the light move and creep across the room like silver, then gold, then red, the soft red light that had fallen across Will's face so many times when he lay beside her. Where is he? Amanda whispered to the light. Then to the stars outside the window as the sky darkened and the stars appeared. Where is he now? The one that really loved me. Where is my old Guy, the one I knew, the one who did not have a silver plane? Where is my child? Where are all the ones who loved and did not love me? Momma, Grandmomma, Guy, Will, Baby Doll and Lavertis and Barrett, Barrett, Barrett, *mon enfant*, my child.

All my languages, all my gifts, all my words and still I am alone. Then lost in remorse and loneliness, Amanda fell asleep still wearing all her clothes. Sometime in the night she rose and drank water and took off the hot wet clothes and slept again and all night long she dreamed terrible dreams. She dreamed she was still married to Malcolm and the girl came and gave her a gift to take him. She carried it to him, thinking it was roses, but when she arrived it became a great swarm of bees and hornets and they were all over him, covering him, and she began to pick and tear the bees from his body. All night long she picked the bees from his sweet face and arms, saying, Forgive me, oh, my God, forgive me.

And the girl stood beside her, laughing at her. There is no boy, she said. There are only the bees.

The other thing was that outrageous pregnancy. For weeks Amanda waged a fierce battle with herself. All day long she faced herself in a Socratic dialogue. When she woke in the mornings she would be thinking one thing. By the time she went to bed she would be thinking another.

She wouldn't ask anyone for help. She refused to see Garth. She made an appointment to see Luke and broke it. She made an appointment with an obstetrician and broke that.

She took walks that lasted one and two and three hours, walking the streets of the little town talking to herself.

This is a problem in logic, she told herself. This is where I decide what my life will be. This is whether I'm free or a pawn of nature.

She would wake from sleep and be filled with a terrible joy, a holy and beautiful wonder.

The next moment it would turn into plain, old terror and she would sit on a chair feeling as though her body no longer belonged to her but was some treacherous thing that wanted to hurt her, wound her, punish her.

A friend from many lives, a son, an ally, a voice sang in her ear. *A special child. A very special child.*

Bullshit, bullshit, bullshit, Amanda said to herself. It's just nature trying to rule us forever. It's a punishment. So I can never be free to do my work, have my own life. It would be an idiot. Something would be terribly wrong with it. I'd have to push a wheelchair all my life. For what? To atone for loving someone for a few weeks one spring. For a few weeks of happiness, if you could call what Will and I did happiness.

Marshall Jordan bore the brunt of Amanda's indecision and morning queasiness.

"Why are you so down on Helene all of a sudden?" he said, looking across the desk at her irritated face. He had been arguing with her for thirty minutes about the poems.

"It isn't all of a sudden. When I first heard about the manuscript I thought it was all so romantic and exciting. Then, the more I worked on them the worse I thought the poems were. Now I think it's her life I object to as much as the poems."

"Her life."

"Goddammit, she was twenty-one years old. I don't know about all this romantic suicide poet stuff. Suicide's a social disease. I've been spending a lot of time this year with someone who got blown off the road by James Alter's death. Will's still recovering from it. I don't like it. I don't think it's justified."

"Well, you can't judge poetry by the poet's life."

"I can if I want to. I mean, what else are you going to judge by that really matters? If someone goes out and gases himself in a garage and lets his kids find the body. Well, that's bad behavior, Marshall."

"I thought you were in sympathy with Helene. Because they took her baby away."

"She should have gone and found the baby instead of killing herself. She was twenty-one years old. I'll tell you one thing. If I'd been that old no one could have taken my child from me. The United States government couldn't have taken it from me."

"You can't imagine what things were like that long ago. Two hundred years ago."

"It's still wrong. It isn't the side I'm on. What did Millay say? I shall die but that is all I shall do for death."

"I like your point of view, Amanda. You know that. But none of this has anything to do with Helene. Stop worrying about the moral implications of it and go on and get the work done. *The Lost Wedding Songs of Helene Renoir* aren't going to lead anyone to suicide. I promise you that."

"I have a lot on my mind right now. Maybe I should put it away and come back to it in a few weeks."

"That might be good. Come back to it with a fresh heart and go on and obey the rules. There are rules, Amanda, whether you like it or not. There are perimeters and prices to pay."

"Do you really believe that?" she said. She was cheering up at the thought of the most eccentric person she had ever known standing up for authority.

"Some days I believe it," he said. "Many days I believe it."

"I'll get my life straightened out and then I'll get back to work and finish it. I'll finish it before too long."

What am I doing? she thought, walking up the long hill to her house through the June heat. What in the name of God am I doing walking along the sidewalk as pregnant as an alley cat? As if I don't have a lick of sense. As if I believed that all I have to do is keep on putting one foot in front of the other and everything will turn out right.

She stopped by a bridge and watched a fat little girl in a

faded dress fishing a narrow creek as if a fish could actually be in such a place. Amanda wanted to go up to her and ask her what in the name of heaven led her to believe a creek in the middle of town was a good place to go fishing but she thought better of it and walked on up the hill. Arkansas, she thought, as she had been doing a lot lately. What a place to make my stand.

✤ ✤ ✤ ✤ ✤ ✤ ✤ *26* ✤ ✤ ✤ ✤ ✤ ✤ ✤

All night Amanda had dreamed she was locked in a room with five other Amandas, six identical Amandas lying on six identical twin beds. The beds were arranged in a circle in a plain room with many windows. It was morning in the dream but none of the Amandas could get up. One by one each Amanda tried to rise from her small bed, then gave up and lay back down. Finally, one Amanda, taller and thicker than the rest, managed to stand up and take charge. She made the thin Amandas get up and make their beds. Then she led them out the door to breakfast.

The real room where Amanda woke up was her same old blue bedroom — pale blue Cannon sheets tacked up at the windows for curtains, blue walls, a soft blue and white Pande Cameron on the floor. A Ross vase stood on a high table holding pussywillow and mayapple and celandine. The room had the clear acrid smell of wildflowers and of cinnamon from the plate of toast Amanda had been eating while she read herself to sleep.

She picked up a half-eaten piece and began to nibble on it, thinking about the dream, then got up and walked out into the hall and stood in front of the dressing room mirror with her hands on her stomach.

Well, she thought. Either I've got to do it or I've got to fix it.

"Fix it!" she said out loud, looking straight into her own eyes in the mirror. "Fix it! No, not fix it. Abort it. Abort it and give it back to the universe. Fix it. Fuck it. Abort it. Whatever. But I've got to make up my mind."

She went upstairs and took off her gown and began to do yoga postures. It was beginning to be difficult to do some of the stretches and her body felt strange and confused and unwell. She stretched out on the floor. Then sat up and pulled her body into a forward bend, sliding her hands down the sides of her legs, laying her head on top of her knees, breathing and breathing, making the blood rush into the hard knot of the solar plexus, where the yogis believe the body stores its problems and its fears.

It's no good, she thought. It's all wrong. It's a parasite. It's going to suck the life out of me. Why hasn't he called me? *He hasn't even called me.* He could be dead for all I know.

She pulled her body into a headstand, balancing beautifully in the middle of the room, trying to concentrate on her breathing, trying to stop all the thoughts.

It's not a baby. A fetus is a fetus is a fetus. When the child is born the parents start dying. It's a hostage. All it will do is kill me. I can't do this to myself. I can't allow it. I can't let it happen. I don't have a choice. I can't have a baby. I'll die. They'll cut me open and I'll die. This time it will really kill me.

The phone interrupted her with its ringing. It was Katie, wanting her to go that evening to a lecture.

"You have to help me, Katie. I want you to go with me to have an abortion. I want to go first thing in the morning."

"Does Will know about this? Have you told him yet?"

"Hell, no, and he isn't going to know. It isn't any of his business. It's my business. It's my body. It's my life. And I'm going to Tulsa and get it over with and I want you to go with me. Will you go?"

"Of course I'll go," Katie said. "Why do you want to go to Tulsa? You could get it done right here."

"I won't do it here. I already called the clinic in Tulsa. I won't do it in this town."

"Okay," Katie said. "If you're sure you want to do it, let's get it over with."

"I'm sure," Amanda said, her voice rising. "I'm too old to have a baby! Tell me something good, Katie. Tell me something wonderful."

"The world is light and air and stone and water," Katie said. "That's all I know for sure."

"I want to leave early in the morning," Amanda said. "As soon as it's light."

"Come spend the night with me," Katie said. "Come sleep in my bed."

The morning felt like fall. Amanda and Katie Vee rose at dawn and drove out of town into the cool white light of the first nice day in weeks. They turned off Highway 71 onto 62, the winding, curving one-lane road that leads west into Oklahoma, into the Indian Nation.

"Look out there," Katie said. They were moving into rolling farm country now, the early morning sun lighting up the summer fields. "God, it's a beautiful day. The whole world washed clean after the rain." Amanda didn't answer so she gave up and they drove in silence. Amanda held her wrist in her hand, tracing the long blue lines of the veins, then moving her fingers up, probing deep below the muscles to feel the long bones of the arm, remembering a vision she had when Luke was massaging her, a vision of the bones of her lower arm, as though it were a marvelous secret just revealed to her. She imagined the baby's tiny half-formed skeleton curled up inside her, deep in the fastness of the soft red world of the womb.

They had come down a long hill to a clear blue lake. It was covered on one end with lily pads like a dark green shadow. Amanda imagined sailing across it in a white sail-boat. I should have taken him to the Virgin Islands to go sailing, she thought, imagining Will on a sailboat in the blue Caribbean, smoking and playing his guitar, smiling at her.

They turned a curve and came upon a field of fescue with a great bare tree in the center, a huge white ghost in a field.

"I love to see the bones of trees," Katie said. "The architecture." Amanda wasn't paying any attention to her so she gave up talking and paid attention to her driving, enjoying the sight of the neat farms with their fields divided like pieces of delicate needlepoint. She drove on, imagining what they must look like from the air, moving down the little white strip of highway between the fields *as if what they were doing was the most important thing in the world, as if what they were doing made the slightest bit of difference to the stars.*

They had crossed the Grand River now. Amanda sighed and looked out the window.

"Go to sleep," Katie said. Amanda did as she was told and Katie drove on into Tulsa, past the huge billboards advertising the Gilcrease Museum and the Zooarium and the Tulsa Ballet, past the signs to Yale and Harvard Avenues and Utica and Delaware and the Cimarron Turnpike and Broken Arrow.

The receptionist at the clinic was a placid-looking girl with black braids. Amanda filled out the form and handed it over and was led back to a bright office with huge Calder prints on the wall.

"Do you want me with you?" Katie said.

"No," Amanda said. "Wait for me out there. I'll do the rest of it alone. I'm not a child. I'm all right. I know what I'm doing."

"I want to explain the process to you," the young doctor said, leaning back in his chair. Behind his head three benign Calder elephants in shades of red and pink were lifting their trunks in salute. "You know most of this, I suppose, but I'll go over it."

"I hate Calder," Amanda said. "He's so lifeless. His stuff always reminds me of Aspen. I was in Aspen one year and every other restaurant in town had Calder prints on the wall. Every time I see Calder I think of matching His-and-Hers ski outfits from Neiman's."

"My wife bought them," the doctor said. "She likes modern stuff."

"I'm sorry," Amanda said. "I didn't mean to interrupt you. Go on. Explain the process. I'm listening."

"You're pretty far along for our procedures," he said. "But there's nothing to worry about, of course. We like to do what is essentially a D and C at your stage, a paracervical block, an IV of Demoral and Valium. Then we'll dilate the cervix and put in a suction curette and suck out the contents. There's no real discomfort." He was looking at her over his folded hands, a young earnest-looking man with wire glasses on his nose. Amanda looked back at him, then lifted her eyes to the elephants, returning their flat glassy lifeless stares.

"Then I can go right home?" she said. "Today, I mean."

"Oh, yes," he said. "Of course. As soon as you're rested." A nurse had entered the room and was standing behind them holding a hospital gown. "It's two hundred and fifty dollars. If you'd like to go on and pay us. Then you can go with Miss Ingersol. She'll help you undress."

Amanda raised her fist to her mouth. She breathed down into her fingers. And leave my baby here with you and these fucking two-dimensional elephants, she thought. And leave his little bones in Tulsa. And be as old and scared as all the other assholes in my so-called culture. No, there's nothing left in me that would let me do that. Amanda stood up. The nurse held out the gown. The elephants breathed down on the little doctor's sandy hair. Amanda looked from the nurse to the doctor. She was shaking her head.

"I don't think so," she said out loud. She was standing up very tall, almost shaking now, looking at the silly well-meaning doctor and the Calder elephants and the plastic uterus and pink plastic reproductive organs on top of the filing cabinets and the expensive antique desk and the green wastebasket and the tacky red carpet and the impassive face of the bored-looking nurse. She wanted to reach out and squash the whole scene together like a cardboard accordion.

"No," she said. "I'm not going to do this. And not because there's anything wrong with what you're doing and not because I know what I'm doing but because I haven't any business in this room, and you'd better let me out of here before I go crazy and kill somebody."

The nurse moved back behind the chair. The doctor slid his hands down to the emergency button on his desk and Amanda turned and moved out the door and down the hall and into the waiting room and grabbed Katie Vee by the arm and led her out the door.

They went out into the bright Tulsa day. Katie went around the car and got in. Amanda followed her to the driver's side. "Move over," she said. "I'm driving."

"Sure, honey," Katie said. "Anything you say."

"Well, don't look at me like that," Amanda said. "There's nothing wrong with me. All I am is pregnant, for God's sake. Women have been having babies for fifty million years with nothing going wrong."

"All right," Katie said. "Who's arguing?"

Amanda drove back down onto the expressway and turned off onto Cleveland Street going into the heart of downtown Tulsa.

"Where are we going?" Katie said.

"Do you have to get back for anything tonight?" Amanda asked.

"I don't guess so," Katie said. "I can do whatever you need me to do."

"Well, I've got three hundred and fifty dollars in cash in that pocketbook," Amanda said. "And I'm going to have me some fun and I need you to have some fun with me. To hell with all this fucking morose dark romantic nihilistic abortion bullshit. I'm going to celebrate. I'm probably the oldest pregnant woman in American letters. I'll bet I'm the oldest pregnant *translator* in the whole fucking world and I'm going to celebrate."

"I'm with you, Amanda," Katie said. "It's your day one way or the other."

Amanda drove down Seventh Street and on down Cincinnati and up to the front of the plush new Williams Plaza Hotel and got out and gave the car to the doorman.

She walked up to the desk, rented a suite of rooms, and told the desk clerk to have flowers sent up. "And a bottle of white wine. A Piesporter if they have it. And hors d'oeuvres. And tell them to hurry. We just got back from Africa. We're dying. You can't imagine what it's been like."

"Sure," the clerk said. "I'll have someone here in a second for the luggage."

"There isn't any luggage," Amanda said. "We had to throw it all away. Had to get rid of everything. We're lucky to be here ourselves. We're lucky to be alive."

A bellboy led them through the lobby to a wall of brass elevators beside a pool. A shining escalator ascended from the pool like a steel waterfall.

"This trip is picking up, Amanda," Katie said. "I think we're finally getting somewhere."

"So we didn't find the Nile. So a few years more have flown by in our search for the elusive Black Orchid. The artist's life, like that of the philosopher, is only in the doing. Come Katherine, the elevator awaits. We will drink and eat. We will rest from our journey."

The bellboy giggled and led them to their rooms, a beautiful blue and beige suite with large comfortable chairs and antique armoires instead of closets. Katie sank down in a chair, watching her friend. "What have you been reading?" she said. "Have you been reading Harrison again, Amanda?"

"This baby," Amanda began, making an elaborate bow in Katie's direction. "This baby was conceived on the banks of the Buffalo River. A holy river, well known for its powers, a fitting place for a pharaoh to make himself manifest. Although of course the river has been kept secret for many years. At the moment of conception I breathed deep of this holy river and therefore . . ."

"Spare me the details of your sex life until after I have a drink," Katie said. "Call that woman and see if she's sending that wine up here."

In a few minutes a waiter appeared at the door. He wheeled in a small table spread with a white cloth. An oriental boy was right behind him with a tray of hors d'oeuvres, liver pâté, fat boiled shrimp and several cheeses.

The waiter opened the wine and served it to them in cold stemmed glasses. Then he and the serving boy backed out of the room thanking them for the tip in deep Oklahoma accents.

"Do you want to talk about any of the events of today?" Katie said.

"No," Amanda said, draining her glass and reaching for the bottle to refill it. "All I want to do right now is get drunk."

They drank the bottle of wine and ordered another one and drank that. Then Amanda decided they should go shopping.

"We can't go out to dinner in this swanky hotel dressed like this," she said. "We've got to buy something to wear. I want to go shopping. I haven't been shopping since I moved to the Ozarks. I've forgotten how to read a price tag. They may take back my citizenship papers."

"That three hundred and fifty dollars isn't going to last very long at this rate," Katie said.

"Who gives a damn," Amanda said. "We'll charge the clothes to Jesus. We'll put them on the old all-American Jesus Visa card. Come on, Katie, I've got to buy me some maternity clothes. Goddammit, I'm the oldest fucking pregnant translator in the Western Hemisphere, maybe the world. I can't go around dressed any old way."

They went tramping out into downtown Tulsa but Amanda couldn't find a store anywhere that sold ladies' clothing. "What's wrong with this place?" she said. "What kind of a town doesn't have any stores?"

"It's a planned city," Katie said. "You have to go to the shopping center."

"Well, then, by God, we'll just go to one." Amanda walked out into the street, hailed a taxi, and told him to drive them to the nearest shopping center. "There's Utica Square," the driver said. "You want to go there?"

"As long as it's got a bar and a department store," Amanda said.

They stopped in the bar for a double martini, then marched into John A. Brown's and took up a big dressing room and started trying on clothes. Amanda tried on a dozen different outfits before she found something she liked, a pair of loose-fitting blue cotton pants and a long gray jacket with frog fasteners.

"How do I look?" she said, admiring herself in the three-way mirror.

"Like a Chinese peasant," Katie said. "Is this what we're in for for the duration of your confinement, Chinese rice field chic?"

"Damn right," Amanda said. "And this is just the beginning. If I'm going to be the oldest pregnant woman in Fayetteville, by God I'll be the best dressed. I've got to find some yellow, Katie. I want to wear a lot of yellow. For the sun god. Well, what do you think? You like these pants or not?"

The salesgirl was standing in the door of the dressing room giggling.

"Come on in," Amanda said. "Join the party. I'm pregnant you know, unbelievable as that may seem. *Enceinte*, knocked up, in the so-called family way, as pregnant as a cat, certified for sure pregnant and fixing to stay that way. That's what I'm doing here, at John A. Brown's. Getting something to wear to a party I'm having. I want you to come to my party. Bring your friends. Bring your boyfriend. What time you get off today?"

"No kidding?" the girl said.

"No kidding. I am. You are at this moment in the presence of the oldest pregnant translator of Middle French in the Western Hemisphere, maybe the world, and this party is going to be going on all day today and into the night. I would like for you to meet Miss Katie Vee-for-Victory-Over-Japan Dunbar, the best potter in the state of Arkansas, maybe the world. Come on and go with us. Come join us as soon as you get off work. I'm telling you you don't want to miss this party."

"Well," the girl said. "I have a date with my boyfriend."

"Bring him," Amanda said. "Bring anyone you want.

I'm taking everyone out to this authentic French restaurant I found right here in the heart of Tulsa."

They had moved out to the cash register. A group of salesladies and customers were standing around, hanging onto every word.

"As I was telling this young lady," Amanda said. "As I was informing her while I chose my wardrobe for my coming confinement I am having a baby, all by myself, for myself. It has a father but he isn't here. I am having this baby for my own self. I will probably never let anyone else hold it. Except for Katie. I am definitely never going to send it to school. As I intend to teach it everything it needs to know right up there on Mount Sequoyah in Fayetteville, Arkansas. Have it all planned. I am going to have this goddamn baby and I am going to make it happy. I am sick and tired of everyone in my so-called culture going around being miserable and unhappy and asleep and dead all the time. Sick of everyone being so goddamn sad all the time. I am going to have this baby and I am going to make it happy. I am going . . ."

"Listen," Katie said to the salesgirl. "How about calling us a taxi. I think I better be getting her back to the hotel."

The taxi driver was a middle-aged man with a crucifix hanging from the rearview mirror.

"I started liking the Pope after all," Amanda told him, leaning up into the front seat. "I used to hate him. I wanted to machine gun him. Well, I changed my mind. I'm going to write him a letter. He's a bad poet though, really bad poetry. What the hell, maybe all he needs is a better translator. I'm the oldest fucking pregnant translator of Middle

French in the Western World, maybe the universe. I am, you will also be glad to hear, the oldest pregnant woman in the state of Arkansas. Any day they'll be having me down to Little Rock to the medical school. Are you a man of babies? Do you have children?"

"Fifteen," he said.

"In that case I would like to meet your wife," she said. "Drive us on over there. Look, you want to come to a party? Look, will you stop off by a liquor store? I can't keep this party going with nothing to drink. You can't keep up a party when you're sober."

But she was fading now and fell back against Katie's arm. By the time they got to the hotel it took Katie and the taxi driver and a doorman to get her up to her room.

"I got to have another drink," she said as they were putting her to bed. "Got to keep the party going. People might be coming any minute."

"Why don't you eat something?" Katie said. "I thought pregnant women were supposed to eat."

"Right," Amanda said. "Got to eat. Got to feed the little fuckers or they suck all the calcium out of your teeth. That's what they taught us at the old baby-stealing home. Feed the little fuckers or they suck out all the calcium. Suck it all out. Holes in your teeth. Holes in your heart. Holes in your skull." She picked up the empty bottle and turned it up to her mouth to drain out the last drops. "Drank all my wine like a good girl, Sister, you fat bitch. Amanda drank it all gone."

Katie Vee took the bottle out of her hand and put her under the covers. She sat beside her holding her hand.

"He's going to be pickled in alcohol, one way or the

other today," Amanda said. "Poor little fucker. He'll be all shriveled up."

"She," Katie said. *"She'll* be all shriveled up."

"He or she. She or he," Amanda said. "What the fuck. What difference does it make?"

* * * * * * * * *27* * * * * * * * *

"*Are* you going to have the amniocentesis?" Katie said. She was trying one more time.

"No," Amanda said. "Because I'm going to have it anyway. Because I'm going to love it if it turns out to be a lump of clay."

"What did she say?" Clinton said.

"She said she wanted to drive to Little Rock to have Drew Kilgore photograph her naked while she's pregnant. She wants to go this weekend. Well, don't look like that.

"Oh, yeah, this week she's a samurai. Did I tell you that? She is turning herself into a samurai."

"She looks more like sumo lately," Clinton said, laughing delightedly at his own joke.

"Well, this isn't funny," Katie said. "She's going to have the baby at home. She and Garth and Luke cooked that up. Luke's going to deliver it. She's over there right now, in something called the Full Warrior Position, practicing her breathing. She's going to invite her friends. I'm not kidding. She's going to invite *you*."

"Well, I'm not going," Clinton said. "I do a lot of things for you, Katie, but I'm *definitely* not going to be the token black at a home birth."

"Well, you have to go," Katie said. "She had a cesarean

section when she was young. If anything goes wrong I want you to be there to help me carry her to the hospital."

"The token *black orderly* at a home birth?" Clinton said. "Wait'll I tell the team."

"She says a birth is a feast," Katie said. "She says you should invite your friends."

"That's because she never worked in a hospital," Clinton said. "Just wait till it starts coming."

"What about the father?" Clinton said. "Has she told him yet?"

"Oh, haven't you heard?" Katie said. "It doesn't have a father. She willed it into being, all by herself, out of light and air. Well, I swear I think she's starting to believe it."

"I heard he was in Africa," Clinton said. "That's what they're saying down at Roger's."

"He got sent to the Sudan with a crew," Katie said. "He wrote her. She finally got a letter. But I don't know if she wrote him back."

"Is she working?"

"All the time," Katie said. "In between childbirth classes and yoga postures and Tai Chi forms."

"I'm going to talk to her," Clinton said. "If she doesn't write to him, I'm going to."

Of course Amanda did write to him. It was November before the letter caught up with him on the *Marilee Breaux*, a supply boat working in the Gulf off Port Sulphur, Texas.

Will finished up his work on the shelves, made some entries in a log, and climbed up on deck. He walked past the generating engines and coiled chain lines and barrels of oil to the far end of the aft deck and climbed up on top of a twenty-by-twenty-foot freezer box to read the letter again. He lay back on one elbow and read it for the tenth time that day. Then he read it for the eleventh time. All around him the dying day was turning into stars. *He wanted to tell someone.* He wanted to tell his mother and father and every friend he had in the world and all his relatives. Most of all he wanted to believe it himself. He opened it up and read it for the twelfth time. It was scrawled in Amanda's huge handwriting on a yellow legal pad.

Dear Will,

I have done an awesome and terrible thing to you, or vice versa.

Sometime in January I am going to have a baby. This is not a joke, Will. Remember that night we camped on the river? I think it was that night.

I dreamed last night we were standing somewhere in a bare field holding on to each other. A wind came up. Then a meadow of soft green wheat began growing up all around us, stretching out in four directions as far as my dream could see.

I wake sometimes from naps so full of ecstasy. I can't describe it to you. It's like the first time you see mountains.

Katie and Clinton insist the baby is half yours under all ancient and modern law. They threatened to write you if I didn't. Therefore, if you polish your boots and come calling I *may* let you claim your share.

Self-centered I am. Stingy, never.

I look gorgeous,
Me

A week later there was another letter. It was longer, sadder, slower, messier. Amanda had written it at dawn on a beautiful fall day.

. . . most of the time I'm completely happy and engaged as if I'm doing everything right. It's like I've figured out how to make it work no matter what goes on outside of me.

The goddamn translations are a bitch. Marshall won't let me break his rule-riddled craft. I'll be glad to be done with them and start on my own work. Well, nothing interesting is easy (I guess). He won't let me change the original even if it helps the poem and let's face it, whatever else she was, Helene was not a great poet. Sloppy, very sloppy. I'm writing reviews for the *Gazette*. I have more than I can do. Dum, dum, dum.

I am lonely for you. Well, I am. My body is strong and lonely. Still, all is well. If Guy would leave me alone. He's begging me to let him call her. Her name is Barrett Clare. How strange to think I know her name. She lives on State Street in uptown New Orleans. Practically next door to where I used to live. I dream of her. I dream I want to take her into the water with me but she won't take her clothes off. I dream terrible things. Still, all is well.

Katie agrees with me that I shouldn't mess into her life. She's married to a lawyer. She could find me if she wanted to. I think she must have some beautiful orderly life. I can't take a chance on bothering her. Oh, Will, I want to bother her. I want to ask her to forgive me. Does she need to forgive me? Oh, well, all is well. I'm starting to like Tai Chi better than yoga. I have an inconstant heart.

Are you sure you'll be here by January? Tell me again. I don't know what I'm saying except I love you. You know all that already. Whatever it means.

-*A*-

⚜

Will put the letter away and began to dream strange dreams about it. He dreamed he was in a gray and white striped car with *Klansman* written on the dashboard. He dreamed he drove to Chicago and killed Guy. He dreamed he was standing somewhere bringing her children, all these naked little children with laughing hands raised to the sky. He dreamed he was alone on the sea plucking children from the water and handing them to her. All night he labored in the water while on a pier his friends played music. Every now and then he would catch the eye of one of them and think they were coming to help but no one ever came.

At night he dreamed such fancy dreams and in the daytime he dreamed other, more practical, perhaps more dangerous dreams.

He was lying on the freezer box one afternoon with his head on a coiled line thinking about Amanda. He thought of what it would be like to go up the hill to her house, all dressed up in a white suit maybe, and she would give the child to him. He tried to imagine taking it in his hands, tried to imagine what it would feel like, all soft and breathing as softly as a trout. That was the best metaphor he could come up with, as he had had very little to do with babies in his life.

Will lay there on top of the freezer box thinking about holding the baby in his hands, trying to imagine Amanda pregnant but he could not imagine it. All he could imagine was Amanda as she had always looked with perhaps a very small football-sized protrusion beneath a negligee.

"Well, I wasn't ready for this," he said out loud. "But I can go with it. I can handle it. I wonder if everyone at

Roger's knows about it. I guess everyone in town knows about it by now."

Will sighed and a dark thought crossed his mind. What if I never get back? What if the boat goes down? What if she doesn't stay there till I get there? Shit, she doesn't need me for anything. She probably only wrote me because she had to. Will's best friend had been deserted by his young wife right after the birth of a child and he had had to get drunk with him a dozen times to watch him suffer.

What if she goes off like that? he thought. What if she goes off like Sue Ellen did? She doesn't need me. I never have been able to figure out what she wants me for anyway. I haven't got any money. I haven't got a thing in the world to offer her. What could I offer her anyway? She's already got everything in the world.

Will sat up and lit a cigarette thinking dark and darker thoughts about Amanda going off to New Orleans or Paris or California carrying his baby. Well, I'll just follow her. It's my kid. She can't go off and leave without asking me. That's terrible, losing a kid like Bobby did. Goddamn, no wonder she's so crazy about all that stuff down in New Orleans.

Well, shit, she ought to go on and see that girl and get it over with. That's one thing she doesn't have. She doesn't have that girl. Well, I'm just going to go find her and tell her about her mother. When I get back to New Orleans by God I'm going to take off and find her and tell her she's got a mother anyone in the whole world would want to know about.

Goddammit, I'm going to do it. I'm definitely going to do it. Will lit another cigarette and lay back on his elbows smoking, looking up at the stars.

Goddammit, nobody could take a baby away from me that belonged to me. I'll find that girl for her. I'll give her something that fucking rich husband of hers couldn't give her or that lousy goddamn football-playing bastard or any man she's ever known.

Goddammit, I'll give her what she really wants. I know she's going to get tired of me like she has every man she's ever fucked with but she won't forget me. No one in the world will do this for her but me. What's that goddamn football player up to, begging her to go with him. Why is he too chicken to do it himself? Well, I'm not scared to do it. If I didn't know who my folks were, I'd be glad to find out. Anyone'd be glad to find out. Unless they were crazy.

I'm getting this fixed up before that baby comes, by God. I'm getting this fixed up as soon as I get back to land.

Will stood up and stretched his arms up to the sky, feeling the long muscles pull down the sides of his body to his legs, full of wonderful feelings of decision and control. He looked out across the calm surface of the Gulf of Mexico and yawned and stretched, pitying the poor confused creatures on the land. He climbed down off the box whistling a little tune and went below and got out his guitar and started making up a song to sing to his baby. It was a song with many bright chords in G and C. C, D, E, F, G, C, D, E. C, D, E, F, G, C, D. How to count from one to eight. One, Two, Three, Four, Five, Six, Seven, Eight. One, two, three, four, one, two, three, four. I'll make a bass player out of him, Will thought. That's the heart of the band. I wish someone had started me out on the bass.

Late in November the *Marilee Breaux* was docked overnight in Port Sulphur, Texas. The first thing Will did was get drunk. It was late the next afternoon before he got up the courage to do what he was dreading doing. It was late afternoon and it was about to rain and in a few minutes the boat was going back out into the Gulf for a four-week stint. He had put it off as long as he could put it off and he was hung over. As usual, he thought. I've really got to quit drinking that damn Jose Cuervo.

He was standing about a hundred yards from the boat, leaning up against a creosoted pole, staring up into the telephone lines. One of the ship's cooks was using the pay phone, hurling Cajun insults into the receiver.

Will was lighting one cigarette after the other staring up into the lines, thinking, those wires go from that phone booth to Amanda's daughter, and all in the world I have to do to put an end to all this sad shit is to get a dime out of my pocket and call information and find out who named Clare lives on State Street and call that number and say, Hello, this is Will Lyons. I'm a nice person. I'm in love with your mother. Please talk to me. And then she'll call the cops. Who do I think I am to mess into the lives of rich people? Well, I'm William David Lyons of Fayetteville, Arkansas and at least I know right from wrong and if Amanda was my mother I'd want to know about it.

The cook yelled one last Coonass command at his wife or daughter, or whoever Michelle was, and slammed the phone down on the hook. The receiver was still warm when Will put it to his ear. I am a friend of your mother's, he said as he dialed. I am a person who usually minds my own business.

"My name is Will Lyons," he said when she answered. "I'm from Fayetteville, Arkansas and I want to tell you who your real mother is. I know this is a terrible thing to call you up like this. I haven't ever done anything like this in my life. Your mother wants to know you. Is there any way you could let me come and talk to you?"

"Who is this?" she said. "Who are you calling? How dare you call me like this."

"I'm a nice person. This isn't some kind of crank call. I wish you would just listen to me for a moment and I could explain why I'm calling."

"What is your name? Tell me your name."

"My name is Will Lyons. I just got back to shore. I've been out on the rigs. I know you don't understand why I'm doing this."

"I don't want to hear this," she said. "I don't want to talk to you. I can't hear you. I can't listen to this. I don't know who you are."

"Please just let me talk."

"Don't do this. Don't do this to me. I don't want to hear anything you have to say." Hang up, she said to herself. You're supposed to hang up. You aren't supposed to let them hear your voice. "I won't hear this," she said and put the phone down on its cradle. She turned and stared up the wide mahogany stairs at the paintings of Charles's grandparents in their ball clothes and on up into the colored light of the stained-glass window in the alcove. It has come, she thought. And it is as terrible as I knew it would be. It is as cold as marble. No, it is colder than that. I am a cuckoo bird. I have no right to be in this house. I have no right to be anywhere.

She tried Gustave's number but the line was busy. She told the housekeeper she was leaving and started out the door, meaning to go to his office and sit outside the door until he let a patient out into the hall. He'll have to see me, she thought. He can't turn me away. Not after this.

When she reached the porch Charles came running up the stairs in one of his rages. "Bill Treen's having David over and they're going to the country club and Mrs. Treen didn't invite me. Now there isn't anyone for me to play with. *Now what am I going to do?*"

"Oh, my," she said. "You can go with me. I'll take you to the club if you want to go. What are they going to do there? There isn't a thing to do out there."

"They're going to have supper. They're going to eat there."

"Then you can too. We'll call Trip to go with you. You and Trip and I'll go." She pulled him into her arms. It was hard to keep him in friends. He made such terrible demands on people. He was going to be better, Gustave said. He was going to be better any day now.

This is my child, she thought, feeling his intense body calming down in her arms. This is my child and somewhere I have a real mother. Not Katherine. Katherine of the big hips is not my mother. I hate to look at her hips. At her fat dumb hips. Danielle has hips like that too. Thank God she is not my mother if it would give me hips like that. And I am going to go crazy. I am going to go stark raving mad.

I can wait until tomorrow to see Gustave. I guess I can wait. I am standing outside the door all the time. I am outside the door forever. It was a line from a poem she had written the year before when she was going through a spell of wanting to search for her parents. Later she had abandoned the idea and the poem.

*"For each of us carries in his heart the Jocasta
who begs Oedipus for God's sake not to in-
quire further."*

SEARCH

*The world lies on its back
beside its oceans.
Beneath its skin hidden rivers
sing to the moon.*

*I am the foundling
waiting to knock at the door
of my mother. Here in my arms
are all of these kisses.
Why is the door knob heavy as doom?
I hear the heart rock in its old soft room.*

*Perhaps she will offer me money
or buy me fine shirts with four holes
in the buttons.
Perhaps she will show me my brothers.*

*We will move together like children in snow,
rolling this new stuff into slick balls
to throw at each other.
Building a fortress of ice
while she stands at the window
baking my lifetime of pies,
wiping her white hands
at the sides of her eyes.*

Six hundred miles to the northwest Amanda rolled over
in the bed and drew her knees up against her stomach and
ran her hands across her body, trying to stay in touch, mov-

ing her hands across her shoulders and legs and thighs. This is my body which is not broken by you. This is my flesh and blood. This is myself. I am going to stop being alone in the world. Already I am not alone. Already a miracle is inside of me. Already a miracle has occurred. My child, my ally, are you listening, I love you so much. I can not tell you how I love you. Be well, be whole, stay well.

Amanda rolled up into a ball. She was swollen now and the baby moved inside her. She could feel its head underneath her hand, or what seemed to be a foot.

Where is the other one? Where is the lost one? Where is my little girl? Oh, shit, I won't think of that. I won't lie here pitying myself. Oh, God, I would like so much to see how she looks. Oh, I would love to touch her with my hand. She won. He said she won.

No, no, no, no, no, don't think of that. Don't ruin the present with the ruined past. Or, oh, shit, you big baby, go on and lie here and cry if that's all you can think up to do.

I know what, I'll pretend I'm in the water. I'll pretend I'm in the bayou swimming to the bridge, singing to my baby, taking him out for a swim.

This is my baby, this is my body which is not broken by anything, this is my own flesh and blood, this is me. All is well. I am well. I am doing exactly what I want to do every minute of my life. Every day is holy. I am in charge of my own life and the life of this child. Nothing bad will happen because I will it so. My will be done, goddammit. My will be done. And when it is over I will go and find her too. I will have her too. I will take back the territory of my life. Now I will take back all the territory. I am strong enough to do anything I want to do. Anything on earth I want to do I'll do.

Not with Guy either. Fuck Guy trying to blackmail me into doing it. I'll do it alone in my way on my own. He didn't help me when I needed him. I'll do it my way because goddammit I want to. I'll tell her what they did to me. I'll tell her what those goddamned nuns did to me.

The deckhands were casting off as Will hurried up the gangplank. What a creepy-sounding lady, he thought. Well, shit, I don't care. I'm going to try again. Goddammit, I'm trying again. We're going to get this stuff figured out before it goes any further.

He threw his bag down on the deck and started helping coil the lines. A storm was blowing in from the south. The sea was beginning to look like a place where a man could forget his troubles. And that suited William David Lyons to a tee.

It was Christmas Eve in Fayetteville. All morning everyone in town had been running around in the cold bright weather taking each other loaves of homemade bread and plates of cookies and jars of tomato relish and artichoke preserves and bottles of wine and liqueurs and whiskey.

Clinton was a sensation playing tennis at the Springhill Club in green pants and a red sweater. The successful town writers were all down at the House of Books signing copies of their books. The rest were down at Roger's telling each other guarded stories about their works in progress.

On the campus everything was deserted except for a few professors hiding from their families behind stacks of papers.

All morning the sky was blue. The air was cold. Many scarves and hats and gloves were being worn and lost and wrapped up. The organist was practicing carols at the Episcopal Church. They were very old carols that almost no one was going to know the tunes to. The young sexton at the Baptist Church was screwing the preacher's sister in the vestry. Divorcees were calling up their old spouses and asking them to come by for a drink. Children were sitting in front of television sets trying to stop asking what time it was.

In the afternoon it began to rain.

⚜

It was 86 degrees in Morgan City, Louisiana. When the boat docked at Pier 23, Will was the first one down the gangplank.

"Come on, Ferriday," he said to his buddy. "Take the hundred and let me get on out of here. It's Christmas Eve. It's fourteen hours to Arkansas and I've got to stop off in New Orleans."

"I'll never see that car again if I let you take it," Ferriday said. "Give me three hundred to make my bad dreams go away."

"I could rent one for half that," Will said. "If I had a license. Well, you got me, buddy. You know that. I'll give you two fifty. How's that? Is it a deal?"

"If that car's not back here by Three Kings Day I'm sending the cops for you."

"I'll have it back by New Year's. Come on. Show me where it is."

Ferriday led him to a blue Ford sedan parked on a company lot. Will threw his bags into the back and slid behind the wheel.

"I won't forget this, old buddy," he said. "I'll pay you back. You'll see."

He headed out of the Nickles shipyards, past the lay barges and a jet barge up on dry dock. It was the *Sally Jolin*. A friend of Will's had lost his hand in the storm that wrecked it, tangled in lines trying to tie up to a rig in twelve-foot seas. Will tightened his own hands on the wheel. Fuck thinking about all that shit, he thought. It's Christmas Eve. I've got thirty-seven hundred dollars in my pocket and I've got some work to do. He touched the pocket with the check in it, hardly able to imagine so much money all his own at one time. A stake, goddammit, I've got a stake.

He headed out Highway 90 from Morgan City to New Orleans, a narrow asphalt strip leading through the marshes. They were still as green as summer in late December. A heron flew up, flapping its scrawny legs. Jesus, Will thought. Jesus, this is crazy country.

Old Highway 90 that the rig workers call Death Alley. Here and there along the highway were small white crosses. At first Will thought they were some weird Catholic thing or markers for dead pets. Then he saw there were names on the crosses. Who put those crosses there? he wondered. What a creepy thing to do. He turned on the radio and stopped at the next filling station for a beer.

When he got to New Orleans he stopped at a bar for a real drink. For courage, he thought. No, not for courage. Just, by God, because I want it. He looked up the address. Charles Clare, 1564 State Street. He sipped on the drink, trying to decide whether to call first or go on over, trying to decide whether to get a haircut. Trying to decide how to do it.

If I'm going to do it, I can't fuck it up. Well, I am going to do it. I am definitely going to do it.

"Do you know where State Street is?" he asked the bartender.

"Sure," the man said. "I used to deliver booze up there. That's the ritzy part of town. Just go down Carrollton until you hit Saint Charles. It'll be off to the side in about fifteen blocks. You can't miss it. What you going up there for?"

"To get a Christmas present for my girl," Will said. "To pick up a surprise."

Barrett was talking to her husband on the phone. He was in Vail, Colorado teaching his legal secretary how to ski.

He was stuck in Vail, Colorado in a snowstorm and it really wasn't his fault he couldn't get home for Christmas.

"Well, you just get as mad as you like because I'm up to my ass in your pouting anyway. So, listen, just shut up a second and listen. That's Mother Nature out there, baby. I didn't make the weather. Now I want you to go down to Adler's and pick up that watch I ordered for Charles. . . . Well, by God, I'll call Gabe Adler and make sure it's ready. All you have to do is go pick it up. . . . Because I'm not there to pick it up. Because I'm stuck in this goddamn snowstorm."

"He's only five years old," Barrett said. "He can't even tell time."

"Look, Barrett, don't go throwing any of your psycho guilt trips on me. Will you get the watch or not? Because I'll call Mother and she'll send Laddy if you're too lazy to do it."

"Do you really mean to tell me you aren't going to be here tonight to go to mass with him?"

"I'm in a goddamn snowstorm. How many times do I have to tell you that? I can't even see out the fucking window. Now are you going to go get that watch or not? Let me talk to Charles. I want to talk to him."

"He isn't here," she said. "He's over at David's. I have to go now. I have a lot to do this morning. I hope the storm lets up." She hung the phone up without waiting for a reply. She hung it up very carefully, then reached up and unplugged it from the wall.

She walked into the front room where Charles and three servants were hanging the huge flocked tree from the ceiling. It was a tradition at 1864 State Street to hang the tree from the ceiling on Christmas Eve. The people the Clares had bought the house from had begun the tradition. Barrett had kept it up. People in the neighborhood liked to walk by on Christmas Eve and see it hanging in the wide front windows as if suspended in air. Every time someone in the neighborhood walked down State Street and saw the tree hanging in its place in the windows of the old Georgian house they knew that one more year had escaped being gobbled up by the cold future. Every time they looked in that window on Christmas Eve they were reassured to know that at least a few people in the world still had enough money to do things right.

The Clares' gardener was up on a ladder pulling the cable through the ring. His wife was measuring the distance from the floor with a yardstick. She was in a bad mood. She had nine children and fourteen grandchildren to cook for if she could ever get through with this silly shit and Dalton was acting like a Tom, something he always did around the Clares, especially at Christmas.

Barrett's housekeeper, Sara, was standing by the window getting irritated about all the flocking that was getting on the rugs and the tinsel Charles was running around throwing on the chairs and sofas as if he didn't have good sense.

"When's Mr. Charles coming home?" the gardener said, seeing Barrett in the door. "I was hoping to get to tell him Merry Christmas before we leave."

"He's in a snowstorm," she said. "He's out of town on business."

"He works so hard," Dalton said. "Mr. Charlie too young to work so hard." Barrett ignored that and started walking around the room picking up pieces of the tinsel Charles was throwing on the furniture. The doorbell was ringing.

"You think this is in the middle?" Dalton said. "Rose, let Miss Barrett see if she thinks this gonna do. Go on, stand back, I got it now. What you think?"

"That's fine," she said. "That's perfect. That ought to be just perfect."

"You want to go outside and see how it looks from the street?"

"No, it's all right. It's fine. Charles, stop doing that. Go find something else to do till we get through."

"Someone's at the door for you," Sara said. "He says his name is Will Lyons. He says you'll want to see him."

Barrett felt the blood rush into her arms and legs, into her face and hands. She stood burning in the center of a still room. All around her the black faces made tiny precise movements and the huge white tree swung on its cable in the window and Charles ran back and forth very slowly and in the center of all that she was alone. She looked across the beautiful walnut floors and the soft pale rugs to the foyer where the morning sun was throwing prisms from the leaded-glass doors all over the walls. Nothing on earth will keep today from happening, she thought. Nothing will keep me from opening that door.

She walked across the room. The young man standing on the other side of the glass doors didn't look like the bearer of bad news. He just looked like a very tall blond boy who needed a haircut.

She walked out onto the porch. Will moved back. They positioned themselves about four feet apart as if they were going to begin a dance. "Why did you come here?" she said. "Why are you doing this to me?"

"Because your mother needs you. Because this has gone

on long enough. Because, I don't know. Because this is what I'm supposed to do. Look, I'm a nice person. I've never hurt anyone in my life. I've never even been in the army."

"Stay here," she said. "Wait here. I'll be back." She went back into the house and spoke to Sara. Then she came back out onto the porch leaving both doors open behind her. "Come around to the side porch," she said. "We can sit down there." She led him to a part of the porch where a set of white wicker furniture was arranged around a swing. She motioned him to a seat, then sat down on a small white sofa. A white china elephant holding a plant with small fernlike leaves was beside the sofa. The shadows from the leaves lay all over her blouse and across her arms. Will felt like he was in a play. A slow-motion play, a pantomime. Everything on the porch was so new, so perfect, so shiny. Everything they were doing seemed so slow, so dangerous, so unreal. Why am I doing this? he was thinking. What in the world made me come here?

Barrett looked up at him and began to cry without making a sound.

"I shouldn't have come here," he said. "I don't know why I'm doing this. Except sooner or later someone had to do it. I can't believe I'm standing here on your porch making you cry. This isn't what I came here for."

"It doesn't matter," she said. "Nothing matters. Tell me everything you know. I want to know. I have to find out anyway. Because of Charles, my little boy. Because he's so high-strung. I have to find out if there're any diseases or anything. I have to know about these things. I don't know what else to say. I don't know what you came here to do to me."

"I'm not going to tell you anything that's bad," he said. "Nothing I'm going to say will hurt you in any way." He was trying to look at her, trying to concentrate, but his mind kept wandering all around the freshly painted porch and into the yard to the severe hedges and the flower beds that looked as though they had been laid out by a geometer. He was thinking of Amanda's overgrown hillside, the jagged paths she and the Traylor boys cut through the wildflowers to the swing. He caught his breath, wondering what it looked like now, in late December, the bare trees, the brush all turned to seed. I'll be there tonight, he said to himself. I'll be there before the sun comes up again.

"Go on and tell me what you came here for," she said. "I don't care what it is. I want to know where I came from. I want to know where Charles came from. He's the only thing in the world that matters to me. I want to know about my mother. I want to know who deserted me."

"She didn't desert you," he said. "She was only fourteen years old when you were born." He folded his long legs around the rungs of the wicker chair until it squeaked from the pressure. "When she talks about you she sounds like she's fourteen years old right now."

Barrett looked up. For a moment it seemed possible. For a moment she could actually imagine such a thing, could imagine being loved and lost and mourned for.

"I came here to tell you that she needs you," he went on. "Well, I don't have any right to tell you this. She didn't send me. I came on my own."

"What is her name? Tell me who she is."

"She's a wonderful person. She has spent her whole life mourning you one way or the other. She's remarkable. She's the most unusual person I've ever known. If she were my mother I would want to know her. The only reason she doesn't come find you is because she thinks it will mess up your life. If she thought for a moment you wanted to see her, she'd be right here. She is . . . I don't know how to tell you about her. She used to live here, in New Orleans. She used to live around here somewhere. She lived on a street called Henry Clay."

"What is her name? I want to know what my name is. *Tell me my name.*"

"Her name is Amanda. Amanda McCamey. That's her real name. She used to be called something else when she lived here."

Barrett dug her nails into her folded arms. Now she was burning again. "*I know her. I met her. You're making this up. This isn't true. If she was my mother why didn't I know? Why didn't she know?*"

"I don't know the answer to that. But I'm going to be with her tonight. If you let me I'll tell her she can call you. She has waited thirty years to talk to you."

"You're going there now?" Barrett said. "To where she is?"

"As soon as I leave here. She lives in Arkansas. In a little town where I'm from."

"I know who she is. I know all about her. You're going there now?"

"As soon as I leave."

"Then I'm going too." She undid her arms and straightened her shoulders and looked up at him and for the first time he saw Amanda in her. "I'm going with you. Will you take me? Will you take me with you?"

"What about your little boy? You can't leave him. It's Christmas Eve."

"I'll take him with me. I'll take him too. Will you take us? Will you let me go?"

"I would like to," he said.

"Then take me." But already Barrett knew she was being deserted again. She had been seeing the expression on Will's face all her life. All her life she had been begging for love and watching the faces she begged from get ready to dole out what they wanted her to have. She knew that weighing. She knew that set of scales. "You won't do it, will you? You won't take me there. You come here to my house and start this and now you aren't going to take me there."

"It isn't that I don't want to," he said. "It's just that I don't know if you should go up there right now. I guess that might not be a real good idea."

"Why not? Why won't it be a good idea? If she has mourned me all these years as you say she has? Why isn't it a good idea? I've seen her. She doesn't look to me like she ever mourned a thing. Why isn't it a good idea for me to go and see her? You said she wants to see me."

"She doesn't know I'm doing this."

"What is it then? Why did you come here and do this to me?" She was almost screaming. She was almost raising her voice to him. "What is it? Why can't I go see my mother? If this is true? If she really is my mother."

"She's going to have a baby. She's going to have a baby in a few weeks. That's why I came here."

"That's impossible. She's too old to have a baby." She stood up from the wicker sofa and began tearing leaves off the plant in quick unconscious little movements, not looking at him now. Not really looking at anything in the world. "That isn't true. None of this is true."

"She's only forty-four years old. And it's true. At least I think it's true. She wrote me and told me that."

"Why would she write and tell you a thing like that? She couldn't be having a baby." Barrett's eyes swept over him, taking in the corduroy pants and the tennis shoes and the old shirt and the unkempt hair. She could not see beneath these things. Nothing she had ever learned had taught her to see anything but surfaces.

"I'm telling you the truth about everything I know," he said. "I wouldn't have any reason to come and tell you things like this for a joke. Your father found out who you are. And he told your mother and sooner or later this is all going to blow wide open and, somehow or other, because I've been out on the ocean I guess, I got it in my head that it was up to me to do this. I'm sorry. I'm sorry as I can be that I came here."

"She's having a baby," Barrett said. "She's having a baby and because of that I can't get in that car with you and go and see my mother. Who are you to come and tell me things like this?" But Sara was there now and Barrett pulled one last leaf off the plant and crumpled it in her left hand and the black woman moved over beside her and put her arm around her waist.

"I should leave," he said. "I shouldn't have come here."

"Did you get Gustave?" she said to Sara. "Could you get him? Did he say he'd call?"

"They said he'd call back in a minute. They said he'd call back soon."

"That's who loves me," Barrett said. "That's who cares for me, Mr. Lyons. Tell my mother that when you see her. Tell her not to worry. Tell her I have the best psychiatrist in the whole world and he loves me no matter what I do. He loves me whether I deserve to be loved or not. He loves me anytime I want him to."

"Should I tell her about this? About seeing you?"

"Why are you asking me?"

"Do you want me to tell her?"

"Could I stop you? Would someone who would come here like this stop at anything they wanted to do?"

"Oh, please. Oh, look, I'm sorry. I'm really sorry. I thought you would want to know. If you knew her you would want to know this."

"Come inside," Sara said. "Mrs. Clare, you come on in now. I think you better be going on," she said to Will. "I think we ought to get inside the house."

"Do you want to talk to me anymore?" he said. "Do you want to know how to call her?"

"I can find her," Barrett said. "If I want to I can find her."

"Forgive me," he said. "Please forgive me."

"Call him again," she said to Sara. "Call them and tell them to find him. Tell them it's an emergency. I don't have anything to forgive," she said turning back to him. He was in pain too. It was something she understood. It was something she knew how to relate to.

"I have to go in now. I have to call my doctor. She was fourteen years old?"

"She was only fourteen years old. She didn't have a thing to do with it. It was done to her."

"I don't know what to think." She started into the house, then turned back one more time, hanging on to Sara's hand as she turned. "Would she love me? Do you think she'd love me?"

"She has always loved you," Will said. Then he walked slowly and awkwardly down the marble stairs to the street and got into the car and drove down Saint Charles Avenue to Carrollton and started the long drive home. He stopped at a doughnut shop on the edge of town and filled a thermos with coffee and took a twenty-milligram Dexamyl Spansule and started driving toward the hills.

I did it, he thought. Maybe it was right and maybe it was wrong but anyway I did it. Sooner or later someone had to do it. I'm going to tell her that I did it. As soon as I see her I'm going to tell her.

When he was gone Barrett stood in the foyer, half in, half out of the doors, holding on to Sara's arm, digging her fingers into Sara's thick, cool skin. Are you my mother? she said to herself. Are you my mother? She was laughing, holding on to Sara and thinking about a children's book she had hidden from Charles because she hated reading it to him. It was a book about a newly hatched bird that falls from its nest and wanders around trying to find its mother. Are you my mother? it says to a cow. Are you my mother? it says to a truck. Are you my mother? it says to a boy. Are you my mother? Barrett said to herself, imagining standing across a room from Amanda saying it, waiting to see what would happen next. "Call him again," she said to Sara. "Tell him he has to call me right away."

All afternoon a slow gray rain fell on the mountain. If Amanda looked out of any window it seemed to her that the little house was floating inside a gray cloud. There was no wind. The rain hardly seemed to fall. Everything was very still except for the sound of wet air moving against the clapboards, with here and there the clear sharp call of a bluejay. Late in the afternoon the cloud lifted a few feet off the earth and the birds came down from the trees and were all over the place frantically hunting for food. Amanda threw all that was left of a sack of popcorn into the yard. Then she walked around the kitchen looking for something to feed the squirrels.

What an old maid I've turned into, she thought. Feeding all the little animals. Jesus. She found a handful of peanuts in a jar and threw them far out into the yard. The movement of her arm brought a sharp quick pain to her right side and she stopped. Oh, God, she thought. You aren't supposed to throw things at the end. Oh, well, that's probably some old wives' tale. Earth mother, feeding her little creatures, hmm. Well, there's nothing here to feed them. Damn it.

Amanda had been trying not to keep food in the house so she wouldn't gain weight. She rummaged around in a cabinet and found a box of Rye Crisp and a jar of peanut butter. She made some very small peanut butter sandwiches and went out on the balcony and threw them down under the tree, trying to make them land in the dry spots.

A fat squirrel came scurrying down the tree trunk, then stopped halfway to the ground, hanging upside down, sniffing the air. He wants it so bad, she thought, but he's afraid to go down there and get it.

Amanda closed her eyes, trying to send good karma to the squirrel but the squirrel wasn't having any. He just kept on hanging there halfway down the trunk sniffing the air.

"All right," Amanda said. "I'll bring it to you."

She made a handful of tiny sandwiches and went out into the yard and started putting them in dry places under the tree.

She felt another pain, this time in her back. She leaned up against the house until it passed. It can't be the baby, she thought. It's too soon. It's two weeks away.

When she got her breath back she went into the house and lay down on the sofa. The pain came a third time. She picked up the phone and called Katie. "I may not be able to come to dinner," she said.

"Why not?" Katie said.

"I think I might be having this baby."

"I'll be right over," Katie said. "Sit still. Don't do anything."

"Don't get excited," Amanda said. "I saw Luke yesterday. He said nothing was happening yet."

"Have you called him?" Katie said.

"No, I called you instead."

"Call him," Katie said. "Call him right this minute. Clinton has the car. I'll have to walk. I'll be right there."

"There isn't any hurry," Amanda said. "It's probably nothing anyway."

The wind was picking up. A front was moving in from the southwest, coming in through the saddle in the mountain. Katie felt it on her face as she ran along the road. She looked up and saw it in the distance. Oh, shit, she thought. That's all we need now is snow.

She came tearing in the house and made Amanda lie down. She built a fire and called Luke and left word for Clinton at the tennis club. He got there before Luke, bringing a sack of groceries. "If I have to help with this birth, at least I'd like to have something to eat," he said. "Amanda never has any food in the house."

He sank down onto the sofa and put his ear to her stomach. "Something's in there," he said. "Sounds like a channel swimmer. Or a fish. Maybe it's a fish."

"What'd you get to eat?" Amanda said. "What'd you bring me?"

"Honey and salt-rising bread and ginseng tea and homemade cookies."

"I don't feel so good," Amanda said. "I feel like . . . I don't know."

"Let me massage your legs," Clinton said. "Come on. Lie down and let my magic hands work on you. I'm not going to hang around this birthing unless I get to do something."

"We don't know it's a birthing," Amanda said. "It could be gas pains from all the junk I've been eating."

She stretched out on the floor and Clinton began to massage her legs. Katie Vee built up the fire and started pacing around the room. "Where in the shit is Luke?" she said. "It's starting to snow."

"Have you ever seen a baby born?" Amanda said to Clinton.

"I've been in the house," he said. "My momma had four after me. But I never looked."

"Where's Luke?" Amanda said. "I want him to get here. And call Garth. I promised him, I swore I'd call him." She stood up. As she did the water spread all over her legs and down upon the carpet and the sofa and on to the pile of old *New Yorkers* lying on the floor with her ballet shoes perched on top like a pair of tipsy sparrows.

The child was on its way. "The baby," she said. "It's coming, Katie, the baby's coming." She stood there watching the water running down her legs and onto the rug, onto her ballet shoes. She looked into the face of her friend. Katie was shaking her head from side to side, wringing her hands, gathering her forces, getting ready for whatever the night would bring.

"It's all right, Katie," Amanda said. "My body knows what it's doing." Then Clinton carried her downstairs to her bed. Luke came in while she was undressing. Garth was there an hour later, carrying a package, wearing a fringed white linen shirt the librarian had made him for a Christmas present. All night he kept sticking his fingers in and out of the fringe, tying little webs around his fingers to keep himself from smoking.

Amanda was wonderful for about two and a half hours, a real heroine, a real samurai.

"It's taking so long," Garth said. "It feels like the longest night of the year."

"The main thing about babies being born is waiting,"

Luke said. "They take their time. They take care of their mothers. The mother is their earth, their safety. It's a closed system, the mother and the child. It has its own time, it knows what it's doing."

"She's doing great, isn't she?" Garth said.

"Oh, yes, she's wonderful. Of course she's been training like she was going out for the Olympics."

"How much longer, do you think?"

"Luke," she called out. "Luke, goddammit all to hell. Where are you? Goddammit, oh, fuck. Luke, get the fuck in here and do something. Call an ambulance. Do something before I die. Do you hear me? Call me a doctor!"

Amanda had gotten tired of being a samurai. She had gone back to being Amanda.

"Goddammit, Luke," she was screaming. "Do something. Call an ambulance. Get me out of here. Get me to a hospital."

"It's too late, Amanda," he said. "Help me now. It won't be long. The head is almost here. For God's sake, Amanda. Come on and help us now."

"Oh, fuck," she screamed. "God damn it all to hell and back again. Call me a doctor or I'll kill you. Go get me some dope. I'll pay anything. Call somebody. Get some dope over here."

"Shut up," Katie said. "I mean it, Amanda. You thought this up. You got us into this. Now shut up that fucking yelling and help this baby get here."

The doorbell was ringing and ringing and ringing. "Go to the door, Katie," Luke said. "Go see who's here."

It was Marshall, leaning on his cane, wearing a white silk scarf and a plaid wool hat, a package of Almond Roca in his hands, staring off into the sky as if at any moment he would spread his cape and fly.

"I say, Katie," he said. "Is Amanda here? I brought —"

"What are you doing here?" Katie said.

"I came by to bring this candy."

"She's having the baby," Katie said. "Right this minute. Right down those stairs. Well, come on in. I've got to go back down there."

"Is there anything I can do?" he said, closing the door behind him, holding on to it for dear life. "Could I go for help?"

"Play the piano," Katie said. "Play anything you know. Go on. Right now."

Then Marshall seated himself at the piano still wearing his scarf and hat and began to play. A Bach toccata began to fill the little house, the clear notes traveling down the stairs to where Amanda was resting between pains.

She turned her head as Katie came in the bedroom door. "Is that Marshall playing the piano?" she said. "Katie, is he really playing the piano?"

"I found him something to do with his hands," Katie said.

The pains began again. "Put your back into it," Luke said. "Breathe with me. Help the child, Amanda. The child is not trying to hurt you. Breathe, breathe, breathe, breathe."

"Goddammit, it hurts," Amanda said. "What the fuck are we doing this for? Please call me a doctor. Oh, God, here it comes again."

The crown of the child's head appeared. "It's almost over, Amanda," Luke said. "The head is almost here. Push again. Oh, you're wonderful. Push against me. Help me.

The child doesn't want to hurt you. The child is doing what your body tells it to."

Now Amanda rose above herself, dreaming she was a porpoise rolling in the ocean, swimming through a sea of pain. She dug her fingers into Garth's arms.

"Once more," Luke said. "We've almost got it. One more push and we've got it."

Amanda pushed and the baby's head appeared. "Oh, for God's sake," Katie said. "It's got red hair." Luke put his hand on the head. "One more shove and we've got it," he said. Then Amanda dove deep down into the sea of herself, gave a long hard push, and the shoulders and arms and body slid out into Luke's hands.

"It's got red hair," Katie said. "Jesus Christ, it's got red hair."

Luke laid the baby against Amanda's breast and her hands found his little body. "It's perfect," Luke said. "A perfectly wonderful baby."

Luke laid the baby against Amanda's body and it fit the curves and volumes of her body as if it had always been there. She could feel the beat and rhythm of its body alike and already strangely different from her own.

Clinton was crying. Standing by the foot of the bed with his long arms hanging down at his sides. Garth went over and knelt beside the bed and touched the child with one hand, stroking Amanda's hair with the other. Then Katie came around the other side and lay her head on her friend's leg, beginning to laugh softly. "Red hair," she said. "That blows my mind. It's got red hair."

Luke stood up with his hands spread wide, nodding to the music coming from upstairs. "Go tell Marshall," he said. "Make him come and see."

Garth stood up and cracked his knuckles. "I'll go," he said. He was glad of an excuse to go upstairs and get a cigarette.

The music stopped and in a moment Marshall appeared in the door still wearing the scarf and hat. "My dearest Amanda," he said. "I don't quite know what to say."

"Thank you for the music," Amanda said. "It was a perfect thing to play."

The excitement in the room was subsiding. Garth and Luke put Amanda into a bath made with herbs Luke had brought from the country. They laid the baby across her, half in, half out of the warm water, close against her skin. She looked down into the child's black eyes and imagined she could see all the way down the line of the generations, could see her father's eyes and her grandmother's eyes and all the ones that came before and the ones that would come after she was gone and the child was gone.

Garth took the child into his arms and wrapped it in a bright red towel. Katie held out a blue robe lined with silk for Amanda.

"Your Christmas present," she said. "Clinton and I made it. He read the directions and I cut it out and we both sewed it together."

"Give me back my baby," she said. Garth handed it to her and she went into the bedroom and lay down on the white sheets.

Outside two feet of new snow had fallen on the mountain. Amanda held the baby against her skin. He curled up against her. He sighed. He moved his hands across her breast. She touched his hand. His fingers closed around her fingers. "Flesh of my flesh," she whispered. "Bone of my bone, blood of my blood. You are kin to me," she whispered, touching his soft hair. Kin to me, kin to me, kin to me. And the memory of the other child was there with them, but it was softer now, paler.

"Katie," she called out. "Come look at him. He opened his eyes. Katie, he's looking at me. Katie, you haven't looked at him in five minutes."

"Do you want me to hold him for you while you sleep?"

"Do you think Will is coming?" she said. "I want Will to see him."

"He'll come," Katie said. "How on earth could he stay away?"

"Jesus Christ," Luke was saying. "Take that tea out of here, Clinton, and get me something to drink. Surely there's something to drink in this house except hippie tea."

Then, in Amanda's little stone house close to the stars Katie and Clinton and Garth and Luke were having a feast. Eating and drinking brandy and cocoa and listening to Marshall play the Goldberg Variations slightly too fast, getting up every now and then to tiptoe downstairs and look in on Amanda and the baby.

Amanda was playing it for all it was worth, lying propped up on nine pillows wearing the new robe open so everyone could admire her breasts. A small fire was burning in the bedroom fireplace, casting flattering shadows on everything. Amanda lay there holding the baby, touching its soft red hair.

"One time when I was young I spent three days trying to write a poem about the fact that a walnut looks like the bark of a walnut tree," she told Marshall. He was standing in the door, not daring to come any closer. "I thought that was the most miraculous thing I had ever noticed. I thought

I was the only one that had ever seen it and that *it was up to me* to tell the world about it."

"It doesn't hurt to remind them," Marshall said. "Especially nowadays. I don't suppose this will interest you much at the moment but I had come over here to bring you some news. I heard from Duncan. He loves the book. The readers all gave you great reviews."

"Then it's going to be a book. A real book."

"A real book. Yours and Helene's and mine too, I suppose."

"I want a blue cover. With a tree. I'll have Ginny draw the tree."

"You'll have to talk to Duncan about all of that. Well, the book will make us all famous. We may be sorry we ever saw it. Now, my dear, what will you name this lovely child?"

"Noel," she said. "It means good news. Noel, Noel," she said, touching his hair. "Now I'll write my novel. I've been making notes for ages."

"I'm sure it will be wonderful," he said, indulging her. Half the people Marshall knew were writing novels. The only thing that surprised him was when someone finished one.

"It's going to be a novel about love," she said. "It will be everything I know about love and everything I can find out from Katie."

Will was not going to make it to the feast. His car had broken down in Alma. He was standing right this minute not two hundred yards from Katie's mother's dry-cleaning establishment, trying not to curse his luck.

"Think you can fix it?" he said.

"It's the water pump," the blue-eyed man said. "I'll rig up something for you, seeing it's Christmas Eve."

"Might as well have a beer while I'm waiting," Will said.

"There's a place down the road that sells it," the man said. "They'll be open another hour. Try down there while I see what I can do."

It turned out to be a pleasant enough country bar. Will pulled up a stool and struck up a conversation with the bartender.

"You're driving into snow," the bartender said. "I heard it on the radio."

"I'll make it," Will said. "It's only an hour. I'm so homesick I would walk to Fayetteville."

"Where you coming from?"

"I was in New Orleans this morning. It's one hell of a drive."

"I was in New Orleans once," the bartender said. "A buddy of mine and I drove our motorcycles down there one summer. We parked at the Superdome and walked to Canal Street to catch a bus. Well, we were standing on the corner by this drugstore. We couldn't have been there two hours. My buddy kept sniffing the air. He turned and grabbed my arm. 'I can't breathe this shit,' he said. 'I'm getting out of here.' We turned around and ran back to where we'd parked the motorcycles and took off across the causeway. We were across the lake by sundown. I never have gone back."

"Well, I'd better be getting back and see if he's got my car fixed. I want to get going before they close the roads."

"Good luck to you," the bartender said. "I'll bet they'll be surprised to see you."

"I'm hoping so," Will said. "That's what I'm banking on."

He took an extra six-pack under his arm and hiked back to the car, small flakes of snow beginning to strike his face.

He started driving up the long hill past Tony Alamo's, fiddling with the radio. He was lucky and found a rock station that was playing something besides Christmas music. "Oh, your kiss, your kiss is on my list," Daryl Hall was singing. It was a favorite song of Will's that had been popular about the time he met Amanda. He fell under the spell of the music, beginning to desire her, thinking about making love to her coming back from the lookout tower at Goshen. He put the cool bottle between his legs while he lit a cigarette.

He rode up over the crest of the hill, the little Ford taking the altitude like a dream, and down over the crest and into the curve, singing along to the radio. "Oh, your kiss, your kiss is on my list. Oh, your kiss, your kiss is on my list." He was around the curve and the lights of the truck were there as if they had been there forever.

As if the truck and the Ford had been traveling toward each other since the dawn of time. They struck and bounced away. Then his hands were loose on the wheel as the little car spun out into the soft white air. The car filled with light. It was all right. It was all perfectly all right. He even had time to regret the borrowed car. Will had always been very careful about returning things he borrowed. The car lifted off into the still white air, describing a long curve like a stone thrown into a lake. Then it began its downward spiral. Then there was nothing at all, "no possum, no sop, no taters," no songs to sing, no games to watch, no beer to drink, no women to love, no stories to tell.

The radio had come from Kyoto, Japan. It was made of sterner stuff and went on playing until long after dawn.

"There's one thing about him," Amanda was saying sleepily to Katie. "He knows how to love. He isn't afraid to go on and love something all the way. Most people don't know how to do that anymore."

"He'll be here," Katie said. "Stop worrying."

"I'm not worrying," Amanda said. "I know he's coming." She ran her hands down the side of the baby, making him stir in her arms. She was cold then and very tired and asked Katie to put another log on the fire.

She snuggled down beside the baby watching the firelight on the wall and the snow piling up on the windowsills, thinking about the snow falling all over the roof and the yard, filling the oaks and the maples, falling all over the mountain and the town, falling all over the whole state of Arkansas.

I'll go find her as soon as I'm well she thought. I'll get on a plane and fly to New Orleans and take a suite of rooms at the Pontchartrain and get my jewelry out of the lockbox and call her up and tell her what was done to me. I'll tell her who she is. How could she be ashamed of me? No one has ever been ashamed of me. I'll be beautiful and wonderful and tell her what they did to me. I'll tell her what those goddamned nuns did to me and she will love me. I know she'll love me.

Then Amanda fell asleep dreaming of herself in a white

silk suit holding her beautiful daughter in her arms. My will be done, she said as she moved into her sleep. My life on my terms, my daughter, my son. My life leading to my lands forever and ever and ever, hallowed be my name, goddammit, my kingdom come, my will be done, amen, so be it, Amanda.